TWO RENEGADE
REALMS

Other books by Donita K. Paul

Realm Walkers series

1 | *One Realm Beyond*

TWO RENEGADE REALMS

BOOK TWO
OF THE

REALM WALKERS

TRILOGY

DONITA K. PAUL

 ZONDERVAN®

ZONDERVAN

Two Renegade Realms
Copyright © 2015 by Donita K. Paul

This title is also available as a Zondervan ebook.
Visit www.zondervan.com/ebooks.

Requests for information should be addressed to:
Zondervan, 3900 *Sparks Dr. SE, Grand Rapids, Michigan 49546*

Library of Congress Cataloging-in-Publication Data

Paul, Donita K.
    Two renegade realms / Donita K. Paul.
        pages   cm. — (Realms walkers ; book 2)
        Summary: "Cantor, Bixby, and Dukmee must band together to find the
    storied realm walker Chomountain after the devastating attack by the
    corrupt Realm Walkers Guild; however, the great wizard is not as he once
    was" — Provided by publisher.
        ISBN 978-0-310-73581-6 (pbk.)
        ISBN 978-0-310-73584-7 (epub)
        [1. Space and time — Fiction. 2. Adventure and adventurers — Fiction.
    3. Best friends — Fiction. 4. Friendship — Fiction. 5. Dragons — Fiction.
    6. Wizards — Fiction. 7. Shapeshifting — Fiction. 8. Christian life — Fiction.
    9. Fantasy.] I. Title.
    PZ7.P278344Two 2014
    [Fic] — dc23   2014032685

All Scripture quotations, unless otherwise indicated, are taken from The Holy
Bible, *New International Version®, NIV®.* Copyright © 1973, 1978, 1984, 2011 by
Biblica, Inc.® Used by permission. All rights reserved worldwide.

The author is represented by the literary agency of Alive Communications, Inc.,
7680 Goddard Street, Suite 200, Colorado Springs, CO 80920, www.alivecom-
munications.com

Cover design: Kris Nelson
Cover illustration: Steve Rawlings
Interior design: David Conn

Printed in the United States of America

14 15 16 17 18 19 20 /DCI/ 19 18 17 16 15 14 13 12 11 10 9 8 7 6 5 4 3 2 1

PROLOGUE

You're Cantor D'Ahma, aren't you?" The soft, feminine voice turned him from the dusty bookshelves.

His light globe didn't reach into the darkness between the library stacks, but a swish of fabric and a slight movement gave away the speaker's position. She stepped into the circle of illumination, and Cantor bowed deeply.

"Your Highness."

Bixby's mother came forward and put a hand on Cantor's arm. She squeezed it gently. "You've grown in the two years since I saw you last."

"I apologize for my hasty departure."

"Bixby was quite upset."

"I haven't seen her since." Though he'd looked for her in every village and city and realm he and Bridger had visited. Their paths had never crossed.

The queen wrapped her arm around his and serenely moved him toward the exit.

Cantor let her lead him. Being rude to the queen of Richra wasn't diplomatic. Even he, without the extensive and formal training of a Realm Walker, knew that. He bent to hear her next comment.

"Well, that was two years ago. I told her at the time why you left so abruptly."

Cantor furrowed his brow. That was interesting. He didn't know himself why he had been in such a hurry.

A buzz in his ear gained his attention. She was probably probing his mind, but he did nothing to put up a guard.

Queen Mazeline patted his arm. "I told her you had been through your first big battle, that you weren't satisfied with the results, and you needed time to discover it was not your personal failure."

Cantor swallowed the harrumph that rose to his throat. Yes, those had been his feelings, though he'd never been able to put them into words. In fact, he'd avoided even thinking about those days.

The warmth of the queen's arm on his spread a soothing peace through him as he listened to her sort out and label the quagmire of emotions he had kept at bay.

"You were injured, dear boy, and not a life-threatening, heroic wound, but small cuts and scratches and bruises. You didn't have a full measure of your worth, and therefore your pride was jeopardized. You believed that your inconsequential injuries showed you had not been engaged in a proper defense of those in your care."

Cantor spit the distasteful word from his mouth. "Pride. Primen loathes a haughty head."

"That's right, dear, and only experience teaches humility. Everyone is born with that particular vice."

Cantor chewed on these words for a few moments as they climbed the stairs to the ground level of the library. He believed her assessment was correct. Bixby had said her mother had the ability to reveal a person's heart. She also said the revelation could be quite uncomfortable.

They approached the door, and Cantor saw Jesha sitting in the sunshine on the wide marble step outside. Her tail wrapped around her feet, making her look like a splotchy statue of a regal cat. As Bridger said, Jesha sat for effect more than comfort in public. In private, she could be most undignified, sprawling in contortionist poses on whatever took her fancy. In fact, Bridger's current position at the bottom of the steps was reminiscent of Jesha at her most unguarded; his feet and tail spilled out onto the cobblestone street.

"You had to go." The queen's voice startled him after the silence in the hushed atmosphere of the grand foyer. "You had to jump into worthwhile activity to drive away the feelings of inadequacy."

He opened the glass door and followed her out into the beautiful day. Cantor knew from an earlier exploration that the street before them ran around the palace wall, then to colorful artisan shops, staid museums, the courthouse, quiet restaurants, and a music shop complete with a string quartet playing out front.

The town was nothing like the small villages Cantor was used to. The only animal-pulled vehicles allowed in this area were the royal coaches. The street had a few handcarts in view. One sold flowers, and another sold cool drinks in pretty colors.

Before the palace, people strolled. Even the children and dogs walked with decorum. The harmony of pastel colors and elegant movement made a pretty scene.

Bixby had explained that the flowering bushes in planters along the walkway infused the air with a calming fragrance. In other words, everyone was drugged. Cantor dismissed the staged tableau and addressed the queen. "I went to continue my search for Ahma and Odem."

Queen Mazeline nodded. Nothing disturbed her serenity.

At the sound of hoofbeats, Cantor's glance moved toward the library at the side of the palace. The wooden wheels of a small trap clattered on the cobblestone street as it turned the corner. Pulled by two guprada horses and driven by a small man in livery, it approached the bottom of the wide marble steps and stopped.

Bridger, roused from a nap, sprang to his feet and looked quickly around. Once he'd collected himself, he bowed to the queen. His court manners outshone Cantor's, but the dragon's clumsiness usually spoiled his elegant poise. Cantor felt a grin tug at the corner of his mouth. He'd grown fond of Bridger.

The queen nodded at the dragon then continued her helpful evaluation of Cantor's previous state of emotions. "Your search for Ahma and Odem was your duty. I would not have thought of you doing anything else. But now another cause must take precedence. And perhaps you will locate your mentors in your pursuit of the information the king requests you to obtain."

She turned a dazzling smile on him. For a moment, Cantor saw the distinct beauty of her daughter, Bixby, reflected in her features. He missed Bixby with a sudden clench of his heart.

The queen's eyebrows arched. "Bixby is on the same mission, has been for over a year. Perhaps she is the one you will discover first."

She let go of his arm and floated down the stairs with one more command tossed over her shoulder in the guise of polite social niceties. "Join us in the palace for tea this afternoon, Cantor. And bring your dragon constant. The king will give his counsel. He probably will tell you to remind Bixby she is supposed to send reports. And I shall tell you to remind her that her mother does need a letter from her. Just once in a while, not daily. Not an arduous demand."

TUNNELS

On his stomach, with his arms above his head, Cantor D'Ahma twisted his large frame and forced his broad shoulders along the narrow passage. A light globe rattled within his wire-cage hat. The bobbling motion sent light and shadow flickering across rough rock walls.

"You coming?" The dragon's voice echoed a bit as it traveled the length of the tunnel.

"Sure." He grunted. "As soon as I wiggle through this rock wormhole you've lured me into." He made little effort to keep the annoyance out of his voice. How, after three years, he was still plagued by Bridger's bumbling ineptitude and ridiculous expectations, only Primen knew.

Cantor's voice rumbled low in his chest and then rolled down the passageway with a heavy resonance. "You'd better have measured these gaps properly, or you'll be off to find miners to chip me out."

"You haven't grown any more this month, have you?"

Bridger asked. "You should be able to make it if your circumference isn't any larger than it was two weeks ago."

"I thought we decided I wasn't growing so rapidly now."

"We, the brains, decided that. I don't know about you, the body." Bridger's voice echoed enough to make Cantor concentrate. With effort, he deciphered the words rolling over each other.

"Yeah, well, this tunnel is a bit snug." Cantor latched onto niches in the wall with his outstretched hands and toed the rough surface behind him. With another grunt, he heaved himself forward an inch. The next shove was more successful, and the one after that broke him free of his wedged position. He squirmed onward until the tunnel opened into a cave.

With a hearty sigh, he rose up on his elbows and surveyed the open space, noting the low ceiling.

He'd seen cabins bigger than this cave. And he'd seen prettier caves. No layered colors of sedimentary rocks striped the walls, no crystals, no unusual geological formations. Just a hollow expansion of the natural tunnels he and Bridger were exploring.

In the middle of this ordinary stone room, his mor dragon sat on a colorful, cushy chair, conveniently provided by his own shape-shifted wings and tail. Bridger liked his comforts. Jesha, the dragon's cat, curled at his feet, slumbering.

With barely a glance at the incongruous scene, Cantor elbowed farther into the cavern, swung his long legs around, and sat up. He eyed the uninspiring room. "I'm beginning to think we've got the wrong mountain."

The dragon nodded, looking thoughtful and wise. Cantor almost rolled his eyes. Bridger could be legitimately thoughtful, but wise only happened by chance.

"Could be we are in the wrong mountain. But do you really want to go back to that council library on Derson? Three weeks reading through dusty tomes is enough for me. Plus, the place was creepy. I always thought someone was watching us."

A small shudder ran over Cantor. They'd spent those weeks oscillating between spikes of fear whenever someone seemed close to identifying them and the mind-numbing boredom of searching through ancient texts for anything that could help them find the Library of Lyme. The King of Richra insisted that this ancient library be found, and supposedly, the only way to find it was to delve through libraries that were merely old, not ancient. It had been the last of a series of similar stops as the pair sought to avert the disaster that would occur when Lyme Major and Lyme Minor intersected their planar stack.

"In my opinion," Bridger continued, "it's a waste of time to try to find another likely hidden place for the oar-REE-ree." He paused, licking his lips and wrinkling his nose as he attempted to pronounce the tongue-twisting word. "Oarry-ree, no, or-er-ree. Another likely place for its library to be hidden."

Cantor cleared his throat and pronounced the word slowly in its parts and then as normally spoken. "OAR-rare-ree. Orrery."

Bridger nodded. "Yes, that. And the library that explains it." He picked up Jesha and stroked her soft and colorful fur. "We kind of like these dry tunnels and caves. But you want us to go back to that dusty, smelly, spooky dungeon-like place with council spies probably lurking among the book stacks?"

Cantor dug into his pocket and pulled out a flat hamper. "No, I'd rather eat." He thrust his hand into the sagging sack, thinking about sausages, and pulled out a foot-and-a-half-long salami. He tried to think of what other foodstuffs he had stored in this convenient access to another dimension.

"Ah," said the dragon. As he sprang up, his body transformed to his normal shape. "It's always good to eat." He carried the cat with him and sat down beside Cantor. "But perhaps your increased appetite means you aren't finished growing after all."

Cantor handed a loaf of bread to the dragon, then reached into the long, flat bag again. He groaned as he drew out a large hunk of very yellow cheese.

Bridger smacked his lips and took the cheese as well. "I thought you liked this cheddar."

Cantor looked up at the dragon and quirked an eyebrow. Jesha's nose quivered at the scent of one of her favorite foods.

"You groaned," Bridger said.

"That was for the growing. In the last two years, I've gained fifteen inches in height. From five foot six to six foot nine. My feet are colossal. If my chest were made out of wood, I'd button my shirts over a barrel. And my voice sounds as if I'm deep inside that barrel."

"Your singing has improved nicely," Bridger pointed out. A mouthful of bread did nothing to deter his speaking.

"My singing was all right the way it was. I'm a cantor."

"Not officially. You're named Cantor, but you don't hold a position in the sanctuary."

Cantor shrugged, took a swig from his flagon, corked it, and took an enormous bite out of a second loaf of bread from the hamper. He then put a saucer down and filled it from a small bottle of milk. Jesha jumped down to lap at the creamy liquid as Cantor put the bottle back into the hamper.

Cantor gestured to the cave around them. "We've seen no sign of life. No writing on the walls. No implements left behind. Nothing to say, 'Hey! People have been here before you.'"

Bridger cocked his head and held up one digit. He whispered, "Did you hear that?"

Cantor closed his eyes and concentrated, fine-tuning his gift of enhanced hearing. "No."

The dragon shrugged. "I don't hear it now either."

"What was it?"

Before Bridger could answer, his eyes opened wider. "There it is again. That sound."

Cantor heard it as well, a scrape of something hard against another hard surface. At the next noise — a human voice, a female human voice — he stood up.

The low ceiling. He'd forgotten. Eyes watering, he squatted and rubbed the crown of his head, glad he hadn't hollered and given away their presence to the owners of the mysterious voices.

Still rubbing his tender scalp, he pointed to the second of the tunnels in the walls of the cave. "That way."

Bridger stuffed the remainder of his bread and cheese into his mouth and approached the entrance of a tunnel they had yet to explore. He nodded, and around the wad of half-chewed snack, he said, "I hear two voices — one man and one woman."

Cantor puzzled over this new development. Wisdom demanded a look at the situation before allowing this man and woman to know they had company. He spoke softly. "I can't make out what they're saying, can you?"

Bridger shook his head. "There's too much echoing in and out of all the tunnels and caves."

"That may deceive us as to where the voices originate." Cantor slapped the dragon on his scaly shoulder. "Let's go explore."

Bridger ducked into the tunnel.

Cantor cupped his hand to his mouth. "Psst."

Bridger paused.

Cantor debated only a moment. An extra measure of caution would be prudent. He placed a general hedge around himself and the dragon, hoping the less complicated maneuver would not alert an enemy of their presence. "Be sure to measure accurately. I'm beginning to think you shift to a smaller size without realizing what you're doing."

"I am always aware of what I'm doing."

Cantor snorted but said nothing. Bridger didn't readily acknowledge the blunders he made, but Cantor had many anecdotes of the dragon's fumbling from their travels. Still, Cantor liked him enough to not want to humiliate him.

In spite of the difficulty discerning which tunnel was filled with echoes and which might lead to the talking people, they pushed onward, at times stooping or crawling, at others walking upright through long and twisting stone corridors.

Bridger stopped abruptly as he reached a turn in the tunnel ahead. Cantor barreled into him, tripping over his tail and landing in a tight spot between the dragon's hind leg and the stone wall.

Without seeming to notice Cantor's predicament, Bridger whispered over his shoulder, "They're in the next chamber. The walls are lined with bookshelves."

"The library? We've found it?" Cantor eased back, removing himself from his uncomfortable position. "Can you see the people?"

"No . . . Yes!" Bridger's lips stretched into a grin, his sharp teeth creating a bizarre picture of gruesome gladness. He jumped forward, out of the tunnel. "Dukmee! Bixby!"

Cantor's heart expanded, and a smile forced its way to his mouth. Bixby! He hadn't seen the little realm walker for two years. The smile fell away as quickly as it had appeared. Why was Bixby traveling with Dukmee?

2

OLD FRIENDS

He heard nothing from the mage Dukmee, but Bixby's cry of delight spurred him through the last section of the tunnel. Following the dragon into the spacious library, Cantor found his friend the same as she had been: tiny, disheveled, fluttery, and beautiful. He quickly made a point of studying his surroundings rather than allowing his gaze to remain too long on the girl.

Glow-orbs studded the room's high ceiling, and cascades of powerful miniature lights decorated the walls from ceiling to floor at intervals around the room. Massive bookshelves lined the outer walls of the room, and freestanding counterparts stood in a haphazard formation around the center. Unlike many of the libraries he and Bridger had delved into, this collection showed no particular dedication to order. Few shelves contained neatly aligned books side by side. Stacks and fallen piles plus small statues and metal twisted into odd sculptures, stuffed every possible ledge. Two massive tables with a dozen wooden chairs dominated one side of the room. Dukmee and Bixby stood there with scrolls, maps, and ledgers spread out before them.

Cantor's eyes skidded over Bixby. She stood too close to the mage. He looked away, studying the spacious room. So this was the ancient Library of Lyme. Here they would find answers to the questions about the renegade planes, the most important being a precise date the trouble would begin. Cantor peered closely at the shelves and alcoves. Where was the orrery?

Bixby's lilting voice interrupted his perusal of the ancient library.

"Bridger, who have you brought with you? Introduce your new friend."

"New friend?" Puzzlement creased the dragon's forehead. "Not new. This is my constant, still Cantor D'Ahma. You didn't think I would forsake him, Bixby? I never would."

Countering the sincerity in the dragon's voice, Cantor laughed. His chortle, deep in his throat, sounded like a frog in a well. No, Bridger would not desert him even when Cantor wanted him to.

Bixby's eyes widened. "Cantor?"

He saw the astonishment on her face and tried not to turn red with embarrassment. He knew she found the change in him disturbing. He wasn't comfortable with this outlandish growth spurt either — not that he would admit it.

Assuming an air of nonchalance, he grinned as he advanced over the smoothed rock floor. "It's me. Two years older than the last time we were together."

"In my parents' palace." Her eyes searched his face, no doubt looking for the lanky adolescent she'd known. Her head was nodding. A tiny rush of pleasure gushed through him. Good. She hadn't forgotten.

He looked at her whitish-blonde hair. The feather-light, lustrous mop topped her small frame like dandelion fuzz. Her outrageous outfit included a dozen layered skirts and dresses, ruffles, lace, and elaborate embroidery, all in shades of brewed tea. "You look just the same."

She laughed, the rippling sound floating around the cave, passing through tunnels and coming back on itself in merry echoes. "Is that my cue to say, 'Well, that can't be said of you'?" She grabbed his wrists in her tiny hands and gave them a shake. Hitching her head back to look up at him, she flashed him a smile, and her eyes twinkled. "What happened to you?"

"I grew."

"Cantor." Bridger motioned him to come to where the dragon stood with the mage. "They're looking for the same information we are. And they found the or — thingamabobby."

Dukmee reached out to clasp arms with Cantor in the traditional greeting of realm walkers. Two years ago, Cantor had been a head shorter than Dukmee. But now the long, lean healer-scholar-realm walker-mage looked up at Cantor.

Dukmee grinned. "I've heard a lot about your exploits."

Bixby hurried to a position beside the two men. She peered up at them, impatience at being left out clear on her face. "I haven't heard anything. What exploits?"

Cantor broke the grasp with Dukmee and turned a little to include her. "Nothing much. Bridger and I have been looking for Ahma and Odem. We've made meticulous searches and discreet inquiries in every realm on every plane in our planeary system. And we failed." He heaved a sigh. "And now your parents have assigned us with the task of finding—" He gestured with an open hand. "What you have already found. Which reminds me ... your father sends a reprimand. He wants you to send in reports. And your mother complains that she doesn't hear from you. Letters, lots of letters, are her request."

"Oh, I'm sorry. I do forget." Bixby gave her head a shake, sending her white-blonde curls into a frenzy. Her expression changed from annoyance to compassion. She reached up to touch Cantor's arm. "I can't imagine the loss of ones so dear."

He liked the feel of her small, comforting hand. But when he looked in her eyes, he saw emotion, and he didn't want to deal with emotion just now. Nevertheless, he felt the frustration rise at his own failures, not to mention the feelings of inadequacy and loneliness he'd cooped up in the same unwanted burden box. Ahma would have counseled him to throw the thing out. Sometimes it was difficult to trash a concept. Cleaning stable stalls was harder on the back, but easier than clearing negative thoughts from the mind.

Frowning, he shook off her hand and took a step back. Dwelling on his failure wasted time and distracted from this mission. He would not let Bixby lure him into such a quagmire.

Bridger lifted his head from examining an old, faded map on discolored parchment. "We still believe Ahma and Odem are alive. We haven't looked for them inside any mountains." He waved his arm around, indicating the cavern. "I bet there are lots of these little hidey-holes around in places we've already been."

A tiny spark of hope flickered in Cantor's heart. "Once we figure out this mess with the renegade planes, we'll look into it."

"Literally." Bridger grinned.

Dukmee laughed, then his face turned somber. "What rumors brought you here?"

All at once the weight of the Lyme prediction fell onto Cantor's heart. As long as no Library of Lyme was found, he could believe that the doomsayers had no ground on which to stand. Now that he was in the very library he'd hoped did not exist, he had to give credence to the rest of the tales.

Reluctantly he related how they'd been lured into investigating the Lyme phenomenon. "Bixby's father related a string of unsettling happenings. Old folklore has been reborn. The Lyme Wars were a legend from an era so long ago that they were mostly forgotten. But men of dubious backgrounds began mumbling about the day approaching when the path of Lyme Major and Lyme Minor would once again intersect our orbit. At first I thought it was some council plot to demoralize the populace."

Bridger perked his ears. "Considering the source of the rumors, that was an understandable conclusion. The council may not be the same as it was, but we've seen evidence that it still promotes discord."

Cantor nodded his agreement. Every once in a while, Bridger sounded like a dragon raised in a proper home, which he was. Proper in that he and his sister were educated, primed with cultural advantages, and expected to become worthwhile citizens. Other times he sounded like he'd missed the point of all that quality background.

Cantor brought his thoughts back to his story. "Then more reliable storytellers began reciting obscure tales of the Lyme Wars. Of course, charlatans latched on to the growing rumor. To them, it was another opportunity to make money. Charm makers, soothsayers, and dealers of amulets sprang up in the marketplaces."

He studied Dukmee, glad to have the mage on his side.

"With all this perplexing activity, it seemed a good idea to verify some of the rumors as true or false. Hard evidence gives us a better foundation for making decisions."

Cantor let his gaze wander around the room, taking in the many volumes of books and shelves filled with scrolls. "What have you found?"

Dukmee crossed his arms in front of him, hiding each hand in the opposite sleeve. "Enough to convince me that there are two planes circling our sun in an orbit that brings them into contact with us in a set number of years."

"Centuries," interjected Bixby.

Dukmee nodded. "Yes, great lengths of time, long enough for the event to fade in the memory of our people. That's why Bixby's father charged us with this search. We've been at it longer than you have, but we haven't been here more than a week."

He paused and let Bixby take over. "This library was designed to record details for future generations. According to these writings, the intersection of our path with that of the two Lyme planes is never fun."

Cantor clenched his jaw. "So now we know that the Lyme planes exist, but do we know the time of the interpass?"

Dukmee sighed. "Three or four months. Probably sooner."

3

ORRERIES

Bixby stood in the arch that separated the library from the next room and gestured to her friends. "Come into the Orrery Chamber."

Bridger and Cantor — she still had trouble believing that giant was Cantor — moved to join her, but Dukmee's nose was already in another dusty book, and he stayed behind. Bixby didn't mind at all. When Dukmee led a discussion, she didn't feel comfortable interrupting. She might be superior in social standing, but his experience and knowledge humbled her. Still, not being able to say what was on the tip of her tongue irked her to no end. When he was with her, she only spoke when he gave her an opening.

She welcomed the arrival of the two realm walkers. Dukmee had been in his scholar mode and not much company. Plus, the prospect of meeting hostile aliens made her nervous, and Cantor and Bridger were warriors in addition to being realm walkers. And to top all that, the sight of them dispelled her fear that the council had taken her friends as prisoners. After all, she hadn't heard anything from them in two years.

Her father had reassured her that he, as king, would have knowledge of any arrest, but Bixby had firsthand experience with the council. Her instincts told her that her mother and father were not as well informed as they believed.

She stepped back from the arch as her two friends approached. She wanted to see their faces the first time they saw the Orrery Chamber. All by itself, the big model in the middle was most impressive. And it was not all by itself.

Both Bridger and Cantor fulfilled her expectations. Their mouths dropped open, and their eyes widened with wonderment. They stood inside the door with their heads moving slowly as they took it all in. The room clicked and hummed as the models moved in tiny increments.

Jesha trotted through the arch and began exploring in and out of the scattered orreries. Bixby wondered if the cat would be enticed to pounce on one of the many moving parts. Some of the instruments were fragile. With a glance at Bridger, it occurred to her that perhaps she should also worry about the dragon's tail. He'd been known to sweep surfaces clean with a single, sudden movement.

"Bridger." She spoke hesitantly. "Be sure Jesha doesn't take a swat at the orreries."

Cantor jumped in before she continued. "And take notice of your tail as well. A swat from Jesha might do some damage. Your tail could take out the whole room."

"Not so!" The dragon's face showed outrage, but after a moment it shifted to serious. "I suppose it could. I'll take care."

The largest orrery stood on the floor. Its arms and orbs and disks gleamed with different colored shiny metals, most of which she could name. Silver, gold, brass, copper, and tin were common. But there was one with a pink tinge she didn't recognize. Dukmee probably knew, but she never remembered to ask him.

Along the wall, smaller orreries made of different materials demonstrated a wide variety of complexity. Fancier models boasted precious metals and gems. Some wooden mockups portrayed the same dynamics but in a simpler form.

Cantor asked the first question. "What energy keeps them moving?"

Bixby guided them to one of the simpler models. "Some respond to a cranking device. This one has a key similar to those used to wind up mechanical toys."

"But others are moving on their own, with no key," observed Cantor.

Bridger approached a model hanging from the ceiling and gently touched a part with his claw. "And nothing could be wound up centuries ago and still be running."

"Right." Bixby motioned for them to follow her to the other side of the room. "Dukmee hasn't determined exactly how it all works, but he's sure that this is responsible for the energy."

She pointed to a round hole in the ceiling. A stream of sunlight shone down on an apparatus in front of them. A wide metal semicircle half surrounded a ceramic orb. The sunbeam hit the metal. As the day progressed, the light would travel around the center on the band of metal.

Cantor held his hands, palms downward, about six inches above the device. "There are a lot of wards around this thing. Some for defense, some for obscuring the mechanics of how it works."

"Exactly. Dukmee decided it was more important to seek

the information we need about the Lymens rather than discern how the creators constructed this." She nodded at the intriguing device.

Bridger had his back to them, examining the biggest orrery in the middle of the room. "Bixby, can you show us how this works?"

"Yes, but let's use a smaller one." Bixby giggled. "I need to be able to reach the planes."

They moved to a glass and metal orrery no taller than Bixby. The different colored disks corresponded to planes. Burnished brass rods held them in position and rotated them in synchronization to the real objects in their solar system.

"You see, the globe in the center is our sun. Right in front of us we have the stack of planes in our system. These don't have any geological markings but they are scale model in size to the real thing." Raised letters on each disk named the plane it represented. "Over here we have the trio planets of Nedian, Narr, and Nosco. Notice they are plump in the middle, not flat like our planes. And they have an additional pattern of movement, rotating within their solar orbit. And out here are Dander and Canady."

Bridger huffed. "Where are Lyme Minor and Lyme Major? I thought the whole point of these orreries was to be able to plot the course of the rogue planes."

"They aren't in this model, but I wanted you to see the normal pattern before we introduce the renegades."

She put a finger on the bottom plane in their stack and pushed it along its course. "Now it's ahead of where it is today. See how the other planes and even the sun have moved more quickly and kept up with the one I pushed? They are still in the correct position, in line with all the other parts."

Bridger had a silly grin on his face. He pointed at the model with obvious pleasure. "So, if our planes are here, then the trio would be there."

Cantor scowled. "How does it get back to where it should be today and at this minute?"

Bixby shrugged. "I don't know. But if you leave it alone, it rewinds or something. In a couple of hours, it will be right on course."

"Fascinating." Bridger put a claw out, then paused. "May I move it some?"

"Go ahead," Bixby said.

They spent a quarter hour moving different orreries, using the keys to energize the simpler models.

Bridger liked the ones he could crank. He spent a great deal of time turning the handles. "These are coordinated with the present position of the planes, aren't they?"

"No." Bixby pointed to the larger models. "With the wind-up models, you can line one plane up with how it is in one of the perpetual orreries. Then for the length of time your turning of the key provides, you will have accurate rotations."

"I agree with Bridger," Cantor said. "Fascinating. But what about the rogue planes?"

Bixby nodded. "Over here."

She led them to a more complex model. "Here's our stack, and here are the Lymes. They've been painted red. I'll speed up the orrery, and you can watch the planes interpass."

She pushed a button on the frame. As she held it down, the planes moved along their orbits at a greater speed. Tracking the red rogue planes as they approached their planeary system proved easy but unsettling. For a moment, the Lymes appeared to be on a collision course. In the end, they slipped between the inhabited stacked planes.

Bridger let out a big sigh of relief. "Good thing they aren't going to crash into us."

Cantor put a finger on Richra and then tapped Derson. "Before they disappeared, Odem showed Ahma how these two planes were in danger of colliding. None of the orreries depict such a happening."

Bixby frowned and came to stand beside her friend. "I think it would take something out of the ordinary to make the planes wobble enough to lose their patterned orbits."

"Out of the ordinary? What constitutes out of the ordinary?"

"We'll have to ask Dukmee for precise answers, but I remember reading about unbalanced mining, like we've had in Richra. It unsettles the polar lines and gravitational pulls."

Bridger scratched his chin. "So how do these rogue planes interfere with our people? Why are they such a threat?"

Bixby waved back at the library. "The tomes say they have vehicles that travel between planes."

"Impossible!" Bridger jerked around to consult his constant. "Right, Cantor? Nothing passes through the space between. Portals must be used. You must be a realm walker to use the portals. Do these people have portals to our planes? Are they all realm walkers?"

Cantor shrugged. "I don't know, Bridger, but we're sure to find out when they get here."

Bixby strolled toward the arch. "The tomes say vehicles, not portals. And a scary thought is, the council seems to be interested in the coming of the renegade planes."

Cantor easily caught up with her. "Any theories on why?"

She didn't answer. One of the things she liked about Cantor was that he treated her like she had intelligence. When they'd worked against the council two years ago, he had included her in conversations, strategy meetings, and the final decisions. She treasured that respect, and didn't want to mar his belief that she could think. She wouldn't put forth an idea that had no substance to back it up.

FOOD FOR THOUGHT

As they moved through the archway into the library, Bixby felt the slight pressure of Cantor's huge hand on her back, ushering her ahead of him. Glancing up at his face, she realized the gesture was unconscious — his brow was knit in a thoughtful scowl. She thought of him as a very special friend. She supposed he thought of her as a friend but with no spice of something special. At least he didn't begrudge her room at his elbow like he did Bridger.

He seemed about to speak when Bridger cut in.

"Remind me, Cantor. Is Dukmee a good cook?"

The mage, it seemed, had abandoned his book and prepared a meal. Bixby hid a smile behind her hand as Cantor's stomach gave a loud growl.

She liked that he was here, even if she did have to batten down the resentment of his leaving Richra abruptly with no goodbye and no explanation. She wondered what their friendship would be like on this new adventure. At one time, she'd thought she, Cantor, and Dukmee could be the three heroes prophesized to come this generation and lead the people to renewal. But it seemed Primen had other ideas. One thing seemed certain — his plans far exceeded anything she could dream up. Her plans fell by the wayside, while reality bubbled and churned with extraordinary possibilities.

In a few minutes, they were gathered around a table, enjoying good food and drink.

"How's your sister, Bridger?" Dukmee asked.

"I don't know. Cantor and I have been busy, so I haven't been home recently. Totobee-Rodolow is a letter writer, but we haven't been in one place long enough for a letter to catch up to us."

"We write back and forth," said Bixby. "We may not have been officially constants, but we have a great friendship. I can tell you a few things Totobee-Rodolow has had in her letters."

Bridger perked up. "Have there been any hatchlings?"

Bixby twisted her lips in a grimace. "I'm sorry, Bridger. No little mor dragons."

He slumped. "What if we are the last of the real realm walkers?"

Dukmee raised his glass. "A toast to the most courageous, valiant, and meager-by-number realm walkers. That's us."

They all laughed.

Soon the conversation turned to their respective travels and the people they had encountered.

The small talk relaxed Bixby, but even under the easy flow of lighthearted banter, the problems of a corrupt government and an approaching enemy lingered.

When their bellies were full and Bixby had cleared away

the dirty dishes, she brought a pot of hot tea to the table with sugar and cream. The men sat in silence, the lighthearted mood broken. The importance of what lay before them rose to the surface. Now they would talk of treachery and danger. And how to fight it.

Cantor sipped at his tea, grimacing as it scalded his tongue. "Who has accurate information on the doings of our illustrious council?" He looked at Dukmee. "What do you know, Mage?"

"The new council building will be finished by the end of the year. The districts whose representatives died in the rebels' blast have been discouraged from seeking replacements."

Bixby passed a plate of sliced cake to Bridger. "Even if they were seeking, finding qualified councilmen would be difficult."

"More than difficult, impossible." Dukmee held his breath for a moment, let it out slowly, then continued. "Totally impossible. Our formidable foe Errd Tos remains in highest esteem among the scoundrels and rogues, crooks and thugs, but has not made a grab for a position of ultimate power. It makes one wonder what he is waiting for."

"It's clear we must speak of the council again even before we ponder the Lymes," said Cantor. "It would be best to know exactly what these evil men are up to. We can't thwart their efforts if we don't recognize one of their strategies when it pops up in our path."

Dukmee wiped his fingers on a napkin. "Bixby's parents get regular missives from the capitol. However, the official notices are worded to obscure the truth rather than to inform the populace."

Cantor rested his elbows on the table and clasped his hands. "Nothing sanctioned by the council is what it would seem to be."

Dukmee nodded. "I do have a bit of verified news. The attempt to murder many of the councilmen was only partially successful. Thirty-three were killed. Out of the sixty-six members still living, there are those loyal to the people."

"There were three before the bombing," said Bridger. "Do three remain?"

"At least one." Dukmee swirled the tea in his cup. "And we can hope all three. Those uncorrupted by the evil leaders are still unknown to us."

Bixby, who had heard all this before, grew excited. "There's to be a closed vote. Then we'll know for sure how many true councilmen remain. Just like before, our men will vote without fear of reprisal. We'll know by how many vote against the majority."

Bridger shifted in his seat. His voice hummed his distrust when he spoke. "And what is the vote on?"

Dukmee lowered his voice. "The last two years have been spent re-establishing the Realm Walker's Guild in a suitable building since the explosions leveled the old hall. Very little overt governing of the realm walkers has been done. But the diminishing number of realm walkers is a worry in all the realms."

Bixby bounced once in her chair before she spoke. "In the days before this council, a dozen or so Realm Walker initiates showed up every year. In the last two years, no one has stepped forward to accept the challenge. We were the last."

Dukmee's hand squeezed gently, and Bixby subsided again. His leadership was unquestioned, but sometimes it was hard to keep quiet and let him guide the conversation. "The council proposes elevating soldiers to the positions that need to be filled."

Cantor, who had tipped back in his seat, jerked forward, and the front legs of the chair hit the stone floor with a thud. "Wait a minute! Soldiers not born to the realm walking service will be plucked out of the armies? They'll be given authority as if they had the stamp of Primen's approval?"

Dukmee nodded. "Exactly. You, your constant, and Bixby never received the approval of the council, yet you function as realm walkers with full authority. Your activities are sanctioned by Primen, but not by men. These soldiers will be endorsed by the council, but not by Primen."

Bridger growled deep in his throat. "How can these phoney realm walkers walk from one realm to another? Seems that would bugger up the council's plans."

"They've got a machine." Bixby refilled Bridger's teacup, which allowed her to move out from under Dukmee's hand.

The dragon's face scrunched up in distaste. "A machine?"

Bixby nodded with her lips pressed in a tight line and her eyes wide. "A machine that creates and sustains portals."

"Impossible." Bridger jerked and spilt his tea. Jesha complained as the hot liquid splattered her coat. She jumped to a cleared part of the table, threw her dragon a scowl, and commenced a clean-up job.

Bixby refilled Bridger's cup. "Impossible as it sounds, they have it. The leaders of the guild are moving to a position of exclusive power. One day, they shall rule all parts of the government, not just deal with realm walker business."

"Until then," said Dukmee, "we have hope. As long as our unknown spies are close to the core of corruption. Although they daily face possible exposure, their presence in the heart of the council allows us to keep informed."

Dukmee finished his drink and allowed Bixby to pour

more tea for him. "They risked sending a message out." Dukmee stirred his brew. "Through these councilmen, we have learned of the guild's interest in the rogue planes."

Cantor leaned forward. "Then they're planning a defense of our realms?"

"In a manner of speaking, yes. Their real goal is to get a hold of these vehicles that travel through a short distance of space. To hop from one plane to another without the use of realm walkers and portals would mean they could invade and conquer the very people they are pledged to protect."

5

AWAKENING

After more than an hour of puzzling over the council's means and motives, Cantor could no longer control his yawning. Bixby, still a fount of energy, laughingly offered to show him a place to sleep. He followed her down a stone corridor as she chattered, watching her graceful bounce. He tightened his cheek muscles, sternly keeping a smile from his face. He didn't want her to think he was laughing at her when the truth was her merry spirit brightened his whole being.

While he and Bridger had been searching the nine planes, he hadn't thought much about her. His determination to find Ahma and Odem had dominated his thinking, followed closely by the pressing need to avoid the notice of any guild representative who may have been lurking about.

Now, though, watching Bixby, he realized he'd missed her. The past two years had brought little time for slowing down, and the near future promised to be no different. Yet Bixby remained as she had always been, bubbling with joy and wonder at life. In her presence, he felt some of his tension fade away. Dukmee and Bixby could be trusted. Perhaps after dealing with the Lyme problem, they would join him in his search.

At one time, he'd hoped to locate and rescue his mentor and her friend on his own, but that didn't happen, and he had come to see that drive for what it was: pride. Finding them would have verified the trust they had placed in him, so each failure had wound him tighter until he thought he would splinter into tiny shards.

Now he was not above asking for help. Using the wisdom Ahma had instilled in him, he was able to see the emotion that had driven his quest — pride — had also blocked its effectiveness. The recent counseling by Queen Mazeline had forced his recognition to the surface. He felt more comfortable with himself than he had since he had walked through the first portal on his search for a dragon constant.

Bixby whirled to face him and glided backward. "The lights in the library are way too bright for us to sleep under. We tried the first night we were here. The next day, I got tired of looking at book after book and scroll after scroll. So I did some exploring."

She twirled with her arms outstretched, indicating the surrounding area. Her light layers of clothing swirled out like many textured fans unfolding. "I found these little alcoves in the tunnels close to the library. I think the original keepers of the Lyme legacy slept in them. They remind me of what I've read about the sanctuary wardens' sparse living quarters."

She pirouetted a few times as they walked, making the little dance-like movements with such ease that it didn't interfere with the process of walking. Any other woman would look odd gliding and skipping while she strolled along. Cantor didn't call Bixby odd. She was light, dainty, full of life, and delightfully unique.

Cantor smiled in spite of himself.

She paused and gestured to the alcove beside them. "How about this one?"

Dim lights along the ceiling of the tunnel illuminated the corridor, but the niche was pitch black. He put the globe-light hat on his head and stepped in.

The room looked to be manmade. Scars from metal tools lined the walls in neat rows. On one wall at knee height, the original rock had been left to jut out in a solid bench. The space could be used as a convenient place to sit or as a bed for someone smaller than Cantor. Protrusions scattered across two walls at random intervals.

"I have a number of theories about those," said Bixby when Cantor reached out and touched one. "They could be hooks for hanging clothes. Some of them might have held a slab of wood for books or various knick-knacks."

Cantor humphed a gentle laugh. "Sanctuary wardens enjoyed sitting on the cold, hard benches while admiring their collection of knick-knacks?"

Bixby laughed. "Maybe not knick-knacks."

"Decidedly not knick-knacks."

"I concede." Bixby held up one elegant finger. "But they could have been hooks for clothes. Or hammocks."

Cantor studied the protrusions for a moment. "So I won't have to scrunch my huge self to sleep on that bench thing? Bixby, you are a wonderful girl."

He took pleasure in the way her face lit up at the compliment.

Ducking his head, he concentrated on his pockets. He

found his camping hamper, and out of that removed a hammock. While he attached the hanging bed to two outcroppings of rock, he asked what would be the routine for the morrow and how could he help.

Bixby wrinkled her nose. "Read books. Read scrolls. Look at maps. Read more books. Read more scrolls. Look at more maps. Until we find the exact date, or rather the way to calculate the exact date of the rogue planes' arrival, we are stuck in the mountain."

"Sounds boring."

"It is."

"But necessary."

With a great sigh, Bixby agreed. "It is."

"Are you going to show Bridger to a sleeping room?"

"Yes. In one of the other tunnels, there are larger niches. I remember how he grows when he sleeps."

Cantor laughed. They'd had trouble moving Bridger when he was drugged and growing with every minute that passed.

"That was a special case. No doubt the narcotic acted as a stimulant to his growth. In two years, he's never topped that night."

"I'm glad to hear it."

She stood in the doorway, watching him. He fidgeted with the hammock, wondering why she hadn't hurried off to do her next assignment. She remained still, and her eyes did not waver from his face. His nerves twitched under the steady gaze.

"What?"

"Do you really dislike him so much? Are you still looking for another mor dragon to be your constant?"

Closing his eyes, he blocked out her pathetic, sad puppy look. Bixby didn't fake emotion or hide her thoughts. She really was concerned about his chafing at having a constant thrust upon him instead of being able to choose. Granted, she was probably also concerned about Bridger's having to endure his disdain.

"He's been with me two years, Bixby. I can't count the times his lack of self-discipline has taken me to the brink of disaster." He wiped his hand over his face. "Though, to be honest, he's never left me in the lurch he's created. He can be adept at rescue, but not necessarily in a quiet, discreet manner." He made a face, just to show how much he didn't want to say the next words. "I like him."

He turned around, looking at her sympathetic face and wishing her away. "Why don't you go usher him to bed?" He smiled, trying to soften his words. "If he manages to drop you in a crevice or pile rocks on your head, give me a call, and I'll come help restore order. I've gotten pretty good at restoring order."

Cantor flipped out of the hammock at the first shriek. At the second, he relaxed. Bridger. Something had excited the dragon. The cry was not of imminent danger but of discovery.

The light globe brightened the room as soon as he removed the covering cloth. He reached for his jerkin as the pattering sound of delicate footsteps came down the corridor. He had it over his head and began to thrust his arms into the sleeves. The person stopped at the entry and gasped.

Annoyed, he hurried. As the neck of his stretchy jerkin popped down around his throat, he studied Bixby. Her white skin flushed scarlet. She blinked rapidly, then whirled to face the other direction.

"Bixby!" He almost laughed. "You've seen me without a shirt before."

Her hair flew as she shook her head. "You looked like a boy then."

"You're making me feel uncomfortable. Turn around. I'm decent."

She obeyed, but her eyes flicked from one object in the room to the next, never settling on her friend. "You were decent be-before. I mean, well, I mean you-you aren't the type to be indecent. In-in words, you know. And, of course, you're decent now, but before, I was in a hurry, and-and you startled me."

Cantor had buckled his belt around his waist, put on his tunic, and now sat pulling on his boots. "What was the hurry all about?"

She clapped her hands and gave a little hop. "He did it. He figured it out."

"Bridger?"

"No! Dukmee."

"Oh, I heard Bridger a minute ago."

"He sort of squealed when Dukmee told him."

Anticipation grew in his chest, along with excitement that wasn't entirely his. He eyed the tiny woman. He'd been a close friend to Bixby two years ago. Renewed proximity must have reawakened the bond they had developed then. That relationship had felt like a sibling rapport. He was well aware that he didn't feel brotherly toward the girl waiting for him now. One more reason to keep the emotions under wraps.

Pushing away the thought, he stood. "Well?" he prodded her. "What news?"

"Dukmee has calculated the date the rogue planes will interpass with our planes."

"How long do we have?"

"Sixty-four days."

Sixty-four days. His heart jumped to his throat. Carefully, he tamped down the desire to cheer. Finally! A problem out in the open, one that could be planned for with exact dates, locations, and participants. And not four months away but just over two. No more mindless wandering and endless waiting.

Maintaining an outer calm, he unhooked his hammock and stuck it in the hamper and shoved the hamper into a pocket. "Then I guess we'd better get moving."

6

WHAT'S NEEDED

Cantor and Bixby found Dukmee in the Orrery Chamber. The mage had placed extra shining orbs around the walls and in between the devices. In the bright light, the machines seemed more alive than before. The orreries hummed, clicked, and glimmered with activity.

Bridger sat on a bench against the wall with Jesha in his arms. He whispered as they came into the room. "We're staying out of the way." The dragon nodded his head toward Dukmee. "This is the third time he's put his theory to the test. It has to do with disproportionate displacement as opposed to formulaic cubic diatrams."

"What does that mean?" asked Cantor.

"I have no idea. I don't know if I even got the words in the right order, or the words that belong together in the same phrase. And there were three other words I can't remember. One of them had six syllables. Saying 'orreries' is easy compared to the one that started with alogor—" Bridger ended his statement with a shrug.

Dukmee mumbled as he worked. Numbers and letters tripped off his tongue in rapid succession. He stood back for a moment, lunged forward, and adjusted a globe that had jerked a bit. Then the scholar paced back and forth with his thumb and forefinger framing his chin.

A grin grew above Dukmee's scruffy jaw. He must have worked all night, with no sleep and no morning shave. Cantor lifted his fingers to his own cheeks. Yes, he was unkempt as well.

The orrery under Dukmee's watchful eye clicked twice and stopped. Lyme Minor and Lyme Major hung on their rods inches away from the nine-stack planeary system. In the gesture of a stage magician, the mage extended his arms wide.

He turned and bowed to his small audience and made his announcement with theatrical flair. "We have the date ... and the hour ... and the *location* of the interpass."

Bixby clapped and bounced. Cantor gave a cheer, and Bridger whooped. Jesha jumped from Bridger's arms and flounced over to Dukmee. The cat did an intricate circling of his legs, weaving in and out from under the hem of his long, elaborate robe.

Dukmee first looked down with pleasure. His pleasure turned to annoyance as Jesha persisted.

Cantor sympathized. The dragon's cat could wear out her welcome in any number of ways. He had been tripped when he'd been her favored person of the moment. She also kneaded with sharp claws. And on occasion, Jesha arbitrarily decided Cantor could be her designated giver of food. Then he received a scratch and shrill meow to announce an empty stomach.

In Cantor's opinion, the cat Jesha was a lot like the dragon Bridger.

Jesha's adoration ended abruptly when the mage scooped the multicolored fur ball away from his legs and into his arms.

Turning his attention to Dukmee's experiment, Cantor studied the location of each plane. "How is it that you suddenly have the answer?"

Bridger stood. "I did it."

Cantor couldn't help but raise a skeptical brow.

"No, really." Bridger looked to the mage for confirmation, and Dukmee nodded his affirmation. "I cleared the table for our dinner last night, and after we washed the dishes and put them away, I returned the papers to the table. Only they weren't in the same order."

"And?" Cantor looked from Bridger's smug face to Dukmee's self-satisfied grin.

The mage stepped to a table and picked up an insignificant looking paper. "He took this paper that had been at the bottom of a pile and put it on the top of the pile next to the one I was working on. They go together, you see. And at one glance, I saw the smaller page held the key to the formulas on the larger."

"And this combined formula tells us — ?"

"Lyme Major will pass between Richra and Derson while Lyme Minor passes between Derson and Zonvaner. So we can now see where to put our defenses and when."

With his fingers templed in front of his chin, Cantor let out a huge breath of air, then turned to face Dukmee. "But do we know anything about the Lymen themselves? How are we to plan our strategy?"

Bridger nodded his huge head. "It's fit and laudable to know when and where we fight. This information enables us to meet them as they invade our planes. However, there is the unaddressed problem. What do we do to repel them? We need an offense as well as a defense."

The dragon stood and paced to the archway, swiveled and returned. His arms lengthened to stretch under his wings. With his hands clasped behind him, his claw-tipped fingers interlaced, he looked like an odd professor brooding over a weighty question.

Cantor leaned his tall frame against the wall, crossed his arms over his chest, and watched Bridger with a reluctant twinge of amusement.

Bixby perched herself on a stool to watch. "Do be careful of your tail when you pivot, Bridger."

The dragon turned neatly at the opposite wall and started back. He didn't answer Bixby.

"Do they fight with spears?" asked Bridger. "Swords? Poison sprays? Bows and arrows? Ball bats? Fleas? Are they afraid of water? Do they lose focus if you sing to them? Do shellfish make them break out in spots?"

Cantor's mouth had drooped open during this recitation. Dukmee looked equally lost. Bridger's musing lacked logic even beyond the dragon's usual standard. Cantor pressed his lips together and tried to make Bridger's rambling nonsense connect to the matter at hand. He couldn't. "Spots?"

Again Bridger's head bobbed up and down. "My cousin gets red welts when he eats crabs or shrimp. All over. Even behind his ears and between his toes. It's a sight to see. He itches and burns and complains."

Bridger ran his hands across his skin, demonstrating how his cousin reacted. "I've thought before that he must be careful not to eat shellfish before a competition."

He looked around at his three friends. They didn't respond. "He's a competitive fisherman."

His audience still stood dumbfounded.

"He's won several tourneys."

"I know!" Bixby's blurted declaration brought Dukmee and Cantor out of their befuddlement.

Cantor examined her excited face. "You know about Bridger's cousin?"

"No. I know about the Lymen warriors."

Various light materials exquisitely sewn into elaborate clothing quivered over her eager frame. Sparkly pieces flashed an array of colors. She didn't wait for the men to respond. "I've been reading the stories."

Cantor wondered if he'd left all sense and logic in the sleeping alcove. He certainly was not surrounded by pillars of rationality. His companions had lost touch with the importance of this mission. Fishing tourneys and bedtime tales? "Stories?"

Dukmee stepped closer to Bixby and put a hand on her shoulder. "Histories." He gestured to the wall lined with bookcases. "Diaries, journals, reports, letters. A thousand different accounts of the Lymen."

Bridger spun around to face Bixby. His tail knocked over a small wooden orrery. "And you can tell us all about them?"

"Absolutely. I have excellent retention."

"What do they like to eat?"

"Cattle and corn."

"Weaknesses?"

"Our sun hurts their eyes."

"Weapon of choice?"

"Anything pointy. Swords, arrows, knives, and spears."

Bridger grinned at Cantor. "This is great."

Cantor agreed, but his mind was already looking ahead. "We'll have to organize the information first, plan our strategy accordingly, and then secure one more thing before we can even hope to slow them down."

"What?" asked Bixby. "What else do we need?"

"An army."

Determined to get numerous projects done before they left, the realm walkers took up different chores. Later in the afternoon, Bixby sat inside a cupboard she had emptied of its store of scrolls. One of the scrolls had caught her eye.

Colors.

Most of the materials she had investigated were black on white or faded brown on darkening yellow. She'd found the latter hard to read.

When she glimpsed a design of yellow, green, and purple, she snatched the scroll out of the tidy pile. With new enthusiasm, she sat on the only uncluttered spot available, the cabinet she had just emptied.

The musty smell tickled her nose. She dug out a lace handkerchief saturated with a light lemon freshening gel and waved it around her head. Tucking it away with a smile, she concentrated on her find. She pulled one end of the neat bow, untying the ribbon. The parchment crackled as she cautiously unrolled the scroll.

Pictures!

Whimsical pictures. The artist conveyed his delight over the subjects depicted on the page, drawing with a light touch of outlining and muted colors giving substance. Bixby wondered if originally these colors had been bold. Now the yellow was murky, the green subdued, and the purple almost black.

As she unrolled the scroll, the pictures became brighter. She bit her lip in anticipation as she ventured on. The last section had only the line drawings, which petered out to nothing. A great deal of room was left, but no more entries.

She frowned.

She didn't have a clear idea of what the maker of this scroll wanted to portray. In order to grasp that concept, she needed to be more systematic in her study. Carefully rerolling the last of the parchment, she began again, this time applying years of studying technique to follow the sequence in more depth.

The depiction of a pod from some plant repeated throughout the manuscript, though only once did the artist actually picture this pod in the branches of a bush. As Bixby explored the scenes, she realized the graceful, willowy limbs and foliage surrounding the pods were actually creatures, more animal than plant. They seemed to crawl in and out of the pods, which begged the question: Were the people tiny or the pods humongous?

Scribbles beside the images began to make sense to her puzzling mind.

Words, but not in a language she recognized and not in a script she had ever seen before. She secured the scroll with its original ribbon and scrambled out of her cubbyhole. Dukmee must see this.

She found him packing up maps on the far side of the library. Dukmee used ornate map weights to spread the scroll from one end of a long table to the other, planting the palm-sized metal statues at regular intervals along the half-blank length of parchment.

The scholar tapped his chin as he slowly perused the document, then grabbed a long-legged metal animal by its middle and shifted it in order to expose an image quite near the edge.

Bridger walked close behind him, peering from his great height over the mage's shoulder.

Cantor stood on the other side of the table, which meant he looked at the whole piece upside down. He pointed to a square of random-looking black marks. "What's this language?"

"The old tongue," Dukmee said.

Cantor's thoughts wisped through Bixby's mind. *"What does he mean?"*

Bixby allowed her cheer to brighten her eyes and face, even in this solemn occasion. *"I believe the next history round we would have taken in training would have covered the theory of the nine planes and only one language. And of course, the old tongue."*

"Ahma and Odem never mentioned these theories."

"Not theories, plural, but theory, singular."

Dukmee bent over the scroll, taking a closer look at some of the writing. Bixby held her breath, waiting for some pronouncement. Dukmee straightened and moved on.

She sighed.

"Why just one theory?" asked Cantor.

"It shouldn't be called a theory, should it?"

Exasperation nipped at Cantor's words. *"No comment. Not enough information."*

Bixby giggled. *"Sorry."*

"It is fortunate," said Dukmee to both of their minds, *"that my coworkers are so considerate. They'd not hinder my thinking by chatting superfluously while I weigh the evidence of this startling discovery."*

Bridger's voice pushed into the cluttered conversation. *"Not using a hedge, are they?"*

Bixby covered her mouth. A ridiculous gesture since the words hadn't been spoken. A bubble of laughter tried to surface. She tamped it down. Her eyes caught Cantor's. His twinkled. The bubble rose again and escaped.

The laugh burst from her lips, followed by Bridger's slow chuckle, then Cantor's rumbling laughter.

Dukmee's eyebrows rose almost to his hairline. He grinned. "Let's have tea and biscuits, and I'll tell you what I think."

The busyness of preparing a snack gave them time to put aside their humor. With hot tea in their mugs, the three turned eager eyes to the mage.

With his free hand, Dukmee indicated the new find displayed on the table. "These are pictures of the devices used to travel from one plane to another. The pods are part of a plant, of course, and therefore prone to lose integrity quickly." He pointed to a picture of a pile of vegetation. On closer inspection, Bixby realized it was not a garbage heap, but old rotting pods.

Dukmee continued. "I tend to think they can make one trip, to and back. They seem to carry only one occupant. So far, I see more problems in using them than advantages."

Cantor ran his finger along the rim of his mug. "Unless you have no portals and no realm walkers."

"Exactly so, Cantor. I doubt they would be useful for our forces, but I can see the guild using them for illegal transport. The evidence of their crime could be buried in a mulch pile."

Jesha jumped into Bridger's lap, eyeing the cheese in his sandwich. Bridger squinted as he thought. Offhandedly, he offered his cat a pinched-off treat while he pondered the new information. "Shall we need an army to repulse the Lymen?"

"I believe so." Dukmee pointed to mid-scroll. "See one of the last pictures — the one that looks like scribble and dots?"

They all directed their attention to where Dukmee pointed.

"That," said the mage in a tone of a grandiose announcement, "is a field. In the field are plants. On the plants are pods."

Realization poured through Bixby's mind and flooded her system with a surge of energy. "Those are pods, thousands of pods."

Bridger shook his head slowly. "Enough pods to deliver an army."

Cantor grimaced. "We need an army."

7

UNEXPECTED COMPANY

Bridger used both arms to gesture at the table laden with books, scrolls, and loose sheets of parchment. "Shouldn't we ask somebody for permission to take all this from the library?"

Cantor shrugged, amused by his constant's desire to follow rules, even when no rules were evident. "Who shall we ask?"

He glanced up from the scrolls he was tying together as the female member of their mission waltzed into the room.

With her garments flowing around her, Bixby came to the work table, carrying several hampers. "Bridger, I'm just glad Dukmee didn't ask us to stuff orreries into these bags."

Cantor straightened and used two fisted hands to rub the small of his back. None of the work tables were the right height for his long torso. He watched Bixby's graceful hands pluck up the smaller tomes and place them in the bag. Bridger's movements resembled those of a shovel digging and tossing garden dirt around. Cantor strode to his side, hoping that with his help they might store the materials with less damage to their frail pages.

While he piled books into small stacks for Bridger to shift into the hamper, he stole glances at Bixby, with her clothes fluttering to the slightest movement and her face in a constant shine of pleasure. She didn't look like someone who would stick to an assignment as dry as plowing through hundreds of old works of literature.

He smiled at her. "Bixby, you constantly surprise me. You've done an admirable job of reading and recording Lymen facts in your journal."

She tossed a frown at him. "I thought you were smart enough to figure out that I'm more than a pretty face. I'm disappointed to find out you didn't think I could study. After all, Cantor, I had my first tutor when I was three."

He laughed and saw her relax. He stretched out his arms and turned in a complete circle. "I know, Bix, but look at this."

Shaking his head, Cantor surveyed the multiple bookcases around the room. He studied the disheveled shelves, noting the empty spaces and the stacks of tomes on various tabletops. "No wonder they called this the Lymen Library. How many books do you suppose are here?"

Bridger answered. "Five hundred sixty-seven."

Bixby's head came up, and she stared at the dragon. "You counted them?"

He smiled sheepishly. "I couldn't sleep the first night we were here."

Cantor grunted. "I'm surprised you didn't put back the ones that Dukmee and Bixby had out."

"Dukmee threatened to lock me in a bottle if I messed

up his piles. I didn't know which were his and which were Bixby's."

Despite the annoyance Cantor sometimes felt at the mage's high-handed decrees, he could not deny the man's good judgment. Especially this last decree to pack up most of the library and take it with them. "Dukmee's right, I know. By taking the unread volumes with us, we can continue to read and learn as much as we can before the enemy lands. There just hasn't been enough time for Bixby to read and summarize all the information."

Bixby kept up her pace of securing the material into hampers. "I think part of his reasoning is that it's better for us to have these than our enemies. What an advantage over the council to know more about our visitors than they do!"

Bixby pushed between the dragon and Cantor as she tidied more bound documents away in another hamper. Apparently, they weren't working fast enough for her.

She thrust her chin toward the tallest bookcase. "I never did get that entire high shelf read. The smaller books came down easily, but I couldn't budge that big, thick monster. It's stuck to the ledge. I couldn't get situated to apply enough leverage." Her head swung back and forth as she looked at her companions. "Maybe one of you could get that last book down."

Cantor left off straightening parchments. Rubbing his palms on his tunic, he approached the ladder leading to the top shelf of a bookcase that almost reached the ceiling. It was twice his height.

"Bridger, come hold the ladder steady," he called as he put his foot on the first rung.

The dragon trotted across the room and grasped the wooden slats with his massive clawed hands. "Got it."

Cantor scrambled up to the top and reached for the volume. He clutched the back binding and pulled. The book didn't budge. He leaned so he could move his body around the ladder and closer to the shelf. "It doesn't look like it's glued down. No sign of moisture that could have caused the edge of the leather binding and the pages to stick."

Bixby had come to stand beside Bridger, her head tilted back so she could see, her hands perched on her hips.

Cantor winked at her. "You aren't a wimp after all." He laughed at the face she pulled.

Cantor tugged again, and the bookcase tilted forward. "Whoa!" He shoved the shelves back against the wall. "Bridger, maybe you should put your shoulder against the bookcase and let Bixby steady the ladder."

Bixby laughed. "You're going to trust your safety to the wimp?"

"Yes, but if I fall, you get out of the way. I'd flatten you. And you'd have to get a new wardrobe. Those clothes wouldn't do for a two-dimensional figure." He reached for the book again. "Are you two ready?"

They chorused an affirmative.

"On the count of three. One ... two ... three!"

The ladder and the bookcase swayed but didn't fall. Cantor held the book up in triumph.

He began his descent but stopped midway. In the distance, a mighty wind rushed through the tunnels. He looked at the tables. None of the papers stirred. The stillness before the storm?

Bridger tilted his head. "I don't like the sound of that. Hurry, Cantor. Get down."

Cantor agreed. He needed to get down fast. Roosting near

the ceiling on an ancient ladder was not the right place to meet whatever approached.

He scuttled down to the floor, wrapped an arm around Bixby, and guided her to a huge table next to a wall. Bridger kept pace with them, pausing only long enough to grab the hampers they had been filling, and all three slid underneath the massive wooden slab.

The clamor escalated. Individual disturbances punctuated the steady rush. Things broke with sharp snaps. Objects slammed into other objects. Crashes, clattering, and solid thuds increased in number and volume. Augmenting that cacophony, the squealing wrench of things pulled apart added a high-pitched din. Still, nothing in the room stirred. At odds with the sound of a raging wind, none of the papers moved.

Bixby squirmed in the circle of Cantor's arm. She twisted her head so her mouth hovered inches from his ear. "Where's Dukmee?"

"I don't know."

Bridger turned to face them and extended his wings as a shield. He transformed his body into a barrier curved over the front of them like a stone shell.

Dukmee's flushed face appeared around the edge of the shield. Cantor and Bixby scooted over as he squeezed in.

Bixby leaned across Cantor to take Dukmee's arm. "You're breathing hard. Did you come far?"

He shook his head. In a loud, clear voice, he announced, "You've torn open a ward."

Cantor nodded. "We pried a book off a shelf."

"This is going to be interesting." Dukmee's face glowed with excitement.

Howls joined the tumult of the blustery wind. Cantor

pulled the trembling Bixby closer as the snapping of jaws and deep-throated growls invaded the bookroom. He reached for his sword.

Dukmee put his hand on Cantor's. "No need. It is all sound, no substance."

"Then why are you hiding with us?"

Dukmee's lips stretched into a wide grin. His eyebrows arched. "Better safe than sorry. I'm quite sure this racket is all bluster. But twice in my long life, I've been wrong. A third miscalculation is overdue."

Booted feet in military cadence joined the din of wind and beasts. If those hiding under the table believed their ears, an army approached, aggressive and prepared for battle.

"I think this is the end of it," yelled Dukmee. "Cover your ears."

Cantor and Bixby obeyed. Even with his ears protected, Cantor winced in discomfort as the decibel level increased.

Bridger in his shield form rattled. The onslaught of reverberation caused the floor to shake, and the dragon shimmied forward and then back. The roar culminated in an explosion.

As if a switch had been thrown, the raucous racket ceased. Cantor lowered his hands. Bixby, sheltered in the curve of his chest and lap, uncovered her ears as well.

Dukmee inched toward the opening between Bridger and the table leg. "Let's see what the ward has brought us."

"Aha!" he said as soon as his head was around the obstruction. He wiggled free. "Bridger, thank you for your protection. You can become your delightful self once more."

As the stone barricade shifted into a dragon again, Bixby and Cantor came out from under the table. Not until they were up did they notice the object of Dukmee's amused gaze.

By the door to the sleeping corridor, a young man in loose white clothing stood looking them over.

Cantor's hand moved to the hilt of his sword. "Who are you?" He stepped forward, maneuvering himself between the stranger and his friends as he took the young man's measure. Smallish, athletic, pale skin, sharp facial features, long hair caught in a leather strap at the base of his neck. No weapons. A friendly expression.

The stranger's gray eyes sparkled, and the protrusion on his skinny neck bobbed as he spoke. "My name is Neekoh. I assume you have come to rescue my master, Chomountain, the right hand of Primen."

8

SIDE TRIP?

Bixby's eyes traveled from Dukmee to Cantor to Bridger, who now held Jesha, and back to Dukmee. Decisions for the group naturally came under his jurisdiction, though she wasn't always sure why.

She eased her small form behind Cantor and drew out her crown hamper. In a moment, she'd switched her organizing crown for a small tiara with tiny points tipped with light refracting crystals. She stepped out, ready to read this stranger's aura.

Neekoh stood with a detached but pleasant expression on his face. His relaxed attitude of extreme good nature seemed out of place given the effect his announcement had on the rest of the group. Could he have played a role in the capture and detention of the powerful Chomountain? Or if he was, indeed, on the side of the righteous, what role did he play in safeguarding the right hand of Primen?

Bixby concentrated, determined to make an accurate

assessment of Neekoh's character. The man shivered with excitement and anticipation. No dark lines of malice lodged among the pleasing colors. No twisted or repetitive strands mixed in with the strands of curiosity, hospitality, and compassion. So, Neekoh harbored no duplicity. He appeared to be a nice young man with a tint of loneliness, a strong dose of duty, and a muddled jumble of confusion.

The man of mystery's straight stance seemed to be his natural posture. One hand clasped the other and rested at his midriff without actually touching his belt. His eyes sparkled and every so often his nose twitched. On the whole, his demeanor reminded Bixby of a friendly field mouse.

She approached Dukmee's mind to report her observations, but Dukmee told her to hush. He probably was making his own assessments. Bixby mentally shrugged aside his easy dismissal and returned to studying Neekoh.

On closer inspection, she realized smudges of dust and various stains marred his white attire. Someone had untidily mended tears here and there in his clothing. The thread, in pale yellow or tan or even blue, did not match the white material. The cloth at his knees and elbows was threadbare. Frayed neck, cuffs, and hems indicated long wear.

Yet Neekoh stood with self-confidence, his shabby appearance unacknowledged. Bixby had seen finely dressed messengers in a similar pose, waiting to deliver their missives to the king.

Intrigued, Bixby wanted to sit the young man down with tea and cake and pry information from him. She knew her curiosity would have to wait, however, until Dukmee gave her permission to become acquainted with Chomountain's champion.

Almost on cue, the mage again took the lead. He stepped

closer, successfully putting himself between their visitor and skeptical Cantor, who fingered the hilt of his sword in a way that made her nervous.

"It's all right, Cantor. Relax. I've read his aura and he's basically a normal person with no hints of sinister intent, but a bit lonely and confused."

"Well, we've all been lonely and confused from time to time."

"That's right, so quit looking like you're going to tackle him."

She heard his gentle laughter from his mind to hers. She saw his shoulder muscles loosen up.

Dukmee took his ceremonial pose, with arms crossed and hands tucked into his large sleeves. "Where is Chomountain?"

Neekoh's face brightened with interest. "In a valley on the other side of the mountain."

"This mountain?"

Neekoh frowned and looked around the disordered library. "Well, it's been a long time since I've been in this room. But I do believe this is the library of the Lymes' legend, isn't it?" He glanced around at the others nodding. "Well then, yes, Chomountain is imprisoned on the other side of this mountain."

Cantor took a step to the side, which allowed him to look straight at the young man. "How can the right hand of Primen be imprisoned?"

"On the one hand, it would be difficult, on the other, quite easy. I'm incapable of using either hand in such matters and had nothing to do with it."

Cantor's lips tightened. "Speak plain."

"Chomountain doesn't remember that he's Chomountain. Therefore, he cannot do any of the things you would expect him to do."

Bixby fidgeted, alarmed. Who could hold enough power to strip Chomountain of his memory? Certainly no one in the guild was capable. And, since this happened many generations ago, no guild member was sufficiently ancient.

Bixby peeked around Dukmee and caught Neekoh's eye. "Have you always been Chomountain's servant?"

Neekoh inclined his head. "My entire life has been in preparation for serving the right hand of Primen. My father and grandfather and my grandfather's grandfather — all the firstborn males in my family have been so honored for years without number. However, we are not servants, but guardians until someone frees Chomountain."

Cantor edged closer to Neekoh. "Who in this illustrious ancestry was the last to see Chomountain?"

"I believe the first Neekoh was the last Neekoh to actually see Chomountain."

Bixby tilted her head, listening to an odd sound. A door squeaked on its hinges. Clicking indicated the latch had slipped into place. The unmistakable scrape of a key in a lock followed.

Bixby looked to her companions. "What was that?"

Dukmee hurried to the table and picked up the heavy book that had safeguarded the ward.

"The ward you tore open is itself protected by wards. With the initial dismemberment, other precautions were activated. These wards are in place to turn back whoever ventured this far."

His voice trailed off as he thumbed through the pages of the book. "Just as I thought, a ward book," he muttered. He pulled out glasses and perched them on his nose. "Very thorough. Whoever wrote this knew far more than the average mage."

He placed the open book on the table and skimmed through the pages. Bixby and Cantor came to stand on either side of him, while Bridger positioned himself between their visitor and the door.

The mor dragon stretched his neck to see over the three lined up against the table. "It's the old tongue again, isn't it?"

"Most certainly," said Dukmee. "A bit of a bother."

Bixby grasped the side of the table as another series of sounds interrupted their search through the large book. Something heavy rasped against something else. The noise ceased and the rattle of heavy chains ended the episode.

"Aren't these just sounds?" asked Bridger. "Nothing is really happening, right? Like the wind and brute animals ... all fury and no substance."

Dukmee shut the book with a snap. "We've got to get out of here. We're hearing the sounds of closing wards. We need to be out before all the exits are blocked."

Bixby placed a hand on his arm. If she hadn't touched him, she wouldn't have realized how perilous the mage considered their situation, but the muscles under her hand bunched with coiled action.

"But if it's just racket, nothing is being sealed."

"I believe this to be true. However" — the corner of his mouth twitched — "remind me to tell you about those two times I was wrong. I think I'd rather be overcautious at the moment."

He turned to the others. "Let's go! The most direct route out of this mountain! Grab the hampers that are packed. We may not get a chance to come back."

Neekoh leapt into action, gathering hampers and shoving them into the folds of his clothing. When the table was empty, he went to another. The others worked as diligently. Soon the five had cleared all the surfaces. Neekoh ran to the door. "Follow me! I know the best way."

Bridger scooped up Jesha and ran through the door leading to the more excavated tunnels. Bixby tossed a look over her shoulder to the two men. "Let's go!"

Cantor shook his head. "How do we know he knows where to go?"

Dukmee hefted the ward book into his arms. "Apparently, he's lived down here all his life."

"He might be part of a trap, a conspirator with the guild."

A great grumble shuddered through the rocks. A spattering of dust and tiny particles cascaded onto their heads.

Bixby shook her skirts to dislodge the crumbs of the cave ceiling. "This doesn't look like the noise is just bluster."

Dukmee took Bixby's arm and guided her toward the door. "Even if the locks are a decoy, the reverberations of noise could destroy the honeycomb of caves and passages. We'd best leave."

"I don't trust this protector." Cantor shook his head and combed fingers through his gritty hair.

Bixby left Dukmee and ran back to grab the front of Cantor's tunic. "Come on! Remember I checked his aura, and he's fine. He doesn't have evil intentions."

Bridger appeared in the door. "Are you coming?"

Accompanied by rumbles, grinding, and miscellaneous pops, Bixby and Cantor ran after Bridger.

Whoever had set up the library with lights and the Orreries Chamber with lasting power had also provided illumination for the halls. At times, the glow came from phosphorescent rocks. Certain stretches had contraptions that hummed but also emitted a steady, radiant beam. Dukmee had expressed the desire to take one down and examine it, but Bixby doubted they'd have the time now.

The shaking walls didn't interrupt the supply of light. For that, Bixby was grateful. She'd packed her caged globe hat in her camping hamper, but she had no idea where she'd put it. Where inside of her clothing had she attached that container?

Bridger stopped abruptly, and Bixby ran into him, finding herself standing on his tail and plastered uncomfortably against his spiny back. Cantor did a better job of coming to a halt. He bumped into Bixby, but it was a gentle bump.

They peered around the dragon to see Dukmee standing under a light, holding the ward book at chin level and scanning the pages with haste. Bixby realized if she had been the one holding the book and searching for clues, her aura would have been frantic. Dukmee's remained calm but hurried. Even patterns undulating with precision.

She often wished the auras came with music. The colored lines fluctuated with a beat. Sometimes she likened it to the pulse of a heartbeat one could feel in a person's neck or wrist. A quick country dance would match Dukmee's present aura.

"What are you looking for?" asked Cantor.

"A stopgap. Something to slow down or halt the guarding wards." He bent his nose to the pages again. "I've found the right section, but I'm having to translate as I read. And I'm reading while I run. These are not optimal conditions for finding, learning, and applying new skills."

Neekoh arrived, having doubled back to find them. "It's only a little more than a mile. We have to hurry."

He took off again without waiting to see if they would join him.

"Let's go." Bridger plunged down the pathway.

Bixby trotted in front of the two men. None of them panted. But Bixby sniffed.

"Cold?" asked Dukmee.

"No, sensing. The air smells damp to me."

Dukmee held the book open, reading and running. He glanced up. "Could be an underground river, stream, pond, or spring."

Cantor sniffed. "You're right. Wet. Hopefully this water won't cause a delay. I think we're going down, not up. Shouldn't we be going up to exit the mountain?"

Bixby stumbled as she looked over her shoulder. She caught her balance and continued but kept her eyes forward. "When Dukmee and I came in, we went around and around and ran into lots of dead ends. Neekoh seems to be headed in one direction. When he makes a turn, we never end up in a cul-de-sac. I don't think he's lost. Maybe this path goes down first and then rises."

From ahead of them, they could hear Bridger's heavy tread slow and then stop. The three realm walkers dropped to a fast walk.

Stepping out of the rock tunnel, Bixby, Cantor, and Dukmee joined Bridger and Neekoh. Everyone stared at the strange sight in front of them. Only Neekoh looked pleased.

The great, dark emptiness felt gigantic. Bixby assumed the vast cavern stretched upward and outward for great distances. They could not see far, and that added to the illusion of considerable space.

Lights hung around the walls, but the lights did not push back the measureless darkness. The light globes reflected in thin straight lines across the watery surface. A placid lake explained the moist air. Without the sun, moon, or stars, the water looked like a sheet of shiny black cloth.

"What is this?" asked Cantor.

"A lake." Neekoh looked over his shoulder with his mobile eyebrows arched to their highest points. "You have lakes above, don't you?"

"Of course." Cantor's eyes squinted. "How does this help us escape the mountain?"

"Well, you've noticed the rumbly-grumblies aren't so ferocious now. We've come away from the protected area."

Cantor scowled. "Did you know the trapping wards would spring into being after we broke the first ward? Shouldn't you have warned us?"

Neekoh looked chagrined. "You see, it has been many years of repeating all the traditions, handed down verbally through the generations. Some of the precise instructions have become untidy. I was trying to remember why the broken ward brought me to the library."

Bixby's soft voice inquired. "Did you remember?"

The young man turned gratefully to the only one who did not look angry. "Yes, a few seconds after the sound of the locks closing. I was sent there to decide if you were friend or foe and to rescue you if you were friends."

Bixby smiled. "Thank you for leading us out."

Neekoh's fair complexion turned red. "You're welcome."

Cantor stepped between the girl and the stranger. "The exit?"

"We go across the lake, through the rough tunnels to the valley, free Chomountain, and leave by the east gate." He looked at them, obviously befuddled. "Isn't that what you wanted to do?"

Dukmee handed the ward book to Bixby. "Put that some-where safe." He turned to Neekoh. "Yes, we want to get out of this mountain. We have an important mission."

Neekoh grinned and nodded. "To rescue Chomountain."

"No, to save the nine planes."

A look of dismay flashed across the guardian's smooth face. "With Chomountain's aid, your mission will be accomplished readily."

Cantor strode forward. "If we have time. We have a limited time to gather the forces to repel the invaders. How do we cross the lake?"

"In a boat."

"What boat?"

Neekoh put a finger to his chin. He never lost his pleasant expression as he looked back and forth. "Ah!" His eyebrows shot up. He trotted along the shore and came back, dragging an eight-foot skiff.

Cantor's low voice came out lower and more growly than ever. "We won't all fit in that boat."

Still cheerful and smiling, Neekoh nodded. "Hadn't thought of that. But something will turn up. Something we can use, that is. There are things that might show up that are not helpful at all."

"Like what?" asked Bridger.

"Toombalians."

9

THE OUTSIDE OF THE OTHER SIDE

Cantor searched his mind. *Toombalians* did not register. Before he could ask, Bridger voiced his question, "What are toombalians?"

"Mythical creatures," Dukmee answered.

The mage crouched by the edge of the lake, dipped his fingers in the black water, and then brought his hand to his nose and sniffed. He looked around at his companions. "Nobody drink this. Keep it away from your eyes."

Bridger lumbered over to the edge of the water. "Mythical? That means fiction, right? Not real?"

"Let me explain." Dukmee wiped his hand on a handkerchief he fished from his pocket. "Nothing has been written of them since scholars quit recording in the old language. However, in careful anthropologic research, myths often are found to have roots in reality."

Bridger sat down with a thump.

His constant's confusion drifted into Cantor's mind and muddled his thinking. Their minds combined, bundling each of their apprehensions into one tangled web of anxiety.

The shared concern drove Cantor to ask for clarification. "So you're saying the animals that toombalians are based upon could exist?"

"That's right, as far as it goes." Dukmee continued in his teacher mode. "A myth is a strong element in a culture. A story in itself does not meet the criteria. To acquire the status of myth, the tale must stand as an explanation of happenings the populace cannot rationalize with their limited means of science. Myths then take part in the forming of the culture's religious beliefs, form of government, and their standards or morals."

A spike of annoyance cleared Cantor's head. Dukmee used an awful lot of words to say something.

Dukmee continued. "In this case, the mythical toombalians are animals floating in the water like upside down jellyfish. Their tentacles look like plant stalks. These appendages impede the movement of anything on the surface, generally a boat. And they also emit a poison into the air when bumped."

Cantor wanted to shake the mage out of his arrogant air and bring him back down to being a friend, not a know-it-all. He drew in a deep breath. He knew Dukmee's scholar persona could disappear as quickly as it had surfaced. In order to tolerate his more obnoxious stances, Cantor attempted to remember how useful the man could be, how generous, how loyal, resourceful, and funny.

Then, as if to deliberately test Cantor's limits of understanding, the mage took a hamper from his robe and sat on the dark soil of the lake's shore. He pulled out several glass vials and took samples of the soil and water. With a pen, he carefully labeled his collection.

Cantor turned from Dukmee's scientific gatherings and looked toward Bridger. The dragon put his hand across his brow as if protecting his eyes from the sun and peered out over the dark expanse. "Does anything live in that lake?"

A smile quirked Neekoh's lips. "You mean anything like toombalians?"

Bridger puffed out his cheeks. A ring-shaped cloud of smoke escaped his pursed lips. The circle floated over to come down over Neekoh's head and settle for a moment around his neck. "I mean," said Bridger in a cool tone, "anything at all."

Cantor stepped between the two, casually blocking any direct contact. He wondered at the rise of impatience in Bridger. His friend rarely displayed anything but the most genial attitude.

"So, Dukmee." Cantor turned the conversation. "Are we likely to run into relatives of the toombalians?"

The scholar held up a finger, indicating they must wait a moment for his answer. He finished writing on one of his tubes and packed it with the others in a cushioned box. "Possible, but doubtful. After all, if one hasn't been reported for an eon, then either they didn't exist to begin with or their species has died out. I think we'd best worry about crossing this lake."

Cantor turned to Bridger, sitting with a discontented look on his face and stroking Jesha.

"Bridge, would you be a boat for us?"

"Maybe. Depends on what kind of boat. I won't be a sail-boat. Too many odd pieces. The sails are most uncomfortable."

Cantor nodded toward the skiff Neekoh had dragged over. "Like this one?"

Still looking grumpy, the dragon approached the small vessel and looked it over. "Sure. I can do this easily."

"I'll go with Neekoh." Dukmee looked up from his work. "I'm done here. Bixby, are you coming with me or going with Bridger?"

Neekoh took hold of the bow and shoved the skiff into the dark waters. "Two passengers to a boat." He jumped into the wooden craft. "That puts your girl with the giant."

"I'm not a giant." A hiss of annoyance carried the words through Cantor's pressed lips.

Neekoh sat down, the cheer on his face unmarred by Cantor's retort. He shrugged and answered, "I didn't know. I've never seen a giant and I've never seen anyone as big as you. I thought you were a giant, but since you say you are not, I look forward to meeting someone even larger."

Bixby tossed Cantor a warning glare, then turned her attention to the unsophisticated man. "It's all right, Neekoh. We know you didn't mean to be insulting. Cantor is a realm walker."

"And," added Dukmee, "there are no true giants."

Bridger and Neekoh chorused, "Really?"

"Really."

"Let's just hope there are no true toombalians." Bridger stretched out his wings, making Bixby and Cantor duck. "Sorry, just getting the kinks out before I shift. I haven't flown in a while, and that's not good for my circulation. Now I'm going to be a boat. Shifting is good for my overall fitness, but staying boatish for a time is not."

"It will only take a day or so to cross," said Neekoh. "I've never had any trouble on the water." He gave a look to Bridger that Cantor took to be an apology. "I've never seen anything living in this lake except some plants."

Cantor glowered at the little man, just to remind him to be more circumspect in what he said. "What is to be our course?"

"Straight away from here. Keep your back to this lighted shore. Just as the glow slides beneath the horizon, look to the shimmer of the water before you. That luminescence gains strength as we travel. After many hours you will be passing over the source of that radiance — tiny, shining water plants. The lake is shallow there, and the tops of these remarkable plants float on the surface."

Out of the corner of his eye, Cantor saw Bixby shiver. He took a long look at his old friend. She almost glowed with excitement.

"It sounds beautiful." Bixby took in a great breath of air and let it out slowly. Cantor smiled at her obvious effort not to become too giddy.

"It is, but don't slow down to gaze at them. The tendrils will weave around your boat, er, um, your dragon and not allow you to go farther."

Cantor mulled through the instructions they had just been given. "We'll be traveling together. But if we get separated, what landmark are we headed for?"

"A beacon. It is said that those who designed the power supply in the Orrery Chamber put it there. The mechanism looks similar. Not that I have ever seen the power supply in the Orrery Chamber, but that is what is said." He held one arm up and circulated his fist. "The light turns at the top of a tower, so from a distance, it looks like it flashes at long intervals. Beyond is a vast plain, with no growth, of course. Not much grows without sun or rain."

Bixby's eyes glittered. Was it the reflected strange lighting or tears? Cantor couldn't read her moods as easily as he once did, and he found that disconcerting. He reached for the bond they had developed during their training in Gilead.

"Neekoh," she said in a soft voice, just a stroke louder than a whisper. "When was the last time you saw the sun?"

"Me?" The young man's eyes grew big in his thin, pale face. "Years ago. My father handed me the responsibility to guard Chomountain, and of course that means living under the mountain."

"Does your family still live in here? Is there a village of your people?"

"Oh, no. There's no one but me. In this part of the mountain, that is. Our habitat is on the side of the mountain, the *out*side, the *other* side, the outside of the other side of the mountain."

He looked around at them with a satisfied grin. He seemed proud of his inept description. He nodded for no reason Cantor could see and continued explaining.

"One day the village will bring me my bride, the prettiest girl ready for marriage. We'll have a child. If it is a girl, my wife will take the baby and place her in the hands of someone in the village. If it is a boy, we will raise him to take my position. She will carry him back and forth to visit me and to have me teach him all he needs to know to be a guardian."

Bixby looked troubled, and waves of emotion swept from her to Cantor. Now he wished the bond between them were not so strong.

"So now that you are in the position your father held, did your parents go back to the outside?"

"Yes. And my wife will escort me out when I hand over my responsibilities to our son."

Dukmee put the last of his hampers away and sprang to his

feet. "All very informative. Shall we go rescue Chomountain, and then our worlds?"

"Indeed," said Bridger as the air cooled and he spread himself out. In only a moment, Jesha sat on one of the three benches within a rustic boat.

Cantor grinned. Neekoh's skiff had only two seats. Bridger hadn't been able to resist outdoing the young man by one hard, splintery wood bench.

Bixby stopped Dukmee as he walked to join Neekoh. "Will the water hurt Bridger?"

Dukmee turned to examine the dragon boat. "I think not. He has his head well above the waterline in that rather ostentatious figurehead. The water is placid and won't splash in his eyes, and he's not likely to drink it as a boat." He patted her arm. "He'll be fine."

10

INTO THE DARK

Bixby circled Bridger's boat shape. "This is much more impressive than the litter. Good job, Bridge. Um ... how do we make you go?"

With a blast of cold air and a screech, two oars popped out, anchored to rowing rings on either side of the middle seat. Jesha yeowed at the disturbance and hopped onto dry land. She parked herself, assuming the stance of a statue for a moment before beginning a wash ritual. Bixby grinned. Many times she could have used a calming process to soothe her own ruffled nerves.

Bixby plunked down on the ground and pulled out a hamper. Inside, she found scarves, mittens, thick gloves, and knitted hats. She shoved it back into her skirts. The next hamper contained what she wanted.

"Here, Cantor. You should wear these."

He came over and took the flimsy brown gloves from her hand. "They're way too small."

She stood and brushed grit off her skirts. "They stretch." She saw his look of disbelief as he dangled one glove at eye level. "A lot," she added. "Try putting them on. Unless you truly want blisters from rowing across the lake."

Cantor grunted and struggled with one glove until it covered his hand. The material clung like a second skin, but it had stretched enough for comfort. He flexed his fingers.

"They feel slippery."

"That's to eliminate friction. The oar won't rub your skin raw."

He tugged the other glove on. "These will be useful if they work."

"Of course they work, Cantor. Dukmee has a pair, and he'll probably give Neekoh a pair if he needs them."

As if on cue, Dukmee called, "Let's get this part of the journey underway."

Cantor gestured for Bixby to jump in. Jesha followed without being asked. As soon as his female companions settled on the front bench, Cantor shoved Bridger into the glassy water. With one long step, he boarded the vessel, then sat on the middle bench. With oars in hand, he pulled out over the waters. He hadn't rowed a boat in over a year, but his body remembered the rhythm.

With his back to Bixby, he had to look over his shoulder to see in front of them. He nodded toward the other boat, a few yards ahead. "For such a small man, Neekoh has powerful arms."

The skiff containing their new acquaintance and Dukmee plowed through the dark water with twice the speed Cantor achieved. He put more oomph into his strokes and tried to quicken his rhythm. The other boat continued to put more distance between them.

"Bixby, can you read his aura this far away?"

She squinted as she peered through the darkness. "No, there isn't enough light, even though Dukmee is holding a glow orb."

"Can you connect with the mage and caution him? He can tell if Neekoh's leaving us behind is on purpose. Once he's read Neekoh, he can either tell him to slow down or warn us of trouble."

Bixby turned on the front bench and stared again toward the faster skiff. Hearing the conversation startled Cantor.

"We're falling behind. Is Neekoh deliberately trying to lose us?"

"No, his aura is pleasant. I think he is unaware of anything that is outside his immediate sphere. I've been puzzling over his attitude."

"Please tell him to slow down. I don't like the idea of crossing this lake, and I surely don't want to do it without you and Neekoh."

"Cantor will take good care of you."

She glanced quickly at her companion and smiled. *"I know. But Neekoh knows where we're going. And you always have a neat bag of tricks."*

"I'll remind him you are following."

Neekoh slowed, and Cantor caught up to the first boat. Looking into their traveling companions' faces and being able to read their expressions helped ease the discomfort of the still, quiet atmosphere. The rings spreading out from each dip of the oars were the only movement on the surface of the water. The only sounds came from the creaking wood of their vessels and the drip of black water from the paddles.

Bixby looked around them and called over to Dukmee. "The lake is kind of eerie, isn't it?"

"Yes. I find myself straining to listen because there is so little to hear." Dukmee waved his hand in the air. "And the stillness makes me long for a breeze or raindrops."

Bixby cuddled Jesha closer to her chest. "I think I would lose my mind if I had to stay here."

Cantor lifted the oars out of the water and rested. "I hope we aren't on a wild goose chase."

"Hardly!" Neekoh's eyes widened in surprise. "I wouldn't steer you wrong. It's my job to escort you. We have the opportunity to restore Chomountain to his rightful place. I've waited all my life for someone to take down the ward."

"I already feel," said Bixby, "like we've been on the lake for hours." She gestured toward the shore they had left. "We can still see those lighted orbs and glowing rocks."

Cantor laughed. "It's probably been all of twenty minutes." He dipped his oars back in the black lake. "We best get going."

"You row very efficiently," Bixby said. "Where did you learn?"

"On the lake at home. Some of the best fishing spots could only be reached by boat." He looked over his shoulder. "Could you and Jesha move to the back bench? It would be easier to talk if you were facing me, and you'll be able to keep watch on Neekoh's skiff from there."

Bixby put the cat down, stood, and moved carefully. When the boat wobbled, she sucked in a breath. She used Cantor's shoulders to help her balance as she eased over the middle bench. Again the craft responded to shifting weight and she swayed. Her fingers dug into his shoulder. She didn't let go until she'd turned around and was ready to sit.

Jesha joined her and they both settled on the wider seat.

Bixby shuddered. "I do *not* want to fall in that water."

"I'm pretty sure you'd be all right. If you fall in, remember to keep your eyes and mouth closed."

"How will I know where to swim?"

"I'll call to you, but a better plan would be — don't fall in!"

She giggled and relaxed. Soon, though, the silence weighed heavy in the air. The moment of peace left them.

Bixby fidgeted. "Are you greatly discouraged since you haven't been able to find Ahma and Odem?"

"I was." A grin spread across his face. "But if we find and free Chomountain after all these years, it'll renew my hope in finding my people."

Bixby leaned a bit to the side to watch the other boat. "Neekoh picked up speed again, and the distance between us is growing." Bixby shook her head. "He doesn't look like he's putting a lot of effort into his strokes."

Cantor said nothing. What could he say? He certainly wasn't weaker than Neekoh. He rowed as well as anyone else he knew of.

He felt a blast of heat from the bow and stern. Bixby jumped away from the shifting wood, stumbling and landing in his lap. He dropped the oars to catch her. He turned her deftly to perch on his knee. "It's only Bridger."

The dragon's great tail swayed above the water. Like a figurehead on a mighty ship, Bridger's head stuck out from the prow. He tilted his head one way and then the other, stretching the stiffness out of his muscles. Then he craned his neck around to look over what would have been his shoulder but was now the side of the boat.

"I think I have too much drag, resistance to the water. I'm going to redo the woodwork of my shell. Instead of rough wood, I'll break out dragon scales. Dragons are fast swimmers, you know."

Bixby giggled. "No, I can't say that I knew that."

Jesha appeared from under Cantor's seat. Bixby jumped again as the cat unexpectedly sprang into her lap.

Cantor grabbed for the oars, thinking they would slide out into the water and be lost. He set them at rest within the boat before addressing Bixby. "What's got you so skittish?"

With his hands on her tiny waist, he lifted her off his lap and put her on the back bench.

She shivered. "This lake gives me the creeps." She looked over the edge of the boat. "Oh, Bridger! The scales are gorgeous."

Bridger beamed a toothy smirk and winked. "I'm also going to bring my sides in and make my hull V-shaped to allow us to move faster." He was quiet for a moment.

Cantor watched the floor beneath his feet narrow, as did the seat he sat upon. Bridger must have created a space between the flooring and the hull in order to structure a V-shape.

"Try it out," said Bridger. "And, Cantor, the oars won't slip away. They're a part of me, and I won't let that happen."

He answered with a grin. "Of course. I should have known that."

Bixby turned to stare at him. "Did you know dragons are good swimmers?"

As he lowered the oars into the lake, he said, "I did." He pulled the oars through the water, and the boat shot ahead. "Works great, Bridger."

The dragon held his head forward like a masthead and took on a wooden effect, looking like scales had been carved on his face and neck and painted with iridescent colors. Bixby exclaimed, "Very nice! Opaque pink. Radiant red. Glimmering green. Shimmering gold. Three shades of blue. I like blue. And that purple is just the right shade …"

A moment later, she looked at his tail. Cantor caught her thought just before she spoke. "Bridger, is there any way you could help with the movement?"

"Not like this. You wanted me to be a boat, remember?"

"Yes," said Bixby in a soothing tone, "but I really don't like this lake, and I know you've been a wonderful boat, but could you be something else? Something *you* want to be, that would take us across the lake faster?"

He didn't even take a moment to think, and that worried Cantor.

The dragon's head swung around to face them. "Bixby, hold Jesha and sit on Cantor's lap. I don't want you to fall out."

Bixby scurried to get in place, holding on to the cat with one arm and grasping Cantor's shirtsleeve with the other hand. "I'm ready."

The air warmed. The vessel quivered, and Cantor closed his eyes. Sometimes when Bridger made a quick shift, the sight of his stretching, twisting, changing color and texture made Cantor sick to his stomach. When he opened his eyes, Bridger was under them, gliding along like a swan with her cygnets on her back. Instead of folding his wings, he had positioned them as high sides to his elegant form.

Bixby clapped her hands and bounced. She slid off Cantor's lap and sat on the long saddle Bridger had provided. The dragon accelerated. Cantor leaned back and relaxed. They had already lessened the distance between them and Dukmee's skiff. And as Bridger propelled himself, his speed caused air to pass through his scales. The slight rattle offset the creepy silence of the lake.

The mage raised a hand in greeting. Neekoh's teeth glowed in the light of the orb, his smile wide and delighted.

"I am so glad you came," he said. "I haven't ever had this much fun. I love watching Bridger's and Jesha's surprises. I hope you stay for a while after we free Chomountain."

Cantor grunted. "Don't forget we're supposed to be saving the nine planes."

"I did forget. Is it something you have to do right away?"

Dukmee looked with surprise at the man seated across from him. "Definitely." He frowned. "Just how long will it take to free Chomountain?"

Neekoh's smile did not diminish as he shrugged. "I have no idea. It's never been done before."

STILL IN THE DARK

Bixby watched as the last of the lights from the distant shore sank below the horizon. She whipped around and leaned to the side to see around Bridger's powerful neck. In the distance, the glow of the underwater plants drew a light line across the horizon.

"Do you think we're halfway there?"

Cantor shifted on the saddle behind her. "I hope so. My legs are getting cramped."

Beside them and just a tad in front of Bridger, Neekoh pulled his oars out of the water and wedged them along the inside of the skiff. "I'm hungry! How about a break for food?"

"Yes." At the thought, Bixby's stomach growled. "I've got all sorts of nice things in my cold hamper. Shall we stop moving for a while? Could Cantor and I come over to your boat? We need to move around and get the kinks out of our legs."

"I can transfer you," said Bridger. "Would you rather I

picked you up with my teeth and lifted you over, or would you like to walk along my wing like a bridge?"

Bixby felt Cantor laughing. He managed not to let on, but his frame shook as he pretended to cough. When he could talk, his deep, rumbly voice sent tremors through Bixby.

"Why don't you just park yourself as close to them as you can? I'll step over first, then lift Bixby."

Bridger used his tail to steer and gently propel himself. They skimmed over the water to the side of Neekoh's boat. In a very short time, the adventurers were comfortably seated, and Bixby passed around chicken sandwiches, pickles, marmalade on rolls, and cold tea.

For Bridger, Cantor had a huge bag of donuts, several watermelons, a gigantic fried fish, a meatloaf baked in a twenty gallon washtub, three chocolate cakes, and a small keg of apple cider. The dragon allowed his arms and hands to come out of his swan shape so he could eat.

Neekoh sat with his eyes closed, chewing his food with a look of utter contentment on his face.

"Are we halfway?" Bixby asked the young man.

He continued to chew.

"Neekoh, are we halfway?"

He still didn't forsake his pleasure but took another bite of the sandwich.

Bixby was both annoyed and tickled. She wanted an answer, but Neekoh looked like he could float away with the next bite.

She turned to Cantor and Dukmee. "What do you think?"

Cantor lifted one eyebrow. "I think we ought to be out of this mountain by now and on our way to do something about the Lymen."

"I think," said Dukmee, "that we should have a piece of Bridger's second cake."

Bridger graciously shared his chocolate cake. Bixby had thought Neekoh's reaction to a chicken sandwich was amusing. His ecstasy over the dragon's dessert had them all laughing.

Bixby felt more serene about being in the middle of the mysterious lake by the time she and Cantor went back to ride on Bridger's back. But it wasn't long before the gloomy darkness, permeating silence, and clammy air again encroached on her.

"Cantor, tell me something about your search for Ahma and Odem."

"I've already told you what there is to tell."

"Then tell me about something you saw on your travels that you'd never seen before."

"Why?"

"I need to hear your voice."

"Oh." He didn't begin fast enough for her. She pressed her lips together to keep from nagging. A sigh escaped after a long wait. "Cantor, didn't you see anything?"

"We saw a lot of things. But you've traveled so much, you've probably seen the things I thought were unusual."

"All right. Then give me hints, and I'll try to guess."

She felt him put up a shield so she couldn't read his mind. She grinned. A wise precaution. Again she thought he'd never speak, but he finally cleared his throat.

"It looks like a desert except there is water. It sounds like a thick bowl of stew over the fire."

Bridger turned his head sharply. "The mud flats on Bondoran."

"Bridger," Bixby protested, "you're supposed to let me guess."

"I might be wrong."

Bixby squirmed to turn enough to see Cantor's face. "Is it the mud flats of Bondoran? Is Bridger right?"

"Yes, I was thinking of the Bondoran mud flats. Bridger, let Bixby guess. It isn't exactly fair since you were with me. It's fresh in your mind."

"I'm ready for another." She faced the front once more.

"Let's see ... taller than a mountain but only from the bottom. Dry up and down, but wet in the middle."

Bridger jerked. "Krossmore Canyon."

Cantor and Bixby spoke in unison. "Bridger!"

"Sorry. It slipped out."

"I'm going to try again. Bridger, pinch your lips together." Cantor breathed deeply. Bixby felt his tension as he puzzled over what to use, and the moment the stiffness left him, she knew he had thought of something. "The father acts the mother, and the child carries a heavy load."

"That's too easy," Bridger complained. "You know what it is, right, Bix?"

"Yes, a cammercon. But I've never seen one. Did you really see one?"

Bridger nodded. "We were in the jungle of Igid at night. Cantor was tucked in his hammock. The father cammercon strolled into our campsite with no more caution than if he'd known us all his life. The baby peeked out of the father's pouch. Along came the mother, and they proceeded to rob us of everything that wasn't stored away."

"Each item," added Cantor, "was handed to the baby, who dragged it into the pouch with him."

Bixby sighed. "They're cute in drawings."

"They're cute in person." Cantor stretched his legs. "But once they've looted your camp, there is no way to get anything back."

Cantor and Bridger laughed.

"What?" asked Bixby, aware that they were sharing a funny memory.

The dragon took a couple of deep breaths to stop his giggles. "With one hand, Cantor clamped the father's mouth shut and held him in place while he stuck his other hand in the pouch to retrieve his flint box. The adult's teeth were out of commission, but it was the baby who bit him."

"Retrieving the flint was necessary. I didn't want to be in that jungle with no fire. Besides, it would have been an awful lesson if the baby had managed to strike a spark inside his father's pouch. But I thought I'd never shake that tiny mite off my finger."

Bridger and Cantor succumbed to laughter once more.

Dukmee called from the other vessel. "It's good to hear laughter instead of silence. We'll be over the phosphorescent plants in a few minutes. Neekoh says in an hour we'll be able to see the beacon, and two hours after that, we'll land."

"Three more hours." Bixby leaned back against Cantor's chest. "I feel like a nap."

Cantor rested his cheek against her hair. "You don't want to miss the pretty plants."

"No, you're right." A yawn stretched her mouth to the point of hurting. "I'm suddenly very sleepy."

"Bridger and I will sing some of the songs we learned on our travels. No lullabies."

"You learned lullabies?"

Cantor chortled. "No, mostly tavern songs."

Bridger sidled up to the other vessel. "Cantor sings quite well. Some day he'll probably take a place in a great cathedral."

Dukmee frowned. "He'd better find something other than tavern songs, if that's his ambition."

Bridger snorted. "He does know a few lullabies."

The mage shook his head slowly. "Still not what he needs."

Bixby pulled a face. They weren't making any sense. If they were teasing her friend, he didn't seem to care. But she took offense and decided to remind them of his ability. "We all heard Cantor sing with the cantors in sanctuary at Gilead. He knows what to do."

"I think," said Cantor, "we'll start with 'Old Man Podder Left His Mouth Turned On and His Mind Turned Off.' What do you say, Bridge?"

"Sounds like an excellent choice."

They entered the waters filled with underwater plants, singing the song of Podder's woes. At the moment, they had no immediate troubles, and Bixby enjoyed laughing at the silly man's trials.

A yawn surprised her, stretching her mouth and pulling an enormous amount of air into her lungs. She vigorously shook her head. What time was it? She tried to calculate how long they'd been on this trek. When had they left the library? They'd eaten on the water, but was it dinner or supper? Her mind felt wooly, packed with fuzz, and uncooperative.

Life in the dark presented many problems. Get out of sync with night, sleep, day, eat, play ... That was the problem. They never played anymore. She stretched and cuddled back. She'd dream about playing.

SNAG

Cantor roused Bixby to look at the glowing plants. She smiled and yawned and leaned to look around Bridger's wing to get a better view. When she slid forward, he pulled her back and discovered she had fallen asleep.

He gently shook her. "Bixby, look up ahead. There's a mist over the lake, and the droplets of water are reflecting the luminous plants."

She opened her eyes and smiled. "Beautiful."

Cantor decided he didn't like the smile. Her eyes usually sparkled with interest. Now they looked empty. Her head drooped. He put a hand under her chin and lifted. Asleep.

"Bridger, there's something wrong with Bixby. Can you get closer to Neekoh? I want Dukmee to look at her."

"I've lost sight of their skiff. I'll speed up."

Immediately in front of them, the mist swirled in shining tendrils. Farther on, the thickness of the radiant fog obscured their view. Although the vapor's slow drifting held a mystic splendor, Cantor saw the beauty as treacherous.

Bixby's pale skin reflected the eerie glow. Under different circumstances, he might have admired the allure it added to her features. He tried to wake her again.

"Cantor, let me sleep."

"You're missing the show. Open your eyes, Bix."

She obeyed. The same vague smile touched her lips, and she dozed off again.

Cantor reached with his mind, trying to connect with Dukmee. Nothing came back to him. He didn't feel any response; not Dukmee and not Neekoh. He probably couldn't speak to Neekoh, but he should at least be able to sense his presence. Aside from Bixby, the only other living entities he could pinpoint were Bridger and Jesha.

He concentrated on his sense of hearing. He used the tricks Bixby had taught him to survey the sounds around them. Beyond the swish of Bridger's tail, he heard nothing, not the dip of an oar, not the drip of lake water returning to where it belonged.

"Bridger, do you know where they are?"

"I've been listening and haven't heard them for a while. Where do you suppose they've gotten to?"

"Can you see the beacon Neekoh said was on the other shore?"

"Not through this fog." Bridger cleared his throat. "How's Bixby?"

Cantor looked down at her pale face. He pulled her closer. "Still sleeping."

"I could clear a bit of the fog if I blow out a flame."

"But if the other boat is right ahead of us, then you'd scorch our friends." He looked around them. They'd entered the dense fog. The worrisome glow in the air isolated them. "Why can't we hear them?"

Cantor had no answer to his own question.

Bridger snorted. "The air smells different here. Perhaps there's some chemical that interrupts the flow of sound."

"I've never heard of anything like that, but that doesn't mean it doesn't exist."

"Remember all that noise we heard when the ward collapsed? Dukmee said that sound existed with nothing making it. Maybe this is the opposite. Something out there should make noise, but there is none."

"Interesting theory. Better than any I've come up with." Cantor looked down. Bixby slept peacefully in his arms. "Bridger, could you stretch your neck so that you can see over the fog? If you can see the beacon, let's head that way."

Cantor watched as Bridger's neck grew longer and skinnier. The thick mist quickly swallowed his head. The dragon had taken his suggestion without a word of complaint. He appreciated that. Shapeshifting from one form to another was a talent, but Cantor knew it was easier on the dragon to shift wholly into another shape rather than half-shifting and maintaining parts of two forms. Bridger currently sustained his swan form, a feathered shape, and the elegant neck stretched like one of those giraffes they'd seen on Bondoran.

A jolt beneath him alerted Cantor to Bridger's forward movement. He must have seen the beacon. Cantor shifted Bixby in his lap. Her tiny frame barely covered his torso. He'd grown over the two years, and she'd stayed the same. Only to him, it felt as if she had shrunk. Surely, two years ago she'd been taller and sturdier.

"Bridger, can you move any faster?"

The dragon didn't answer. He reached with his mind and could not find him.

"This is ridiculous. I can see you. I can touch you. Why can't I hear you? Can you hear me? Bridger!"

He'd loosened his grip on Bixby. She started to slide off his lap, and he managed to catch her. As he pulled, he discovered a stem of the shimmering plant wrapped around her ankle. Reaching down, he grasped the tendril and tried to pry it loose.

The vine tightened. Cantor pulled his knife and sliced the plant. He quickly unwound the part clinging to her leg. Another stem snaked up and entrapped his booted leg. He swung his blade before it tightened. As the plants invaded Bridger's back, reaching and twisting and threatening, Cantor realized the dragon's forward motion had stopped.

"Bridger!" he yelled between flashing his knife through one green rope after another. "Bridger!"

He gained footing on the saddle and dragged Bixby higher, away from the black water. That seemed to flummox the shining vines. They reached only a foot or so out of the lake. If they did not come in contact with Cantor or Bixby, they withdrew.

Cantor peered up the column of Bridger's neck. He could see it only so far before the glowing mist hid the rest.

"If I climb his neck, I can find out what he's doing, and why he can't hear me, and why he's stopped." He harrumphed. He still held Bixby's light body under one arm. "You're no help, Bixby. You can't even tell me if my ideas are worth trying."

He lowered her to the saddle. Pulling his heels closer to her body, he anchored her, hoping she wouldn't slip while he looked in his hampers for a rope. Soon he had her lashed to the horn and pommel Bridger had provided. Now if the dragon didn't shift to some other shape while he climbed, Bixby would be safe. Perhaps he could figure out what needed to be done.

"Where's Jesha?" His head whipped around. "Jesha!" Had the vines dragged her underwater? Surely not. She would have put up a fight. He would have heard her. He hoped. Losing Jesha would devastate Bridger, and Cantor admitted to himself he'd grown fond of the cat as well. But he didn't have time to locate her using his mind. He had to hurry.

He took one last look at Bixby. She looked secure.

With a heavy sigh, he dug the toe of his boot into the soft flesh of Bridger's neck. Using the feathers for handholds, he scaled the dragon's neck through the fog. By the time he broke through the cloud at Bridger's chin, his breath came in shallow pants. The climb had not troubled him, but the thick moist atmosphere clung to his airways.

He coughed and cleared his throat. The first thing he saw, besides the swan's bill, was the beacon. The light poured over the fog-covered lake for a few moments, then slid off to the side to disappear and reappear on the other side as it made its rotation.

"Bridger."

The dragon jumped. "What are you doing up here?"

"The question is what are *you* doing up here. You've stopped moving."

"I have?" He grumbled in his throat. "I have! Why did I stop?"

"What do you remember?"

"Looking at the light."

"We've got to move. Can you shorten your neck, extend your wings, and fly above this fog?"

"Where'd this fog come from? My feet feel wet."

"The fog is over the light plants in the black lake. We've lost

Dukmee and Neekoh and Jesha. Bixby is in some kind of deep sleep, and you're confused."

"I can't see you, you know," said Bridger. "It's strange to talk to you when you're so close but I can't see you. Could you climb on my nose and sit there?"

"Right now your nose is a swan's beak and isn't big enough for me to sit on. And we have other things to do."

"Did you see the light? It's coming around again."

"I did see the light. Maybe you've been looking at the light with too much focus."

"My feet still feel wet. My tail feels wet as well. And I think my stomach."

"Yes, your stomach is wet. We have to get out of here." Cantor fought down the urge to shake his dragon. "Pay attention. I need you to fly over the fog. Bixby is down on your saddle. I've tied her on, but when you shift to being a dragon, please keep her safe."

"Bixby's here? Why didn't you say so?"

"I did. It was practically the first thing I said. She's asleep! I can't wake her up!" His voice rose. "Dukmee and Neekoh are gone. So's Jesha!"

"Jesha is here somewhere. I can feel her. I feel Bixby too. And my wet feet. And tail. And stomach. The light is coming round again."

"Don't look at it!"

"You're very cranky."

"I'm not having a good day, Bridger. Give me a little help here."

"All right. Hold on. I'm shifting."

Cantor hastily closed his eyes, but Bridger was so quick he

almost didn't need to. He felt the dragon's neck thicken, making it hard to hang on. Then Bridger's head sank to a reasonable height above his body. At the same time he extended his wings, flapped several times, and rose into the air.

Cantor found himself straddling Bridger's neck in front of the saddle. He turned carefully and sighed his relief at seeing Bixby in almost the exact position he'd left her in.

"Prrowl!"

Bixby's skirts moved, and Jesha's head surfaced. She pulled her elegant body from her hiding place and repositioned herself, stretched over the girl's back. Her haughty gaze told Cantor she deplored his lack of control over her comfort.

Bridger hummed, stretching out his word on one note. "Here—"

"—comes the light again. I know, but don't look straight at it."

"It's a pretty light."

"I think it hypnotizes you."

"Oh."

"Just oh?"

"Oh, dear. It's hard not to look."

"Don't look."

"Here comes—"

"Bridger!"

"I'm not looking."

"Can you see the shore? Focus on the shore."

"The other boat is there. Neekoh is standing beside it. I don't see Dukmee."

The fog beneath them thinned. The black lake shimmered with light from the beacon, but no more plants glowed under the surface. Neekoh had bedecked the boat with bright orbs.

Cantor pulled light globes from his hampers and positioned them around the saddle.

In the new light, Bixby looked paler than ever. Cantor hoped Dukmee would have a cure for her unnatural slumber. He leaned to look around Bridger's neck and his heart sank. Dukmee lay in a still heap in Neekoh's skiff.

13

BRIGHT VALLEY

Cantor jumped off Bridger's back as soon as the dragon's feet hit the sand. Jesha followed with a cross mew as a final complaint about being on the lake. Above them, at the top of a round tower, the beacon still circled. A faint hum penetrated the silence. Cantor welcomed the sound after the unsettling stillness of the lake. He hurried to the skiff Neekoh had pulled completely out of the water.

"He's sleeping!" He bent over the boat and shook Dukmee. "What happened? What have you done? How long has he been like this?"

Neekoh wrung his hands. "Since we were in the fog. It's never been so thick before. I've never had problems. I was nervous. Really nervous. But we got to shore, safe and sound."

"If you call this safe and sound. Bixby's out as well. Do you know how to wake them?"

Bridger bent his neck to sniff Dukmee. "Maybe it was the toombalians."

"Why would the poisonous air affect only Dukmee and Bixby?" Cantor continued to shake the sleeping mage.

"Well, you can't deny they are both odd, and sometimes odd in the same way." Bridger prodded Bixby with his snout. "They are both smarter than they should be, and they seem to know what people are feeling and why they feel that way. That's odd."

"Queen Mazeline is odd that way too."

Cantor turned on Neekoh. "What do you know about this? Did you allow this to happen?"

"No. It's never happened before, as far as I know. But usually we're down here alone, just one from the family Neekoh. All the stories I heard about our vigil never mentioned this." He waved a hand over Dukmee. "But usually we're down here alone. No outsiders like you, just our immediate family."

"You said that before." Neekoh obviously wasn't trained for emergencies. If Bixby were awake, she could read his aura. She'd seen nothing in the previous readings. She'd want him to be gracious. Cantor bit down his impatience.

He put a hand on the young man's shoulder to lend him a bit of emotional stability. "Let's get them to Chomountain. I'm fairly certain the right hand of Primen will know what to do." Cantor picked up Dukmee and started toward Bridger. "Bridger, can you carry two?"

Neekoh followed him for a few feet, then turned to pace back and forth.

Bridger shapeshifted to devise two body-sized sacks hanging over his back like saddlebags. He surrounded Bixby with one. "They should be fairly comfortable in those."

He wiggled as if his skin itched. "Take off the ropes. I'll

contract the covering to keep her safe." He peered at Cantor. "We don't want her slipping away. I missed her while we were on our own. Not to mention you need her influence. She's good for you."

Cantor jogged around Bridger to get to the empty carrier. "All right, Bridger. I get your point. You're happier with more than just me to keep you company."

"I do have Jesha. She's a good companion."

Cantor didn't answer. Bridger had tried this tack before. But Cantor wasn't going to recognize Bridger as his constant just to satisfy the dragon's whim. He still believed he should be allowed to pick his own dragon, even if he had grown accustomed to Bridger.

Dukmee's tall frame weighed little, and Cantor had no trouble maneuvering the mage, feet-first, into the sack.

He returned to Bixby's side, intent on taking off the ropes he'd used to secure her to the saddle. He glanced up to see what Neekoh was doing. The ward guard stood gazing across the lake, his eyes distant.

"Is something wrong?" Cantor asked.

Neekoh startled and turned to face him. "You realize that I have never seen Chomountain. I only know where he is. Until you broke the ward, there was no way to get in."

"But you can take us to the entrance?"

"Yes, of course. That's my job. Well, the rest of my job. The first part was just being here. I'm not sure about what is involved in the second part." His pensive expression suddenly gave way to his normal cheerful appearance. "I'll take you through the tunnel. That's what I'll do. No one in my family has ever taken anyone but one of our own to the entrance.

This is something new. I shall be known as the Neekoh who guided the rescuers to Chomountain."

He gathered the light orbs from his skiff, placing them in a cloth bag at the stern of the boat. Bridger had taken care of the orbs Cantor had used. He redistributed them so that he was illuminated from head to tail. Cantor grinned but refrained from telling his constant that he looked like he belonged in a parade. Jesha sat on Bridger's head between the dragon's ears.

With two lights attached to his clothing, Neekoh gestured for Bridger and Cantor to follow. They entered a tunnel unlike those on the other side of the lake. In these passageways, no marks made by the hand of man smoothed the walls or floor. No manmade lights brightened the route. Their orbs and globes illuminated the gray walls where flecks of minerals sparkled. Jesha prudently moved to ride between Bridger's shoulders.

The rock tubes were uniform in width, but varied in height. Cantor and Bridger walked carefully to avoid stubbing toes and falling forward. After a few whacks to their heads, they soon became adept at spotting low-hanging outcrops. Constantly looking down and up made Cantor's neck hurt.

Neekoh was short enough to charge through.

"Neekoh," Cantor called down the tunnel. "Slow down."

In a moment, their guide was back, facing them with a contrite expression. "I am so, so sorry. I'm excited. We're going into the valley. We'll see Chomountain. Everything will be different from this day forward."

"Don't leave us behind, or it'll be just you going into the valley."

Neekoh bobbed his head in eager agreement. Before they actually got to the last tunnel and the archway that led outside the mountain, the poor man had to return many times. He just couldn't keep his feet moving at a sedate pace.

Bridger stopped when they could see the light from outside. "Check on Bixby and Dukmee, Cantor. I thought I felt them twitching."

Cantor doubled back and squeezed between the dragon's side and the rocks. "Bixby looks the same."

He pushed into the slim space on the other side. "Dukmee has shifted, but he's still asleep."

Bridger grumbled and ambled forward. "Neekoh is coming back. I bet that little man has traveled twice as far as we have with all his backtracking."

"Probably." The passage widened, and Cantor could walk beside the dragon. He placed a hand on the beast's shoulder. "We are nearly at the end of this part of the journey. We'll find Chomountain. He can wake Bixby and Dukmee. We'll help him out of his trap, get his advice, and move on to the defense against the Lymen."

"Sounds like a good plan." Bridger made a moue with his scaley dragon lips. "Nothing is likely to go wrong with such an unassuming agenda. No likelihood in that outline of events for mishaps, mischief, misfortune, and miscellaneous mayhem."

Cantor turned to give Bridger a disapproving stare. "Mmm? Are you quite finished with your sarcasm? It doesn't suit you, you know?"

"So you've said before. Yes, I am finished."

Neekoh stopped in his return trip and waited for them, his form bouncing and fidgeting in silhouette against the light from the cave entrance. Cantor couldn't see his expression, but he could imagine his silly grin.

"I wonder what Neekoh will do now that he no longer has to guard the entrance to the valley."

Bridger exhaled a puff of smoke. "He'd be free to go to his village. All the Neekohs from here on out will live ordinary lives." Again Bridger puffed smoke. "I wonder if they know how to do anything practical to support themselves."

Cantor batted a wispy cloud from in front of his face. "Why are you smoking?"

"I don't know." Bridger cleared his throat and touched his neck with his hand. "It feels a bit ticklish."

"I hope you aren't coming down with something. This mountain is bad for one's health. First, Bixby and Dukmee succumb to some sleeping sickness, and now you're catching cold."

Bridger dragged his feet, slowing down the pace. "I suppose Chomountain will be able to cure a sore throat."

"Let's hope so." Cantor scratched the dragon under his jaw in a place that Bridger always found comforting.

They came up to Neekoh, who rubbed his hands together as if unable to contain his excited energy. "I can't get through the archway without you. I tried, but it held me back."

Cantor scratched his head. "Are you sure that our being with you will allow you to enter?"

"Of course! You broke the ward. You'll be able to go through, and I'll just go with you."

For a fleeting moment, doubt assailed Cantor's peace of mind. Suppose they couldn't get through. Suppose Chomountain wasn't even in the valley. Suppose if he were in the valley, he chose not to help them.

He quickened his stride. When they got to the entrance, he strode straight through onto a large stone shelf jutting from the mouth of the cave. Stopping at the edge, he looked back just as Bridger and Neekoh passed under the arch.

Relieved, Cantor turned and raised his hand to shield his eyes as he surveyed the vast, lush valley before them.

Green trees crowded most of the view. In spotted areas, massive blooms in bright colors stood out clearly against the dark, verdant backdrop. Rivers and streams crisscrossed the terrain. An outcropping of rock poked through the tree line, looking organized enough to be the remnants of a building. The cliffs on the opposite side had a similar appearance.

"There it is." Neekoh spread his arms out, indicating the view before them. "It's called Bright Valley, and it's the resting place of Chomountain."

Cantor grunted. "Don't you mean the prison of Chomountain?"

"It's never looked prisonish to me."

"It looks vast and full of hiding places to me," said Bridger. "It'll take days to cover all that territory. But I suppose you're going to say again that you just know he's here but you don't know where."

Neekoh looked as cheerful as Bridger looked grumpy. He nodded. "You're exactly right. I say, you're clever. I've never known a dragon before, but I didn't expect one to be so smart."

The young man looked back and forth between Bridger and Cantor. "Let's make camp. I like sleeping out under the stars, and even though I could, I don't. I know how to make a good fire too, and how to cook. It will be fun to camp with friends rather than all by myself."

Cantor nodded, then pointed to the towers of rock. "What

do you know about that, Neekoh? Is it a ruined palace, a temple, a fortress, or just rocks?"

Neekoh shrugged. "We'll have to go see. I've never been past the tunnel entrance."

Bridger led the way down the sloping valley wall. No trail guided them on their descent, rather the dragon slashed at the heavy underbrush and cleared a path.

Once Cantor's eyes grew accustomed to the bright light and the endless shades of green that confronted them, he discerned patches of meadowland, acres of bushes, and different varieties of trees. Some foliage clustered with like kind. Others mixed with a wide assortment of plant life.

Bridger stopped at the first clearing on level ground. Neekoh and Cantor freed Bixby and Dukmee and laid them on the thick, soft grass. Cantor gently shook them each in turn, trying to rouse some kind of response, but in vain.

Neekoh hovered behind Cantor. "What do you think is wrong with them? Why aren't you asleep? You look like them."

His suspicions that Bixby and Dukmee were cut of the same cloth seemed validated. Bixby, with her remarkable talents, and Dukmee, with his different roles in life, excelled at many tasks. In the ancient times, beings existed with unimaginable gifts. The strain had died out, but occasionally a "throwback" would surface. He knew Bixby's mother had astounded her generation with her abilities, and Bixby had surpassed her mother.

How much should he share with Neekoh? He still didn't trust the young man. "If the toombalians are real and made an effort to end our journey across the lake, then their efforts only partially succeeded. I suspect there's something in Dukmee and Bixby's bodies that makes them susceptible. Like some people are allergic to a particular food. Or those people who always catch a cold twice a year while others never get sick."

Neekoh rubbed his hands together, a happy gleam in his eye. Obviously, sticky little problems were not as exciting as tackling a monumental search. He grinned at Cantor. "I'll scout the immediate area."

Before Cantor could respond, Neekoh had taken off into the thick woods.

Bridger lumbered back into the clearing, carrying an armload of sticks. "I'm thinking that the temperature will drop once the sun goes down behind the rim of the valley. What kind of geological formation do you think this is? It's so much like a bowl, I first thought it might be a dead volcano. But that can't be right. There aren't any volcanoes on our planes, only on ball planets like Ether and Elyn."

Cantor's eyes widened. "Have you been to those planes? They're in another galaxy."

"No." Bridger rolled his eyes. "Of course not! But my sister was able to open portals we could see through. She couldn't overcome the problem of the portal not opening *on* the planets but *above* the planets. So we could see but not touch."

"Amazing. And what's a volcano?"

"Ball planets have a core of liquid rock, and it spews out to make cone-shaped mountains. Totobee-Rodolow has been helping scientists examine Ether and Elyn. Yes, my sister is a lot more competent and a lot less flighty than she appears. And those scientists! The things they figure out just by looking. It's amazing." He paused in his arrangement of the kindling. "Unless their theories are all wrong. Then it's just a waste of time."

He breathed fire on his pile of sticks and set it ablaze. "I'm starving. And I don't want to wait for the fire to settle into nice coals. Let's not cook a dinner. We have enough to snack from your hampers, don't we?"

Neekoh came into the camp with a handkerchief full of berries. "There's lots to eat in this valley. I bet Chomountain has been cultivating plants that can be harvested. I saw fruits, vegetables, and grains. Perhaps tomorrow we'll find him."

Cantor's suspicions swirled in his thoughts. "How is it you know about cultivating and harvesting?"

"Books. There are two more libraries in the mountain."

He handed the berries to Cantor and picked up a stone. Busy with his own thoughts, he worked to put several flat rocks around the blaze. "We can cook with these."

Cantor stifled a yawn. "Good idea, Neekoh, but we're skipping cooked food tonight. We need rest more than stew."

Neekoh's face fell in disappointment. "I could cook while you rest."

"You wouldn't be able to wake us up. Just put it on hold for tomorrow morning. We'll need nourishment then. This is a huge basin. Our best option is to send Bridger up to look over the valley to pinpoint likely spots. If we're lucky, maybe even find Chomountain." He held back a yawn. "I'm going to eat and turn in."

Cantor looked away from Neekoh's disappointed face. He was too tired to fuss with a campfire and he'd made a reasonable decision. Neekoh's sad eyes wouldn't work on him tonight. He admitted to being a little chagrined and said, "We'll worry about tomorrow when the sun comes up."

14

TROUT

Bridger's raspy voice stirred Cantor from a deep sleep. He pried his eyes open. Streaks of sunlight burst from the trees and crossed the clearing with thin stripes. Cantor sat up, shook his head, and rubbed his hand over his face.

Bridger coughed.

"Are you all right, Bridge?"

"Sore throat, deep cough, achy all over."

"Sounds miserable."

"I feared you weren't going to wake up. Bixby and Dukmee have not stirred."

"Where's Neekoh?"

"Getting two more buckets of water from the stream."

A rustling among the bushes announced Neekoh's return. Soot streaked his face, but his lips stretched in a wide grin. "I've put out two fires caused by your dragon's coughing. He seems to have it under control now. But it was exciting. I like having others around."

Cantor turned back to Bridger. The dragon sat beneath a tree, and Jesha crouched beside him, tilted ears showing her grouchy mood. The cat's favorite perch was on Bridger. Apparently, she didn't like his hacking and sniffling. She stood and strolled with an elegant air to settle down beside Bixby.

Cantor wanted Chomountain found. He looked at Bridger's red nose and eyes. "Do you feel well enough to scout the area?"

"Sure. I'm hoping Chomountain has a cure for this cold. Neekoh gave me some herb tea, but it tasted like boiled swampweed, and I had a hard time swallowing it."

Neekoh stirred up the coals from the night before and added wood. "It has to taste bad to do you any good."

Bridger growled, or maybe he just cleared his throat. "You said that before, Neekoh, and I told you it isn't true."

Cantor stood. "I know both Dukmee and Bixby carry medicinal herbs, but I wouldn't know which ones to give you. Neekoh, could you watch our sleepy friends while I go with Bridger to look for Chomountain?"

"I'd be delighted. Do you want me to try to wake them periodically? It would give me something to do."

"It wouldn't hurt." Cantor pushed aside a pang of reluctance. Neekoh hadn't been with them long enough to have earned his trust, but Bixby said he had no unpleasant auras. He'd have to give the young man a chance. "Remember, be gentle."

Bridger rested against the tree. "You're not ready to go. I'll take a nap."

Neekoh shook his head with his ever-present smile in place. "Everyone is sleepy. You people from the outside are peculiar."

"I'm not tired, and neither is Jesha. The others aren't

normally so sluggish. Once we find out what's wrong, and if Chomountain has a cure, we'll be alert and lively. I promise."

Cantor washed and shaved. He changed into fresh clothing and checked on Dukmee and Bixby one more time. With a bread and cheese sandwich in his hand, he approached the dragon.

"Let's go, Bridge, if you're sure you can make the flight."

"I'll be more comfortable doing something, instead of lolling around moaning."

Cantor climbed on. Bridger had provided a saddle. As they took off, Cantor waved to Neekoh, who hopped around with enthusiasm over watching the dragon take flight.

"He certainly is a happy fellow," Cantor observed.

By mutual and unspoken consent, they started a zigzag search pattern. Cantor felt Bridger's fatigue and wanted to head back to the camp after four sweeps of the valley. He was just about to make the suggestion, when Bridger tensed beneath him.

"Would you look at that?" Bridger swooped toward a larger river. "There's a fisherman."

Cantor spotted the man standing in the shallow water. "Could we have found Chomountain this easily?"

"Neekoh didn't say there was anyone else in Bright Valley, so I suppose we have."

He banked and circled, coming at a good angle to land. A sandbar jutted out into a bend in the river. As they approached, the fisherman pulled in his line and waded ashore to meet them.

Of a wiry and slim build, the man was old, with short-cropped white hair and a long white beard. Suntanned and spry, he wore blue pants tucked into rubber waders and a plain green shirt, also tucked in. His belt was of fine leather tooled with a fancy design.

He waved as he came near. "You're the first visitors I've had in a very long time."

"You have visitors?" Cantor slid off Bridger's back and onto the sandy bank.

"Once in a while. They always try to lure me out of the valley, but I like it here." The fisherman reached out a hand to shake as he crossed the last few yards. "Welcome to Bright Valley."

"My name's Cantor D'Ahma, and this is my friend Bridger-Bigelow."

Bridger grasped the man's hand. "Thank you, sir. You're Chomountain, if I'm not mistaken."

The old man laughed. "Well, you are mistaken, sonny. My name's Trout. Old Trout, nowadays. I've more than a few winters under my belt."

"You're not —?" Cantor paused to gather his wits. Were they in the right valley? Was Chomountain here? Anywhere? Was the right hand of Primen still alive? Had they been delayed on their mission for nothing? "Do you know Chomountain? Is he here?"

"Chomountain? Seems like I knew something about a Chomountain years ago." Looking at the ground, the old man appeared to be thinking. He shook his head. "Can't say he's here, if you mean here in the valley. I rarely cross paths with anyone. I live here. Have lived here for many years." He looked up.

Cantor thought his expression very sad. Surely this old man knew something. Hadn't Neekoh said that Chomountain had lost his memories? Maybe these sad eyes testified to having forgotten who he is.

Trout grimaced. "Sorry I can't help you. First time I've had visitors in lo these many years, and I can't give 'em what they need." His face brightened. "Could be you need something else. And I can help you with that."

Cantor frowned. "When did you come to the valley? How did you get in?"

"I came with my parents through the East Gate. I was just a wee lad and had seven brothers older than me. Over the years I've laid each to rest, everyone, one by one." He looked from Bridger to Cantor and back to the dragon. "Now isn't there some way I could be a good host and help you out?"

Cantor gestured toward Bridger, who had stepped back, observing. "My friend here has a cold, and I have two more traveling companions who have been struck down with some kind of sleeping disorder."

Trout snapped his fingers and pointed to the sky. "Now that, I can help you with." He turned and strode toward the water. "Just let me get my fishing gear, and we'll go by my house to pick up a few things."

"We also have a young man with us. He's part of the ward that protected Chomountain. His name is Neekoh." Cantor watched Trout closely in hopes that Neekoh's name might register with him.

The man's stride never faltered. "Do you like to fish?"

Apparently, Old Trout didn't know anything about Neekoh.

"Yes, I fished at a lake near my home on Dairine."

"I fish a lot." Old Trout pulled his catch on a string out of the water. "Where are the rest of your party?"

"We camped at the base of the ridge, near the tunnel that leads to the outside."

"There's a tunnel leading to the outside, you say? Never knew that."

"It's been closed. With a ward. To keep Chomountain inside."

Old Trout motioned them to come along as he followed a track through the woods. Bridger had to shrink a bit before he could manage the trail.

The old man set a brisk pace, and he talked over his shoulder as they went. "Must not have worked very well, because obviously, he got out. If he's still here and I can, I'll help you to find this man, Chomountain. Why do you think he's in Bright Valley?"

Cantor ran his hand through his hair. He didn't want frustration to make his voice sharp. "Well, because there was a ward designed to trap him in here. If he wasn't here, there would be no need for a ward."

"That sounds logical. Here's my home, humble and cozy."

They broke through the last of the trees and came into a small meadow. A log cabin stood to one side with a garden, an old-fashioned water well, a chicken coop, and a seven-by-seven-foot animal pen. Rabbits hopped among the plants in the vegetable patch.

Old Trout spoke to the two goats in the pen and waved a greeting to the rabbits and the chickens. He left his fishing gear on the porch. "One minute and I'll grab my herb satchel."

"Do you want us to chase the rabbits from the garden?" Cantor asked.

Old Trout stopped suddenly and turned about. "Why would you want to do that?"

"So they won't eat all your food."

The old man frowned. "But that's not my food. I only take the leftovers."

He ducked inside and came out with a wide-brimmed, floppy hat on his head and the strap of a green leather bag over his shoulder. He carried a pair of soft leather shoes. Using a boot jack built into the wood slats of the porch, he pried off his waders, then sat on the steps to put on his shoes.

"Have you got a frying pan, a kettle, and eating utensils?" Old Trout stood and hitched up his trousers.

"Yes, we do."

The fisherman grabbed his string of fish. "Good. Let's go make some breakfast."

He headed off through the forest, and Cantor followed. Bridger fell in behind, grumbling.

"What did you say, Bridge?"

"I said I'm tired. Slept all night and I'm tired."

"You're sick. I hope Old Trout's remedy works. It doesn't look like he'll be of much help finding Chomountain."

Bridger coughed. "What if he is Chomountain and just doesn't remember?"

"Then we'll have to find evidence that he is and convince him."

The trail led to their camp, although the place where they stepped out of the woods wasn't obvious from the other end.

Neekoh jumped up when Old Trout stepped into the open area. "Chomountain!"

The old man held up a hand. "No, no, no. Name's Trout. Your friends made the same mistake. I brought breakfast. Get out a frying pan and we'll cook this fish. I've got herbs for the dragon's cold too, so heat up some water."

Neekoh looked at Cantor with his face twisted in disbelief.

Cantor sympathized. The poor young man had just been disillusioned in his life's work. Neekoh studied the fisherman.

His voice squeaked. "Do you know where Chomountain is?"

"Can't say that I do, but I'll help you look for him. I've been thinking of some places he might be, places in the valley where I wouldn't run into him."

Neekoh's face stiffened. "Who told you your name is Trout?"

Old Trout tramped over to look down at the two sleepers. "Oh, I suppose it was one of my brothers. Older brothers do tend to give little brothers strange nicknames."

Neekoh wasn't ready to give up. "What did your parents call you?"

"Young Trout. Now people say Old Trout." He paused in examining the sleeping duo and concentrated his attention on Neekoh. "For obvious reasons, don't you think?"

Cantor came up beside Trout. "Do you have any idea what could be wrong with them?"

He shook his head. "No spots or fever or delirious caterwauling?"

"No, just sleeping."

Old Trout shrugged and turned back to the business of making breakfast. "Could be they're hungry. That might be what ails them."

Cantor shook his head. "They fell asleep right after our noon meal yesterday. I don't think hunger put them to sleep."

"That doesn't mean hunger won't be what wakes them up. Let's get this food on. Nothing beats the smell of sizzling fish, and I brought dough for biscuits as well."

He crouched beside the fire, opened his satchel, and pulled out a small cloth bag, a rag, and a larger sack. Neekoh placed the kettle, a frying pan, and a large fork on the flat rocks he'd brought close.

Old Trout opened the lid of the kettle and peeked inside. He hummed as he pinched herbs from the smaller bag and scattered them over the water. He pushed both rock and kettle closer to the flames.

He grabbed the oily looking rag and wiped the inside of the frying pan.

"Anything I can do to help?" asked Cantor.

The old man handed him the string of fish. "Yep. Clean these and keep the innards. I'll dig the guts into the garden soil. The bunnies have the biggest and best vegetables in the valley." He sat back on his heels and looked around with one eyebrow quirked. "Of course, they're the only ones who've got a garden."

Chuckling at his joke, he stretched open the drawstring top to his larger sack. Out of the coarse-woven cloth came a double handful of whitish dough. Old Trout pinched off bits of dough to roll in his hands and plop into the pan.

By the time Cantor returned with the cleaned and filleted fish, a pile of golden biscuits sat on a serving platter. Cantor didn't recognize the dish, so he assumed Neekoh had produced it. He'd used a tin plate from his own hamper for the fish.

Bridger leaned against the tree he'd claimed earlier. A huge mug with steam rising over the rim rested in his cupped hands under his chin. The dragon alternately sipped the brew and breathed the steam. His lips curved in an understated smile.

The powerful aroma of bacon wafted from the frying pan.

"Bacon?" Cantor quickened his step to peer over Old Trout's shoulder.

"Just to give us some nice grease for the fish."

Cantor handed him his plate. Bixby moaned, and Cantor rushed to help her sit up. He wanted to squeeze her in a tight hug, but held off. Perhaps she was fragile after her ordeal.

"Something smells wonderful," she said. "I'm starving."

Cantor pointed to the fire.

Bixby caught her breath. "Chomountain."

"He says his name is Trout."

"But?" She looked confused. "Shouldn't he be Chomountain, or are we someplace other than I expected us to be? Where are we? Last I remember we were gliding over those pretty plants in the water."

"That was yesterday. Today we're in Bright Valley."

"Isn't that where Chomountain is supposed to be?"

"Supposed to be, but apparently isn't."

Dukmee struggled to sit. Neekoh quickly gave him a hand, and the mage stood. He stretched and groaned. "I feel like I slept for a month."

Neekoh grinned. "Only a day, sir."

Dukmee squinted at the old man. "Chomountain?"

"No, sir." The young ward guardian stood as if on duty, stiff and proper. "Old enough to be, but not. He remembers things. Chomountain would have forgot. He's Old Trout, and he's making breakfast." Neekoh's stance melted with his enthusiasm. "There's biscuits already, and tea. And another kind of tea if you have a sore throat. And bacon, and there's going to be fish."

"Good. I'm starving."

"That's what Bixby said. And Old Trout said you were probably hungry. He thought the smell of breakfast cooking would wake you up, and it did."

Dukmee finger combed his hair. "Does he know where Chomountain is?"

"No, but he says he'll help us look."

Dukmee walked over to the fire and extended his hand. "I'm Dukmee. Pleased to meet you."

"Hands are busy right now, but pleased to meet you as well. Grab yourself a biscuit and fill it with bacon. Neekoh, get this man some hot tea. Fish'll be ready in two ticks."

"How long have you lived here?" asked Dukmee.

"For as long as I can remember, and I suspect some time before that. Love it here. The fishing can't be beat. Do you fish?"

"No."

"Well, you and the other folks can look for that Chomountain fellow. That young man Cantor and I'll bring in lunch and supper."

"We do have some other things we need to do." Dukmee took a bite of his hasty sandwich. "Oh my, that's good."

"Yep. Most everything in Bright Valley is good."

15

NO PLACE LIKE TROUT'S HOME

Bixby marveled over the old man's home and garden. "Look, Cantor, he makes his own shoes and cloth and everything. He made this furniture. He made the rug. It's all homemade. Even the oiled paper in the windows."

Cantor and Dukmee sat at Old Trout's table with their scrolls from the Library of Lyme spread out. Cantor didn't seem to be sufficiently impressed, so she went on. "There's a smokehouse and a drying shed for his herbs. And he showed me where he has cold storage in a cave nearby."

Dukmee looked up briefly. "We're only going to be here a short while, Bixby. We need to move on to building defenses against the invasion."

"What about finding Chomountain?"

Cantor turned in his chair to look at her. "I think this was a case of being led astray by good intentions. Chomountain is probably not here and never has been. Trout would know.

We'll look around for a day or two, but then we must remember our primary goal."

"Trout wouldn't know. He's old, but not as old as Chomountain. And besides, what if he is Chomountain and doesn't remember?"

"Then he wouldn't remember things that didn't happen, would he? And Trout remembers coming here with his family and settling in this house."

Dukmee pulled another scroll closer. "Try to focus, Bixby. Remember our goal."

Bixby tired of the repetitive declarations of their priority. She and Dukmee had talked of nothing else for months. Then Bridger and Cantor had arrived, and that's *all* they talked about. "I know, I know. Stop the invasion. Save the world."

Old Trout came into the room holding Jesha. He had invited them all to stay with him, and when he discovered the cat, he fussed over her, greatly pleased with a new animal. He stopped abruptly when he saw his littered table, and put Jesha on the floor. "What have you got there?"

"Histories and maps." Dukmee picked up a scroll and offered it to the old man.

He put his hands up and waved a "no thanks" gesture. "Those would be of no use to me. I can't read."

"Can't read?" Bixby looked around the room. No bookshelves. How could he live all alone and not have books?

"Don't need to read." He indicated the cabin around them. "I've got plenty to keep me busy. I'm always thinking of something new to make. Sometimes the ideas just come to me in pictures, like I've seen the thing before, only I can't remember exactly where." He made a thoughtful face, then shrugged. "And I enjoy fishing. I *really* enjoy fishing."

If the joining of their voices in a three-way silent conversation made a noise, it would have been a resounding clang as Bixby, Cantor, and Dukmee rushed to consult with each other over this revelation.

Bixby's eyes nearly popped. *"He can't be Chomountain if he doesn't read. How can the right hand of Primen not read? He'd read and read in every language there is, wouldn't he?"*

Cantor looked swiftly from Dukmee to Bixby. *"How can he build all of this without plans or even pictures? Surely only Chomountain would have that knowledge in his head and ability in his hands."*

Dukmee twisted his mouth and then relaxed it. *"If Chomountain forgot, then he wouldn't remember how to make things. If Trout can't read, then he's not Chomountain. It appears to be obvious even as we try to force Trout into the role of Cho. He is not."*

Dukmee put the scroll back on the table. "These histories tell us of a time when the planes were invaded by people from the two realms known as Lyme Minor and Lyme Major. Their planes interpass with ours at great intervals of time because of their different orbit around the sun."

Trout rocked back on his heels. "I know where there are scrolls like that here in the valley."

"I knew it!" Cantor snapped his fingers. "Bridger and I have been to so many ruins, we should be able to sniff them out. Those towering rocks away from the valley walls are part of an ancient structure, aren't they? Do you know what it was?"

"No, but I thought this Chomountain fellow might be there. I've never been interested in it, so I haven't explored much. But there are stairs going underground." He pointed to the table. "And there are rooms still intact where there are those things and pictures and statues. I do go to look at the art, sometimes."

Cantor stood. "Let's go check it out."

Old Trout shook his head. "I have some snares I need to set. We might have quail or pheasant for dinner. You don't need me to look at that sort of thing." He nodded toward the maps.

"I'll go with you." Bixby moved to stand between Cantor and Trout. "I'd like to go, and I think Bridger should stay here and rest. The tea has helped him a lot, but a nap this afternoon would be better than flying us to the ruins."

"I've got horses you can ride, if you know how." Old Trout went to the door, stuck two fingers in his mouth, and whistled, a high, sharp sound that made Bixby want to cover her ears.

Trout turned back. "Now these are wild mountain horses, or their ancestors were, anyhow. When I first took to riding 'em, they were skittish as water on a hot pan. But these, well, they grew up knowing me. We'll wait a bit and see how many show up. You have to ride without saddle or bridle. I'll show you, and if you take to it, you can ride all over the valley."

Cantor moved to the door. "We've ridden before, with and without tack."

At the sound of hoof beats, a smile broke out on the old man's face. Following Trout outside, Bixby joined Neekoh, who stood on the porch with his mouth dropped open and the beauty before them reflected on his face.

Two dozen small horses and five large steeds thundered across the meadow and stopped in front of the house. The horses whinnied, and Old Trout whinnied back. They shuffled for position as close to the old man as they could get.

Bixby laughed. "They're beautiful, and they have such nice manners."

Dukmee and Cantor paused on the porch to watch.

Trout continued his round from horse to horse. He greeted each one, petting their noses and necks, and talking to each in turn. Now and then a horse paused as if they understood his words and would speak back to him. A few stayed in the yard before the house and some left, loping back to the woods.

"These here're people," said Trout, gesturing over his shoulder. "Like me, but not as old. They want to go to those old rock buildings. I figured you'd tote 'em if you got a mind to."

Trout turned to his company. "Any of these three will do for Neekoh and Bixby. Probably Dukmee wouldn't be too heavy a load, but his feet would pretty near hang to the ground. The two bigger horses would do for him and Cantor."

The horses pranced a bit, and one of them playfully butted the old man with his nose.

He laughed and pushed the pretty roan away, instead singling out the light ginger horse and petting her lovingly as he went to her side. "This is Dani. She's a good girl. Look here now, and I'll show you how to get on and give you some pointers.

"These horses are smart. They almost read your mind." Taking the mare's mane in one hand, Trout gave a hop and swung himself onto her back. "A little squeeze of the legs to go, sit back a touch to stop, lean if you want to turn." He demonstrated, and Dani went in a tight circle until he sat up straight. "Like I said, they're smart. But I will say they don't like to stand around. If I ride one to a fishing hole, by the time I'm done, he's gone. But you can always whistle 'em back."

The horses nickered as if gossiping among themselves, then stared across the meadow.

"Eager to get going. We'd better hurry." Trout made introductions to the larger horses and assigned a horse to each rider.

"I don't think I'll go," said Neekoh. "I've never been around horses, and I don't think I'd be any good as a rider."

Trout patted his shoulder. "You'll surprise yourself. You got just the right temperament to be a natural rider."

Bixby exchanged a look with Cantor and hid a smile behind her hand. His face plainly said he, too, wondered what kind of temperament made a horseman.

"Come here, Neekoh, and meet Taffy." Trout led the reluctant young man to a glossy brown mare. "She's just right for you. She has a sense of humor, and I feel you appreciate a lively, happy attitude toward life."

"*That is a fair assessment of Neekoh.*" Bixby spoke just to Cantor's mind. "*Do you still have doubts about his reliability?*"

"*Yes and no. I don't see him as malicious. But I don't think he's dependable, because I don't think he has all the facts. He just has knowledge that has been handed down from father to son. After so many generations, a few details are bound to have been lost.*"

Trout had Neekoh mount Taffy. "Just sit there and get used to her being underneath you. You don't have to go anywhere on her until you're comfortable."

Neekoh gave a nervous laugh. "Does *she* know we aren't going anywhere?"

"She does."

Trout had each of them mount up and watched them as they gave simple directions to their horses. Bixby sat on Dani and quickly fell in love with the sweet horse's personality.

Cantor rode the largest horse. Olido frisked a bit under his weight, as if showing that the big man was not a problem to the stallion. Dukmee had ridden bareback before and easily communicated to his horse, a handsome mare named Breez.

Neekoh lost some of his timidity while watching the others. With his grin back and his excited voice under control, he followed Trout's instructions, growing visibly more confident with every turn and halt Taffy accomplished.

When they felt sufficiently practiced, Trout gave them instructions on the shortest, easiest route to the ruins and waved them along.

"I think he's glad to be rid of us," said Bixby when they were out of sight of the cabin.

"Probably," Dukmee agreed. "After all this time alone, five visitors and a cat must be overwhelming."

Bixby laughed. "He likes the cat."

"He does, indeed," Dukmee agreed with one of his rare smiles.

"I wonder if Trout would like to go with us when we leave."

Cantor, riding on the other side of her, spoke up. "I don't think so. I think he's content here."

"He's very old." Bixby shook her head, and her wild white curls flailed her cheeks. "What if he were to get sick, or fall and break a bone?"

"If he were to die, I think he would prefer to die here." Cantor sounded reasonable, and it irked Bixby.

"If I were to order the universe, I would arrange it so that we find Chomountain and introduce him to Trout, and the two of them would become fast friends."

"Don't we need Chomountain to come with us?" asked Cantor.

"Well, he could do that. Then after we have quelled the

Lymen invasion, he could come back here and do his right hand of Primen business from the comforts of this valley."

Dukmee chortled. "Bixby, the purpose of the right hand of Primen is to walk among the people, acting as judge and mediator and educator. It would be difficult to share his wisdom from isolation."

"I suppose that's why I'm not arbitrator for the world. I forget important details."

Dukmee laughed. "Bixby, when you become a mother, you'll have the ordering of a small universe. It's a weighty job. But you shall excel. You have the right temperament to be a natural mother."

"What does that mean, exactly?"

"I have no idea, but it sounded good when Old Trout said it."

Dukmee sat up straighter. "I find it very satisfying to be a mage."

Bixby laughed. "When you aren't being a realm walker or healer."

"Or a scholar," Cantor added.

"I find it good to be content in whatever role I find myself." Dukmee ignored Cantor's humph.

Bixby laughed again. That's one of the things she liked about Dukmee. He had something to say for every occasion. And she liked Cantor because he would never let Dukmee get too full of himself. They made good companions.

16

COMPANY

In a forest, the path narrowed. Dukmee and Neekoh led the way, and Cantor fell back to ride beside Bixby. In green lace and brown ruffles, she looked as lovely as she ever had. He watched her handle Dani, touching the pretty mare's neck and speaking quietly to her. Not that the horse needed soothing. Even when a fresh breeze stirred some of the trailing bits of Bixby's clothing, neither her horse nor his took exception.

"I'm glad you're back," he said.

Bixby tossed him a puzzled look. "What do you mean? I didn't go away. You did. You left me at my parents' palace and went questing with Bridger."

"I meant while you were sleeping." Oh, no. He'd opened the door. Now he would have to talk about her feelings when he left so abruptly.

"Oh." She shrugged. "That didn't feel like going away. In fact, it didn't feel much like anything." She tilted her head. "However, two years ago, it did *not* feel good when you went away with

Bridger." Her eyes met his for a moment before she looked away. "I resented your sudden departure. We'd been partners in trying to stop the council. I thought we'd go on being partners."

Cantor reached to put a hand on her shoulder. "Your father gave me a list of places I might find Ahma and Odem. It never occurred to me that you'd be ready to leave home so quickly. I'm sorry."

He watched for her expression to change, to lose that hurt look he'd caused. Since they'd met again in the Library of Lyme, she'd acted like the same friendly Bixby. He'd had no idea she carried a pain.

"I'm so glad you told me, Bix. You know I wouldn't hurt you on purpose."

She smiled and tossed her hair. "Now that would be something. Here I saw a little bitty old slight as something to moan and groan about. *Insensitive* was one of the kinder words I used to describe you. If you were to hurt me on purpose, I'd have to come after you and make you see the error of your ways."

"I remember how well you fight." He smiled. "I'll be sure to be on my good behavior." He made an observation about the beauty along the trail and led the conversation to a safe topic. He liked Bixby a great deal, but he didn't want to form the habit of emotional talk. He'd do a lot for her, but he wasn't ready for that.

He hadn't shielded his thoughts carefully enough against their strong connection.

"Don't worry, Cantor. I'm not going to be mushy. I tidily stored your act of callousness into a little mental box and refused to bring it out. Now that you've apologized, I can toss the box."

They rode beside the river for a while, then crossed at a wide, shallow point Trout had described. The terrain on the far side was hilly and dotted with small clusters of trees.

A road of sorts cut through the foliage, leading away from the ford. Under the horses' hooves, odd-shaped slabs of stone made a rough path. Chunks were missing. Dirt obscured some of the flat rocks. Grass and squatty shrubs forced their way up in the cracks.

As they approached the ruins, Cantor became uneasy. He sensed Bixby's apprehension as well. When Dukmee and Neekoh stopped and dismounted, Cantor and Bixby followed suit without question.

Dukmee spoke quietly when he joined them. "We've got company."

"Impossible!" exclaimed Neekoh in a voice too loud.

All three of his companions said, "Shhh!"

They all listened intently for a moment.

Bixby shook her head. "They didn't hear us." She looked at Neekoh. "There's quite a few of them, and their activity is centered on the ruins."

Neekoh whispered, "What are they doing?"

Dukmee patted Breez on her nose. "We're going to find out. Neekoh, you stay with the horses. See if you can keep them from wandering off. We'll sneak into the ruins and learn what our visitors are up to."

Neekoh's neck knob bobbed up and down. "You're going to walk right in among them?"

Cantor nodded. "We're trained for this sort of thing, Neekoh. Don't worry, and keep your head down."

The young man scrunched his head down and his shoulders up.

Bixby giggled. "It's just an expression. It means don't get caught."

"Ah, I get it. I keep my head down behind something so they won't see me."

"That's right." Bixby had her hampers out and was looking through her different crowns.

Neekoh gasped. "You wear a crown?"

"All the time."

His eyes darted to her hair.

She raked her fingers through the blonde tangle and pulled out a thin silver circlet adorned with tiny gold leaves.

Cantor suppressed a laugh. He imagined the young man was overwhelmed by all the things they revealed. No company for years, then suddenly a realm walker, a mage, a princess, and a dragon show up on his doorstep.

Neekoh's eyes were twice as big as normal. "You're a princess."

"Well, yes, but these are utilitarian crowns."

"Utila ...?"

"Useful. They have attributes that help me as a realm walker."

Neekoh collapsed to the ground, sitting with his legs crossed and astonishment on his face. "You're a realm walker too! Bixby said so."

Cantor took Neekoh's arms and hauled him to his feet. "And Dukmee as well."

The man's muscles quaked under Cantor's hands. "Neekoh, are you all right?"

"Just happy. Just happy. Nothing ever happens. For generations, nothing happens. Now. Everything! I am the Neekoh who gets to see it all. It could have been just nothing for me too. But no, I get to be here when you're here."

Cantor spoke calmly and quietly, hoping to settle Neekoh's euphoria. "But if we don't find Chomountain, the Neekoh destiny will not be fulfilled. Stay with the horses. Be quiet. Wait. Try to keep the horses here."

"Yes, sir. I can do that."

Cantor gently patted Neekoh's thin arms before he let go. "Good. Good. You'll do a good job."

He looked up to see Bixby smirking. *"What?"*

"You're being kind."

"Stop it, Bix. We've got work to do."

Dukmee had been standing, focused on what was farther down the shattered road. "There are thirty-three men at the ruins. Twenty-seven are laborers. Four are guards, providing a harsh incentive for the laborers to work. One is a realm walker. And one is from the Realm Walkers Guild. They have a portal open. I can't tell to where from this distance. And they are looting the buildings. The councilman is under the mistaken impression that they have found the Library of Lyme."

He faced Bixby and Cantor with raised eyebrows. "Shall we go take a look at what they are carting off?"

Eagerness to outwit the enemy coursed through Cantor's veins. He and Bixby would slip in and out without causing a stir. Dukmee would probably stand close by and do his spying with his mental powers.

"Where'd she go?" asked Neekoh. His head swiveled as he tried to look everywhere.

"Bixby's right here," said Dukmee. He pointed, and Neekoh sighed his relief.

"I thought she'd gone."

"She has on an obscuring crown. It helps her blend into her surroundings and confuses the minds of anyone around."

131

"What about you?" Neekoh's eyes took in Cantor's huge form from the top of his head to his boat-sized boots. "Surely you'll be seen."

"I'll tell you about it when we get back."

The three finally got away from Neekoh and his questions. They crept up the hill and hid in a thickly wooded area. Within the confines of the forest, a strange and breathtaking plant grew. Each vine reached from the decayed vegetation on the floor to the lowest limbs of the tree and climbed out of sight into the canopy. The rope-like tendrils supported flowers the size of Cantor's hand and in a variety of brilliant colors that had Bixby starry-eyed.

She touched one of the blooms tenderly. "I shall embroider this flowering vine on a piece of clothing. I wonder what it's called."

Dukmee pushed aside a curtain of foliage to pass through. "We'll ask Trout when we return. I think we best hurry. I believe they are almost done with today's work."

When they reached the edge of the woods, they saw the trees had encroached upon the boundaries of the crumbling edifices. Bixby stepped right out of the forest and into one of the smaller buildings.

Cantor slipped around the side and stealthily made his way to a large structure. By hiding in the dark space between, he could watch the laborers come and go as they carried objects to the portal.

He spotted a large, shambling giant of a man and plucked him out of the line. With little effort and no noise, he simultaneously pinched the man's nose and a nerve at the base of his skull. He then supported the man's weight as he laid him on the ground. Taking his long tunic and headscarf, Cantor soon looked enough like the laborers to take a place in the procession. He matched the tired men's shuffle and posture, resting his chin on his chest and allowing his shoulders to slump.

A guard stood at the door to the building they would enter. Hopefully, the guard had been on duty all day and was not as sharp as he would have been in the morning. Cantor passed the man without arousing even a second glance. Once inside, he stepped out of the line and crouched behind a broken half wall to wait for an opportunity to advance to another room, out of the path of laborers.

Moving swiftly and without a sound, Cantor darted to an open area to the side. In this tiny alcove, he found treasure. Books had been gathered from the shelves and piled on a table by one wall. A dirty cloth next to the tomes indicated an effort had been made to clear away some of the dust. Pulling out a hamper, he quickly filled it with the lot, then tucked the hamper away and started for the door.

Footsteps from the corridor interrupted his departure. He saw an open gap in the outside wall. At one time, the partially squared hole must have been a window. The sill crumbled at his touch, but he swung out just before two men entered the room. His position was not a good one. Anyone walking the shabby streets would see him, and shards of rock littered the ground beneath his feet. If he moved, the crunch would alert those inside to his presence. He stayed still.

An oath broke the silence from within. "They've already taken this collection. I don't remember authorizing the removal. Could it be one of the muscle-headed oafs took the initiative?"

Another voice sounded ill at ease. "I didn't direct them here. It must have been one of the other guards. Do you know what time this happened?"

"No, and it doesn't matter. I'm sick of this dusty place. We can go as soon as they empty the room they're working on now."

"Do you want them fed and watered before we return?"

"No, waste of time. What made you ask such a thing?"

"You mentioned dusty. They haven't had a break all day. I'm sorry I mentioned it, Mr. Councilman. Just mindful that the jailer will want them returned in the same condition as they went out. He'll charge more if he can't work them tomorrow."

The other man sputtered a bit. "Well, all right then. I don't want the money to come out of my pocket. Water them. Dole out a portion of food and find some shade. Ten minutes out of the sun. Keep watch. If we don't take the same number back as we brought, that will cost me even more dearly." He paused as if thinking. "No, it won't. It will cost you."

The men walked away.

Cantor took the long way around to get back to the laborer he'd waylaid. The men had been gathered for their allotment of food and water and the ten-minute rest. The guards stood around with eyes trained on their charges. Cantor dressed the man with the clothes he'd borrowed, then propped him in the shade in clear view of the portal.

He thought for a moment about whether or not it was safe to mindspeak to Bixby. Their bond had strengthened, which meant less leakage to an outside listener. The realm walker at the portal put out a very discordant vibration, meaning he would be a poor receptor. He decided it wasn't much of a risk.

"Bixby?"

"I'm done."

"Meet you where we left Dukmee."

"Give me five minutes. I found something interesting."

A flash of exasperation accompanied his realization of what she was packing. *"Pencils? Bixby, you don't have to bring them."*

"Yes, I do. You'll see why."

"Put them in your deepest hamper so they won't bother me."

All he heard was her giggle in his mind.

17

WHAT DO WE KNOW?

Dukmee silently welcomed Cantor and Bixby back, and together the three of them moved farther from the ruins, walking all the way to where Neekoh kept the horses.

Neekoh jumped to his feet. "The horses are still here. All I had to do was talk to them. When I stopped talking, they started walking, so I have told them everything I know about Chomountain."

Cantor blinked. Had he heard correctly? "That couldn't have taken long, Neekoh. You've never even seen Chomountain."

"But my family tells the tales of Cho. It is part of our destiny to keep alive what is known. When each son takes his father's place, they go back to the village and become the historian. Only I will have no successor. But I'll still get to tell the stories. My story will be last. The story of your breaking the ward and taking Cho back to the outside world."

"There are a few problems with that story, Neekoh."

"What?" The young man looked befuddled.

Cantor looked to Bixby and Dukmee for help, but neither offered to join the conversation. Dukmee looked so preoccupied, Cantor believed he must be thinking of something totally unrelated. Bixby's face shone with anticipation, also unrelated to Neekoh's naïve rendering of their actions. She had something to show them, and the something had to do with those pencils she had stowed away.

Cantor heaved a sigh. He didn't bother to muffle it. He wanted the other two to know he was frustrated. "Neekoh, it's true we broke the ward, but that's all we've done. We haven't found Chomountain, and we haven't rescued him. We will leave here soon whether we find him or not, because the Lymen invasion is imminent, and we must stop it."

Neekoh opened his mouth, obviously to pour out his opinion, but stopped when Dukmee put a hand on his arm. "Peace. You've done well with the horses. We'll ride back to Trout's in a minute. Right now, we three have to exchange information."

Dukmee pinched his upper lip, shuddered, and set his face in a mask of solemnity. "These men were here under the orders of Errd Tos."

Bixby gasped, and Cantor moved a step closer to her. The high councilman had almost uncovered Bixby's spying two years ago, before the bombing. He'd left her brain and body frazzled. Dukmee had managed to save her life and her mind.

"Why?" asked Cantor. "And how did they know the ward was broken? Is it just a coincidence that they came at this time?"

"Hardly a coincidence. The realm walker with them had

been monitoring the ward-protected portal. He knew it had opened as soon as you took the book off the shelf."

"Do you think they have Cho?" Neekoh's hands came together in a loud clap, and he proceeded to wring them until Cantor thought he'd pull his fingers off.

"No, I don't." Dukmee peered at Neekoh through slitted eyelids. "You swing to extremes, young man. Stick to the happy side of your pendulum. Optimism carries people much farther than pessimism. The worst thing that could happen rarely does."

Dukmee's gaze took in all of their party. "It seems Errd Tos expects to find information about the vehicles that transport the Lymen warriors."

Bixby stirred beside Cantor. "We already knew that, but did they truly find anything?"

"What they found was a lot of material about Chomountain."

"I have books I pilfered from one of the rooms." Cantor patted his tunic where a hamper held what he'd gathered. "They looked to be about Cho. I didn't take time to read the titles closely."

Bixby bounced. Her light clothing glittered in the sunshine. "The room I looked into must have had works of art. I could see by the clean spots in the dust where statues had been. There were also places on the wall where pictures must have hung. I collected the pencils, quills, ink, and paper left behind. I thought Cantor could give us an idea of what these writing utensils had been used for."

Cantor nodded to her. Yes, that would be useful, but the practice of his talent still gave him the willies. He likened it to dead people whispering in his ear, or some ghost moving his hand. It wasn't that, Dukmee had assured him, but it did feel odd.

A loud cracking noise interrupted them.

They first looked at each other as if one of them would have an explanation. Cantor saw their puzzled expressions and focused his mind on hearing anything that would explain the explosive sound.

"There's a commotion going on at the portal. People hurt, and the cracking noise was the portal shutting unexpectedly."

Bixby stood with her head at a tilt, her face pensive as she listened. "The realm walker is on the other side." She gasped. "He wasn't the one holding it open. The council has a machine that serves the purpose of a realm walker. A machine!"

Disgust pulled at Dukmee's face. "Yes, a mechanical device, something they've made instead of using the course of action given us by Primen. As you would expect, it hasn't proven to be reliable. That's why they had a realm walker with them. But he was unschooled and of no use when the portal started collapsing."

"Shouldn't we go help those who are injured?" She looked to Dukmee.

Cantor's jaw clenched. Of course, Dukmee was the oldest and the most experienced, but no one had assigned him as the person to be in charge. It grated, after two years of being the one making the decisions. He consulted Bridger, true, but the ultimate choice was his.

He chastised himself. Arrogance helped no one, and if he had to step aside in order to work well with Dukmee and Bixby, then that's what he had to do.

Dukmee didn't answer Bixby's question but stood collecting information. Cantor watched his thoughtful expression and knew exactly when the mage had left his mental assessment of the situation at the portal. With eyes bright, Dukmee addressed his friends.

"The injuries are minor. One of the laborers seems to have enough training to patch the scrapes. The councilman believes the portal will reopen in a matter of minutes." Dukmee chuckled. "He's distraught, and I don't think our aid would be anything but more disruption. And I do think it's prudent to keep our presence a secret."

"I want to see them," said Neekoh. "Can I sneak close and watch them for a while?"

Cantor gave the hamper holding the books to Dukmee. "I'll take Neekoh while you look at these. I hope there's something useful in there."

He smiled and gestured with his head to the ward guardian. "Come on."

"We'll be here when you get back." Bixby's wave was cut off by her eagerness to see the contents of the hamper. She and Dukmee sat on the ground with Cantor's unpretentious sack between them.

Cantor took one last look, then hiked up the hill toward the ruins. "Stay close. I'm taking you to a rise in the land on the far side. We should be able to look straight at the portal area from there."

Neekoh followed. His stealth impressed Cantor. When they reached the place where they could slither under some bushes and peer over the crest, Neekoh kept taking big breaths and holding them.

"Trying to settle your nerves?" Cantor whispered.

Neekoh nodded but said nothing.

"Look." Cantor pointed. "The portal is just now opening."

The area in front of the waiting men shimmered like heat waves on a desert. A dark color separated from the undulating center and looked like it solidified in a frame around the portal. The hue and formation didn't look right to Cantor. He counted himself as an experienced realm walker, but his skin crawled at the sight.

Cantor could tell that Neekoh had never seen such a thing. "That doorjamb is not really there," he explained. "You could pass your hand through it."

The realm walker stepped through. Cantor took a good look, first trying to recognize him and then etching the man on his memory. He wanted to know who this man was. If he ran into him again, he'd be wary of any connection.

The councilman shoved in front of the laborers and spoke to the realm walker, his hands moving in rough, angry gestures. After a moment of apparent bickering, the subordinate bowed and led the councilman through the opening. The realm walker came back, and with the guards herding the laborers, they all filed through the portal.

"I'd like to go through that."

Cantor chortled. "How did I know you would say that?"

"What's on the other side?"

"Excellent question. It's important to find out what's on the other side *before* you charge through. In this case, I think I recognized a farmhouse a few miles outside of Gilead on Dairine."

The portal slipped shut with a faint shooshing.

Neekoh backed out from under the bush and stood up. "Let's go look at the ruins."

Cantor objected. "Dukmee and Bixby are waiting for us."

"They're looking at those books. They won't mind if we

take a quick walk through the abandoned buildings. Maybe we'll see something else to take back and examine."

The idea appealed to Cantor. Spotting likely items was easier when you weren't watching for guards.

"All right. But a quick look — the emphasis on quick."

Neekoh plunged down the hill, his shoes slipping on loose stones. Somehow he managed to get to the bottom without tearing his clothes or his skin. Cantor followed at a slower pace, eyeing the area. It would only take one straggler or one man left on watch to ruin their effort to be unseen.

"I think this was a city," said Neekoh as the two men passed in and out of one of the decrepit buildings.

"I'm guessing a university or some center of learning." Cantor pointed to the big structures in various states of decay. "There don't seem to be any dwellings for common folk."

"They'd have to have some kind of servants. Smart people don't have time to cook and wash and tidy up."

Cantor laughed out loud. "You're right, Neekoh. They aren't always very savvy at taking care of themselves. But in the biggest buildings, the stairways probably lead to servant quarters beneath the ground."

"I'll go see." Neekoh ran down some steps, then did an about-face and raced up. "Do you have a light orb? It's very dark down there."

Cantor obliged, and Neekoh returned to his quest. Cantor took out a light for himself and followed slowly, looking at carvings on the wall.

"Help!"

Neekoh's cry transformed Cantor from a casual observer to a warrior. He pulled his sword and charged down the rest of the steps. At the bottom, he stopped and surveyed the short hall before him. It came to a T. A light glimmered from the right turn.

Cantor took the time to listen. He heard Neekoh sputtering, possibly from a hand over his mouth. He also heard labored breathing.

Mumbled words came from Neekoh. Cantor strained to interpret them.

"I can't breathe. Take your grimy hand off my face."

The one holding Neekoh muttered through uneven panting. "Hold still or I'll stick this knife in your throat."

"Don't do that. That could kill me."

"That's the idea, rat."

"You're bleeding, aren't you? I can smell it. And I think your blood is soaking the back of my shirt. It's very uncomfortable."

"You talk too much."

"But I'm very good at stopping blood and cleaning wounds and making bandages and finding herbs to ease the pain."

Cantor crept to the end of the hall, being careful not to be seen by the men around the corner. "If you're injured, let us help you."

"Why would you want to do that?"

Neekoh piped up. "They have these codes of honor and vows of integrity and other noble things. They have to help you, or their consciences will hound them."

"They? How many?"

Cantor cleared his throat. "No need to say how many, Neekoh. Tell me, are you one of those who were here at the ruins today?"

"I am."

Neekoh shuffled his feet. "Ow! I just needed to get my leg in a better position. Why didn't you leave with the others?"

"They left me here to die. I was held responsible for some thieving the laborers did."

"So they aren't your friends anymore?"

"Friends?" The man scoffed. "They were never my friends, but I am now no longer in their employ."

"Oh, well then, how do you do? My name is Neekoh. I was employed —"

"Neekoh! You don't have to tell this man your business." Cantor turned the corner and allowed the injured man to see him.

The guard swayed. His face gleamed with sweat. Blood stained his tattered uniform. The whites of his eyes barely showed under heavy eyelids. His injuries must be many and deadly.

Cantor took a step forward. "I think we can help you. Let Neekoh go, and we'll take you back to our friends. One of our party is a healer."

"Who?" asked Neekoh.

"Dukmee."

"He is? I thought he was a mage and a scholar."

"He's also a healer."

"Amazing. I'm so glad you came looking for — um, someone. I have not been bored for even an hour since you broke the —"

"Neekoh!" Cantor ground the name out between clenched teeth.

"I can't say anything about that, either?"

"No."

The man behind Neekoh groaned. As Neekoh stepped forward, the wounded man slipped to the floor.

"Well, that's good," said Neekoh. "Now we can help him without having to talk him into it."

18

A PATIENT

Cantor communicated to Dukmee and Bixby, telling them about the wounded guard and asking them to bring the horses. He lifted the man and carried him up the stairs.

Neekoh trailed behind, chattering about the ruins, the visitors, and the guard. "That talking with your mind thing sure is convenient. Do you suppose you could teach me to do it?"

"I don't think so." Cantor laid his burden down in the shade of one of the less-worn walls. "I think you're born with the ability, and then you learn to use it." He crouched beside the guard and examined him.

Neekoh clasped his hands together. A frown etched his face in unfamiliar lines. "Is there something you need me to do to help?"

Cantor sat back on his heels. "He's been beaten severely and sliced every which way. No method to their cruelty, just random infliction of pain."

"Will he die?"

"His injuries are beyond my skill, but Dukmee and Bixby may be able to pull him through. And Trout had a cabinet stuffed with dry herbs."

The guard groaned.

Cantor put his hand on the man's shoulder and spoke. "Help is coming. Neekoh, prop him up some, and I'll give him a drink."

"Respectfully, sir, it would be easier if I gave him the drink while you held him up."

Cantor nodded. "Good thinking."

Neekoh's chest puffed up with the casual praise.

Cantor noticed. *He's been alone too long.* He wondered who had set up the strange tradition of one of the Neekoh family guarding the entrance to Bright Valley. It seemed a rather pointless task, since the wards kept intruders away, and apparently Chomountain wasn't even in residence.

Cantor supported the guard's head and shoulders easily. Rousing him so he could drink was another matter.

Neekoh touched the man's arm and shook him gently. "Wake up!"

The guard's head lolled from one side to the other, and he groaned.

"Splash some water on his face."

Neekoh obliged, and this time, the man opened his eyes.

"Drink." Cantor nodded to Neekoh, who held a flask that had been filled at Trout's well. The old man had claimed the water had special qualities. It tasted like plain water to Cantor.

The guard eagerly downed the water with quite a bit of dribbling. He sputtered, and Neekoh pulled the flagon away from his lips.

"It's good." His words slurred.

"The water?" asked Neekoh. "You've lost a lot of blood. You need to drink."

The guard clumsily shook his head. "No. It's good I'm dying."

"Oh, well ..." Neekoh shot a panicky look at Cantor. Cantor merely shrugged.

Neekoh's neck knob bobbled. "We don't know that you're dying. We've got traveling companions who are pretty clever with medicine and such."

Cantor looked beyond Neekoh. "They're coming now. You just hang on a little longer and let them help."

The wounded man wheezed. "Nothing will help. The guild ... full of evil men — " Coughing interrupted his attempt to speak. By the time the hacking subsided, the guard was once again unconscious.

Dukmee and Bixby rode into the abandoned street with the other two horses following. The healer and girl dismounted and came to inspect their patient.

Neekoh hovered behind them. "He just passed out again. We gave him some water, and he tried to talk."

Cantor watched Dukmee's solemn expression as he checked the guard's injuries. The healer paused for a moment over the swelling at the man's side and above his waist. That was the same wound that had troubled Cantor when he'd first done a cursory exam. He knew the damage done there would likely kill the man.

Dukmee looked up at Cantor and nodded. *Internal bleeding.*

The healer stood. "Cantor, can you summon Bridger? That would probably be the kindest way to transport this man back to Trout's cabin."

Bixby jumped to her feet. "He's badly injured. We shouldn't move him."

Dukmee turned his somber eyes to hers.

Cantor overheard Dukmee's explanation. *"None of us has the skill to heal him."*

She stilled. "Oh."

Bixby watched the dragon rise into the air. Her heart beat with slow deliberation. She always wanted to help, but sometimes Primen put before her circumstances where she could do nothing. Even with all her talents and the years in which she'd polished those skills, she often fell short of her own expectations. Her limitations reminded her she could help only within the confines of Primen's providence.

She hopped up on Dani and urged the horse back along the trail toward Trout's home.

Dukmee rode with his patient on Bridger's back. The dragon had shifted his shape between his wings to form a safe cradle for the man to lie in. He provided a saddle behind the patient to accommodate Dukmee.

Bridger had not complained about being called from his sickbed to aid a stranger. He came, loaded his passengers with grace, gave an encouraging word to Bixby, and left. He was only a speck in the sky now. She hoped the guard would still be living when they returned on the horses.

Cantor rode just ahead of her, his back straight, his body swaying with the horse's gait.

The trail widened, and she urged her horse to catch up. "I'm really impressed with Bridger."

"Why is that?" Cantor's voice still held a reservation when talking about the dragon he had not chosen.

"Well, hasn't he proven he's useful? Hasn't he helped you out of many scrapes?"

He snorted. "Scrapes that were usually the result of his uncanny ability to make a simple task complicated, or a simple plan explosive, or a simply worded instruction a maze of double meanings. In other words, he makes his own disasters."

"He flew out here to help an enemy guard even though he's sick. And he didn't have a thing to do with that calamity."

"I like him!"

Neekoh's voice from behind startled Bixby. She turned and gave him her biggest smile. "I like him too."

Cantor twisted to glance back at Neekoh. "I admit to liking him. But that doesn't mean he's an adequate constant."

Bixby decided if she said anything else, it would be caustic. She didn't think using cutting words to point out how unfair Cantor was to Bridger would help her fellow realm walker suddenly appreciate his dragon.

Just a little way from the old man's cabin, Trout passed them on the trail. His rod hung over his shoulder, and he had a knapsack with his fishing paraphernalia.

"I'll be back before sundown with our supper." He waved a hand, seemingly as content and happy as usual. "That man hasn't died yet. Your healer friend has him tucked up in my bed."

Bixby frowned. She hadn't thought about where they would put the soldier if he made it this far. Trout's bed was a frame hung by its corners from the roof beams. An odd mattress of thick homespun material stuffed with longstem grass swayed back and forth like a stiff hammock. Any pressure set the contraption in motion. She'd found it a fun place to sit, but she doubted it was a practical place to nurse a wounded man.

They rode up to the cabin's porch and slid off the horses. Bridger lifted his head, briefly interrupting his nap under a spreading nester tree. Bixby figured he was still suffering from the cold and needed to rest after his flight. She'd talk to the healer about it. They should be able to do something. Jesha lay curled in a basket on the porch, and the slight raise of her brow as Bixby passed seemed to suggest the cat agreed.

Dukmee came out to greet them. "He's unconscious," the healer reported. He eyed their mounts. "We're grateful to have had such fine rides. Neekoh, would you be willing to give them a good rubdown?"

Neekoh stood straighter. "Certainly."

Cantor looked puzzled. "Do you know what it means to rub down a horse?"

"I figure you rub them." The young man shrugged. "That shouldn't be too hard."

Cantor laughed. "I'll show you." He strolled over to a place where the grass grew tall. The horses followed, whinnying as if carrying on a cheerful conversation. Cantor took out his knife, grabbed a bunch of stiff green stems, and cut off a handful. "This is what we'll rub them with."

Bixby took her eyes off the two men and stared into the dark cabin. "Is there anything I can do?"

Dukmee put his hand on her shoulder and urged her toward the door. "Let's make him comfortable."

Bixby had worked with Dukmee enough to recognize his proposed treatment. The herbs he took from a pouch and crushed into powder form would put the guard into a deep sleep. With the first application of pestle to mortar, the strong fragrance of wide-leafed pomerune burst into the cabin's air. Just breathing the scent calmed Bixby's agitation. Dukmee added ersal and cremusm, and the fresh scent of summer days in open fields filled the room.

Bixby turned her mind to what she could do. At present, the man stirred and mumbled. Obviously, Dukmee had been washing the sweat and grime off the patient before she arrived. She took a bowl of cool water to the bedside, knelt, and crooned a soothing tune as she dabbed a damp cloth on his face. His red complexion cooled and paled. He mumbled more and thrashed less.

Dukmee soon came to stand beside her with a paste of herbs. She put down the bowl to help steady the man so the healer could open his mouth and put the concoction under his tongue. Dukmee was quick. He stood back, watching to make sure the guard did not push the medicine out.

Satisfied, he wiped his hands on a towel. "I'm always grateful any time I administer that compound and don't get my fingers snapped off."

Bixby smiled up at him. She started to get up.

"No, stay where you are. I want you to use your gifts to determine what's happening inside the poor man's body."

"You mean we can help?"

Dukmee shook his head. "No, but while he's in this deep sleep, you can make some adjustments so that when he awakens, he'll be more comfortable. Also, I want you to become more familiar with the techniques I've been teaching you."

Bixby paused, her gaze on the silent man. "You want me to practice. That doesn't seem right."

Dukmee made an impatient sound in his throat. "Yes, Bixby. You must practice. It will not hurt him. Your gift will

151

relieve him of some stress. Next time your healing hands are needed, you will perform with more confidence. You help him a little. He helps you and the next patient a lot."

Bixby pulled in a deep breath, but she couldn't make herself lay her hands on the guard.

"Start at his head, Bixby."

She expelled the pent-up air and cupped her hands over the guard's crown of curly brown hair. Dirt clung to the dark, matted locks. She urged her awareness to sink deeper, past the unwashed hair, past the scalp crusted with dried blood, and through the thick bone of his skull. The rhythm of thoughts pulsed through her fingertips. The medicine had eased his tormented mind. He appreciated the slight swaying of the hanging bed. It reminded him of visits to a loving aunt. The images of a hammock soothed and comforted him. For the moment, he was at peace.

Bixby smiled at her erroneous assumption that Trout's awkward mattress would be a poor place to put the wounded guard. The pleasant thought skittered away as she recalled her purpose.

She moved her hands to his forehead, his eyes, his nose, and his mouth. Gently probing for distress, she found that he breathed with effort. But the problem was not in his airways above the neck. With her hands on his chest, she located two broken ribs.

"His right lung is punctured."

Dukmee nodded. "What would we do if we were going to save him?"

"Pull the rib back into position. Strap his chest to keep it immobile."

"Reposition the two ribs to alleviate the pressure."

Carefully minding her energy flow, Bixby coaxed the broken bones back in place. If the patient moved more than a trifle, they would slip again. If they kept him sedated, he probably would not reinjure himself there.

"Continue," Dukmee said.

As she moved her palms along the guard's sides, she came to the injury that would kill him. Even if this had been the only wound, they could not have helped. This massive bleeding around his kidney and across his lower abdomen could not be dealt with in a cabin high in the mountains.

"Don't linger on this, Bixby. There are numerous flesh wounds on his arms and legs. You can squelch the bleeding and apply soothing balms so that he won't be tormented by pain when he comes to."

She nodded, unable to voice the despair she felt. She let go of the tiny hope that something her hands could do, some medicine they could produce from their stores, or a fluke of nature would suddenly heal this man. She busied herself with cleaning, medicating, and binding his many slashes and gouges, wondering, as she did, if the guard had family and friends to miss him.

19

WARNING

Cantor didn't go into the cabin until the next morning. They'd cooked dinner and eaten outside the night before. Trout's one room had been crowded with the patient in bed and Bixby and Dukmee on thick floor pallets. And for some reason, Jesha had abandoned Bridger and insisted on keeping watch inside all night.

Bixby and Dukmee were up and seeing to the comfort of their patient. Cantor stepped through the door and allowed his eyes to adjust to the dim light. Jesha perched at the foot of the bed.

He smiled at Bixby. "Neekoh and Trout have been fishing."

Bixby groaned. "Let me guess. We're having fried fish for breakfast."

"Right, but he said there was some cornmeal in here, and I thought I'd make some corncakes."

"That's a wonderful idea. We've had fish at every meal since we met Trout."

Dukmee looked up from the mixture in his mortar. "He did tell us that he liked to fish."

They all chuckled, and the man in the bed cleared his throat. "Who is that old man?" His voice was stronger than the night before, and he didn't gasp between every few words.

Jesha now sat on the bed at the guard's waist. He had one hand resting against her back. The cat lifted her head to look over the humans in the room. She must not have seen anything of interest, because she closed her eyes and ignored them.

Bixby hurried to her patient's side. "You're awake. Let me give you a drink."

"There was one brew you gave me last night that tasted like it'd been dipped from a frog pond. The other one was all right."

Bixby wrinkled her nose. "I'm afraid it's the frog pond for now. It eases your pain and allows you to think clearly."

And in just a minute I'm going to ask you all sorts of questions, starting with your name.

"What does the other one do?"

"Helps you sleep and keeps you from vomiting."

"Well, I've got something to tell you, so I guess I'll swallow the pond water. It would help if I could hold my nose."

"Your nose is broken."

"I know."

Cantor heard the humor in the wounded man's voice. He stepped closer and caught the man winking at Bixby.

"I'll help hold him up so he can drink." Cantor positioned himself at the head of the bed, where he could brace against the frame and keep it from swaying. He could also redirect any inappropriate conversation should the man feel like one last flirt with a pretty girl.

155

Bixby squinted her eyes at him. *"Cantor, he's dying."*

"These guards can be rough individuals. I just don't want him talking to you like you were a bar room floozy."

She giggled. *"Bar room floozy?"*

Cantor refused to be diverted. *"Doesn't this man need a drink? His medicine?"*

She went away to fix the potion. When she came back, Cantor held the guard, gently lifting him by the shoulders and supporting his head against his chest, careful not to shift his torso and disturb his broken ribs. Jesha moved aside, hopping off the bed and exiting the cabin.

The guard drank the smelly brew all at once.

Bixby smiled at him. "I put a spoonful of Old Trout's honey in it. Was it any better?"

Cantor lowered him carefully before the patient answered. "It was sweeter ... but still pond water."

Bixby heaved a big sigh. "I'm sorry."

"Don't be. I figure you won't be able" — he grunted — "to pour many more of those down me before I die."

Bixby remained silent for a moment. Cantor thought the sorrow on her face would tear a hole in his heart.

She summoned a cheerful expression. "You're in for a treat this morning. Trout makes the best pan-fried fish I've ever eaten. Even after three days of fish at every meal, it's still tasty enough to anticipate. And Cantor said he would make us corncakes for a little variety."

Dukmee stood and gestured with the hand holding his mortar. "I'm taking this medicine out to Bridger. His cold won't last much longer."

He left, and Bixby got to her feet, rubbing her knees. "I'll find the cornmeal."

Cantor rose to fulfill the promise he'd made for hot corncakes.

"Wait," said the guard. "I want to know who the old man is."

Cantor pulled up a stool and sat next to the bed. "He appears to be an old man who loves fishing and doesn't mind being alone. He has an excellent knowledge of animals and plants. He's resourceful and has built himself a comfortable home with some amazing conveniences."

"Conveniences?"

Cantor nodded as he looked around. "Everything in this room, he's made. The bed, the stone oven in the fireplace wall, the carved spoons and forks, even the skillet." Cantor shook his head in disbelief over the list. "He's shown me how he forges metal, and to think that he starts from scratch on everything is amazing."

"He must be smart."

Cantor agreed. "Smart and patient and handy with tools."

"And all alone?" The guard looked concerned. "I couldn't handle being alone. That's why I joined the guild's new military." He snorted, then winced. "I didn't find the fellowship I expected."

Cantor agreed but didn't want to waste the man's energy on their negative assessment. "Another odd facet of our host's character is that he doesn't read. You would think that someone who is intuitively intelligent and lives all alone would devour books."

"For a fact? Doesn't read?"

"True."

"Humph," said the guard. "I can read."

Dukmee called from the porch. "Neekoh and Trout have

just come out of the woods. Looks like they have quite a catch. We'd all appreciate those corncakes."

Cantor got to his feet. "I'll be back."

Bixby came to the side of the bed. "Before you go to sleep again, I want to know your name and if you'd like me to write a letter, you can tell me whom to send it to."

The wounded man's eyes were half shut, but he smiled. "You're a tiny thing but your heart is big. Beautiful. That hair. Shining."

Jesha scooted in through the open door and took up her position on the bed. This time she settled near his chest, and the wounded man put an arm around the comforting cat.

"Sir." Bixby touched his cheek. "Your name?"

She stood and looked at the cat. "Next time. Because there may not be a time after that."

The next time Cantor checked on the guard, he was sleeping. Bixby beckoned him outside, and he followed her to the forest where she handed him a basket and pointed to the ripe berries on mountainsweet vines. "I'm going to make a pie."

Cantor remembered Bixby's cooking from their last adventure together. He willingly took the container and began picking the ripe red fruit. He popped a few in his mouth as he went, testing to see if they were sweet, not tart.

She worked beside him, picking more and eating less. "I have to admit I like working outdoors much better than under the mountain."

"I do too. Sometimes" — he glanced at her — "like now, I wish we could stay here awhile. But we're running out of time.

We have to leave this tranquil valley and search out an army to face the invasion."

"And soon," she agreed. "Before we go, though, I want you to experiment with the pens and paper I found. My intuition tells me there's something for us to learn."

Cantor didn't want to think about using his gift to find out what the pens and pencils had traced out before. "How's your patient?"

"He's dying. He doesn't feel it, except now he finds it hard to breathe. And he sleeps."

"Did he say any more about what he wanted to tell us?"

"No." Bixby went down on her knees in order to reach into the lower branches. "He seems to think he should tell you, not a girl, and not a healer."

Cantor quit picking, overcome by a sudden urgency. "Bixby, we need to hear what the man has to say. Right now."

Bixby craned her neck to see his face way above her. She said nothing for a moment, then pushed herself up to a stand. "I think you're right."

They left the basket on the porch and went directly to the patient's bedside. Jesha no longer slept, but sat with her eyes trained on the man's face.

Bixby wiped sweat from his brow and spoke softly. "Wake up. I have a cool drink for you."

Cantor helped position the man so he could swallow from the cup she held. Jesha moved only long enough for them to give him the drink and lower him back on the mattress.

His labored breathing hushed his thank-you. Bixby put down the cup and took the man's hand. "What was it you wanted to tell us?"

For a moment, Cantor thought the man would not have the

strength to answer. But he licked his lips, took shallow breaths, and opened his eyes briefly to look at Bixby. "They … they didn't beat me for the theft. They couldn't let me … go back. I overheard something." He mumbled, cleared his throat, and took another glimpse of Bixby. "Cause them a lot of trouble if I told."

His eyes closed again. He'd used too much breath to speak so many words at once.

Cantor put a hand on his shoulder. "Take your time. We won't leave you." He moved to the side of the bed so he could look the guard in the eye. "Why don't I ask you a few questions, and you can just say yes or no or nod?"

The patient closed his eyes and nodded.

"Did you hear this conversation while you were at the ruins?"

His lips parted, and he whispered, "No."

"Did the councilman and realm walker who were here take part in the conversation?"

"No. Not important enough … in the guild."

"He's sweating harder, Cantor. Maybe we should let him rest."

"Get that water you use to bathe his face. I don't think we have time to wait, do you?"

She shook her head and left to replenish the bowl and get clean cloths. Jesha edged closer and rested her chin on his scruffy cheek.

When Bixby returned, Cantor moved aside so she could reach the man's face. Jesha reluctantly sat up. With his eyes closed, he did not respond to Bixby's first dabbing of his forehead and cheeks.

Cantor leaned forward. "Are you still with us?"

His nod barely moved his head. "The cat?"

"She's here," whispered Bixby.

Cantor touched Bixby's arm. He hated to push the man like this, hated what it was doing to Bixby too. But he had no choice. "Does the conversation have to do with the Lymen's invasion?"

"Yes, but there's more." He wheezed as he spoke. His eyes popped open, and he stared at Cantor. "I don't know — do any good — tell you. You may be bad like 'em."

Bixby took his hand again. "We've run into some evil men in the Realm Walkers Guild. We've chosen Primen's ways. Not evil."

He snorted, something that must have been a derisive laugh. He choked and took a moment to regain control of his breathing.

His words came out in a breathy whoosh. "Sixty-six councilmen left. Inner circle called Kernfeudal plan to assassinate all those they can't recruit." He pulled in a couple of shallow, shaky wheezes and continued. "Explosion at the guild — two years ago — first attempt to kill 'em. Next 'cleansing' — during the Lymen attack."

Cantor nodded. "The chaos of the invasion should give them plenty of cover for their nefarious plans."

The patient's mouth quirked up at one corner. "I do like the way you talk."

"And the Lymen attack?" Cantor prodded.

"Want what aliens use to get from one plane to another. True realm walkers to be killed. Not all at once. One by one — out on missions. The kernfeudal have filth, scum — follow any command." He swallowed, choked again.

When the stranglehold subsided, he started to speak again.

"No," said Bixby, squeezing his hand. "That's enough. You need to rest."

With his other hand, he held up two fingers. "Brosternhag. Vattledorn." The words were indistinct.

Cantor leaned closer. "Brosternhag?"

He nodded.

"Vattledorn?"

He nodded again. Smiled. "Go get 'em."

"We will."

The guard didn't respond. His eyes closed as his face relaxed into contented peace. His breathing slowed, then stopped.

Cantor put his hand on Bixby's shoulder, feeling it tremble with her tears. "You did all you could for him, and he has done all he could for us. We now have two cities in which to begin our probes."

Jesha stood, bumped the man's chin with her head, and then sprang from the bed to saunter out into the sunshine.

20

END AND
BEGINNING

The funeral was an impromptu affair. Old Trout went to a shed and pulled out a shovel. "I've got a place." He started for the woods and Bixby, Cantor, and Neekoh followed.

Bixby tried to shake off the sadness that dampened her spirits. "We didn't even ask about his family, where he lived. We don't know his name."

"Keast Manbro." Trout spoke over his shoulder. "No family, and few friends since he left his village on Dairine."

Bixby exchanged a look with Cantor. As far as she knew, the old man had never been near the patient. "How do you know?"

"Talked to him." Trout changed directions. The trail became narrower and overgrown.

Bixby pulled her wispy clothing closer and sent a shimmering cover over her sleeves and skirts to keep them from catching on branches. "I didn't see you come in the cabin. Were we asleep?"

"I don't know if you were sleeping. I didn't go in."

"Then how—" Bixby turned a questioning face to Cantor. *"He's Chomountain. I know it."*

Old Trout's voice was calm and roused no doubts that this was an ordinary occurance. "I heard him calling. So I answered."

Cantor's face lit up. "There you go, Bix. He can mindspeak, not so earthshattering about that." He spoke over the sounds of the bush being beat back. "You can converse with your mind. We can do that too."

Neekoh made a noise in his throat.

Cantor sent him a sympathetic look. "Well, some of us can."

"Yep. Neekoh has other talents." Trout plowed through the undergrowth.

Neekoh's smile returned.

Bixby slipped behind Cantor and spoke to Neekoh. "Will you trade places? With the three of you tramping ahead of me, you'll break down the weeds. It'll be easier for me to walk."

"I could carry you."

Bixby smiled at his enthusiasm. And his smile grew when Bixby refused the offer.

"No, that's all right. It's important on a quest for everyone to pull their own weight." She didn't tell him that with his back to her, she'd be able to float, skimming across the tops of the trodden plants.

She sighed, the solemnity of the situation rocking her usual lightheartedness and natural optimism. She needed time to reflect on life and death, on the path Primen had set before her. Death made one reevaluate one's priorities. She was determined to serve and be a positive influence in a negative world. Her goals were lofty.

Neekoh thwarted her plan by walking backward in order to carry on a one-sided conversation.

She hid a scowl. Her goal for this moment was to shake off this yappy young man without it sounding like a reprimand.

Was that sufficiently lofty?

She laughed at herself and gave him an order. "Turn around and march on, Neekoh. You're making me dizzy."

He laughed too and faced forward.

In the silence that followed, her mind returned to meditation on noble endeavors. Did she fall short of being an honorable realm walker? Unfortunately, she could recall many areas where she needed improvement.

They came upon a clearing, and Bixby caught her breath at the serene beauty of the glade. Sunshine spread a golden hue over grassy swells in the small hollow. Tiny yellow flowers and bigger white blooms swayed with the breeze. She could watch as a zephyr flowed from east to west with a gentle ruffle of every plant. Orange and black butterflies flitted back and forth.

Bixby glimpsed deer and rabbits, then counted three different species of colorful birds before the wildlife took note of the humans' presence and darted to the safety of the woods.

Old Trout tramped back and forth, with his head bent to examine the turf beneath him. He seemed to waver between two spots, then made his decision, jamming his shovel into the ground. He cut a rough rectangle with the blade and then scooped up the grass and flowers as if they were a blanket. After clearing sod in the rough outline of a grave, he began to dig in earnest.

Cantor took over, the shovel looking comically small in his grasp. He could have lifted larger amounts if he'd had a bigger shovel, but he worked rapidly and soon the hole was deep. Bixby thought he was shaping it now, not so much a rectangle, but an oblong that fit within the boundaries Trout had first hewn out of the sod.

Neekoh sat on one side of Bixby, and Trout sat on the other. Neekoh had drawn his knees up and circled them with his arms. He didn't watch the digging. His head swiveled as he considered many birds, butterflies, and small furry creatures. He, in turn, was scrutinized by those who peeked out between trees at the edge of the glade, including a fox who sat beside a bush, watching them with no apparent fear.

Old Trout had been rummaging through his knapsack. He now had thin thread, feathers, fur, and hooks laid out on a rock.

Still carefully avoiding the sight of dirt being thrown out of the hole, Neekoh looked at the old man's collection. "What are you going to do?"

"Tie flies. Lately, I've left some of my best lures in trees and tangled in water plants. Time to make some more."

Neekoh got up and moved closer. "Show me."

"Don't need to show you."

"Why not?"

"'Cause you're sitting right there. Don't need to show you because you can't help but see."

"I see." Neekoh looked pleased.

"Well, of course you see. That's what I'm saying. You don't have your eyes closed."

Trout's faced puckered in a sorry scowl for a moment, then the wrinkles smoothed out, revealing his usual calm, friendly demeanor. He slapped Neekoh on his arm and went back to his flies.

As in many cases, Trout was accomplished in what he was doing. His old, gnarled fingers twisted, wrapped, and arranged a slither of feather and a tiny fluff of fur together onto a hook. In a half hour, fourteen flies sat in a row. He told Neekoh the name of each one as he finished.

"This one is a yellow-bellied twisty worm." Trout held up the decorated hook.

"It doesn't have a yellow belly, sir."

Trout scowled and looked closely at his fly. He turned it every which way.

"No yellow anywhere, sir." Neekoh repeated in a respectful tone.

"Not important." Trout's gruff voice disturbed several birds that had come quite close to peck at seeds. They fled with a flurry of wings. The old man's tone lightened. "Quite right. But fish don't see in color, only black and white."

Neekoh tilted his head. "How do you know?"

"Nothing mysterious about that, son. I just go inside the fish's brain and see what it sees."

"Does that help you when you fish?"

Trout stiffened and picked his lures up one by one to store them in a special heavy cloth folder. "That would not be sporting, now would it?"

A shadow fell across Bixby's lap. She saw Cantor's dirty boots first and followed his muscular frame up past trousers, tunic, and a day's growth of beard to look into his solemn eyes.

Trout lifted his head and tilted an ear toward the trail they had blazed. "Bridger and Jesha are coming with Keast Manbro's body."

Crackling of bushes on the path brought them to their feet. They turned to see Jesha marching into the glade. Behind her,

Bridger bore the guard's body, cradled in his arms. Dukmee, who had changed into more formal attire, brought up the rear. Bixby looked down at her layers and skittered into the woods to put something frillier on top.

Returning, she saw Cantor join Bridger beside the grave and leap into the hole. He reached up, and between them, they placed the body with dignity in the earth.

Old Trout paced over to stand at the head as Bridger gave Cantor a hand climbing out. Jesha solemnly took a place beside the old man's feet. Trout nodded to Cantor and Bridger on one side of the grave. He briefly glanced at Bixby, Dukmee, and Neekoh on the other. Bixby's eyes opened wide when she saw the twinkle in the old man's eye.

"A few words," said Trout, "as befits the occasion."

The others nodded. Bixby had been to state funerals and village funerals, one type prim and proper and the other not. She couldn't imagine what Old Trout would say.

He cleared his throat. "We stand beside a hole in the ground. At the bottom is a broken jar. We will bury the remains of one we barely knew.

"Keast Manbro has escaped. He's cast off the encumbering frame that served him while he needed it. Now he does not need that frame. Now he is free, not only of a merely passable imitation of what he really is, but also free from the wounds inflicted upon that vessel. Wounds that hurt in the flesh, wounds that ravage the emotions, wounds that scar the mind, and wounds that would convince us to wither and hide and be no more.

"Keast Manbro, in this new freedom, knows what it feels like to be a seed responding to the warmth of the sun, the nourishment of the soil, and the nurturing of gently flowing water. He knows the joy of soaring like an eagle. He knows the delight of a minnow in a meadow brook. He knows the satisfaction of a rabbit burrowing to make an underground home.

"We cannot mourn for Keast Manbro. It would be more fitting for Keast Manbro to mourn for us.

"But with patience, we walk. With hope, we continue. With confidence, we face trials. With joy, we anticipate the end that is no end but the beginning."

Old Trout dropped to his knees and scooped up two handfuls of the newly turned dirt. He dropped it into the grave. Cantor used the shovel. After a moment of uncertainty, Bixby also knelt and joined in burying the guard's body. Bridger turned his back to the grave, but he used his tail to carefully push the hill of dirt next to him into the hole. Dukmee took Neekoh by the arm and returned to the hillock they'd used earlier for a seat.

Jesha sat in her stoic pose, watching the burial with an excess of decorum. Bixby looked up from time to time and smiled at her. The cat didn't respond.

The last of the dirt was shifted. Cantor, Old Trout, and Bridger laid the pieces of cut sod over the little mound. Bixby took a seat between Neekoh and Dukmee.

"Look." Neekoh pointed to Jesha.

Beside her, two rabbits sat with their ears alert and their noses constantly twitching.

Bixby blinked twice. "I never — "

"Neither have I," said Dukmee. "I can coax a wild thing to accept me as you can, Bixby. But I've never seen one come out and join a foreign group on its own."

When the three working on the grave had made final adjustments, Old Trout picked up his shovel and headed back on the trail without another word. The rabbits departed, and Jesha came to rub against Bridger's side. Bixby stood as Cantor came to join her.

She looked over the meadow with its subtle crests and valleys almost obscured by the thick, flowering grasses. Serenity hovered in the warm, sunny air. With a sharp intake of breath, she looked at the grave and again at the glade.

She put her hand on Cantor's arm. "This is a graveyard."

He looked puzzled. She pointed to the small swells in the land and then pointed to the new grave. "They're the same size."

Neekoh came to his feet and offered a hand to Dukmee. Bixby wondered what her healer friend thought of being treated as an ancient. She shook the thought away as Dukmee's face took on his own particular expression of discovery. She'd been with him for two years, and she knew him well enough to recognize his glee at the sudden solving of an intellectual puzzle.

He turned on his heel and started down the path. Bixby sighed. She also recognized Dukmee's behavior. He wouldn't share his finding until he'd worked out all the details and given himself enough time to regain his majestic composure.

21

CHOMOUNTAIN

Bridger had widened the path as he came. Now, on the way back, he trundled along ahead of the others to further beat down the trail overtaken by abundant plants. Neekoh carried Jesha as he followed the dragon. Their new friend had a tendency to get too close and then had to leap over Bridger's tail as it swished from side to side, something that seemed to annoy the cat exceedingly.

Bixby tugged on Cantor's sleeve, a gesture which he had come to like. "Who do you think is buried back there? Trout's family?"

"I think it's entirely possible. When we get back to Trout's cabin, why don't you ask him?"

"He might not want to say anything about it."

"Even if he gives you no answer, you won't be worse off than you are now."

She scowled at him. "What do you mean?"

"You're all tied up in knots, trying to make sense of Old

Trout, the valley, the ruins, the meadow, everything. You need to start finding answers so you can relax or just let it all go."

"What about you? Don't you want to know as well?"

"I'm more interested in finding concrete answers to what we can do to thwart the Lymen invasion. We have to leave this place and get on with our mission." He knew the frustration he felt had sharpened his words. He tried to think of some way to tell Bixby he hadn't meant to be curt.

Bixby walked silently for a few steps, then tugged on his arm again. "Dukmee saw something or figured out one of the riddles of this place at the end of the funeral. Do you suppose he thinks Chomountain is buried in Old Trout's 'place'?"

Cantor's face screwed up in reaction, and he quickly returned it to a mask of neutrality. If those were graves, then Old Trout hadn't owned up to having visitors previously. He had said that he didn't get many visitors. So some had wandered into this valley. But he hadn't been forthcoming. Did he not remember, or did he lie? He didn't seem to take anything seriously enough to bother with prevarication.

Cantor felt Bixby's thoughts poking at his own. He looked at her with mock chastisement. "Bixby." He had made it a habit lately to keep his mind shielded. Too many people in his present company could read his mind.

Bixby squeezed his arm. "Sorry. What are you thinking?"

"I was considering what you said. I don't think Chomountain is buried in the meadow. The previous mountains didn't die, did they?"

"No. One was scooped up by the hand of Primen. One was standing in a field, and a chariot pulled by flaming horses stopped and took him aboard. And when another one climbed a ladder past the clouds, the ladder fell when another man tried to go up. The second man and the ladder turned to dust, and the wind carried them away."

"It would seem that those who hold the office of the mountain, the right hand of Primen, skip physical death and are taken to be with Him in a more comfortable way."

"I'm not sure climbing a ladder that tall would be exactly comfortable. And I would think hard before getting in a chariot pulled by horses on fire."

He laughed. "Well, we aren't as close to Primen. I imagine the mountains have a good idea of what's going on."

Bixby tilted her head, popped a hand up to straighten her slipping tiara, and hummed. She stopped abruptly and asked, "If Chomountain is not buried in the graveyard, was he ever in this valley?"

Her blue eyes opened even wider, making her look about twelve years old. Cantor shook his head, not so much in answer to her question but to dislodge the protective feeling that rose in his chest.

"I'm beginning to doubt even the existence of Chomountain. And if he doesn't exist, were all those others before him myths made by man?"

Her fair eyebrows wrinkled together as she thought. She repeated the hum.

"Why are you doing that?"

Startled, she looked straight into his eyes. "What am I doing?"

"Humming. I don't remember your humming in the Library of Lyme, but since we've been in this valley, you hum."

She looked perplexed. "I guess I picked it up from Trout. He hums."

Cantor put his hand on her back and propelled her forward.

"I haven't noticed him humming. Why does he hum? And why do you have to hum just because he does?"

"I don't hum *just* because he does. He believes that humming organizes his thoughts. So I thought I'd try it. Humming quickly becomes a habit."

"And is your thinking more organized?"

"I don't know. I think I don't think much at all when I hum. Or at least I don't think about thinking."

"So instead of organizing your thoughts, humming eliminates your thoughts."

She shook her head. "It can't do that, can it? I mean, totally abolish my thinking?"

"I wouldn't think so, but I have noticed you've been preoccupied some."

"Well then, that proves it doesn't. Because if my thoughts were done away with, then I couldn't be preoccupied."

"That does make sense." Cantor became aware that he was staring at her. Her puzzling expression was endearing. He had to stop being so interested in the way she looked. He was beginning to categorize her expressions, filing them away to remember later. He was the one not thinking. If he didn't watch out, she would cause problems. He scowled at her.

She smiled. "I don't think you should worry."

For a half-second he feared she had followed his train of thought. But he was guarded. She must have been referring to the humming problem.

Cantor wasn't convinced that the humming was benign. The thought that this habit might somehow hurt her compelled him to object. "I don't think you should hum. Why not do an experiment and don't hum. Take note as to how efficiently your mind is working as you do without humming for a while."

"I don't see why you're making such a fuss." Bixby preceded him into the meadow where Trout lived. She stopped just beyond the end of the path and whirled to look up at him with her fingers twisting a clutch of ribbons hanging from her belt. "But I'll do what you ask, even though your concern seems silly."

"Maybe it is and maybe it's not. It won't hurt to follow my instinct on this."

"Speaking of instincts, I'm sure there is something to learn from my loot pillaged from the ruins."

He nodded and gestured for her to go on toward the cabin.

Bridger had already settled under the tree he liked best for napping. Jesha cuddled against his chest on his crossed arms. Neekoh had gone to the animals.

Cantor grinned at the young man's enthusiastic greeting to the pig and goats. "He really should be a farmer."

"Yes, that might be his calling." Bixby nodded toward the porch, where empty pegs showed that the old man had taken his fishing gear. "Trout has gone to catch our supper."

Dukmee came out the cabin door, holding an open book Cantor recognized as one he'd brought from the ruins. The scholar sat on the edge of the wooden porch.

Cantor's nose itched as he contemplated poring over those ancient volumes. He knew why Dukmee had come out of the cabin. Not only did the sun provide good reading light, but the fresh breeze helped stave off fits of sneezing over the musty tomes.

As Cantor and Bixby walked toward the cabin, Dukmee jumped to his feet, closed the book, and tucked it under his arm. He marched past them without a word and went straight to the resting dragon. He spoke quietly to Bridger, who stood with a long-suffering sigh. Jesha sprang to sit on Bridger's head.

As the scholar climbed along with his book onto the dragon's back, he called over his shoulder to anyone who might be listening. "We're going to make a quick trip to the ruins to check on something. A matter that needs to be investigated before we quit this valley."

With her fists planted on her hips, Bixby watched them take off. She turned her solemn face to Cantor. "If you insist on us leaving soon, I'd like to remind you to have a go with the writing instruments and paper I picked up at the ruins."

Cantor's mind immediately conjured up a half dozen things that he really should do at once in order to leave the next day. But they hadn't really decided the time of their departure. And he recognized stalling techniques even when he wasn't consciously trying to get out of this duty.

"All right." He sighed as if he was making a sacrifice as great as Bridger's foregoing his nap to provide transportation for Dukmee. "Bring the lot out here. Perhaps it won't be so stifling done out in the open."

He sat on the steps as Bixby disappeared into the cabin. He heard her shifting things, banging around, and stacking something heavy on the table. When she came out, she had dust on her nose and carried a light green hamper decorated with lace flowers, ribbons, and a frill of shiny pink material.

She held it up for him to see. "I put the writing utensils and paper in this so you could work with one thing at a time. Perhaps stowed away like this, the others won't bother you."

Cantor nodded. She sat beside him with her legs dangling off the side of the porch. Reaching into the bag, she brought out a pencil and a small sheaf of paper.

The urge to put the chore aside warred with Cantor's curiosity. Dukmee had first taught him about the strange feelings that crept up his skin and worried his mind whenever he came in contact with writing instruments. He'd learned then that he had the ability to retrieve movements made long ago from a pen, pencil, quill, or even a burnt stick. Thus he gathered information that was lost to all those who did not have this talent. That stipulation seemed to encompass everyone else existing in their world.

He took the pencil Bixby held out and held it over the paper. Within seconds the pencil made contact, and with the guidance of those disturbing vibrations, Cantor wrote out a list of words.

"Ha!" He slanted the paper for Bixby to see. "A grocery list?"

"More like the ingredients for a specific dish. Try again."

Once into the experience, Cantor moved on without all the dread he'd manufactured before he got to work. Under Bixby's encouragement, he tried out different writing tools she had in the hamper and different types of paper. Sometimes he couldn't get a reaction from a pen held over one paper, but when they changed to a different sheet, he produced what the pen had last done. He drew buildings, a diagram for an aqueduct, herbs with names and uses printed beside the sketches, and people.

One lot of paper and a particular pen evoked the images of many citizens of the ruined community. Beneath his hand, a sheaf of papers displayed a staff of professors, a number of scientists, a good many servants, a few children, and horses, dogs, and cats. The images were grouped according to activities and packed closely together.

But the last one he drew took up the entire sheet. He drew with tiny precise lines, and the muscles of his hand cramped. He tried to rest, put this drawing aside for a bit, but he returned to the task as if driven.

The picture was of an old man wearing a wizard's hat. Long hair covered his shoulders, and a beard spread out over his chest. He wore priestly robes and carried a carved staff. The pencil hovered over the face, and then Cantor drew the telling details of eyes, nose, and mouth.

"That's Trout," whispered Bixby.

Cantor's hand dropped down to the bottom edge of the portrait.

The pen spelled out, "Chomountain."

22

SORTING THINGS OUT

Bixby took a deep breath and let it out slowly. "Do you think Old Trout knows?"

Cantor shook his head. "No. Neekoh said that Chomountain doesn't remember who he is."

He ran his fingers through his hair. "And we haven't seen any evidence that he is constrained in any way. People were kept out, but he willingly stayed here and fished. Taking his memory was sufficient to impede his travels."

"I suppose they could have instilled the obsession with fishing."

Cantor nodded thoughtfully. "I bet you're right."

"They changed his focus." Bixby shuddered at how easily they had made sure Chomountain would not be involved in Primen's business. Of course, the execution of the idea required more expertise than most people possessed. Who was behind this? And who were the people in the graveyard?

"Do you think that somehow Trout's responsible for all those graves?"

"It seems likely he dug them, but not that he slew the people in the graves."

"I guess we should ask him."

Neekoh approached with a piglet in his arms. "Bixby, he's injured his foot. Do you have medicine for him?"

"I suppose so." She pulled a hamper from her skirts. "Do you know where Trout might be?"

"Fishing." He sat on the edge of the porch, holding the piglet securely. His glance traveled past Bixby to the paper Cantor still held. "You're quite an artist. I didn't know. When did you sketch Old Trout?"

Cantor held the picture out for Neekoh to inspect. "It isn't Trout. Or, rather, it is, but it isn't."

Neekoh's mouth fell open. "It says Chomountain. Did you find it in the ruins? But the paper doesn't look as old as the others you brought back."

Bixby swabbed the injured hoof, making the little one squirm. "The paper is old, but it was well preserved in a stack of unused art materials. Cantor can feel what a pen has written or drawn before and reproduce it."

She smiled at Neekoh's look of disbelief. "I was astonished as well, but I have read about wizards who could do the same."

"Cantor's not a wizard, is he?" Neekoh shifted the pig in his arms, clutching it tighter against his chest. "I thought he was a realm walker."

Bixby studied her friend, who had become engrossed in another drawing. Grinning, she nodded to Neekoh. "He is. But realm walkers come with different talents. I can fashion clothes, wraps, purses, shoes, and other useful things with my fingers. That comes in handy." She waved a small pot of ointment in front of Neekoh. "Hold piggy closer to me so I can smooth this over the wound."

He obliged while Cantor looked from his drawing to the two people beside him. "You could ask me your questions, Neekoh. I'm sitting right here."

"You're busy."

"Not *that* busy." He picked up a clean sheet of paper and another writing instrument, this time a device holding a sliver of charcoal. His attention riveted, without an ounce left over for Neekoh.

The piglet squealed another objection to Bixby's tending of his foot.

"Oh, stop that," she said. "The salve doesn't hurt."

Neekoh scratched behind the pig's ears. "You think Old Trout is Chomountain after all."

Bixby pulled out some strips of white material. "Pretty sure he is."

Neekoh's body quivered with excitement. "Then we will be able to free him. I will be the Neekoh who released him." He hugged the pig, then turned a sincere face to Bixby. "With your help, of course. And Cantor, Dukmee, Bridger, and Jesha."

Cantor put aside another completed drawing. "Only Trout won't leave as long as he doesn't believe he's Cho." He changed writing instruments and selected another sheet of paper.

The piglet squealed. "Oh, sorry!" Neekoh loosened his grip. "How do we get Trout, I mean Cho, to believe us?"

"I have a feeling we only need to trigger a memory to break the spell that took his past. Dukmee should be able to help with that."

"Where did Dukmee say he was going?"

"To the ruins."

Neekoh thrust out his chin, indicating a new drawing in Cantor's hand. "What's that?"

Bixby neatly tied off the binding and turned to study Cantor's work. "It looks like vegetation."

"Those aren't like any plants and flowers I've ever seen." Neekoh shifted his gaze to Bixby's face. "How about you? You've been to lots of places besides this mountain."

"I don't recognize them. But I do know this picture was originally drawn by a different artist than the one who drew Chomountain."

"How?"

"A different style."

Neekoh nodded as if he understood what she meant. "Cantor sure draws fast. Why aren't all the pictures in Cantor's style?"

Cantor held the picture away from him and stood. "Because it's not my talent that produces the picture. I'm only a conduit of the original artist, whoever held this charcoal."

He put the paper on the porch boards and bent over. With quick, sure movements, he labeled the picture and read the words aloud. "Flora, Lymen Major."

Bixby gasped. "Someone from here has been to Lymen Major?"

"It would appear so." He displayed the charcoal encased in the convenient holder. "This contraption is practically jumping in my fingers, seeking more pieces of paper."

"You're not upset about that?" asked Bixby.

Cantor put the pen down and dug a scrap of parchment out of the hamper. "I seem to be getting used to it. Each time is easier than the last."

He grinned at her and stood to stretch. When he sat down again, he gestered to the pile of pictures. "I think I can probably spend several more hours working." He turned to Neekoh. "You've been fishing with Trout a lot. Do you think you could find him and bring him back?"

Neekoh's lips stretched into a goofy smile. "I think I've been to every one of his fishing holes. He's fun to follow around. He talks all the time. And hums too. I guess both of us have had to make do with little company."

"I'll go with you," Bixby volunteered. "Unless you want me to stay here, Cantor. I could cook something to go with the fish."

Neekoh laughed. "As long as it isn't more fish. Trout's meals do get monotonous."

Although Bixby could tell his attention had already shifted to his next picture, Cantor laughed too. "Go with Neekoh and help find the old man. Dukmee and Bridger will return and cook." Cantor picked up a different pen. "I'm actually going to enjoy what these tools will reveal. It's exciting."

Bixby patted him on the arm, an act which he ignored. She rolled her eyes and started off with Neekoh.

Their first stop was the pigpen and livestock shed. Neekoh put the piglet in a stall rather than in the outside mud hole. He left food and water. As they left the stable, he patted the animals within reach. "I'll feed the rest of you when we get back."

The animals looked attentive to his voice.

Bixby grinned to herself. The men on this quest continually surprised her. Cantor now wanted to draw. Neekoh had found an affinity for animals. Dukmee preferred research to his healing profession. And humble Old Trout was the most powerful being among the planes, though he didn't know it.

"Where do you think he'll be?" asked Bixby as they followed a path in the shade of the trees.

"He likes to rotate among his favorite spots. I've gone with him enough to be able to guess. Two places are due for another visit."

The afternoon sun brought out the fragrant scent of the forest. Green plants and colorful flowers swayed a bit in the breeze. Birds with fancy feathers darted from branch to branch. Plentiful insects provided their afternoon snack and kept up a rattling percussion softly in the background of other natural sounds. All unexciting, normal noises of the forest. But Bixby felt that she would burst with the exhilaration flowing through her.

Extending her hearing out around them, she tried to locate Trout. Keen as she was to find him, she could barely contain her impatience with Neekoh's vague notion of where the old man might be.

She gave herself a mental shake. She would get used to this outrageous development. Cheerful, simple Trout being the ancient, wise right hand of Primen tickled her sense of the absurd. But circumstances in the very near future were too severe to allow anything to be taken lightly.

She reminded herself of the trust that had been placed in her. For too long, the prophecy of three realm walkers thwarting evil and pointing civilization in a different direction had hidden dormant under the tasks of every day. Bringing Chomountain out of retirement would be monumental. Was this what the prophecy predicted? Not if Trout remained in Bright Valley.

Hopefully, Trout would accept his change of circumstances. With the invasion coming and the guild councilmen perpetrating evil schemes, all the planes needed the personal guidance of Primen. Chomountain had a big job to tackle.

They had walked several miles when Bixby heard a soft song like a lullaby being sung in Trout's whispery voice.

"I hear him," she told Neekoh. "He's singing."

"Ah, he's trying to catch a big fish he's been after for several years. He's grown to be monstrous compared to the others in the lake. Trout thinks if he sings a croony tune, the fish will be lured into carelessness." Neekoh tsked. "He's going to miss fishing."

They hurried, not bothering to go quietly among the tangled undergrowth and scurrying creatures.

When he saw them emerge from the forest, Old Trout abruptly reeled in his line and waded out of the river.

He scowled as he splashed to the shore. "Won't catch that old coot with company standing on the banks. When are you and your friends moving on? You're welcome here, of course. But I'm used to solitude. And you people eat a lot. Don't mind fishing. Love fishing. But keeping the frying pan full has taken some of the joy. The relaxing part of fishing. The sitting and absorbing the sun, the sounds, the smells. Fishing for four more people, a dragon, and a cat is almost work."

Neekoh went to the old man and rested a hand on his arm. "Is something wrong? You don't sound like yourself."

Bixby agreed. The old man's creased face frowned at everything in sight. Usually his bright eyes snapped, and his mouth turned up in a cheerful grin.

Old Trout shook his head and jerked a shrug. "I feel twitchy, like something's going to happen. Can't tell if it'll be pleasant or not."

Bixby took hold of his other arm. "Let's hope it's pleasant. Cantor has something to show you. Shall we go back to your cabin?"

The old man squinted at her for a long moment, then nodded. "Might as well. I'm supposing whatever your Cantor wants to show me is part and parcel of this creepy feeling under my skin."

Usually, Old Trout hummed a bit randomly as he walked, and he spoke a few words to critters he passed. Now though, he was silent.

Questions tumbled in Bixby's brain. Was Old Trout really Chomountain? Would Chomountain regain his powers along with his memory? Would he regain his memory? After hundreds of years, was he physically, emotionally, spiritually fit to assume the duties of the right hand of Primen?

She gazed at the back of his scrawny neck as he tromped down the path ahead of her. Had this been a necessary side trip or a colossal waste of time? She'd be happy to turn the whole situation over to Dukmee's capable hands. Let him tell the old man he wasn't a fisherman, but the most high priest, the right hand of Primen, the advocate and intercessor between Primen and his people, the chosen arbitrator representing the one and only true and living God.

23

SORTING
OTHER THINGS
OUT

Dukmee peered over Bridger's shoulder at the land passing below them. Not one sign of human life. At least those soldiers and others from the Realm Walkers Guild would not interrupt his exploring.

As he perused the books in the cabin, he'd thought that the secret rooms and hidden library mentioned in the literature referred to those in the mountain. But bits and pieces of odd statements had slowly come together in his thinking. The city was established during the same era as the Library of Lyme. The same scholars worked at both places. They'd divided the wealth of information to keep it safe. If one source fell into the wrong hands, the villains would still need the details from the other site. In order to use the knowledge, both stores of information must be at hand.

His conclusion: the castle harbored a room of interest, one with Lymen artifacts and eyewitness accounts. Evidence from this location would dovetail with and perhaps expand upon the reports he'd found in the mountain.

Since his troop of investigators had been sidetracked into this lonely valley, the find of a store of information would do much to justify the loss of time. Now he understood why he'd resisted the inclination to shake the dirt from his shoes and urge everyone out and away. Something in this valley was important, very important.

The wise men who left it here probably warded it to repel evil, designing men. But perhaps it was also warded to attract followers of Primen. Cantor had been determined to leave, but he'd not made the final push to see his desire fulfilled. He'd probably been influenced by the ward. Dukmee intended to discover this last clue in the mysterious valley.

The westward wall of the valley rose before them, showing clearly that this side of the mountain was rugged. Sparse vegetation dotted the steep rock inclines. Rock had fallen off in sheets of colorful shale. In the distant past, settlers must have depended on the abrupt cliffs to protect their backs.

"There's our destination, Bridger. Circle once to spy out any intruders."

"The portal isn't open." Bridger huffed over his shoulder. His lungs hadn't cleared completely of the infection he'd had.

"And that's a good sign. Hopefully, we'll be alone." Dukmee tapped the scales on Bridger's neck. "I have a good feeling about this. Land at the far end, close to the broken walls that look like they once enclosed large rooms."

"Looks like a tumbled castle to me." Bridger slowed his speed and started his descent.

"Exactly! It's easier to see from up here."

As soon as Bridger's feet hit the ground and he folded his wings against his sides, Dukmee threw his leg over the ridge and slid down the pale bronze scales. He stood so the dragon could look over his shoulder at the book he held open.

"That's a history book of a city." Bridger leaned closer, his chin touching Dukmee's head. "Is that this city?"

"Yes, and the whole purpose of this settlement was to offer sanctuary to scholars. One big university. They called it the Whirl of Knowledge. Or just the Whirl."

Bridger grunted. "A strange name."

"Not when you know its history and the thinking of the founding fathers. They believed that knowledge held power. As information is acquired, it builds momentum. They had left what they called a maelstrom of learning. Those with the most data in their time used it for evil. These pilgrims wished to isolate themselves and use intelligence for good."

"Sounds fanciful."

"It was. They repudiated the Maelstrom of Madness. They had lots of names for it. Maelstrom of Malice. Maelstrom of Mayhem. Malevolent Maelstrom. They sought to establish a World Whirl of Benevolence."

Bridger lifted his head and surveyed the crumbled walls, deserted buildings, and piles of stone rubbish. "Did they succeed?"

Dukmee closed the book with a snap. "Initially. In the beginning, their premises were centered on Primen's teachings. Then they became engrossed in saving the world from physical destruction. Their people became frenzied, unfocused, and weak."

"Did the outside maelstrom discover their whereabouts and conquer the city?"

"No. Not as a fighting force." Dukmee marched to the front opening of the castle. "Strangely, the outsiders came seeking help from the Whirl. A mutual threat had overcome three of the planes. These grandiose warriors of the Mayhem Maelstrom discovered that their knowledge had no muscle in battle. The methods they had used to develop a ruthless army failed to give them men with fortitude. Without a moral core or commitment to something, they could not withstand a constant conflict against this stronger force."

"They had to care about something in order to fight for it."

Amazed at how the simple dragon comprehended these philosophical concepts, Dukmee finished his summation. "And it seems the loyalty did not have to be attached to something of real merit, although that helped."

"What was this threat? Dragons?" Bridger's voice picked up enthusiasm. "There are stories of monstrous dragons eons ago."

"Not dragons." Dukmee opened his book once more and walked into the desolate courtyard.

Bridger followed. "Beasts? Ogres? Massive serpents? Poisonous spiders without number?"

"No, Bridger." He looked down at the page and over to the shadowed side of a crumpled wall. "I think the room we seek will be over there." He strode with purpose and spoke over his shoulder as he went. "They were decimated by Lymen, Bridger. The Lymen we face in a few weeks."

The crunch of Bridger's steps stopped. Dukmee glanced over his shoulder. The dragon stood for a moment, thinking, then continued following Dukmee. "You know," he said, "that doesn't sound like good news to me."

"I don't suppose it is. But if we can glean knowledge from

this source and rightly combine it with the information we already have, we should be ahead of the invaders in battle."

Dukmee concentrated on the dimensions of the rooms, walls, and even the doorways. Some of the drawings in the book lined up with what he could see, but too many variables made it hard to judge.

"What's wrong?" Bridger hung at his shoulder again. His hot breath smelled like peppermints.

Dukmee turned to the side, away from the cloying sweet exhalations of his fellow researcher. But Bridger put a claw on his shoulder and moved him back.

"It's a puzzle book, isn't it?" The dragon took the tome from him. "Imagine one this old. We have them on Effram. I've seen them in the markets, and I've played with them with the children."

Bridger doubled the two facing pages in half, tucking the outside edge into the center binding. "Sometimes it only takes one fold, but this puzzle is trickier."

He folded the top of the left side down to make a triangle of that part of the page, then did the same thing to the bottom of the right side. Dukmee took the book back.

The lines on the folded pages now lined up to make a new drawing, a perfect drawing of the rooms around him.

"Well done, Bridger." Dukmee marched through a doorway, turned right, and hurried down a narrow stairway. He stopped at a heavy wooden door.

"This is it?" asked Bridger from behind him.

"This is it."

Dukmee read for a moment, then examined the right side of the doorjamb. He pressed in a square tile, then found a matching design on the door itself. When he pressed on that square, a loud, complicated clicking clattered beneath his fin-fingertips. The door moved, and he was able to push it open.

A waft of stale, damp air hit them in the face.

"Light," said Bridger.

He plucked a torch from its holder on the wall and breathed on it.

Under its glow, Dukmee stepped into the gloomy room. "We pass through this room, and two more, then come to the one containing the materials we seek."

A fine settlement of dust coated the floor. No tracks, not even a rodent or insect. The stone walls had been smoothed by men who excelled at their craft.

Bridger cringed.

Dukmee noticed. "What's the matter?"

"I don't like having all that rock on top of us."

"You were all right in the mountain."

"Well, yes. Primen made the mountain. Men made these buildings."

"Look at the beams in the ceiling. The men were master builders."

"Still not Primen."

Dukmee tsked. "We're fine. These walls have stood for thousands of years."

"The ones outside didn't."

"That's because they were exposed to the elements — rain, wind, hot, cold."

Dukmee took the last steps to the next door quickly. He didn't want to give the dragon time to work up a stronger case of nerves.

Since he had a good idea of what he was looking for, he managed the mechanical trips for the following two doors easily. Each room consisted of the same smooth rock walls and beamed ceiling. Each progressive room smelled mustier than the one before.

Dukmee paused in the last chamber. This final door had a different set of instructions. He pushed three right side tiles in the proper order, then the corresponding left side tiles in the reverse order. A lever eased out from the adjacent wall.

Dukmee grabbed hold and pulled, but it required more strength than he had available.

"I can't do it one-handed, Bridger." Dukmee nodded to the metal rod. "Push that down, if you will."

Bridger grasped the lever with his free hand and smoothly moved the rod from a forty-five degree angle upward to a position much closer to the wall downward.

The heavy door grated against its frame and rose into the wall above. The air in this room was no more unpleasant than the last. In fact, the atmosphere was less dank and gloomy. Dukmee ducked under the lifting door, and Bridger followed.

The sound of metal grinding against metal reached their ears as the door finished its ascent.

Bridger lifted the torch and turned slowly. The room appeared to be much like the others, perhaps bigger. And along the opposite wall where another door would have been, round ceramic pipes thrust out from the wall at regular intervals.

"I wonder what those are." Dukmee took a step forward.

The section of floor beneath his feet sank with a suddenness that upset his balance. He fell forward and dropped the book, which skidded across the floor. The thud of his impact and the scraping of the leather binding across the fine grit on the floor sounded strangely loud in the isolated chamber.

"Are you all right?" Bridger came to his side and bent to examine him, poking and prodding and irritating Dukmee.

Dukmee did a quick check. He'd knocked his chin on the hard floor, slamming his jaws together, but none of his teeth wiggled. One palm had lost a bit of flesh. He'd barked his shins against the side of the hole made by the falling segment of stone. He stood and the front of his legs protested.

"I scraped my shins, but other than that I seem fine."

He eyed the recess he stood in. One square had fallen, but by design, he was sure. Three foot by three foot, perfectly square, and with the sides made out of identical material.

He took Bridger's outstretched hand and climbed out of the knee-deep depression.

A screech rent the air, and the heavy door dropped, slamming against the floor. For one moment Dukmee and Bridger stood balancing as the room reverberated.

"Master builders," said the dragon.

Behind them, trickles of water fell from each of the pipes.

Dukmee's stomach clenched. "Indeed, they were, Bridger. This is a well-designed trap."

24

A FLOOD AND A GLOBE

The pipes' trickling flow increased. Dukmee snatched up the tome before the water could reach it. The pages fell open to the puzzle folds. He turned the page and read on.

In his peripheral vision, he saw Bridger fidgeting, shuffling his huge feet, twitching his long tail, drumming his clawed fingers against his sides, rotating his head every which way, and darting glances here and there.

The dragon twisted his lips. "I don't suppose knowing how to swim would be helpful, since there's no place to swim to."

More interested in the book than Bridger, Dukmee muttered, "Probably not."

His fingers fumbled through manipulations of the next two book pages. None of his experiments worked.

"Let me try." Bridger took the book. This time he made triangles of the upper edges, then folded each page in half lengthwise. He handed it back to Dukmee. "The pages after this have been torn out."

Dukmee sighed. Things just weren't going smoothly at all.

As he bent over the book once more, Bridger waded through the ankle-deep water to inspect the pipes. His swishing tail sent small waves splashing against Dukmee's legs.

He held the book higher.

"Whoa, this water's cold," Bridger complained.

"Mountain snow melt-off collected somewhere. Brilliant builders," said Dukmee. He held up the book. "It would have been prudent to have read ahead before entering this room."

Bridger gave him his attention.

He tapped the bit he'd just skimmed. "These paragraphs explain how to avoid triggering the trap."

Bridger grunted. "And the pages telling how to get to the next chamber are missing?"

"That's right." Dukmee closed the book and turned in a circle, looking closely at all aspects of the room. "No windows, of course. The scholars would not have wanted their work to be submerged in water — soaked, sodden, and unsalvageable. This is not the last room, but how do we get to the next level? And where is it?"

"Up." Bridger tilted his head to survey the ceiling. "Up, because the water would go down if we opened something in the floor."

"Could you fly up and get a closer look?"

The dragon placed the torch in a holder on the wall. "I'm not built to hover. I'll stretch my neck instead."

After only a minute, Bridger announced, "I don't see anything."

Dukmee stood in water up to his knees. "How about along the top of the walls, just under the ceiling?"

Bridger eased his head over to the side and began a

studious search along the walls. He sidled through the water. As he approached the closed door, Dukmee remembered the hole in the floor.

"Be care—"

Bridger fell into the pool.

Dukmee dodged, unsuccessfully avoiding the splash of cold water. He managed to protect the book with his body.

Bridger's neck telescoped back to its normal length as he thrashed awkwardly.

"Calm down," said Dukmee. "Just put your feet under you."

Bridger stood, looking sheepish.

The water now covered Dukmee up to his waist. He held the book out from his soaked shirt. He was almost as wet from the dragon's splashing as Bridger was from his dunking.

"Come on, hoist yourself up. We need to find a way out of this predicament."

Bridger lurched but didn't gain higher ground. "My foot's stuck on something."

Dukmee pushed his way through the water to Bridger. "There was nothing in that hole when I was in it."

"Something has my foot."

"Something alive?"

"No." Bridger struggled.

"Well, at least that's good news." With a sigh, Dukmee took Bridger's arm to help him balance.

The dragon twisted, his tail popped up for a moment and managed to knock the book out of Dukmee's grasp. Dukmee clamped his teeth on biting words of annoyance and only let out a heartier, blustering sigh. If they drowned in this trap, the book wasn't going to do him any good, anyway.

With both hands wrapped around Bridger's skinny arm,

he tugged. His feet slid across the smooth floor toward the hole. He quit pulling and the dragon surged upward.

"I'm out," he said, "but something is still wrapped around my ankle."

He leaned back, presumably on his tail, and lifted the entrapped limb. A chain dripped water as he raised it above the pool.

"Now, what's that hooked to?" Dukmee took hold of the chain and tested its strength. "Point your foot. I'll try to slip it off."

Bridger tried, but it was a clumsy maneuver getting the foot out of the water and allowing Dukmee to manipulate the chain. He fell sideways with a splash. The chain jerked taut, then suddenly relaxed.

Dukmee pulled it out of the water, revealing a large metal disk, while Bridger righted himself once again. The pool's surface undulated with waves. Bridger shivered, and tiny droplets sprayed Dukmee's face. He wiped a hand across his eyes to clear his vision.

Dust filtered down from above. Both turned their faces upward, blinking the grit away as they watched a shaft open in the ceiling.

"Look." Bridger pointed. "There's light up there."

"I see." The water now touched Dukmee's chin. "I also see some problems with this escape hatch. You're too big to squeeze through, and the sides are smooth — nothing for me to hang on to as I climb."

Bridger smirked. "Obviously, these master builders weren't expecting one of their captives to be a shapeshifting dragon."

The dragon changed swiftly. He propelled his head upward as he elongated his entire body. His top half had disappeared up the shaft by the time his tail left the water. The tail, now resembling a thick rope, wrapped snugly around Dukmee, pinning his arms to his sides. Bridger pulled him along and, once Dukmee popped out of the shaft at the top, put him down gently.

Dukmee frowned as Bridger dipped his tail back down the shaft. He heard swishing, and just as he was about to ask what the dragon was doing, Bridger pulled his tail up. The dragon had retrieved the water-soaked book. He gave it a shake, sending a scattering of droplets around the room, then laid Dukmee's treasured tome on the floor.

Bridger returned to his normal shape and looked around. "Great. We're in another room with no exit."

Dukmee grinned at the dragon's doleful expression. "Except the one at our feet."

He shivered, still wet and cold. If they got to the surface, the warm summer air would be welcome.

Bridger stood erect, pursed his lips, and blew. Dukmee cringed, but instead of a blast of fire, a pleasant, drying breeze issued from the dragon's mouth. Dukmee turned, eyes closed, soaking in the luxurious warmth that chased away the goose bumps. His hair, no longer plastered to his scalp, responded to the tepid air with ripples like grass in a sundrenched glade. His clothes dried and undulated under the flow of Bridger's breath.

"Thank you, Bridger. I'm comfortable at last."

The dragon smiled, took in a deep breath, and sneezed. A spout of flame licked Dukmee's arm, leaving a scorched stretch of sleeve.

Dukmee flicked his fingers over the cloth. "No harm done. No harm done."

He turned away, avoiding eye contact with Bridger that might add to his embarrassment.

A buzz of excitement quickened Dukmee's breathing as he scanned the walls. Neat printing and pictures covered every inch of the floor, ceiling, and four walls. "This is it, Bridger. We found the mother lode."

"Can you read this?" Bridger peered at the words on the wall. "It's different."

"It's written in code, but I already broke the code in a volume I found in the Library of Lyme."

"So are you going to copy all this down? Or can you memorize it like Bixby can? And what good is it going to do if we can't get out?"

"Oh, there are bound to be instructions among all this. We'll get out."

"I hope you have a hamper of food with you."

Without commenting, Dukmee removed a storage sack from his inside pocket and handed it to the dragon. Bridger sat and explored the contents, chomping on his favorite foods as he pulled them out, putting others aside.

A companionable silence fell over them. Bridger contentedly eased his hunger. Dukmee strolled around, reading the words and examining the pictures inscribed on the walls so very long ago.

The light in the room never varied. It occurred to Dukmee that there must be an unusual source. No one object supplied the soft glow. The only oddities in the room were the hole in the floor and an orb stuck to the ceiling.

"I wonder what that is."

Bridger, sated and collapsed against one wall, opened his eyes and squinted in the direction Dukmee pointed. "Is it important?"

"It might be. Why don't you go up and get it?"

"Wouldn't you like to read for a bit longer while I take a nap? Remember, I've been sick. If it isn't urgent, I could get it after a restorative snooze."

"Be a good fellow, Bridger, and get it now."

He groaned and shifted to his feet. "All right."

A couple of flaps of his wings, and he plucked the orb from the stem that held it out from the ceiling. He settled down next to Dukmee and offered the prize to his companion.

Dukmee's skin tingled as he reached for the globe. He'd never seen anything like it. The smooth glass slipped from Bridger's claws into his grasp. A shock sprang from his hand, traveled up his arm, and threw him to the floor.

He tried to speak but his mouth wouldn't move. On his back, with his arm outstretched, his head turned to one side so he looked over his shoulder and down his arm, he was incapable of the slightest movement. The thought rushed through his mind that he wasn't breathing, but with concentration, he discerned that he did breathe with a shallow, steady rhythm.

He could see.

He could hear.

Bridger shuffled back and forth, muttering, "You told me to get the globe. I got the globe. It didn't do a thing to me. You told me to get it. I got it. You wanted it. Now you have it."

Dukmee felt Bridger poke his side. "Wake up. You have to read the walls. You're supposed to figure out how to get us out of here. Wake up and do your job."

He poked Dukmee again. "This isn't my fault. You said get the globe. I got the globe."

Dukmee concentrated on the hand holding the glass orb. If he could just get his fingers to relax and release the globe, he'd probably be able to move. If he could just communicate to Bridger to take the globe from his hand. He focused on forming a message to send to Bridger's mind, but words didn't leave his head and penetrate the dragon's skull.

His attention returned to the globe. It held the key.

In a flash, he saw the purpose of the sphere-shaped instrument. Like a library, it held all the information from the mountain and all the writings and pictures on the walls. Everything.

As he peered into its center, the words spun as if suspended in a liquid. He could stop them at will and read. He could skip forward as if flipping pages in a book. He could return to a word or phrase he'd seen previously. He wanted to shout with triumph, but he couldn't move.

He swallowed.

He blinked.

He wasn't going to die.

Bridger's poke redirected his thoughts. Would the dragon be able to get them out?

"Wake up." Bridger's head came into view between Dukmee's head and his hand. It was upside down. He frowned. "Hello?"

25

I HEARD YOU COMING

Standing under the shingled porch roof, Cantor tacked the last drawing on the outside wall of the house. Bixby and Neekoh had been gone on their search for Trout over an hour before, and he'd drawn for much of that time, stopping only when his hand cramped so badly he could no longer hold the writing instrument. He'd laid his work aside almost reluctantly and turned his attention to sifting through the piles of drawings he'd created and pinning the most relevant to the wall.

The burro brayed in her paddock. She probably wanted her dinner. In the two days they'd been with Trout, Neekoh had taken over that chore. He got along well with all the animals, but the burro and the goats particularly liked him. The horses came when he whistled.

Cantor had always had an affinity with the birds and small creatures of the mountains, but he'd never had at his feet a rabbit, a fox, a turtle, and a raccoon, all at the same time. To see Neekoh sitting on the stump by the garden, surrounded by these creatures, filled Cantor with amazement.

They showed no fear of the human and no tension between animals prone to hunt or run from one another.

Cantor frowned. In his mind's eye, he could also see the young man sitting year after year in the dim caves of the mountain. What had been the purpose? Guardian of Chomountain? That was laughable. Generations of his family had gone through a ritual of sacrifice that kept no one and nothing safe. The wards had been sufficient.

No longer absorbed by the writing tools, Cantor took a deep breath, let it out slowly, and surveyed his surroundings. The late afternoon sun sifted through the trees west of Trout's little homestead. He rotated his head, stretching his neck muscles.

Jumping off the porch, he landed squarely on his feet in the wide area of grass and dirt just in front of the cabin. With the ease of long practice, he began the forms that limbered his body and kept him ready for combat, a habit he'd neglected lately. With the invasion coming, he should be all the more diligent in taking care of his fighting skills. He'd broach the subject with Bixby and Dukmee when they returned.

Another frown creased his face. Where were his friends, and what delayed their return?

Before he'd really gotten started, he almost abandoned his exercise. That was his problem. He was too easily distracted. He lacked commitment, lacked discipline. Stubbornly, he stretched his arms above his head and pivoted to the fifth stance of the first form.

Forty-five minutes later, the sun had eased toward the

western mountain peaks. Cantor blew out his last large breath and strolled toward the animals. He'd feed them before the others returned. That would be one less thing keeping them from the major issue they must face this evening.

The gentle beasts greeted him, obviously counting his arrival as the harbinger of grain and fresh water. Cantor wandered among them, seeing to their simple needs and adding a gentle hand of appreciation. Shooing the chickens into the henhouse and shutting the door was the last chore of the evening.

As he headed for the cabin, the burro made her happy, grunty noises. He turned to see her small hoofs beat a happy tappity-tap on the packed dirt as she danced back and forth, her head swinging over the short fence. Cantor grinned and looked to the trees. Bixby, Neekoh, and Trout strode out from the woods and crossed the open space at a fair pace.

Cantor walked to intercept them. Old Trout charged past without a word. Neekoh shrugged as he went by, with his hands splayed palms up in a gesture that claimed no understanding of the old man's mood. Bixby raised her eyebrows as she walked past with a little less sass in her lively steps.

Cantor fell in beside her, his long stride kept in check so he could take her hand and slow her down. He leaned over to whisper, "Did you tell him?"

She looked up with mischief in her eyes. "No, I thought you better suited for such a revelation. Or Dukmee."

Cantor sighed. "Dukmee, definitely Dukmee."

"We could argue that Neekoh was officially appointed his guardian, and therefore, it's his responsibility."

As they came up to the cabin, Trout stood on the porch, looking at the drawings one by one. Neekoh sat on the edge, the cat already ensconced in his lap and receiving a thorough ear rub.

Cantor and Bixby stayed on the grass and watched as the old man sidestepped along the wall, slowly. Very slowly. Occasionally he rubbed his hand through his hair or squeezed the back of his neck. He set his fists on his hips, crossed his arms over his chest, fiddled with his beard, hummed a monotone ditty. He didn't speak.

Neekoh got up, the cat in his arms. "I'll go see to the animals."

Cantor observed the lad's uneasy expression. "I've already done that."

"Then I'll just keep them company a bit. Maybe sing something mellow as a lullaby. They like that."

Cantor cocked an eyebrow but didn't stop him.

Bixby sighed and tucked her tiny hand in Cantor's massive one. "I wish Dukmee and Bridger would return."

Cantor silently agreed.

Bixby's thoughts intruded. *"Where did they say they were going?"*

"The ruins."

"What had Dukmee found in the books? What was he checking on?"

"You know he didn't say."

"Typical."

Cantor grunted.

"What do you think he's thinking?"

"Probably pondering some great archaeological discovery and not thinking of us at all."

He heard Bixby's thoughts whirr and sizzle for a second.

"Not Dukmee." She thrust the words at him. *"Old Trout. Chomountain."*

Cantor bent his arm and stuck his thumb in his belt. Bixby still held that hand, so she floated up with the movement and hung beside his leg.

He looked down. "Oh, sorry."

He lowered her so she stood on her feet. She glared at him, but then her eyes lost the flare of indignation and a sparkle of humor replaced it. They looked at each other. Then succumbed to a fit of laughter.

Bixby jerked her hand out of Cantor's grasp and covered her mouth, using the other hand as well as if that would help muffle her giggles.

Cantor pressed his lips together and looked away from her, up toward the treetops and mountain. He studied anything his eyes fell upon, trying to tamp down the inappropriate mirth.

When he thought he could control his emotions, he lowered his gaze to the porch. Old Trout stood on the edge, facing them, arms crossed over his chest and a glower showing through his straggly gray beard and bushy eyebrows.

Cantor cleared his throat, partially to alert Bixby to the changed circumstances. "You don't look like Old Trout anymore . . . sir."

"This," said Chomountain in a commanding voice totally unlike Trout's pleasant rumble, "is what I heard coming."

"Sir?"

"Not clear, of course, but a mumble in my memory, a whisper in my conscience." He rubbed his hands together with vigor. "Primen has called me back. Don't tell me how many years. Knowing won't change a thing."

He turned abruptly, strode into the cabin, and came out

again, clutching the bit of polished silver he used for a mirror. He placed himself in the strongest of the fading light and inspected his face.

He shook his head. "That doesn't help a bit. I look just as I always have, not a day over two hundred."

"But ..." Bixby said.

He flapped a hand at her. "Yes, yes, I follow your line of thought. But I took up my position as right hand of Primen somewhere around my two hundredth birthday, and I haven't aged since." He winked at Bixby. "One of the advantages."

He paused and tilted his head as if listening. All Cantor heard was the soft soughing of the wind through the trees, the mellow calls of a few night birds, insects and tree frogs with their rhythmic clatter, and Neekoh's soothing tenor working wonders with a pleasing melody.

Bixby shifted to stand closer to Cantor's side. "What do you hear, sir?" she asked.

"I hear the symphony Primen began at the dawn of time. And Neekoh missing the high B every time he comes to it. I must tell that boy to lift his eyebrows when he approaches the top of his range."

Chomountain turned his back on them and returned to his perusal of the pictures. "Not all of these are of me." He pointed to a sketch of a tall, thin man in flowing robes. "Arbinaster. A scholar from Alius. And with him is Borneodeme, an astronomer from Derson." He moved to a set of buildings. "These are structures housing the parliament of Tatumknol. Why did the artists include these?"

He whipped around, focusing on Bixby and Cantor again. "Who was responsible for shutting down my memory and isolating me? And to what purpose?"

Cantor didn't think he expected an answer. His own theories revolved around the Realm Walkers Guild.

Chomountain nodded at him. "I know. With your animosity toward the guild council, it would be convenient for their involvement to have begun so long ago. But you've come to the conclusion yourself this isn't feasible. A more powerful force has to have masterminded this."

Bixby bounced, something she often did when a thought had taken hold in her fervent mind. "We have to look behind the evil we can see to something bigger. Something outside of normal. Life like Primen and the mountain servants and the Primen warriors. They transcend time. Are there entities of evil like Primen's force for good?"

"There are entities who once served Primen but fell away in pursuit of their own interests. We rarely deal directly with them, but with those mortals who cater to their demands in hopes of gaining power."

Cantor narrowed his eyes. "There are plenty of those in the Realm Walkers Guild."

"You're right, son, and we'll deal with them. Presently, our focus must be on the Lymen invasion."

Cantor's mind skipped to the dragon and the scholar. Where were they? Dukmee usually handled any crisis that came up, but that silly dragon fell into trouble like a mouse fell into a pail of milk. Suppose Bridger had dragged Dukmee into some serious difficulty?

He reached with his mind for contact with the dragon. Nothing. Of course, Bridger might be in a sound sleep. Since he'd been fighting this cold and taking Dukmee's and Bixby's elixirs, he'd been less responsive than usual.

Cantor couldn't shake his concern. "I'm worried about Dukmee and Bridger."

Chomountain nodded, then closed his eyes, tilted his head, and seemed to listen. In a moment, he opened his eyes. "There's no disturbance in the air. I would think your friends have taken shelter at the ruins. We'll look for them in the morning."

Neekoh approached the cabin cautiously. "I thought I'd help with dinner." He held out the egg-gathering basket. "We've got an abundance of eggs. And I picked some vegetables to make omelets."

"Excellent, dear boy!" Chomountain gestured for Neekoh to come up on the porch. Clapping him on the back, he said, "You know, I think I'll go off fish for a while."

Neekoh grinned. "You're all right, then? I mean, you aren't upset? You can be Chomountain and not Old Trout without a fuss?"

"Certainly. It's poor form for the right hand of Primen to go all fussy on people."

26

A LONG NIGHT

Dukmee was not going to wake up. Bridger had been watching him for hours, and, though his eyes stared ahead, he only blinked once in a while. That was not awake—that was something else.

Bridger wondered if the sun had gone down yet. The light was the same intensity it had been when they first entered the room. For a while, to relieve the boredom of watching the mage, he'd searched for the source, but even after careful examination, he'd not been able to detect where the strange light came from. He did notice that he cast no shadow, and neither did Dukmee. Air flowed through the room without windows, doors, or vents.

But the puzzling room soon lost its fascination, and ever since it had been a long, dull wait. Bridger had satisfied his hunger several times now, but boredom put an edge back on his appetite.

"I should feed you," he said to the nonresponsive scholar.

"That'll give me something to do, and perhaps food will stimulate whatever is choked up in you, and you'll come round. It worked when Old Trout prepared food for you and Bixby."

He removed a tin pot and a bottle of water from the hamper, then dug around until he found dried meat. He held it up to show Dukmee. "Not sure what this is. Probably deer or cow. Or maybe turkey."

He broke the jerky into bits and dropped it into the pot with water. Blowing a tiny flame, he warmed the thin soup. "Ought to have something else in there, but you may not be able to swallow."

He reached into the hamper and brought out carrot, cabbage, and onion. "Now that will taste more like a stew. Of course, it won't be thick. And I'm not going to give you the chunks."

By intermittently blowing a thin stream of fire on it, Bridger set the stew to simmer. In between flames, he sat back and looked around.

"Nothing's different. No way out. I don't suppose the passing of day changes anything. You know, the slanted sun rays hitting a trigger outside and doors opening up in here. That sort of thing. If I had been the master builder who's so skilled and all, I would have set up something astonishing like that. Just so the innocent people trapped inside, through no fault of their own, would have a delightful surprise at the end of the day."

Since Dukmee didn't offer any conversation, Bridger hummed a few tunes as he waited for the vegetables and jerky to soften and flavor the water. He sang two of the songs he knew all the words to and skip-sang through several he didn't know so well. Of course, the choruses were easier, and he sang those louder.

He looked at Dukmee, wondering if the scholar enjoyed his efforts to entertain or wished he would stop. At that moment, he missed Cantor. Cantor would be full of advice. Sing softer. Don't sing that one. It doesn't make sense. Start singing lower so you can reach the high notes at the end. Stop singing.

On rare occasions, Cantor would sing with him, and he had a wonderful voice. Of course, his name referred to someone who sang during worship ceremonies. They'd heard cantors in sanctuary in Gilead.

"Soup's almost done, Dukmee. I'll have to move you. I hope it doesn't hurt."

He left the pot simmering and picked up the unconscious scholar. "Only I don't know for sure if you're out, 'cause your eyes are open, and it feels like you're watching me. Which is kind of creepy. Hmm, you're shivering. I wonder if you have a blanket in one of your hampers."

Before putting him down again, Bridger used his breath to warm the stone floor and wall where he would prop Dukmee. He then sat him down as gently as possible, returned to heat the soup again, then came back to look for hampers that might contain blankets.

"Pillows would be nice too."

He found a bag of Dukmee's clothing. Another sack held books. "This is almost an entire library."

Bridger read the spines he could see. "All astronomy."

In the next hamper he found a wool blanket and a small pillow. "Right!" Bridger cheered. "Later, I'll shift into a bed and use these to tuck around you."

He inhaled deeply. "Ah, that does smell good."

Bridger drained the soup through a sieve so Dukmee would only have to drink the broth. Hopefully he wouldn't choke. The dragon really did not want the scholar to sip the soup down his windpipe instead of the food pipe.

He brought the mug over to Dukmee and tried to hand it to him. "Just not going to be able to do it, are you? Okay, but don't complain later that I did a messy job."

Bridger sat against the wall, took Dukmee into his lap, and leaned him back against his scaly chest. He tucked a cloth under the scholar's chin, then picked up the mug again.

"Good. It's cooled off some. I don't suppose you could open your mouth and then close it. That does seem like a very minor request."

He nudged Dukmee into a position where he could see his face from the side. Guiding the cup to Dukmee's mouth, Bridger tilted it just as he reached his lips. With the rim of the mug, he parted the lips and poured a drop or two in.

"At least we didn't spill it. Did you get anything?"

Dukmee swallowed.

"Hey! You did."

For the next half hour, Bridger dribbled the soup between Dukmee's parted lips.

"I've got an idea," said Bridger when he almost finished the second mug. "You're doing a great job of swallowing. We can use that to communicate. I'll ask a question and if the answer is yes, you swallow once. If the answer is no, swallow twice. What do you think? Is that a good idea?"

Dukmee swallowed once.

Bridger put the mug down. "Do you want to do it now?"

Two swallows.

"Why not?" Bridger watched his friend. "Oh yeah, yes or no questions. Do you want to have some more soup?"

Two swallows.

"Do you want something?"

A lone swallow.

"What?" Bridger waited. "Oh, do you want dessert?"

Two swallows.

"A drink?"

Two swallows.

"Well, that makes sense because your dinner was all liquid."

Bridger cast around in his mind for what Dukmee might want. *What do I usually want after a busy day and dinner?*

"Sleep?"

Dukmee swallowed once.

"Okay, let me clean up the mess, and then I'll settle us down for the night."

He eased the man off his lap and went to put things away. Dukmee had finished all the broth, so Bridger downed the cooked vegetables in one gulp. He put the unwashed pot, the knife he'd used to cut ingredients, the spoon he'd used to stir, and the mug to one side. He didn't have any means to wash the items.

He warmed the blanket, then the stones where he intended to sleep. Finally, he shifted his lower half into a soft mattress and pulled Dukmee into his lap. He'd left the blanket just out of reach so he stretched his arm to get it. Covering Dukmee was no problem, but the dragon fumbled as he raised the scholar's head and tucked the pillow underneath.

"Goodnight, Dukmee. It sure would be nice if you'd move around a bit in the morning. And talk too. Remember, you're going to read the walls and get us out of here. Well, goodnight. Don't worry about things. You need to relax and sleep. Things have a way of working themselves out."

Bridger wiggled a bit to get more comfortable. "And things always look better in the morning."

First thing in the morning, Cantor looked under the tree where Bridger usually slept. The dragon had not come back during the night. Cantor turned full circle, eyes squinted and examining the sky. No sign of the dragon flying back. He transferred his gaze to the toes of his boots, contemplating where that blasted beast could be.

Looking under the tree again, he noticed the small, multicolored Jesha doing her morning wash. Her face, whiskers, and ears looked fresh.

"Where's Bridger, cat? Come to think of it, where have you been since yesterday?"

Jesha paused in her ablutions long enough to give him a disdainful look. Her eyes shifted to somewhere behind him. Cantor turned, fully expecting to see Bridger and Dukmee crossing the field. Instead he saw Chomountain.

The old man had tossed aside his plaid shirt, blue pants, and old boots. He wore long, flowing robes in colors that rivaled the beauty of a peacock. He smiled as he approached.

"Still anxious about Bridger?"

"Not anxious, sir."

Chomountain cocked an eyebrow.

Cantor knew the right hand of Primen saw right through him. "Not *exactly* anxious ... sir."

The old man didn't say anything, but waited.

"I've traveled with him for three years, one year with Bixby and two years on our own. I know how much trouble he can fall into without trying."

Cantor reached under the tree limbs and picked up the

cat. "I'm worried about Dukmee. Bridger might have led him into a fix."

"Dukmee is well able to take care of himself."

Cantor found himself blustering. Chomountain hadn't had time to assess all of Bridger's peculiarities. "Under normal circumstances, I would agree. But he's not attuned to Bridger."

"You are?"

"Yes, but not willingly. You have to know how Bridger thinks, or more often doesn't think, in order to keep him and you out of trouble."

"And you know Bridger this well?"

Cantor nodded. "Three years. I'll repeat, not willingly."

"And Dukmee? How well do you know Dukmee?"

"I know more about Dukmee than actually know him. He's a healer, a scholar, a realm walker, a mage and, I suspect, a wizard."

Chomountain nodded. "He's a savant."

Cantor searched his memory. "I think I've heard that word before. But I don't remember in what context. It has something to do with the brain or how it's used, doesn't it?"

"That's pretty close. A savant is a person who can use his or her brain with more efficiency than most of us. A savant can be brilliant in one area or many. A very long time ago, even before the last invasion of the Lymen, one particular race of people was known to produce many savants. In their society, a savant was more the norm than an ordinary child."

"Is Bixby a savant as well?"

"Yes."

"But she doesn't know it, does she?"

Chomountain shook his head. "Her mother is gifted and found the talents burdensome. I believe she never told Bixby,

217

in the hope that the awkwardness that plagued her life would not touch the life of her daughter."

"How can you know all this about Bixby and her mother? You've been sequestered in this valley since before they were born."

"As the right hand of Primen, I have access to a lot of knowledge — knowledge filtered through Primen and therefore reliable. I deemed it prudent to acquire background information on the people who came to rescue me."

Cantor shoved that new revelation aside. He needed to concentrate on answers to the particular questions that already spun in his head. "Primen told you that Bixby's mother didn't tell her she was a savant to protect her?"

"No, that was a conclusion I drew for myself from what he did tell me." Chomountain put a hand on Cantor's shoulder and studied his face, his own expression grim. "What is it that troubles you?"

"I had hoped I could ask you where to find Ahma and Odem, and you would be able to tell me. But that's not so, is it? Like Feymare, the Primen warrior, you communicate with Primen, but he doesn't tell you what you want to know."

"He tells us only what we *need* to know. He is authority without being boss. He is provider without being domineering. He is leader without being despot."

With anger tightening his throat, Cantor's voice dragged out of his mouth. "And he keeps secrets."

"Not in a bad way, Cantor."

"Well, since Primen isn't likely to point us to Dukmee and Bridger, we'd best begin our search for them."

"Right." Chomountain used gentle pressure on Cantor's

shoulder to turn him and urge him toward the cabin. "Breakfast first. Bixby's already cooking. The ruins next, don't you think?"

"Do you feel something from the ruins? I haven't been able to pick up anything from Bridger."

"No, haven't felt a thing. I guess I must be rusty. A long time has passed since I exercised the talents Primen bestowed upon me."

"Or it could be there's nothing to feel, which would mean —"

"That they've moved on and left us."

"Or they're dead."

Chomountain arched a bushy eyebrow at him. "No need to be gloomy."

Breakfast was quick. Bixby served coffee, bacon, and biscuits. With crumbs still in his beard, Chomountain went out to gather horses for the ride. Bixby and Cantor did a sketchy job of cleanup, and Neekoh joined them after doing the morning chores for the other animals.

He sat down to have more biscuits. "Your biscuits are better than any made by any of the rest of us." He shoved another one into his mouth, chewed quickly, then drank from the pitcher of water. "I hear Chomountain coming."

Bixby hung the rag she'd been using on a hook near the stove. "Sometimes your manners are atrocious, Neekoh."

He grinned, picked up another biscuit, and headed for the door.

Chomountain sat astride Olido, the biggest horse. The size of the stallion reminded Cantor of Bridger when he was shaped as a war horse.

Neekoh walked in front of them, petting each, and

whispering to them. They nickered in response, obviously liking the attention.

He grinned over his shoulder at Cantor. "I can ride any of the horses now. We're all friends."

Chomountain cast a fatherly eye on the young man. "You've made good use of your time here."

"Thanks to you, sir. You've taught me so much."

Cantor stepped forward and claimed Breez. "Let the lesson today be finding misplaced friends."

Bixby laughed, skipped to Dani's side, and leaped to a riding position on the horse's back. She turned the mare toward the ruins and prodded her into a run.

"Well," said Chomountain. "Are we going to let Bixby have all the fun?"

27

KABOOM!

I wonder if it's night or day." Bridger's voice woke Dukmee.

His first urge was to stretch. He couldn't. Nor could he yawn, shout, whistle, or release the globe still grasped in his hand. Awareness of his situation came quickly.

Using the blanket he'd found last night, Bridger propped Dukmee on his side on the floor of the chamber. He felt the cold, and the hardness of the floor pressed uncomfortably against his body. His hip and elbow on his down side ached.

Desperation clawed at his peace of mind. He needed to escape the physical imprisonment of his body and of the room. He had to be able to move, and they had to be able to leave this chamber.

As he had for hours the day before, he forced himself to concentrate on the globe and scan the information flowing before him. The words ran like ribbons crisscrossing up and down, and diagonally through the round instrument. He'd found that if his mind latched onto a phrase, that stream of words separated from the chaos and presented itself in page form closer to the front of the glass. When his attention lagged, the sheet slipped off, line by line, to become once more a part of the whole crazy, jumbled conglomeration of data.

Bridger passed his range of vision, jarring his concentration. He realized the dragon was feeling his way around the room, touching the wall as if hoping to trigger some sort of release mechanism.

That might not be such a bad idea.

When Bridger moved out of his peripheral vision, Dukmee returned his attention to the globe. This time he located a section he wanted to read with greater ease. His confidence rose. He extracted the next page in half the time. If he could have crowed, he would have when he discovered he could mark the information to come back to after putting it aside.

On the dragon's second pass, Dukmee saw that he'd lowered the band of his tactile search. He gave a tacit approval of Bridger's strategy.

As he again scanned the crystal, he spotted a ribbon that might lead to answers. He followed that information trail and found a startling revelation.

Oh no! Bridger must stop. Stop now! How do I reach him?

Dukmee focused all his efforts to speak to Bridger's mind. He began the connection weakly, first feeling the dragon's frustration. Next, he snatched a few stray thoughts from his mind. Just as he finally grasped a solid line of reasoning from Bridger, a flash of light jarred Dukmee's concentration. Simultaneously, the thoughts faded away and visions emerged.

What was that? A ward *breaking*? A new ward springing into action?

Dukmee gasped. He could see exactly what Bridger saw,

but the barrier to speak to the dragon's mind still blocked his efforts. While seeing through Bridger's eyes, Dukmee could not see the orb.

Large dragon hands with long, pointed claws eased along the wall, running across words, numbers, and symbols. The signs before the dragon duplicated the images Dukmee had seen within the globe.

Probably it's the other way around. The globe has stored all the wall data. Oh, Bridger, you are so close. How can I warn you? No, no, no. There it is. Skip over the block with the crack drawn through the center. No!

Too late. The ground trembled, and with it Dukmee completely lost his connection with the dragon. A rumble rose from beneath Dukmee's prone body. Dust and bits of stone showered down on his back.

Dukmee felt himself gathered into a ball. He expected his stiff joints to shatter as he folded in on himself, but with Bridger providing the energy to change positions, he felt no discomfort.

He'd closed his eyes against the debris, but opened them just a slit to see Bridger's arm in front of his face. He still felt the disturbing shake of the world around him. He still heard the scrape and clattering of the shattered walls and ceiling. But he no longer felt pummeled by rock and grit. Bridger had made a covering out of his body and protected him.

As if intensifying in a planned crescendo, the noise surge peaked, then exploded. *Kaboom!*

Tremors resonated for ten, fifteen seconds.

The earth stilled. The building around them shifted and settled. Bridger's body pulled away from its sheltering stance. Coughing, the dragon picked Dukmee up and carried him out to the expanse beyond the annihilated stone vault, where grass covered a little meadow and then climbed with the rising hill to the forest that towered over one side of the ruins.

Bridger, still coughing, placed Dukmee on the soft blades of fresh, green grass.

"I'm going—" He coughed and wheezed before he could finish. "Water."

Dukmee heard the flap of leathery wings. Without thinking, he moved his head so he could follow the dragon's flight. Realizing his freedom, he carefully sat up. He looked at the globe in his hand, grateful that it had not broken, then he set it down on the ground between his knees.

Laughing, Dukmee stretched out on his back and tilted his head to see the tops of the trees behind him. He rolled onto his stomach, then rolled again and sat up. Bridger approached from the opposite side of the city, gliding effortlessly as he came in for his landing.

"You're sitting!" He thunked down on the ground beside Dukmee. "Are you thirsty? I can take you over to the stream."

"I'm sitting, and I'm thirsty, and you can take me to the stream in just one moment." He held up the sphere, which appeared golden and opaque in the sunshine. "I want to tell you what this thing we found is."

Bridger nodded, his eyes trained on the globe.

"Inside this ball of glass," said Dukmee in his most scholarly tone, "is all the information that was written on the walls of that chamber we were in."

Bridger glanced at the building that was more ruined now than the rest of the ruins. "The walls that are no longer there."

Dukmee followed his gaze. "Yes. I should think that the

only way to access that data now would be by using this globe. Take it and gaze into its center for a minute."

"It's not going to strike me down, will it? Like it did you?"

"You've held it before. You're safe. I want to see if you can delve into it, or if it takes a wizard to see the contents."

Bridger gingerly took the globe, hastily looked inside, and then tried to push it back into Dukmee's hands.

"Bridger, it's not hurting you. Take a good look."

The dragon twisted his face in protest, but peered within for a full minute. "Now can I give it back? I don't see anything."

Dukmee clasped the sphere and glanced within. The flow of words and pictures continued. This time he was able to break away at will. "The minute I touch it, I see what is within."

The dragon didn't seem to appreciate the wonder of the globe.

"Bridger! I glimpsed parts of the tomes we uncovered at the Library of Lyme. That could mean that not only the contents of that chamber, but the accounts from all those scrolls and books and everything are also in this sphere."

Bridger slanted his eyes at Dukmee. "Did something fall on your head before I got to you?"

He reached over, and using a claw, carefully lifted Dukmee's hair, examining his scalp. "You've got layers of grit, but I see no blood. Let me take you to the stream. You can get a drink, wash off the dirt, and you'll feel better. Then we'll go back to Trout's — "

"Chomountain's."

"Cho's place?" Bridger squinted his eyes as he examined Dukmee from head to toe. "We haven't found Cho's place yet. Are you sure you're all right?"

Dukmee laughed, thoroughly pleased with himself for

being able to move and for holding a library he could access in the palm of his hand.

Bridger frowned and put a steadying hand on the mage's shoulder. "You might be a bit sick from that trance you were in. Bixby or Cantor or even Chomountain himself can talk to you about what you see. I'm taking you back to them right away."

"No need." Dukmee nodded toward the ruins. Neekoh, Bixby, Cantor, and Chomountain rode through the streets. The horses' hooves clattered on the old stone pavement. As they passed the crumbled building, Bixby spotted them and pointed. Her grin brightened her face even from that distance. She waved, and the others turned to follow her lead up the grass slope.

Bridger stood. He waved back and gave a gasp of pleasure. "Oh, good, Neekoh has brought Jesha." His glance swept the whole city. "Did you notice that none of the other buildings shattered like the one we were in?"

"The manufactured earthquake was designed to disintegrate the chamber if the wrong people were about to get their hands on the globe. You pushed a button that a scholar of the building would have known not to touch. The falling rocks were supposed to kill us."

Bridger chortled and looked a bit smug. "Again, they did not count on a shapeshifting dragon to be one of the prisoners."

"You're right. And thank you for saving my life. You did it twice, you know."

"I can be useful. Cantor doesn't always think so."

The small party on horseback trotted up the hill.

"Bridger!" Cantor's voice rang across the distance. "What did you do?"

Dukmee stood, and leftover debris fell from his clothing.

As he rode up the hill in front of everyone else, Cantor frowned. He examined Dukmee's state and turned to give Bridger a once over.

Dukmee brushed some of the dirt off the front of his tunic and then finger-combed his hair. Bridger had dunked himself in the stream and looked decidedly better than he did.

Cantor pulled up several yards away. "It looks like you tried to bury Dukmee alive."

"No," said Bridger, wagging his head back and forth. "I just pushed a button. That's all."

The dragon turned to Dukmee. "Climb on. I'm taking you to the stream now. It'll give Cantor some time to cool off."

"I can just tell him . . ."

"No, you forget that I'm his constant and attuned to him. He's just happy I'm not hurt, and he's angry because he's been worried about me. It'll be all right. Just climb on."

Dukmee hoisted himself onto the dragon's back.

As Bridger sprang into the air he called, "Going for a drink and a wash. We'll join you on the trail back to Cho's."

28

INITIAL PREPARATIONS

Bixby sat with her legs dangling off the table. With all of her friends in the cabin, there weren't many choices for seats. Dukmee and Cantor sat on the edge of the bed. Every time Dukmee set the swinging mattress in motion, Cantor cast him a cantankerous look and stopped the swaying with a foot on the ground.

Dukmee hadn't stopped fidgeting since Chomountain told him to wait a bit before sharing what he found in the ruins, and Cantor had been almost surly since the return of his dragon. After stopping the bed's motion once again, he glanced up at the light over the table, disapproval clear on his face. Bridger hung from a beam. The dragon had shifted into a lovely chandelier with Bridger's face looking down and a nice show of candles all around his head.

The only calm person was Neekoh, who sat on the floor, content to hold Jesha in his lap and gently rub her soft coat.

Amidst it all, Chomountain brought out a flat bag from under a cabinet. From inside the bag, he pulled out a dozen or more hampers of different sizes and shapes. He arranged them on the table next to Bixby. She hoped the contents were more remarkable than the containers, nearly all of which were very plain and boring.

Cho held a bag in his hands, examining the plain stitching. "One of the interesting aspects of my entrapment was the total lack of curiosity. I know I've stumbled across this collection of hampers three or four times a year, but I was never intrigued enough to open them."

"I could embellish them for you if you like." Bixby picked up a dull brown hamper. "Perhaps a yellow bird on a leafy green branch for this one — with lace, of course."

"The bird and branch appeal to me, but not the lace." Cho smiled at her, much as her favorite uncle did. Love covered the gaze that held just a bit of tolerance for a precocious child.

Tamping down resentment at his condescending humor, Bixby schooled her features into a cool smile. She did not appreciate being patronized.

He raised his eyebrows. "A bit of judgmental attitude being thrown back at me? Why do you think that because you amuse me, I am looking down at you?"

Bixby ducked her head. She'd rarely been caught before. Her nanny had taught her well to hide her more rebellious thoughts behind a neutral expression. "I'm sorry, sir. Many times people have scorned my offer to help, thinking my time spent in creating beauty is frivolous. Wasted time is a sin."

"Is it, now?" Chomountain glanced out the window. He smiled.

Bixby followed his gaze. Sunshine brightened the meadow

grass as it rippled in the breeze. Birds and butterflies swooped over the garden. Wildflowers and Trout's cultivated roses, wisteria, and morning glories vied for the most colorful accolade.

Chomountain's huge hand rested lightly on her shoulder. "I wonder if Primen knew that he was wasting his time as he created the frivolous beauty we see out there."

Bixby worried her lower lip between her teeth for a moment before answering. "Primen is without sin, so I guess his creating of beauty would be permissible."

"Yes, Bixby. And Dukmee's passion for playing with weeds, and Bridger's quick response to those in trouble are sometimes seen as ineffective and therefore a bother. They don't earn the scorn heaped on them, but their reaction to such ignorance proves their character." He glanced upward. "Every one of us has smacked into walls of discrimination at one time or another."

Bixby avoided looking at Cantor. Her realm walker friend always treated the dragon with disdain. Well, not always. Since they had joined in this venture, she'd noticed he had mellowed some toward the dragon, although he still refused Bridger as his constant. And right now he was peeved with Bridger, and she wasn't sure why.

"I'm giving each of you one of these hampers." Cho distributed the storage devices. "Make note of what's inside so that we have an inventory of what we have and can make up a list of what we need."

He stopped before Dukmee. "While we work, Dukmee will tell us about this glass ball he found. Do pay attention to him. He believes this object to be of great worth to our mission."

Dukmee stood, impatience clear on his face. Bixby longed to dip into his mind to find out what troubled him, but from long experience with the healer-mage she knew she probably couldn't circumvent his barriers, and if she did, he'd scold her. And now, hints of his being a wizard, even more learned than a mage, had been dropped by Bridger and Chomountain. She hadn't a chance of outmaneuvering him.

Once Dukmee displayed the globe, his demeanor changed. Enthusiasm sparkled in his eyes. A slight tremor gave away his excitement.

"This is what Bridger and I discovered. It was embedded in the ceiling, so Bridger had to retrieve it. Once he placed the sphere in my hand, the power within literally knocked me off my feet."

A swift glance around showed Bixby she was not the only one who'd abandoned the small chores Chomountain had given them. If they were to be chastised for sloughing off at the job, she wouldn't be alone.

She turned back to study the glass ball. She couldn't see through it, yet occasionally she saw a spark of light, almost as if a lightning bug were trapped within.

Cantor spoke up. "What's inside?"

"Pictures, diagrams, maps, entire books, scrolls, encyclopedias, and everything arranged for easy access. It's extraordinary. There are streams of ideas that can be arrested and focused upon. Ribbons of words that weave in and out among the others as if in an integral dance. It'll take awhile to master the retrieval system, but once we do, we'll have the combined knowledge of the Library of Lyme and the reference chamber within the ruins."

Dukmee offered the globe to Cho. "Try it. It didn't work for Bridger, but that might just be because he's a dragon."

Chomountain shook his head. "I don't read. And anyway,

I don't want all that knowledge running loose in my brain like tapeworms."

Bixby screwed up her face at the image.

Dukmee harrumphed and offered the globe to Cantor. He took it, peered for a long moment into the glass, shrugged his shoulders, and gave it back. "I didn't see anything but an occasional spark. Pretty little lights that Bixby will no doubt like."

Bixby smiled at him. That was better. His tone of voice hadn't sounded so harsh and unyielding.

Next, Dukmee carried his treasure around the room to Neekoh. The young man turned the sphere smoothly in the palm of his hand. "It feels cool, nice, but I don't see anything."

Dukmee's sigh sounded impatient. "Try holding it still and studying the inside."

Neekoh did as he was told, then held the ball close to Jesha's face. The cat flicked her tail, turned away, and yawned. Neekoh handed the globe back to Dukmee.

Dukmee turned to the table in the middle of the room. "You're the last one, Bixby."

She took the globe, eager to see what was inside. She saw the flashes of light Cantor had described, and they were as pretty as he said. Frowning, she squinted and tried to focus. Still nothing but those occasional, sparkling bursts of bright color.

Her studies before, during, and after her short stint at the Realm Walkers Guild had given her plenty of practice in concentration. If determination and perseverance could have shown her the words and numbers Dukmee talked about, she would have seen them.

With a sigh of disappointment, she handed the precious sphere back to Dukmee.

Astonishment raised his eyebrows, widened his eyes, and left his mouth hanging open. He did not look dignified, and if Bixby hadn't been crushed by her inability to use the globe, she might have giggled.

"You didn't see *anything*?" he asked.

"The lights."

"Cantor, you're sure as well?"

Cantor glanced to the chandelier. "Did Bridger actually try?"

Dukmee leaned against the table next to Bixby. "Bridger held it twice."

Bridger spoke from above. "I didn't see what Dukmee saw. I think Chomountain should try."

Cho held his hands in front of him, palms out in a physical refusal. "No, no, no."

"But why not?" Bridger asked respectfully. "Even if you can't read, you could say whether or not you see the script."

"That object was made for mortals, and I'm not quite a mortal. It's designed to aid you. I doubt the thought ever crossed the minds of the makers that a right hand of Primen would ever see it."

Chomountain cleared his throat and straightened his vibrant, multicolored robes. "I believe Dukmee should be given twenty-four hours to study the thing. Then we should be on our way. We do have a mission. We must stop the Lymen from invading and prevent the evil guild councilmen from blowing up any more of their fellow members."

"I've had a thought," said Bixby. It wasn't a pleasant thought, and perhaps the others would think her dreaming up problems.

Chomountain put a hand on her shoulder and looked patiently into her eyes. "Tell us, dear."

All eyes turned her way. She swallowed.

"Having all the knowledge from both places is very valuable. Being able to read that information and understand it makes Dukmee a dangerously valuable person. If the villains among the Realm Walkers Guild find out about Dukmee and the globe, then they will want him in their hands."

Cantor stood and moved to her side. "And they do know, or at least suspect, the information is here. That's why they sent the expedition to explore the ruins."

Bixby took in a long breath and let it out slowly. Cantor understood. Replacing the tension of voicing her idea, pleasure from his support brought on a different tension. A warm glow tightened her muscles in an entirely new way.

She tilted her head back and looked way up to the underside of his chin. He took a sidestep, effectively moving away from her. His following her logic and backing up her idea felt like an extra cord binding them to a common goal. She liked the connection, but she realized Cantor did not.

With pops, crackles, and a sudden warmth in the air, Bridger jumped down to the floor as himself. "We shall have to protect him. He's actually not all that good at taking care of himself." The dragon tapped a claw on his own forehead. "Mind's on other things when he should be alert to danger."

Dukmee's outrage was clear in his expression. "Wait just a minute. I — "

Bixby cut in. "I agree. In the everyday, no-conflict kind of day, you do well. But we've been working together for almost two years, and you do get a bit sidetracked."

Cho pulled on his beard and cleared his throat. "I just told Cantor that you're able to take care of yourself. But in these times, I would feel more comfortable if you would allow us to be your guardians." He placed a hand on Dukmee's back. "You are much too valuable to let a stray thought betray your safety. What do you say, Dukmee? Will you be sensible about this?"

"Of course, I'll be sensible." Dukmee mumbled something under his breath.

Chomountain tilted his head back a bit and looked down his long nose at the mage. "What was that?"

Bixby's eyes widened. She was sure Cho had lengthened. His hat almost touched the rafters. Perhaps he only stood straighter, but she'd never noticed him stooping. He still had Dukmee pinned by that penetrating stare.

Dukmee actually squirmed. "I said, 'I'm probably the most sensible of the group.' Begging your pardon, sir."

Cho raised his chin, threw open his mouth, and guffawed. He clapped Dukmee on the back.

Dukmee half smiled, still looking unsure whether he'd overstepped the line of propriety.

Bixby frowned as she tried to puzzle out Cho's behavior. She had years of court experience with nobles of different ranks and diplomats from unevenly valued nations. But her family had never had the right hand of Primen in their palace. She had no experience with a fisherman turned immortal being.

Chomountain showed no more signs of offense. "You read, boy, and the rest of us will prepare for the journey."

As each turned back to his task, Bixby carried the hamper she'd been given to the porch. Her mind whirled with new discoveries. Cantor's gentle smile, his strong voice, and the sheer power of his presence had almost knocked her off her feet. He seemed like a new person, someone more than the friend she'd grown to rely on in their last adventure together.

She pushed Cantor aside with great effort, and pictured Dukmee in her mind. Nervous? He'd been unsure in his conversation with Chomountain. And Cho had called him boy! Bixby had never thought of the healer as "boy." Getting a glimpse of Chomountain's perspective, she realized that they were all young and inexperienced compared to him. They were like a group of children being sent out to conquer the bullies on the playground. Only the bullies destroyed, pillaged, and murdered. They all needed to be more than they were. The only way to do that was to infuse themselves with Primen's might.

With a sigh, she settled on the porch. She'd muddle through her thoughts in an attempt to assign rank and duty to each member of their team. She knew enough to realize that a group worked better together if they felt the natural hierarchy of command.

Oh, Primen, I'm making a mess of this. I'm taking on more than I need to, aren't I? You've provided all these companions with different talents for different purposes. And I'm trying to take all the responsibility. Is that part of being a princess? I mean I come from a family of rulers. Do I just barge in and take charge because I've seen Father and Mother do that? All right. I'll remember I'm a child of Primen, not the queen of the universe. You always listen to me, don't you? Thanks.

29

GATHERING FORCES

Cho sat on the porch beside Bixby. His elaborate robes didn't blend as well with the rustic background as had his pants and plaid shirts.

The cloth of the sleeveless tunic shimmered with each movement. Up close, Bixby could see tiny circles of reflective metal scattered in the weave of the fabric. The bits near the hem lay in a pattern of waves.

Underneath this long outer garment, Cho wore a robe that at first glance looked to be a solid blue. But as Bixby watched, the blues faded and swirled, mixed and flowed with iridescent shades of green and purple. The same material on the sleeves held audacious hues, and the shimmer was more pronounced.

In spite of the fantastic garb, when Cho smiled, he looked like Old Trout, but in fancy duds. "What's your hamper's resource?"

"Injury and illness, sir."

"Is it well stocked?"

Bixby furrowed her brow and pressed her lips together as she reached in to locate a certain bottle. "Some of the items are very old. I don't recognize them."

Shaking her head so that her white-blonde curls bobbed and swayed, she handed Cho a small brown bottle with a cork stopper. "This one says oil of Prahlay. I've never heard of it. Have you? Do you know what it's for?"

Chomountain turned the bottle around in his hand, examining all sides. "Prahlay comes from flower nectar found in the tropical fields of Richra. Most probably, it's a remedy for something of tropical origin. A rash, a bite, something hard to digest but tempting in appearance."

"I'm from Richra. We have two bands of tropical terrain. I should know this."

Cho leaned back on his arms. "Now, don't be so hard on yourself. You didn't spend much of your time on Richra as you grew up. A couple of weeks from time to time, between your jaunts off to learn from another wise man interested in yet a different spectrum of truth."

"You know about that?"

"I do."

"Do you know why I was originally sent out? What my father asked me to do?"

Cho pursed his lips and looked at white clouds billowing in the eastern blue sky. They grew rapidly and overflowed the horizon, spreading toward the west. "I know you have a mission, but I wasn't told what it is."

"Oh." Bixby followed his gaze and watched the quickly changing tabloid of white and gray clouds. Puffed up and clinging to each other, they darkened.

"Storm coming." Chomountain stood. "If you need help for your task, you can ask. I won't interfere unless you want my aid." He paused, studying the clouds once more. "You have to ask."

He gestured toward the animal shed. "I think I'll visit with my old friends." He sauntered off, his posture reminding Bixby of the fisherman, not the right hand of Primen.

Cantor stepped out of the cabin as if he'd been waiting for Chomountain to move on. He sat where the old man had been and plopped his hamper on the wooden slats of the porch floor.

Bixby flashed him a smile. "What's in your bag?"

"Cooking and Cleaning. Pots, knives, sponges, soap, frying pan, mixing bowl, even a recipe book."

"No staples like flour, sugar, beans, or coffee?"

Cantor shook his head. "Nope, but I have another hamper here. Dukmee would have taken this one, but he's busy."

She looked over her shoulder, listening for sounds from inside the cabin. Jesha purred near the open door, but other than that, the tiny building might have been empty. Yet she knew Neekoh and Bridger hadn't come out the front door. They must have gone out the back way.

Cantor offered her the bag. "Shall we look inside?"

When she was slow to take it, Cantor opened the top, pulling the drawstrings loose. He held it out again, and she reached to plunge her hand inside. She jerked to a stop and squinted at her friend. "Did you put something nasty in there for me to grab?"

Cantor's belly laugh surprised her. He was shaking his head, but the more he denied it, the harder he laughed.

"Humph! Cantor D'Ahma, you can examine the contents of that hamper yourself. I don't trust you."

Cantor sobered, wiped tears from his eyes, and forced his face to stop twitching with the inclination to fall back into hilarity.

Bixby watched his efforts, steeling herself against being duped. Acting would never be Cantor's forte. His mischievous streak made a blatant lie of the pious expression he tried to stick to his face. He was a rough country boy playing true to his colors. He hadn't grown up so much after all, even though he'd been away from his home for three years.

Probably a wet, stinky fish. Maybe a skunk tail. Old Trout had a number of animal pelts in various stages of tanning. A slithery grass snake? A cracked egg?

She leaned away from him as he reached into the bag.

He started to pull his hand out but stopped with his wrist even with the top of the hamper. "I really didn't plant an ugly surprise, Bixby. You can trust me to treat you with respect."

His carefully modulated voice convinced her of his insincerity. Her squint came back full force, and her lips pressed into a perfect line.

Cantor tucked his chin against his chest and looked dejected. Bixby's heart softened. She doubted her certainty of his duplicity. She could be wrong about him. In fact, it wouldn't be the first time she'd underestimated him or misconstrued his intent.

Her shoulders relaxed, as did the terrible scowl she'd held in place.

Cantor's head whipped up. He roared. His arm appeared as fast as the flick of a whip. A shapeless brown object dangled from his hand. He thrust it into her face, and she screamed.

Cantor fell off the porch, laughing.

Bixby jumped down and stamped her foot on the hard-packed dirt. "Childish," she raged. "Pure childishness. Wicked. Fiendish. Not childlike at all. Bully. That's what you are. You're nothing but a bully. Bully!" She kicked at the ground, aiming to shower dirt on his worthless hide as he rolled around, unable to control his laughter, gasping for air.

She flounced away from the cabin. They had to go together on this mission, but she wouldn't be paired with him to do anything.

She'd thought he'd matured somewhat, even hoped he'd developed some tender feelings for her. They'd always had a special bond, could read each other's minds as if they were speaking out loud. He was handsome and manly, and she could easily start thinking of him in terms of hero to her heroine.

"Phooey!" She clenched her fists. "What's wrong with me?"

She stopped. Cantor had never disgusted her as much as he had just now. Never.

She turned around quickly and caught him watching her. He plastered a silly grin on his face ... but not fast enough.

On purpose. So they wouldn't be more than friends. Wary friends.

Cantor was smart. She did another about face. He must not see her expression. He'd know she'd figured out what was behind that silly stunt. He wanted to protect her.

But now she knew. He'd overreact if he knew her priority mission. If she needed to tell someone about the little job her father had given her, it would be Chomountain she would tell. Not Cantor.

Cantor watched Bixby enter the animal shed. A proper barn, really — long and low and filled with stalls and feed rooms, an animal infirmary, a tack room with more fishing tackle than tack, and a tannery. He'd discovered it was buildings that had been connected on to one another. So a string of sheds took up half the building with a door in the front and one in the back of each unit. Another part held a string of rooms connected to each other.

He dropped the woolly brown mitten back in the hamper of coldwear. He twitched for something to do. His emotions had set him on edge. A realm walker never lost compassion, but never succumbed to passion either. Emotional fervor inhibited thinking. Lack of control could get a realm walker killed ... and the people he'd vowed to safeguard.

The best thing he could do for Bixby was treat her like a little sister. And that's what he'd done. The prank sprang into play at the sight of her suspicious face. No premeditation, just an opportune answer to an awkward situation.

He knew he hadn't frightened her. He'd seen her fight and knew within that frail body, hidden under yards of feminine frippery, a valiant heart drove Bixby to do courageous things. But he'd startled her. She hadn't really expected him to be such a teaser.

Teasing was better than flirting. Flirting could get them killed.

He wouldn't lie to himself. In the past few weeks, he'd found himself thinking about her in too many unguarded moments, fighting the urge to protect her — even from Chomountain's gentle chastisement, watching her for the sheer pleasure of her dance-like moves.

But they would never dance together. He was more than

three feet taller than she was, and his thigh was probably bigger around than her waist. And more than that, her parents were king and queen of Richra. He didn't know his parents, but the two elderly people who had raised him were peasants. There had been legendary realm walker couples, but very few, and none from such divergent backgrounds.

He stood and went into the dimly lit cabin to fetch another hamper.

He'd forgotten Dukmee and his mysterious sphere. When Dukmee leaned back in the only chair, Cantor jumped enough to bash his head on one of the low beams supporting the roof.

The mage came to his feet to offer Cantor his sympathy. "Here, sit on the bed. Let me look at that. It's bleeding a little. You'll have a goose egg in a bit."

Cantor sat with his teeth clenched. He'd let the mage coddle him until the stars left his vision. Then he'd tell Dukmee to quit acting like an old woman.

"Old woman?" Dukmee laughed. "Your thought shield slipped there, my friend, and that came through loud and clear. You won't consider me an old woman if you need a healer after battle."

Cantor watched him pour a solution on a cloth and then felt him slap it on his small wound. He expected it to sting, but instead the cool, wet potion eased the pain.

He sucked in a breath and shot Dukmee a rueful smile. "Thank you."

"So, sounds like you're in a bit of trouble with our friend the princess. Don't worry, I'm sure she'll forgive you soon enough." Dukmee sat in the chair, picked up the globe, and tossed it from hand to hand.

"Should you be doing that?"

Dukmee grinned. "It's unbreakable. I've already dropped it. Well, it rolled off the table while I was getting a drink. Since it didn't shatter when it hit the floor, I hammered it with the fire poker."

"Naturally." He didn't think he would have beat something that valuable. "At least it's one less worry. When the guild soldiers swoop down to capture you, we only need keep your skin intact and not protect a fragile orb." Cantor shifted the pad on his head, off center a bit, to where the flesh still tingled. "Have you discovered something to help us?"

"As a matter of fact, I have."

"Well?"

"The founders of the society that populated the ruins liked to make things complicated. Rather, they believed that obscuring information and making it hard to find protected it from their enemies. Therefore, they didn't just write the book. They wrote the book, hid the book, and then hid two stones that tell where the book is."

Cantor stared at Dukmee. *How can he be pleased with this information? Lymens are due to invade, and we have no defense. Now we have to go chasing around after two stones? And the two stones aren't even the goal but tell us another place to chase down?*

So far, being a realm walker reminded him of a dog chasing his tail. The dog seemed to enjoy the activity, but nothing was ever gained.

Light flashing off the shiny bits of Chomountain's magnificent robe announced his arrival through the back door, with Neekoh close behind. He stopped to survey the room. Holding the lapels of his robe at his chest, he looked to be a man sure of himself and the authority he could wield, yet enough of Old Trout's demeanor remained to keep him from appearing pompous.

"Ah, a quest! Nothing more invigorating than having a quest as the first step in a venture to save the world. A quest should be the beginning of every endeavor."

The right hand of Primen looked intently at the three men with him. "Don't you agree, Neekoh?"

"Yes, sir." The former guardian of Chomountain bobbed his head to emphasize his agreement.

"But, gentlemen, I must inform you," said Cho in his most authoritative tone, "Neekoh will not be going with us."

Cantor stifled a groan. *Now what?*

"Neekoh has been promoted to guardian of Bright Valley. Next time I come for a small vacation, my caretaker will have everything in order, just as it is on the day we leave."

Cantor couldn't escape his negative reaction to this statement. *Providing the world is still traveling through space, not occupied by Lymens, and not blown up by councilmen. And when is Cho due a vacation? Hasn't he been off fishing for a thousand years or more?*

Cantor stood. "I need to talk to Bridger. Excuse me."

30

CHO'S SURPRISES

Cantor sighed his relief when he saw Bridger sleeping under his favorite tree. The dragon had stretched forward with his chin resting on his crossed arms. Shaped as his dragon self, Bridger was the size of a bull. His ears twitched as Cantor neared.

One eye opened, exposing an intelligent gaze. Bridger opened the other eye, lifted his chin, and shook his head, making his scales from the top of his head down his neck and shoulders rattle. A stiff spurt of wind clattered through the leaves in the tree above. The dragon sniffed the air and cast an eye toward the darkening clouds. He appeared to be ignoring Cantor's approach.

Cantor stopped just a few feet in front of the dragon, who slowly turned his head and looked at his visitor. Cantor shifted from one foot to the other. He needed to get this done so they could get on to more important things.

He looked straight into Bridger's eyes. "I overreacted."

Bridger nodded.

Cantor smiled and sat down cross-legged in front of him, glad Bridger was not going to be awkward about his outburst. Sometimes the dragon got huffy and made Cantor's life miserable for days. But often Bridger just brushed off Cantor's ill temper.

Stretching out his legs, Cantor leaned back on his arms and looked up at the rolling clouds. The air smelled fresh, with the scent of rain carried on a sporadic breeze. The day promised change. No more static waiting around.

Cantor reflected that not having to deal with a disgruntled dragon was one more point toward a positive shift. He glanced at his companion and noticed Bridger's glittering eyes positioned to peer down his nose. A haughty dragon.

Oh, so he wasn't going to get off without a reprimand, after all. A chilly breeze ruffled Cantor's hair and sent a shiver down his back.

Bridger's tone matched the temperature of the air. "Dukmee might decide to put his other skills to the side for a while and concentrate on being a realm walker."

Cantor understood the meaning behind this comment. "And if he does, he'll need a constant. And you just might be available."

"There aren't that many mor dragons willing to leave the comforts of home."

"And that's why I'm here to talk to you."

Bridger tilted his head at the unexpected comment. His words tumbled out as he backpedaled his hint to switch allegiance. "I'm not eager to change constants at this late date. We've been together for three years. Official or not, we're bonded."

Cantor sat up. "And Dukmee has no desire to put aside everything to be exclusively a realm walker."

"Well, you're right in that he hasn't mentioned it lately, but he has suggested such a thing from time to time."

"For now, Bridge, we have to work together." Cantor pulled his jacket tighter and buttoned the few buttons he had left. He'd scraped off quite a few when sliding through uncomfortable tunnels, looking for the Library of Lyme.

He rubbed his hands together and wished the dragon was in the mood to blow a little warm air on him. Since Bridger wasn't taking the hint, Cantor returned to laying out his plan. "We need to enlist at least two more dragons. Dukmee says we must go on a quest before we have enough information to thwart the Lymens."

Bridger scratched behind his ear. "It won't do much good if we get the information the week after the onslaught."

"My thinking exactly. I'm going to suggest we split up. You and I can go to Effram and find some of your kin to help."

"That's going to be a tall order." Bridger frowned. "Being taken on as a constant used to be every little mor dragolet's dream of glory. But corruption in high places sullies the water downstream. Few eligible dragons in these times think the job worthy of our righteous race."

At Cantor's grunt, Bridger continued. "Think of it. We know the guild is corrupt. Although the councilmen are not realm walkers, they influence those under them. No noble dragon wants to be associated with a morally weak realm walker. The number of hatchlings is down because the guild no longer nurtures young prospects into fulfilling their destinies."

Cantor picked a blade of grass and wrapped it around his finger. He must choose his words carefully. He unwrapped the blade and tossed it to the ground. "I see all the problems, Bridge. However, I don't think our mission can be successful without the mor dragons, bonded or not."

He paused and allowed himself to reach out to Bridger with the essence of his spirit, a type of communication practiced between constants. Loathe as Cantor usually was to admit it, Bridger was right. The length of their association had created a bond Cantor most often chose to ignore.

The rhythm of the dragon's body revealed to Cantor how receptive he was to the idea. He felt Bridger's pleasure at realizing how vital his kinsmen were to the defense of their world. Bridger's embarrassment that the other dragons might not respond to the call to arms rippled through both the dragon and Cantor. Bridger's desire to make the request was hampered by his fear that his kin would let him down.

A rumble in the distance reminded Cantor of the storm coming. "It would be good to have a mor dragon paired to each member of our party. But even one additional mor dragon would substantiate our forces. Three would be a boon for our side in any fray we entered."

He stood. "Let Dukmee and Cho and Bixby seek some vague bit of knowledge that may not be of any use. You and I will seek warriors who will make a difference."

Bridger stood as well, and the hamper Cho had given him fell to the ground.

Reluctant to press the dragon any further, Cantor swooped up the dropped container. "What was in your bag, Bridge?"

The dragon smacked his lips. "Snacks."

"What kind of snacks?"

Bridger shrugged and ambled toward the cabin. "Tasty snacks."

Cantor followed. "A goodly supply?"

"At the time I opened the hamper, it overflowed."

Cantor pulled the drawstring loose and reached inside.

"Ahem." A twinkle brightened Bridger's eye. "Quite possibly enough fare for five grown men on a three-day expedition. Or seven lonely women having tea each afternoon for a month. Or one hungry dragon who, for a long time, had been without delights such as cinnamon fudge, lemon-frosted tangerine cookies, buttered popcorn, candied peanuts, or long strips of bacon-flavored dried banana."

"And how long did it last the hungry dragon?"

"An hour, perhaps. And perhaps fifteen minutes more. I became too drowsy to keep an accurate accounting of the time."

Cantor laughed at Bridger's haughty tone. The dragon mimicked people as well as objects.

Lightning flashed. Thunder boomed. Bridger stretched a wing over Cantor just as huge pellets of rain smashed into the ground.

"We're going to get soaked," yelled Cantor. "Run."

They charged across the lawn to the bare ground in front of the cabin. Clattering up the wooden steps on the porch, Cantor laughed at all the noise they made. He stopped and looked down at the plank floor beneath them, the railing, and the steps.

"Don't look, Bridger, but tell me how many steps lead up to the porch."

"Three."

"Look."

Bridger obliged. "Five?"

"You're not crazy, my friend. When I left less than an hour ago, there were three."

"Wizardry," Bridger said. "Dukmee or Cho?"

A gust of wind brought a sheet of rain across the porch.

Cantor sidled up to the wall. "Why bother?"

"Practice," Chomountain said from the doorway. "I need to polish my skills of space and matter management. Come in."

He held the door wide. Bridger entered first and paused.

"Move." Cantor poked him. "I'm getting wet."

Usually when Bridger entered the cabin, he deflated himself. Cantor noticed as he squeezed through that the dragon had done nothing to shrink.

When he looked around, he understood. "Oh."

Chomountain had done some remodeling. The swinging bed, scarred table, corner kitchen, and storage shelves no longer crowded the little room. And the little room was no longer little. A table large enough to accommodate all of them sat to one side under a real hanging lamp. Large comfortable chairs circled a rug close to a stone fireplace. Stairs led to another level. Doors on each side of the main room hinted at yet more space.

"Come in, come in." Chomountain ushered them forward with an odd combination of Old Trout's quirky friendliness and the great Chomountain's dignity. "I've prepared a meal from recipes I've half forgotten, but I believe I've done well enough. This might be our last meal together for a while."

Cantor frowned. "Why do you say so?"

"You and Bridger are going to Effram. An excellent idea. Bixby will go with you, of course. She and Totobee-Rodolow can aid in persuading the mors that this is a worthy cause with no nefarious characters attached to it."

Cantor and Bridger exchanged a look and a feeling. The

right hand of Primen knew a bit too much of their business. By what means did he acquire it? Eavesdropping? Mind mining? Messages from Primen?

Chomountain crossed the room to a door that had not been there before. "The kitchen's in here. Come help load the table."

"Where's Dukmee?" asked Bridger.

"In his bedroom, reading the orb."

Cantor turned toward the door. "Bixby and Neekoh are in the shed. I'll go get them."

"No, no. Too much rain." Cho stopped for a minute, his eyes cast to the ceiling. "There. I've moved them."

Tramping of feet on the ceiling drew Cantor's attention to the stairs. Bixby and Neekoh banged down the newly added steps.

"We were in the barn," Neekoh began, his breath coming in gasps.

"He moved us." Bixby snapped her fingers. She peered around the room, then at Chomountain. "Cho?"

He nodded.

Her delicate features glowed with excitement. "No warning. Just blink your eyes and you're someplace else. I'd like to be able to do that."

A door opened, and Dukmee entered the room. "I was concentrating, and when I put down the globe, I was in another room." He gazed around the altered space. "Have I been asleep?"

They all turned to stare at Cho.

"No, Dukmee, not asleep." His hands gestured his desire for them to calm down. "Now, don't be upset. It's rather fun to do these things after such a long time of fishing every day."

"Can you move people over great distances?" asked Cantor.

"Can you build prisons around select groups of invaders?" asked Dukmee.

"Can we have dinner?" asked Bridger.

A TRIP TO EFFRAM

When they walked through the portal and into Effram, Bridger cheered. Bixby covered her ears to save her hearing from the thunderous roar. With a yeowl of protest, Jesha jumped away and ran to hide behind some rocks.

Bridger widened his grin until even his fist-sized, multi-pointed molars gleamed in the sunlight. A dragon's smile always touched Bixby's heart — with fear. With Bridger, though, familiarity with his comical nature prevailed. She grimaced at her friend and pulled her hands away from her ears.

"Sorry, Bix!" Bridger beamed as he looked around his home plane. "I got excited. We haven't been here in a long time."

Cantor stretched, did a few forms to limber his muscles, and then stood looking off to the west. "I wonder if the dragons still keep to themselves."

When he had been to Effram before, all the dragons

congregated in Tinendoor by the poisonous Sea of Joden. The mor dragon population had shrunk in recent decades. They now numbered fewer than any of the other breeds.

"My sister has communicated that our kin are even more reclusive than they were two years ago. Most of the other dragons mix freely with your kind, but our race has always been a bit standoffish."

Cantor tipped his head to the side, looking at Bridger with a quizzical expression.

"Do you mean self-righteous?"

"That's exactly what I mean," said Bridger. "Shall we be on our way?"

Bixby sat in front of Cantor on Bridger's back. Even without access to Cantor's thoughts, she'd sensed his reluctance to let her join him and Bridger in Effram. After what had passed between them, she shared his hesitancy. But Chomountain had quietly repeated that she would go find Totobee-Rodolow. Something about his understated authority was hard to defy.

Bridger accepted the "suggestion" and adopted his casual, friendly demeanor. Cantor, sitting directly behind her, acted like a wood carving, stiff and unresponsive. She tried to pry into his thinking and again met a barrier. Jesha, sitting between Bridger's ears, gave her a look that Bixby labeled sympathetic. After all, Jesha was a lady cat and perhaps male cats were as unfathomable as male humans. When she developed the skills her mother had, Cantor would not stand a chance.

Once in the air, Bixby had time to ponder Cantor's strange behavior. He often treated Bridger in a cold manner, but since yesterday he had extended that attitude toward her as well. She missed the warmhearted fun of their past adventures. She understood that Cantor wanted to make sure they didn't get any closer. They would be better warriors without emotional ties. But she wanted emotional ties — warm, cozy, loving ties.

She brightened. Perhaps she had it all wrong. Perhaps this bout of sullenness grew out of Cantor's past experiences in this land. Dunked in the poisonous Sea of Joden, he'd endured a long, painful convalescence. And, of course, Effram was where he'd hoped to find his chosen constant ... but instead wound up with Bridger.

Before she could come to any definite conclusions, Bridger burst out in song. He chose a rollicking tune about ships, waves, and the mysterious girl who seemed to be in every port. Bixby joined in on the chorus, and then sang along for six more songs of the dragon's choosing.

"Save your breath, Bridger," Cantor commanded at last. "We'll be going over the Tinendoor mountains soon."

Bixby swiveled a bit in order to see Cantor's expression.

He quirked an eyebrow. "He gets winded in the thin air at a high altitude. Singing and flying at the same time would be no problem if we were closer to sea level."

"You've learned a lot about each other."

He gave a curt nod and didn't answer. Bixby sighed heavily and faced forward again.

Three years earlier, they'd stayed in Tinendoor quite a while, not long after she and Cantor had been through one adventure together. Bridger had already attached himself to Cantor, and they had come to this valley to seek the dragon's sister. They'd stayed because Cantor got mixed up with the wrong people and got himself thrown into the Sea of Joden. They'd finally found him being tended to by a family of Brinswikkers. She began to laugh at the thought of the rather large Cantor in the home of his very short caretakers. Behind her, Cantor remained stoic.

Bother Cantor and his morose ways! This was a moment to be happy.

Bixby allowed herself to feel the thrill of places she remembered as they sailed easily down the inward slope of the mountain. Green grass carpeted most of the valley, except where outcroppings of colorful limestone striped exposed cliffs.

The treacherous sea — really, a very big lake — stretched out to their left. The vibrant colors of mineral bits in the water sparkled in the sun, making it appear innocently attractive. On closer examination, Bixby saw no bird or animal anywhere near the shore.

Supposedly, no fish could live in the tainted water. That would have disappointed Old Trout, but Chomountain cared nothing for fishing, a transformation brought about simply because Trout remembered who he was.

As Neekoh pointed out, Trout didn't act like a mountain, an immovable standard of Primen, when he didn't remember he was supposed to act that way. Bixby recalled a multitude of times when her nanny would give her a soft pinch and say, "Remember you're a princess. Act like one."

Farmhouses dotted the land. Scattered along the foothills, small villages kept themselves away from the poisonous waters. Tinendoor boasted only one metropolis, Tidoor, which perched on mountainous terrain in the southern part of the valley. Merchants carried their goods from town to town, going between the designated markets. Tinkers made a fine living by reaching those who had no time or means to travel.

One of the fairgrounds decorated the landscape ahead.

The bright colors of banners, tarps, and canvas enclosures couldn't be missed from above.

Bridger, gliding lower, made a small, excited jump in his smooth flight. "That would be a good place to start looking for Totobee-Rodolow."

Anticipation zinged Bixby's nervous system, running a pleasant shiver up and down her spine. She smiled at the prospect of seeing Totobee-Rodolow again, and at the chance to wander up and down the aisles of the open-air market.

Some of the vendors had colorful canopies over their stalls, but most merchandise lay out on tables with no sun shelter. Bridger flew low as Cantor and Bixby did a spot check of the crowd. They sighted no mor dragons, but they did encounter the tantalizing smell of the food stalls.

"This faire requires a closer examination." Bridger banked and landed in the field adjacent to an area where buggies, wagons, carts, and horses waited for their owners to return.

Bixby and Cantor slid to the ground. Bridger shape-shifted the saddle out of his back and slimmed down his bulk. He could easily roam through the faire at a size no bigger than Cantor.

Cantor pointedly nodded toward Bridger's back. "Mind your tail."

Bridger's tail thinned and snaked out eight feet. Then he pulled the ropelike appendage up and wrapped it around his waist twice. As a final restraint, he tucked the end in behind the broader part below his chest.

Cantor and Bridger started toward the hustling crowd. Jesha trotted to catch up and chose Cantor's shoulder to perch upon.

"Wait!" Bixby almost stomped her foot at her male companions. "I need to change."

"You look fine to me." Cantor paused and grinned. "What do you say, Bridge?"

Bridger's nose was in the air, his nostrils flexing as he smelled different faire foods. "We'll wait for you in front of the fried pastry booth."

She lost sight of them as soon as they passed the first perimeter markers.

Turning around in one spot, she searched for a private place to take care of her grooming. She probably wouldn't be able to pass a comb through her curls, even though she'd worn a cloche hat that fit closely to her head.

She spied some covered wagons parked close to each other and headed that way. Just as she suspected, someone had set up two privacy chambers complete with toilet.

The old woman outside the first canvas cubicle took her coin. "You've got ten minutes. Every minute after ten costs you a pintrap more."

"That's very reasonable." Bixby smiled at the woman. "You probably see most of the people who come to the faire."

"I do." Her eyes narrowed as she looked more closely at Bixby. "You ain't from the King's Guard, are you?"

"Oh, no. I'm here to find my friend Totobee-Rodolow. She's a mor dragon."

The old woman's mouth twisted. "Of course I know who Totobee-Rodolow is. She was here this week." She flapped a hand above her head. Her action implied she had better things to think about. "She might come again. They sell fine-quality goods at this faire."

"I hope she does come again. If you see her, would you tell her Bixby is here?"

To the woman's indifferent shrug, Bixby said, "Thank you," and lifted the tent flap to enter the shelter.

The woman kept the space clean. Bixby had no problem with pulling her layers of clothing off and piling them on a chair.

She opened her clothes hamper and withdrew more colorful garments. Smiling with anticipation, she then folded and stored the multi-shaded brown, white, and peachy skirts and dresses she had been wearing.

Her fifteen minutes in the tent satisfied her need to match her clothing to the joyful feeling she had. She looked forward to seeing Totobee-Rodolow, and perhaps she'd find some bits and pieces to add to her wardrobe. Plus, paired with a small amount of black, the colorful garments made a wonderful dancing costume. She hoped this faire had a dance every evening. She hoped they'd still be here.

Out of one hamper she rarely used, Bixby pulled three long, mirrored panels. Propped against the chair in a row, they made a decent looking glass. She inspected her selection of clothing, adjusted a hemline that was too straight, and then began the important business of finding the right crowns.

She would want to be able to tell if someone represented the truth or not. Or even if they fashioned lies out of half-truths. She picked out a slim circlet of woven vines embellished with emeralds and peridot stones. The vine was dotted with blue, red, and yellow gemstone flowers. She settled it on her abundant curls. Very pretty, and useful too.

She had the listening diadem in her hand when voices drifted through the canvas at the back of the little room. Plopping the circle of small bronze flowers atop the other crown, Bixby leaned in the direction of the conversation and tuned her hearing to catch every word.

"Bridger's here." The male voice sent a chill down her spine. Errd Tos, the leader of the Kernfuedal.

"We've got his sister tidily tucked away." This woman's voice Bixby had never heard before. Malice coated her words to the point Bixby could almost see a spiteful smile on the lips that spoke them. She knew, if she put on a different crown, that could be a reality. The problem was that the picture she would capture would be the woman's image of herself. Rarely was such an image accurate.

The woman spoke again. "Who's with him?"

"Cantor, the unauthorized realm walker."

"Should we let them wander around, or do you want them out of the way?"

"Oh, out of the way, my dear."

"I'll see to it."

"Do so."

Just like Errd Tos to send someone else to do his dirty work. I've got to warn Bridger and Cantor.

With quick, jerky movements, she tidied up the mess she'd made. Then, with the extra pintraps she needed in her hand, she pushed out the tent door.

The old woman lay stretched out on the ground.

"Oh!" Bixby dropped the coins and knelt beside her. "Are you ill? Hurt? Can you hear me?"

"Doubt she can," said a voice from behind, just as a cloth bag slipped over Bixby's head.

PLANS FOR DEFENSE

Bixby had positioned herself beside the fallen woman to the best advantage. With her weight on one bent leg, she anticipated the attack from behind. As the hood came down over her eyes, she whipped her right leg out in a high sweep and caught her attacker's knee. The thwack her leg made against his was a satisfying sound. So was his grunt. As he went down in one direction, she rolled to her feet in the other. By the time she stood facing him, she'd dispensed with the hood, throwing it down on the ground.

A quick glance told her she had accurately perceived the situation. Only one had been sent to ambush her. He stood, anger in his eyes and in his stance. Too much anger. He wouldn't be thinking clearly.

She smiled at him, and that brought him charging right into the knife she'd turned out at the last moment. His eyes bulged, and he jerked backward, tripped over the old woman, and landed on his backside. The impact jarred a grunt out of him.

He clamped his hand on his thigh. Blood trickled between his fingers. She heard a low growl as he rolled into a crouch. He'd managed to get himself stuck in the same leg where her blow to his knee already impaired his movement.

Bixby took a good look at him while he was struggling to get up. Dressed in ordinary clothes, he could have been a farmer. Except he was cleaner than any farmer she'd ever met on a weekday. They cleaned up well for Sanctuary, but why get spiffy in the middle of the week?

Her attacker had overworked biceps, and his thigh muscles bulged. Clean light brown hair nicely cut belied his role as ruffian. Overall, he didn't have the appearance of any tough she'd ever met.

"Who are you? Why did you try to kidnap me?"

He gritted his teeth as he stood and let out a hiss. With that gust of air, all the anger and belligerence seemed to leak out of him as well.

"Name's Tegan. I'm looking for a wife."

Bixby cleaned her blade on a rag and tucked it back in the hidden sheath between her skirts. "Your proposal needs some work."

"No maid on Effram would have me." Tegan's fine, broad shoulders had slumped. He stared at the ground. With his brow furrowed, he looked confused.

Bixby studied him. Her crown indicated he told the truth. Unfortunately, the information didn't come with any elaboration. She knew he was unmarried, but she didn't know why. He was a handsome man. She decided to resort to the direct approach. "Why?"

"Because I'm ... odd."

Again, she took a moment, trying to see what would be so repellant that the man had to forcibly capture a bride. His strategy was odd, certainly, but the rest of him seemed normal enough.

"I'm sorry. You look fine to me."

His face relaxed, and good-looking turned into strikingly attractive. "Then will you marry me?"

"No, I'm busy."

She bent to take another peek at the woman. "What did you do to her?"

"A whiff of Starnaut juice."

Bixby stood. "She'll not be too happy when she comes around."

"I didn't want to hurt her."

"Well, you didn't." Bixby glanced at the woman. She didn't trust this man enough to take her eyes off of him for more than a second. "Starnaut juice wears off quickly. You might have damaged her some when you fell."

"I didn't land *on* her."

She dismissed his statement with a frown and listened to the chatter from the faire. She needed to find her friends, and she didn't need Tegan coming along. "You should stay here until she wakes."

Bixby's skirts flared as she twirled around to march past the wounded man and between two tents. The old woman groaned but Bixby refused to be delayed any longer. Moments later, she heard the limping gait of Tegan behind her.

He caught up to her. "She's all right."

Her head almost came to his shoulder, which was a nice change from Cantor and Dukmee, who towered over her.

"Could you slow down a bit?" he asked. "Or stop while I bind up this wound? It's just a scratch. It won't take but a minute."

Bixby stopped and stared at him. Her tiara helped her define his general character — basically a moral man with a high level of frustration. She discerned intelligence stifled by something she could not identify.

And she didn't have the time to explore his temperament!

"You're going to tag along behind me, aren't you?"

"Yes."

He couldn't attack her in the crowded faire. And her friends would defend her if he got unruly. She didn't really need his help, but he was big, and it never hurt to have help.

She sighed. "Sit on that barrel, and I'll fix your leg. Be quick. I have to tell someone something."

Tegan sat. Bixby knelt beside him and pulled out her hamper for illness and injury.

As she cut away the material around his wound, she noticed he hadn't given the hamper a second glance. A flat bag containing bulky objects sometimes disturbed people. Obviously, he'd seen hampers before. That would mean association with more than cows and chickens.

She put aside her assumption that he was a farmer.

The knife had sliced along his lower thigh and had not plunged into the flesh. Stitches would make the scar less noticeable but weren't absolutely necessary. She wiped the blood away, applied a cleanser, then smoothed a creamy ointment over the long cut.

Bixby tidied away the things she had used so far and extracted a roll of linen from her hamper. Again, she wondered at his lack of curiosity. Surely he didn't know many people who carried a hamper specifically for ministering to medical needs. But Tegan showed no interest. Not one word of inquiry. Actually, he didn't speak at all.

She cut a length of the linen and folded it to make a pad to absorb the oozing blood.

Taking his hand, she put it over the bandage. "Hold that wadding against the wound."

He did as he was told.

She wrapped the cloth strip around his thigh, tightly enough to keep pressure on the wound, then tied it off. She stood, looking at the top of his head as he examined her work.

"I really have to go." She rammed the last of the scattered supplies into the hamper and turned to sprint away.

She intended to leave him behind, but Tegan kept pace with her. Bixby stopped at the perimeter barrier. Tegan plopped down on the wooden rail and leaned forward, panting. Bixby surveyed the immediate area, then shut her eyes to reach out to her friends.

"What is it?" asked Cantor, dropping some of his barriers.

"Errd Tos is here, and he's ordered your capture."

"Are you coming to join us?"

"Yes, we'll be right there."

She felt Cantor's confusion. *"We?"*

As Bixby moved into the faire, her companion pushed away from the rail and caught up with her.

She gave a resigned shrug. *"Tegan is with me."*

"Tegan?"

"He wants to marry me."

She giggled at the strength of Cantor's bewilderment.

"Don't worry, Cantor. I told him I was too busy."

Bixby let go of her connection with Cantor so she could concentrate on moving through the crowd, keeping her eye out for brutes working for Errd Tos. Far more weary, lonely, hopeless people roamed through the faire than those who were looking for trouble.

Normally, so many people in despair would have captured Bixby's attention. She would have spent some time studying this crowd to determine what common element in their lives caused their distress. She steeled herself not to allow her curiosity to upset her agenda. Top priorities were finding Cantor and Bridger, rescuing Totobee-Rodolow, and persuading more mor dragons to join them in the battle against invaders. Then off to save the world.

First, the pastry booth.

She and Tegan found the food court, and then the stall selling cakes, cookies, meat pies, and sausages wrapped in dough and baked until nicely browned.

A small version of Bridger stood beside Cantor. The dragon's belly protruded as if he hid a large game ball inside.

"You're going to be sick," she scolded.

Bridger licked his claw tips and smacked his lips. "Never sick."

"You just had a beastly cold. You do get sick."

He shook his head. "I never get sick to my stomach."

"I have something to tell you that might make you queasy."

Cantor elbowed in between Bixby and the dragon. He pointed over Bixby's shoulder. "Who's this?"

Bixby barely gave the man a glance. "Tegan."

"What is he doing here?"

"Following me."

"Why?"

Bixby beetled her brow. "I don't know why." She faced Tegan. "Why are you following me?"

Tegan looked confused, an expression that often came to his face. He frowned as if in deep thought and finally answered. "I forgot."

He wandered off and sat at one of the tables provided for those who had bought a meal.

Bixby gave him a last puzzled look, then dismissed him from her thoughts and returned to the important matters. She switched to mindspeak so only the two could hear her. "*Errd Tos is here.*"

Moving closer to the dragon, she put her hands on his arm. "*Totobee-Rodolow is captured.*"

Bridger grunted. "*Seems to me my sister was kidnapped the last time we had a mission together. Maybe we shouldn't take her along.*"

Bixby had no experience with brothers, but she had heard that they could be quite callous toward their sisters. Bridger had just confirmed that. She took away her hand and glared at him.

"*We've got to free her, even if she isn't to come along.*"

Cantor broke in aloud. "What's he doing?"

Bixby followed his gaze to Tegan. "He's reading a book of some kind. Looks like a journal."

"I'm not comfortable with his going with us. There's something odd about him."

Bixby screwed up her face and studied her attacker-turned-suitor. "That's what he said about himself. I don't see it." She jerked on Cantor's sleeve, and spoke to his mind. "*Totobee-Rodolow! We've got to rescue her.*"

"*Do you know where she is?*" asked Cantor, his eyes still on Tegan.

"*No.*" Bixby turned to Bridger. "*Do you have any idea where these villains would be able to keep her?*"

"*Juicy kumquats! I've been gone three years. How would I know?*"

"Well, we've got to find out." Bixby used a reasonable voice, not at all the one that hovered in her throat. "*Whom can we go talk to who might have information? Any of your relatives? Your friends?*"

"*There's a hot spring where my kin often visit. It's a nice place to relax and catch up on things happening around the realm.*"

"*Let's go there.*"

"Wait." Cantor put his hand on Bixby's arm. "*Maybe there are mor dragons here. We should find them and talk to them first.*"

"*What about Errd Tos? His men are looking for you.*"

"*We're probably safe in the middle of the faire. When we go to leave, we'll be in danger.*"

Bixby nodded and pulled out her crown hamper. "We'll try to connect with one." She pulled out a fancier crown with a high rim, with no jewels but plenty of twists and elaborate sculpted metal. It wasn't her best crown for locating the mor dragons, but the other was way too conspicuous. She placed the two she had been wearing in the hamper.

Bridger and Cantor already had the faraway look of someone reaching with his mind to find someone. Bixby closed her eyes, took a deep breath, and allowed her consciousness to escape the boundaries of her brain.

Her search came up with nothing. In a moment, she opened her eyes. "That's strange, isn't it?" She looked at her two friends.

Cantor quirked an eyebrow. "I didn't find one mor dragon, but Bridger should have had better luck."

The dragon shook his head and looked at Bixby.

"I didn't find one either. Do you think they've isolated all the mor dragons?"

Cantor looked skeptical. "Takes a big jump to get to that conclusion."

"What do you think?" asked Bixby.

"I haven't decided. Let's go check out the springs Bridger mentioned."

Leaving the crowded market, they headed back to the field they'd landed in. Just before they turned a corner, Bixby looked back. Tegan followed them but read as he walked, absorbed in his book. She wondered why Primen had caused their paths to cross. Curiosity niggled at her brain. Why did he think he was odd? What kind of odd? She doubted he would disappear and never enter their lives again. That just didn't seem to be the way Primen worked.

She had just a twinge of anxiety. Nothing in their future looked safe. A small conundrum like the interesting Tegan would be an easier problem to solve. A lighter burden. More fun, at least.

But she wasn't making the choices for this journey. And to tell the truth, considering what was at stake, she would gladly leave the whole thing in Primen's hands. His problem. His responsibility. She would be the minion.

33

FINDING HELP

Nothing in the Tinendoor valley was far away.

A dragon could fly end to end in the morning and side to side in the afternoon. The poisonous Sea of Joden accounted for most of the distance in the middle. Bridger glided south along the mountain range and soon came to their destination.

A rise in the foothills pushed upward, then dipped before the mountains, creating a bowl-shaped valley. In the center of this geological formation, a myriad of stone columns shot upright. Obviously made by some force of nature, the grouping looked like people gathered for a celebration of some kind.

"It's called the Family," said Bridger over his shoulder.

At the feet of statues carved by the environment, green and blue water bubbled out of the earth. One side spouted green foam, and down the other side trickled miniature blue falls.

"Very pretty," said Bixby. She held Jesha and stroked the kitty's back.

"But no dragons." With alert eyes, Cantor did another sweep of the area. "Any other ideas?"

Bixby pointed to a ramshackle building about a mile along the hills. "Let's ask at that inn if they've had any dragon custom lately."

Bridger banked and began a descent.

Close at hand, the hostel looked better than it had from the sky. Small repairs, fresh paint, and seedlings planted in a long border of the property showed someone had recently invested some time in the old place.

Two children ran out the front door and dashed across the lawn to greet them. They came to a skidding stop just yards away.

The elder, a girl with rosy cheeks, pale blue eyes, and neat brown braids, curtseyed. "Welcome to Halfway There Inn."

Cantor laughed. "Where are we halfway to?"

The boy, grubbier than his big sister but just as polite, pointed in one direction. "If you're going south, sir, you're halfway to Tidoor." He switched arms to point in the opposite direction. "If you're going north, you're halfway to Blendit."

The girl curtseyed again. "Won't you come in and have tea? My mum makes the best cakes and pastries in Tinendoor."

Not to be outdone, the boy bowed. "My pader makes his own brew. It's tasty."

The girl turned disbelieving eyes on her little brother.

He looked down and scuffed his shoe against long, healthy blades of grass. "Or so I've been told." He peeked up at Cantor and winked. "Mum also makes sandwiches and soups and things."

Bixby turned a laugh into a cough, not wanting to belittle the delightful boy.

A voice called, "Jory, Mack, bring our guests inside."

In a window with billowing white curtains, a young woman waved. Bixby waved back.

"We have a cat. May we bring her in?"

She had addressed the woman but the children chorused, "Yes!" At the woman's nod, Bixby started to the door with Jesha in her arms.

Bridger smacked his lips as they followed the children toward the inn. "Tea and trimmings." In the fastest change Bixby had seen so far, the dragon became a smaller version of himself. He didn't bother to secure his tail.

Bixby decided to wait until they saw the inside before deciding whether the tail would be a menace.

The inside of the building enveloped them in cool, dark simplicity, brightened only by natural light from the windows. Wooden chairs clustered around several tables. A singing bird hung in a pretty cage. It ceased its delightful warble and cocked an eye at them. Cantor pursed his lips and whistled the same pattern as the bird's song.

Sister and brother stopped as they wove through the furniture and turned surprised faces to Cantor. The realm walker stopped his tune, and the bird took it up. As soon as it stopped, Cantor had a turn. Jesha ignored the bird and claimed a space on the hearth.

The children laughed, bounced on their toes, and clapped their hands.

Their mother came out of a back room, carrying a tray with mugs and a big teapot, creamer, and sugar bowl. She set her heavy load on the nearest table. Bixby went to help her.

"I'll be back in two ticks." The woman headed toward the

curtain-covered door again. "Just need to get the pastries and some spoons."

Bixby poured the tea, sweetened the dark brew with lumps of brown sugar, and lightened it with the cream. Bridger came at once to sit at the table, and Cantor joined them when the innkeeper brought two plates of sweet breads.

"Thank you very much," Bixby told the mother.

Cantor, Bridger, and Bixby bowed their heads as Cantor thanked Primen for his provision and asked for help in finding the mor dragons.

The mother and children had stood quietly waiting, but at the mention of mor dragons, the woman drew in a sharp breath.

"Go outside now," she said to the children when Cantor had finished. "Make sure none of the chickens have pushed through the fence and gotten into the garden."

The children giggled and playfully bumped one another as they left the inn.

Bixby smiled. "What is your name?"

"I'm Mistress Cane."

"I'm Bixby D'Mazeline. This is Cantor D'Ahma and Bridger-Bigelow." Bixby tilted her head. "There's something you want to tell us?"

She hesitated a moment. "How did you know?"

"I just noted little things. For instance, there must be a reason you suddenly cared so much about the chickens."

Cantor stood. "Won't you join us?"

He pulled out a chair then returned to his when Mistress Cane settled.

"There are only five mor dragons left." She looked at Bridger. "Six."

He nodded and took another fried pie.

Mistress Cane took in a shuddering breath. "They gathered at the Family. My husband knew they were there and went to introduce himself. We just bought the inn, and he wanted them to know we would be pleased to have their custom."

She paused. Her teeth worried her lower lip. "Before he reached the spring, he saw men hiding and spying on those in the bowl. He thought that strange."

Bixby and Cantor nodded, their attention fully on the innkeeper. Bridger poured himself another mug of tea. Then, showing his manners, refilled the two other mugs.

"So my husband, Makki, ducked down and spied on them — the ones who were spying on the mor dragons."

At Bridger's elbow, a pile of crumbs collected as he ate. Mistress Cane brushed the tiny bits off the edge of the table and into her waiting palm. "He couldn't have stopped them. He counted a dozen ruffians as he followed them. But he was brave enough to follow them. Or foolhardy enough."

She looked down in her lap where her hands rested, one clutching crumbs.

Bixby knew the disjointed sentences came from the woman's distress. Using her ability to scope the woman's thoughts, she got a clearer picture. The men had overcome the dragons and marched them out of the Family Springs. Her husband couldn't stop them, so he followed.

She reached over and patted her arm. "Go ahead. You can tell us. We mean you no harm."

"They're keeping the dragons locked up. Makki's been going there every day, to take them food and check on their welfare. He'd help them escape if he could. He's there now."

"Crista!"

Everyone turned to see a young man standing at the door to the back room. Bixby detected a strong mixture of outrage and fear for his family.

He strode into the inn. Tense muscles hardened his jawline as he stared at the group around the table. "What are you saying? Who are these people?"

Mistress Cane stood and went to his side. "It's all right, Makki. They can help us." She leaned closer. "I think they're realm walkers."

Makki groaned. "Oh, Crista, that could make matters worse. You're too trusting."

She took his hand and guided him to the table. Cantor stood. After Bixby kicked him under the table, Bridger stood as well.

"Pleased to meet you." The dragon extended his hand.

Makki cautiously took it. When Bridger let go, the man examined his palm as though to determine if it were still intact.

Bixby bit the inside of her cheek to keep from laughing. Obviously, Master Cane had never shaken the hand of a dragon before. He held his hand before him, marveling at not being scratched by those vicious-looking claws. But the man had been willing to invite the dragons to his inn. Fear unsettled him. It shivered around him.

Cantor shook his hand as well, but it was Bridger who talked. "My sister has been captured, they tell me. I wonder if she is with those who were kidnapped from the Family Springs."

Bixby saw the young man start to question the dragon, then stop himself. She easily guessed his thoughts. He'd been on the brink of asking what the dragon's sister looked like. A foolish question for a mor dragon. They shape-shifted.

Unlike Bridger, however, most mor dragons could shape-shift to only a limited number of things. And her friend Totobee-Rodolow, who spent too much time using her shape-shifting abilities to design and decorate her body, could only shift into different forms of herself.

Bixby decided to help the conversation along. "Totobee-Rodolow is a fashionable dragon, usually decked out in jewels and brilliant colors."

Makki's eyebrows rose. "I know Totobee-Rodolow." His gaze wandered back to Bridger. "This dragon is brother to Totobee-Rodolow? That's hard to believe."

Bridger nodded. "Totobee-Rodolow got all the looks." Smug and self-satisfied, he looked directly at Makki. His fearsome grin showed pointed teeth. "And I got all the talent."

FIVE DRAGONS—
FIVE BARRELS

They were herded into a small cavern. Soon after the ruffians had them trapped, the King's Gaurd showed up."

Makki pointed to a dark shadow in the face of the cliff. The moon shone much too brightly for this rescue mission, but Cantor knew they didn't have time to wait for the moon to wane. Crouched behind Bixby and beside Bridger, he listened carefully to their guide's layout of the land.

"We can enter from over there." Makki pointed to the end of a trailing rock formation that looked somewhat like a tail coming off a huge sprawling beast. "I doubt the King's Guard even know of its existence. I've been going in and out of the cavern through that tunnel all four days that they've been in there."

Bixby spoke quietly at Cantor's elbow. "Why don't the dragons shift shape and leave?? Surely one of them could get out and procure a key or go for help."

Cantor shook his head. Makki needed to know more about

the dragons. "They must not have the ability to shift into things small enough to ease their escapes. We know Totobee-Rodolow can't."

"I think they're drugged," Makki said.

"Why?"

"They don't seem to be upset that they're being held against their will. In fact, at times, I think they don't even realize they aren't allowed to leave."

"Drugged, for sure," said Bridger. "My sister hasn't been shopping in four days. That's not natural."

Makki pointed in the other direction. "That's where the beast comes from. The hole that looks like an eye socket on the skull of a steer."

The cave had a rock ledge before it, but other than that, it was a sheer drop to the ground below.

"It flies?" asked Bixby.

"Yes."

"Then it's a dragon." Cantor stated his opinion as fact. He didn't care for the fanciful interpretation Makki had put on the animal. The innkeeper thought it resembled a demon's dog.

Makki shook his head. "It doesn't look like a dragon."

"But it has wings?" Cantor asked.

"Yes."

"It's big, you say?"

Makki nodded, the muscles in his jaw tensing.

Cantor worked to keep his tone patient. He really wanted to snap this man out of his delusion. But when a realm walker came into a situation that required his help, there was no room for lording over the people in need.

"Can you think of any animal that has wings to fly?"

Makki sighed. "Just dragons."

Bixby had been biting her lower lip. A sure sign of deep thought. "Maybe it's a dragon who has shape-shifted into this beastlike thing."

Bridger growled. "That would be abhorrent to any mor dragon. We are raised to fulfill a destiny. There are a few who've gone astray. But they chose to live far, far away rather than face the scorn of the rest of the clan."

A shrieking cry echoed off the walls of the cliff and sent painful shivers along Cantor's arms. Bumps on his skin rose where he'd felt each of the stinging pricks. His eyes sought the cave of the beast. No bird had made that strident sound.

The creature made no appearance, however, and Cantor soon forced his mind back to the task at hand. "Makki, you lead the way to the tunnel. Bixby, you're with us. Bridger, you keep that beast off our tails should he come out ready to tear us up."

Bridger nodded and shifted into a mountain goat. He nimbly passed over the rocky terrain, heading for the beast's cave.

Cantor had to poke Makki to bring him out of his stunned reaction to the dragon's turning into a goat. They began their stealthy trek. Bixby followed Makki. He moved confidently, having traversed this ground every day. The entrance to the tunnel was small, but once through the narrow way, they could easily stand. Inside, cool damp air smelled clean and fresh.

Bixby passed out light orbs. A whiff of air trailed over Cantor's cheeks and out the small entry behind him. He sniffed the air. Fresh — a good omen.

He held up his light. "Let's get on with our plan."

"Step around that shaft." Makki pointed to a hole in the ground right in the middle of their path. "I don't know how deep it is, but there's water at the bottom. I dropped a rock in and heard it splash."

Cantor felt a measure of comfort. Once they'd convinced the innkeeper and his wife of their integrity, Makki had turned out to be a valuable man to have on their side. He knew this area well. And he was eager to free the dragons. Alone, Cantor's party would have wasted a lot of time. With Makki's help, they could hope to rescue the kidnapped dragons before dawn.

The rock walls were carved out of limestone, not by man but by water. The height varied, and Cantor minded his head to keep his scalp from being scraped against the low places. The path cut back and forth, showing where the water had traveled the course of least resistance. Uneven places in the floor cropped up at intervals and caused Bixby and Cantor to stumble.

Makki took them along the main passageway and then turned off to the right. "The barrels are down here."

Cantor heard the waterfall before they rounded a corner and saw it. Only about five feet tall, the steady flow fell from halfway up the side wall and disappeared into a huge crack at the base.

Five barrels stood against a weeping wall. Puddles dotted the jagged floor. Cantor smiled at the thought of Dukmee. Their friend would have become engrossed in the geological formations, theorizing about how the water had changed the inside of the mountain over the years. Cantor allowed himself a moment to wonder how Dukmee and Chomountain were doing on their mission.

Makki picked up one empty barrel and thrust it under the spout of water. "I've only been able to take each dragon one barrel of water each day, but with three of us, we could probably manage two. They always seem more awake a little after drinking."

"Another reason to suspect drugs." Cantor moved to a second cask, rolling it closer to be filled next.

With water lapping against the brim of the first barrel, Makki and Cantor shoved it out of the way and set up the next to fill. Bixby took on the task of fastening a tight lid into the opening of the full container.

When the second lid slipped into place, Bixby looked at the two men. "Now what?"

Makki tipped a barrel over on its side. "We roll them to the dragons."

Cantor hadn't been able to visualize Makki's description of the opening between this tunnel and the small cavern where the dragons waited. Now he could see the roots tangling in the gap. Makki had hacked away enough to be able to stuff the casks through one at a time.

Bixby leaned as far into the other side as she could without actually going in. "They're all asleep."

Makki scratched the back of his neck. "I usually come in the afternoon. I prefer to be with my family when night falls."

Bixby backed out of the hole. She looked at Cantor. "I'll go through and wake Totobee-Rodolow."

"There's no guard in the cavern." Makki leaned against a wall. "Miss Bixby probably won't see any of them. The dragons have told me they keep to themselves at the entrance. The guards do bring back food and water, but I've never seen them in the cavern itself."

Bixby pulled out a hamper.

"I haven't said you can go, Bix." Cantor wanted to think through this change in plans.

She stopped all motion, with eyes wide and mouth open.

"Why couldn't I go? What's wrong with my going? I'm

small enough to fit through. Totobee-Rodolow knows me, and I daresay I know some dragons in there. I met them when visiting with her two years ago, along with many of her other dragon friends who aren't mor dragons. Look, Cantor, we need to get the dragons awake without making a lot of noise. When they wake up and see me, whom they know" — she emphasized this point with individual words distinctly pronounced — "they won't put up a fuss, thinking I'm part of those who kidnapped them."

"Hush for a minute and let me think."

"Why do you have to think?"

"Why do you have to talk?"

She planted her fists on her hips, pressed her lips into a thin line, and glared at him.

He sat on his heels, mulling over the things they knew. All of their information came from Makki. Everything he'd said so far had proven true, but the guards were an unpredictable element. Even if they had never entered the cavern before, tonight might be the time one of them wandered in.

He stood. "I want this hole big enough for Makki and me to follow you if there's a need. Then, I agree, you are the most logical one to go rouse Totobee-Rodolow."

They worked as quietly as they could. Cantor hacked at the top of the opening where the roots were thickest. Makki sawed pieces from the sides. Bixby sliced away the bits and pieces at the bottom. She grumbled when the others dropped stringy roots and chunky stubs on her head and back.

"I wonder if we're killing a tree aboveground." She wove her fingers through her hair, knocking loose some of the debris.

"A tree with roots this big and this deep must be a very large one." Cantor looked down and grinned at the top of her head. She really was a good companion, not squeamish. Despite her lace and frills, Bixby had a warrior's heart. With a polished overlay of feminine charm. "I don't believe cutting out a small portion of its root system will even be noticed."

Bixby laughed. "None of the trees I know notice anything at all. They respond to climate changes, the length of the day, how much rain they get. But they do not chat about the weather or recommend a lotion to keep their bark smooth and young-looking."

Cantor stepped back and examined their work. "I think that does it."

Bixby stood immediately and jiggled her skirts, scattering specks of tree root on the floor. Holding her crown in her hand, she bent over and wildly shook her hair. Then she picked up the hamper she'd retrieved from her skirts earlier, put one crown away, and pulled out another.

"What's that one for?" asked Cantor.

"Seeing in dim light."

He nodded. "Good choice. Makki and I will take turns with the barrels. As soon as the dragons start drinking, Bixby, you can come back to this side and help with the relay for getting them filled a second time."

He put his hand on her shoulder and gave a gentle squeeze. "Off you go."

As soon as she'd slipped through, Cantor positioned himself so he could watch her.

Makki peered through the roots next to him. "Gotta keep an eye on her, eh? Same with my Crista and the tots."

Cantor blustered, but Makki had already turned away. And all Cantor could see of him was his outline made by the light orb he carried in front of him.

Cantor wanted to explain, but that would have made matters worse. He and Bixby were realm walkers. They were comrades in the service of Primen. Part of their duty was to watch out for one another, and this need to protect her arose from their partnership, not a romantic complication. Romance, flirting, affection would be counterproductive to their mission.

Maybe after.

35

THE BEAST

Weaving around the sleeping dragons, Bixby skimmed across the cavern floor. Of course, Totobee-Rodolow slept against the opposite wall. She wanted to talk to her friend before waking the other dragons. As with all mor dragons, these had increased in size during their slumber. The cavern was small and overly full. But none of the sleeping dragons stirred as she glided by.

When she reached Totobee-Rodolow, she stopped and stared. The previously stunning dragon looked worn and frayed. Bridger's sister had always set the standard for fashion and grooming. Now her scales were dingy, her claws ragged, and her tail unadorned with gemstones. The dragon Bixby loved wouldn't be caught dead in the shape she was in.

Bixby put a hand on her hip. She needed to get the dragons awake and watered and out of this prison.

She started to touch Totobee-Rodolow but pulled back, noticing just in time that the dragon's scales had taken on the sharp edge that protected her while asleep.

Bixby leaned toward her ear. "Totobee-Rodolow, wake up."

The dragon lifted her head at once. "Who? Bixby! Darling, it is so good to see you."

"We've come to get you out."

"Out, my dear?"

"Yes — you've been captured."

Totobee-Rodolow sat and scooted to lean her back against the cavern wall. "I think you must be mistaken." She looked around the dim room. "Although I must say, I'm not sure where I am. Now, that's rather unusual, isn't it?"

"You were captured and brought here. The King's Guard are stationed outside to keep you from leaving."

"I do remember a walk, an unpleasant trek across some rocky terrain. We couldn't fly, but I don't remember why."

"Starnaut juice."

"Now, don't be absurd. We dragons know better than to …" She broke off to yawn, a most inelegant gape not even hidden behind her massive hand. "I'm tired, Bixby. Come back tomorrow at a decent time, and we'll have tea."

The dragon slipped down the wall to stretch out once again.

Bixby had to stop her. "Totobee-Rodolow, look at your hands. Your claws are a disgrace. When did you last have a manicure?"

Totobee-Rodolow glanced at her hand, looked again more closely, and sat upright. The look of horror on her face would have made Bixby giggle if their circumstances were less dire.

"Well … well." Totobee-Rodolow examined herself and obviously did not like what she saw. "There might be something to what you say." She looked around the room. "There's that nice young man who brings us fresh water every day. I thought I saw Cantor a moment ago."

"That's Makki, and Cantor is here too. We've got water for you and your friends. You must drink it and pull yourselves together so we can escape."

Totobee-Rodolow stood and shook. Her scales rattled loudly. Bixby cringed, hoping the guard would not come to investigate.

As they crossed the room, the dragon nudged her sleeping friends and explained each time she got one on its feet. Bixby said, "Quiet, please," and, "Do be quiet," and, "Hush," to no avail. The dragons muttered and rattled their scales and trudged the short distance to the hole in the wall. They sounded like a herd of dragons.

Although a group of dragons is a watch, not a herd. Bixby glanced toward the front of the cavern. No movement. *The guards have surely heard all this commotion.*

Bixby slipped through the hole and ran down the tunnel to the waterfall, where she resumed her job of recapping each cask as it was filled. Makki and Cantor rolled the barrels down the passageway.

"Last barrel." Cantor pushed it under the waterfall. "They are definitely awake now and very indignant."

"Do they remember? Can they shape-shift?"

"Oh, yes, they remember, all right. Lots of throaty threats and growly intentions being expressed. As to shape-shifting, I don't know the length of time it takes for a mor dragon to recover from starnaut poisoning."

"Mad mor dragons." Bixby thought for a moment. "There's a nursery rhyme about mad mor dragons eating porridge with a knife."

The water flowed into the cask at Cantor's elbow. He

288

checked the level and spoke over his shoulder. "I vaguely remember it, but only a couple of phrases come to mind."

He shoved and scooted the barrel over to Bixby.

She maneuvered the round lid into the ridge that held it and tightened the bands to keep it in place. "It's going to bother me until I remember."

"I think we're going to be so busy, you won't have time to fret about an old poem."

While Makki helped Bixby dispense herbs to lessen the drug-induced headache that bothered some of the dragons, Cantor scouted the area right outside the tunnel's entrance. The moon had shifted, but it still shone brightly. Cantor spotted tracks in a dirt trail. He followed and came within yards of the main entrance to the cavern.

Ducking behind a pile of boulders, Cantor stilled and stretched his senses to gather information from his surroundings. The dry air smelled of the nearby bushes. With a bit of concentration, Cantor picked up the smell of mineral water from the Family Springs.

From the entrance of the cavern, he heard snores and heavy breathing and footsteps. One guard must be the night sentry. The man paced, either trying to stay awake or worried about something. Cantor hoped he wasn't worried about all the noise the dragons made as they recovered from the effects of starnaut juice.

He covered his ears at the sound of the eerie screech he had heard earlier. The noise ripped through him and effectively shut down his ability to hear small sounds. A nudge from behind startled him. He spun around, sword in hand.

"Bridger! I could have killed you."

The goat sidestepped, whirled, and darted off. Cantor sheathed his sword and followed. "Slow down, Bridge. I'm not as nimble on my feet as you are."

The goat headed across a steep slope.

"Not only can I not cross here, if I did, I'd be in plain sight."

Cantor looked for an alternate route and saw one lower and among bushes. He started to climb down, lost his footing, and slid. At the bottom, he froze and listened. He heard the goat complain in a very goaty bleat. Puzzled, he reached for Bridger with his mind.

"What are you doing?"

"Watching the beast's lair."

"Where are you?"

"Not far. Keep coming along the trail you'll find a few yards to the north of you."

Cantor stood carefully, brushing off the dust and checking to see if he'd lost anything on the way down. He had his sword, a knapsack, various hampers, and his skin. Good inventory.

He moved with stealth. Although after all the commotion he'd made, he thought the guards must be deaf or drunk.

But the beast was awake. It growled in a sustained rattle, sounding somewhat like a cat's purr. Cantor tried to catch the beast's thoughts. If this was a mor dragon, then the task should be simple. He gathered a sense of malice and anticipation.

The hair on the back of Cantor's neck stood up. The beast knew they were there. It was simply waiting for them to make a mistake.

Coming to the edge of a scruffy stand of trees, he found goat Bridger waiting for him in a small open space beyond.

Keeping to the shelter of the wood, Cantor kept his voice low. "You're in plain sight, you know. Suppose this beast gets hungry and wants to have goat for an early morning snack?"

The goat yawned.

"Why are you talking to a goat?"

Cantor jerked his head to see his dragon friend standing against a huge boulder. He'd changed his scales' color to match his background. Cantor glanced at the goat and back to Bridger with narrowed eyes.

"Last time I saw you, you were a goat."

"When I was a goat, I could see only as well as a goat." He signaled Cantor to follow. "Have you got my sister out yet?"

"No, but the dragons are awake. We gave them water and Bixby's treating them to counteract the drug. Your sister is unharmed but disheveled."

Over his shoulder, Bridger tossed him a look of disbelief. Cantor grinned. The beast let out another of the high-pitched screams.

"Have you seen it?"

Bridger nodded. "It paces to the front of its den and sits on the stone shelf. I don't know why it doesn't just fly off."

"Did you try to communicate?"

"No. If that thing was once a mor dragon, there is nothing left of its beginning."

"I brushed its mind and came up with feelings and attitudes. Anger, hatred, the desire to destroy. Nothing about why it stays."

"I suppose this is its home." Bridger crept behind some rocks.

Cantor bent down as well and inched into the narrow space.

Bridger pointed. From their vantage point, they could see the beast. It reclined on the ledge Bridger had mentioned. Its ropelike fur tail hung off one end, and its chin rested at the very edge of the other side.

The moon muted its colors. Dark and darker scales with no shine to reflect the soft glow covered its body from the neck down. Where the scales left off, dark fur covered its head. Feathered wings batted the air sporadically as if chasing off bothersome insects.

It moved its head slightly, and Cantor shivered. The cold yellow eyes could have been staring right at them. Bridger and Cantor both withdrew from the lookout point of their hiding place.

Bridger whispered, his voice trembling. "It saw us."

"It already knew we were here."

"What is it?"

"Lion, eagle, and dragon?" Cantor guessed.

"Lion, eagle, and horse?"

"Why horse? It doesn't have horse legs."

"Horse because I don't want the last part to be dragon. It's a disgrace to all dragons to be a part of such a monstrosity."

"Monstrosity? It doesn't look that bad. In fact, that's a rather pleasing combination."

"Pleasing?" Bridger shrieked, then clamped a clawed hand over his mouth. He continued in a fierce whisper. "I'm not talking about the way it looks. I'm talking about its heart."

Cantor could not think of one thing to say.

"Mor dragons stand for something good. Our teachings center around virtues approved by Primen. Nobility, self-sacrifice, generosity, patience, forgiveness, tolerance of those weaker, desire to help the unfortunate. How will people know what mor dragons are unless they see them acting like mor dragons?"

He looked over his shoulder toward the beast. "If it was a mor dragon, and I find that hard to believe, then it has been corrupted past all recognition. However, the ignorant will look at it and think it is the norm for mor dragons."

Cantor gave his friend a long look, his heart constricting as Bridger's sorrow flowed over into it. For a moment he glimpsed his friend's mourning for his dwindling kind and under it his fear that mor dragons were headed for extinction. Cantor still didn't know what to say.

"I'm sorry, Bridge." He put a hand on Bridger's shoulder. "But there are still those who know the difference between the pretender and the true mor dragon."

The dragon let out a great sigh, then he nodded his great head.

Cantor had never seen his lighthearted friend so solemn. "What do you want to do?"

Bridger wrinkled his brow and looked at him. "Save my sister, of course. Let's get on with it."

36

DRAGON FIGHT

Cantor eased up to peer over the shortest rock. The beast stood and stretched its wings.

"What's the plan?" Bridger nudged his back. "Should we lure him down here so we can fight on the ground?"

Cantor dropped back down to sit on his haunches. "I was hoping to go straight to the rescuing part and skip the fighting. Much less chance of mishap."

Bridger settled beside Cantor. "You know the guard isn't going to let my sister and friends just walk out."

Cantor nodded but continued following his own line of thought.

Bridger stretched his neck so he could peek over the rock, then telescoped it back down.

A plan had come to Cantor's mind, and he pondered the details.

Again Bridger rose up, looked over the rim, and slumped down.

"Quit being a jack-in-the-box." Cantor scowled. "You distract me."

Bridger managed to sit still for two minutes, and then he popped up and down again. "He's still there." The dragon matched Cantor's glare. "I'm supposed to keep an eye on him. I've got to move to keep an eye on him."

Cantor said nothing. Bridger hunkered down and waited. It wasn't a full minute before he spoke. "I'm thinking about using their starnaut juice against them. Bixby can put that crown on that makes her unnoticeable and sneak into their camp. Now, the smell of starnaut juice alone puts humans to sleep. She finds the bottle, tips it over, and they topple, snoring without interruption."

"Including Bixby." Cantor wiped one hand down his face.

"Oh … well … that wouldn't be so bad. Because then my sister and friends can run out, snatch her up, and fly away."

"We've discovered that starnaut juice inhibits a dragon's ability to fly."

"Then, they can run away."

The flap of wings, a strident cry, and a thud against their protective rock jolted the two out of their conversation.

"I told you." Bridger straightened as the sound of flight moved away. "I should've been watching that beast."

"Why did he attack?" Cantor looked from the empty cave on the cliff to the cavern entrance. Two of the King's Guard stood outside, watching the beast in flight. "Did those two order the strike? Or did they just come out to investigate the disturbance?"

The beast circled the sky, passing in front of the full moon. Its stark silhouette reminded Cantor that they were handicapped by having no knowledge of how this creature fought. It wasn't one of the enemies they studied in training. Ordinarily, he would know the attacker's strengths and weaknesses, its preferences in battle, and its measure of cunning.

Cantor touched Bridger's mind and found his friend puzzling over the same things. He chose to speak aloud. Speaking silently from mind to mind required concentration, and he wanted both of them focused on the enemy.

They kneeled side by side, considering the beast as it strutted back and forth on the thick trunk of a downed tree. The beast, in turn, seemed to be watching for them to make a move.

Bridger sighed. "I suppose it wants to draw us out."

"We need to find out how things are going with Bixby and the other dragons. Could you shift into something small and fast? Something that wouldn't look out of place in this area at night?"

"A weasel? I haven't been a weasel in a long time."

"I guess that would do. Tell Bixby and Totobee-Rodolow what's going on out here. Bring back a report of how ready they are to move." Cantor clapped Bridger on the shoulder. "You do come in handy from time to time."

Bridger's grin was as wide as Cantor's. Cantor pulled his hand back as he felt the scales under his hand move.

Bridger's weasel was a tad big for the ordinary critter, but with luck no one would observe him as he made his dash. Cantor prayed for his safety as he darted out. At least the moon had moved far enough toward the horizon to provide long, deep shadows. Bridger kept to the murkiness that clung to the rocks and bushes between them and the tunnel entrance.

Cantor held his breath and kept up his silent prayer until Bridger disappeared into the safety of the cliff's secret door.

Bixby sucked in a startled breath when a furry creature tumbled into the cavern from the tunnel. The animal expanded and shifted to become a recognizable visitor.

"Bridger-Bigelow!" Totobee-Rodolow exclaimed. "How good to see you, brother."

"Hello, Tote. Do you know what kind of beast that is out there? It's complicating the rescue."

"Do you remember Great-Uncle Pootanner?"

Bridger nodded, then his eyes widened as her words penetrated his thinking. He looked aghast at his sister. "No. You don't mean it."

"I'm afraid it's so." Totobee-Rodolow's voice held shame as well as sadness.

"Did he recognize you?"

"I haven't seen him."

"Then how do you know?"

"Rumors. And if you listen closely to that horrible screech, you can hear him giving orders to his division of soldiering dragons."

Bridger cocked his head as he thought. "Now that you mention it . . . What made him turn feral?"

"They say it was when his third wife left him, and the army retired him for overzealous discipline."

Another dragon broke into their conversation. "Mor dragons are meant to go with realm walkers. When young Pootanner chose to align himself with the roc dragon army, he set his foot on the wrong path."

The dragon Bixby knew as Lupatzey wiggled closer. "That's right, Ethelmin. It was only a matter of time."

A male dragon approached. "You women quit the gossiping and get to work making yourselves dainty again. We need to be small enough to fit through whichever exit is chosen."

He turned to Bridger. "Sorry about that, son. You have a report?"

Bridger's chest enlarged as he faced the head male of his clan. Bixby listened carefully to Bridger's well-worded account of the happenings outside.

She called out to Cantor. *"You should hear Bridger. He's doing such a good job of detailing the circumstances. You'd be proud of him."*

She didn't receive a response. No wonder he'd sent Bridger instead of just communicating through their minds. Was it distance, rocks, interference from the rogue dragon? Something was not right.

Tamping down her worry, she focused back on Bridger, and caught the end of his report. Bridger turned to her. "Do you have a message to send to Cantor? I'm supposed to tell him when you think you'll be ready to travel. Vankorge says half an hour. Do you concur?"

"Yes, half an hour should be plenty of time. I haven't told them a thing about Chomountain or the Lymen invasion. I thought it best to wait until they are quite themselves again and feeling self-confident."

"No problem for Totobee-Rodolow or Vankorge, but the three others are timid."

"It will all work out. Take care on your journey back."

He saluted her, did a fancy back flip, and departed through the root-lined hole in the wall.

The beast had swooped over Cantor's hiding place several times. Undoubtedly an attempt to rattle his calm. His calm was already rattled, but Cantor would not allow that to interfere with his determination to free the prisoners.

He'd come up with several plans while waiting for Bridger's return. The best would be to distract the flying menace far from the cavern, then have the dragons battle their way out in its absence. Makki would lead them off to a protected area. He and Bridger would join them when they'd ditched the beast.

"I'm on my way."

Bridger's thought broke through his concentration, and he turned a searching gaze on the underbrush beneath the cave entrance.

Just as Cantor spotted the weasel, a scream rent the air, sending a shiver down his spine. He stood and surveyed the area for the beast.

There, just lifting off from the downed tree. It gave another raucous cry as it thrust its mighty wings down and soared into the sky. Circling, it came lower and lower.

Cantor cupped his hands on either side of his mouth. "Bridger, it sees you. It's going to attack. Hide!"

He'd hoped the beast would dither between its first target and him, a fool shouting out and standing in plain sight, but the beast folded its wings and plunged toward the weasel. Cantor ran. He had to intercept Bridger before the creature caught him.

"Bridger, hide!"

Why didn't the dragon slip into a narrow gap between rocks? Why didn't he duck under a bush?

Cantor scrambled over a small ridge of tumbled rocks and

pulled his sword. He had a straight path to Bridger. No obstacles would slow him down.

The weasel stopped and stood on its hind legs, looking at Cantor. "Move, Bridge. It's coming."

He heard the swoosh of air and a wicked chortle. Cantor jumped down to the path and ran. The hind claws of the beast encircled the weasel's head, and both predator and prey bolted upward. Cantor swung his sword at the empty space above where his friend had just stood.

He yelled his frustration and looked up. The weasel transformed into Bridger. The larger head forced the beast's claws to widen, but it managed to hang on. Bridger grabbed its legs above the claws. He swung his tail up and delivered a hefty blow to the beast's hindquarters, then dug his hind claws into both legs above his handhold. The creature screamed and opened its claws.

But Bridger didn't fall. He held on and allowed his body to swing under the beast's belly. Switching hands, he turned neatly in the air so that they both faced the same direction. The creature shook its feet in an effort to dislodge its cargo.

Bridger lost his grip on one leg, and the beast used that leg to slash downward, striking the dragon's face. Bridger cried out.

Cantor hopped in helpless rage.

He heard a rumble from the cavern. Half a dozen guards ran helter-skelter for cover as five irate dragons charged out of the entrance. Bixby followed with her knife drawn but no one to attack. Makki followed her, fairly bursting with fervor for the fight. He jumped around and yelled encouragement to the watch of dragons.

Cantor looked to the sky again and saw the dragons

hurtling upward toward the beast. Circling, they shot in one by one, landing stunning blow after stunning blow. At times, two would attack, one from above and one from the side. Bridger had a grip with both clawed hands on one of the beast's legs. The other leg had been struck in the melee and now hung as if broken.

Bridger swung forward, lifting his hind legs and slicing at the beast's chest. As he watched, Cantor saw the next swing would have a longer arch than the previous ones. Bridger kicked up and drove a claw into the creature's neck. A squirt of blood shot out, and the beast faltered and went limp.

Cantor's heart caught in his throat as beast and dragon fell toward the rocky terrain. Two of the dragons swooped in and grabbed the falling corpse. A third flew beneath. At just the right time, Bridger let go and landed on his sister's back.

For a moment, Cantor wondered why his dragon friend had not let go and flown on his own.

Bridger's sagging body told the tale. Cantor stretched his thoughts to his constant and learned the rest. Bridger was unconscious.

THE FIRST STONE

The dusty road wound down the hill and approached a large wall around Higtrap, the capital city of Derson. Standing at the crest, Dukmee examined his gray mage robes.

He looked over at his traveling companion, Chomountain, who had donned his most magnificent robes, with brilliant colors and flashy metallic embroidered designs on a dark green background. He used an elaborately carved staff so artistically contrived that the play of light and shadow on the animal figures and thick vegetation gave the appearance of movement.

Sweat trickled down Dukmee's back, between his shoulder blades. His shirt clung to him. Dampness spread at the waistband of his trousers.

Why wasn't Cho hot? Why wasn't he, too, covered with the fine grit of the road? And why did all those they passed on this trade route ignore them?

Not that he minded. Being mistaken for a mundane mage never disturbed Dukmee. Nor did he mind the label of hum-drum healer or stuffy scholar or routine realm walker. The fact that he was all of these and a bit more did make him extraordinary. Chomountain had called him a savant. He would admit to that. But being extraordinary got in the way of doing all the things he liked to do. People tended to want to talk about what he could do instead of letting him go off and do it.

Chomountain stepped off the road and sat on a large flat boulder, conveniently just the right height for a bench and located under a fragrant shade tree. The sweet smell came from large white blossoms, flowers as big as dinner plates. And the oversized, waxy dark green leaves rattled in the breeze with a very rhythmic clatter.

Dukmee blinked. A moment ago, there had been no tree and no bench, but he was growing used to such occurrences. Chomountain definitely possessed more skills, more highly developed skills, than he.

The two men sat on the rock and watched the people pass by.

"They don't look at us." Dukmee waved to a child, but the child did not respond.

"Two men taking their ease," said Chomountain. "What's to see?"

"I'd expect the children to come look at the pictures on your robes. They're attractive."

"Are you suggesting that I would lure them to my side?"

"No! But you must be doing something to make them ignore you."

"I'm not doing anything. Surprisingly, people can be

surrounded by the glorious creation of Primen and not see it. Just as they don't see the colors of my robe."

A toddler, riding in a pouch on his mother's back, cooed and waved tiny fists in the air. His merry eyes were locked on Dukmee's companion.

Chomountain laughed, blew a kiss, and waved good-bye.

Puzzled, Dukmee could not let that pass. "He sees you."

"The very young often do. But as they grow older ..." Chomountain shook his head, looking sad. "Sometimes they don't hear. I can introduce myself as Chomountain, and even though they know the significance of the suffix *mountain*, they don't realize they are talking to the right hand of Primen."

"Doesn't that anger you?"

"It's not my place to be angry. My work is to bless people, not curse them." He stood and stretched. "The curator should be back from his midday meal now. We can gain entrance to the museum."

"That's what we were waiting for?"

Chomountain grabbed his staff from its resting place against the tree and tapped the end twice on the ground. "You had better stand."

Dukmee stood. Chomountain tapped twice again. The tree and rock bench disappeared. Dukmee watched the people on the road. No one seemed to have noticed.

"How do you do that? How is it possible?"

"The principle is the same as your hampers. You put something inside the hamper, and it's stored somewhere else in the universe. It's not gone, just relocated temporarily. I merely do this with larger objects and without a physical hamper. The hamper is simply a prop, you see."

Dukmee didn't see, but he knew Cho well enough by now to sense further probes would get him no better answers.

They walked into town with no interference from the guards at the gate. No matter which way they turned, the crowds in the market town parted for them to pass. The people in front of them stepped aside without any apparent recognition of the two walking toward them. As Dukmee looked over his shoulder, he saw the people merge. He had the uncanny feeling that these people did not even know they had stepped aside to allow him and his traveling partner to pass.

Dukmee had never been to Higtrap before. The city had once been the agricultural center of this vast plain of rich soil. The Port of Ponduc had taken over that claim as more and more produce was shipped across the ocean to foreign countries. The Higtrap markets were said to have been reduced by half. If that were so, the crush of people, carts, and animals must have made life in the city miserable.

As they walked freely through the crowded marketplace, Dukmee eyed the wares for sale in the booths. He chuckled to himself as he thought of what Bixby's reaction would be if she were with them. He hoped they would find Totobee-Rodolow and persuade the luxurious dragon to join their group once again.

Bridger's sister delighted in shopping as much as Bixby did, though the mor dragon bought less frequently. She stored away design and color combinations and textures, which she later copied as she shape-shifted her body into various styles. She did enjoy acquiring necklaces and rings.

Cho guided them straight to the museum doors. The sign carved on one of the stone pillars supporting a porch overhang read "Artifacts of Antiquity."

At the bottom of a wide set of steps, Cho stopped. He smiled as he surveyed the front of the building. "I helped gather some of the items in exhibits here." He placed a hand on Dukmee's shoulder. "I can't tell you how good it feels to be able to remember things." His hands dropped to his sides as he stared down at the stone step before them. His head wagged from side to side in slow disgust. "Fish!"

Blowing out a blast of air, he put a foot on the first step, then withdrew it. He patted his beard, straightened his pointy hat, and twitched the folds of his robe. He then turned a critical eye on Dukmee.

"How did you get so dirty?" Cho followed his words with a flurry of activity. The old man slapped away the dust on Dukmee's robe. He finger-combed the younger man's hair, which instantly fell into neat locks. The last gesture toward restored decorum involved swiping his hand across Dukmee's face.

His face felt wet. Dukmee repeated Cho's final motion across his forehead, nose, cheeks, and chin. Not wet. But his skin no longer felt like sandpaper, dry and covered with grit.

"There you are." Cho took Dukmee by the arm and walked with him up the stairs. "Now we're both fit to be introduced to the head curator. Not Diggertommy — he died years ago. Current man's named Hartenbar."

They entered the building to find solemn silence, dim lighting, and cool but slightly stale air. Various items showed artistic talent in lighted glass cases or hanging on the walls under directed light.

Several people roamed the rooms. One man had three boys in tow and explained to them in a hushed voice the importance of the item they stood before. A very old woman leaned on the arm of a younger version of herself as they moved to a bench where they could rest and look at a massive painting.

A man in curator robes came out of a side room. He altered his course the moment he saw Dukmee and Chomountain by the door.

"Welcome. I'm Curator Hartenbar." His low, mellow voice hardly stirred the air. He gestured toward a raised table with an open book and a pen. "Are you first time visitors? We'd like you to sign our guest book."

"I am," said Dukmee, and went to leave his signature. The amount of information asked for surprised him.

Name, place of birth, date of birth, currently residing in, occupation.

For name, he put Dukmee R'Binion S'Cratmoor D'Latheren. He was born on Richra, and he decided that was all the authorities at the museum needed to know. He put the pen back in its holder and turned to see Cho clasping the curator's hand as that man sputtered.

Chomountain smiled kindly. "Settle down, now. Collect yourself. I'm not in the least offended, and the pleasure is mine in making your acquaintance."

With his complexion growing redder and redder, Curator Hartenbar shook Cho's hand. Sweat poured down the small man's forehead and off the nape of his neck, wetting his neat hair so it hung in spikes over his collar. He looked as if he'd faint.

Moving quickly so he could catch him if he should pass out, Dukmee took a position beside the curator. "Is something wrong?"

Grinning with great satisfaction, Chomountain nodded toward the curator. "We've found one!"

Dukmee raised his eyebrows. He searched his mind for an idea. To what did Cho refer? "The stone?"

"No." He pulled one hand out of the man's grasp and pointed to him. "He recognized me. It took him a second or two. But he sees the robes, and he sees me."

Giving a slight bow in the curator's direction, Dukmee spoke sympathetically. "He's an eyeful, isn't he? But we've got to find a certain stone, and we're hoping you know where it might be."

The man took a deep breath and seemed to be coming out of his stuttering awe of the right hand of Primen.

"Yes, yes, I'd be glad to help."

Dukmee decided he'd do the talking. The man tended to quiver whenever he looked at Cho. "We've been to the ruins in Bright Valley."

"The Whirl Temple."

With effort, Dukmee damped down his excitement. The man was already aware of the background. He saw the curator's confidence take hold.

"We are looking for a stone, actually two stones, but the archives say that one of the stones was taken to the Artifacts of Antiquity in Higtrap."

The man was nodding. Could he possibly know where the stone was? Dukmee had assumed it would be shelved in some underground storage space beneath the museum.

The curator turned. "Follow me. We have an exhibit of the Whirl Movement. You'll be interested in several of the artifacts."

They walked past the old woman and her daughter. The curator turned a corner.

"Ah!" Cho clapped his hands together.

Dukmee suppressed the smile that came bubbling out of his astonishment. The walls were covered with drawings of the temple and the surrounding city as they must have looked before they became ruins. In glass-covered displays, many objects lay on rich materials to show off their fine points. Placards gave the particulars of each piece.

Curator Hartenbar crossed the room to a shadowbox display on the wall. "I believe this is the stone you are referring to."

Dukmee took slow steps, examining the item as he drew closer.

"Well, Dukmee?" Cho's voice sounded as if laughter hid beneath his calm. "Is this our prize?"

"I believe it is, sir." Dukmee stopped in front of the glass. He removed the orb from his pocket and held it up. The globe glowed, and images within spun. They came to a halt with one image focused in the center. "Confirmed. The orb authenticates the stone."

Cho was at his shoulder, looking at the stone and not the globe.

"How can it be so simple, sir?" Dukmee put the orb back in his pocket. "Isn't this too easy?"

The right hand of Primen sighed, but still the feeling of pleasure, even delight, permeated his demeanor. "Odd, isn't it? We often expect problems and trials, only to find Primen, to the contrary, has laid a straight path over an easy terrain."

HIGTRAP ONCE
AGAIN

People on the trade road below stared up and pointed. Bixby waved from Totobee-Rodolow's back. Cantor looked indecisive, then lifted his arm to wave as well. He frowned as Bridger, flying beside them, also flapped a hand in greeting. Sometimes Bridger's sociable inclinations didn't suit the dignity of a realm walker and that irritated her friend.

Cantor's mild treatment of his dragon pleased Bixby. She knew Cantor found it hard to fault his dragon friend. Bridger'd been injured by the beast, neary fallen to his death, and was still too weak to carry a burden. Hopefully Dukmee and Chomountain could complete his healing.

Bixby grinned and glanced over her shoulder. They'd be a sight to see any place they went. Behind her and Cantor, three additional mor dragons flew side by side. Lupatzey, Ethelmin, and Rollygon had joined them in the mission to turn back the invaders.

Vankorge's decision to remain behind had surprised her. As the head of the clan, he claimed his highest priority was the need to hold the mor dragon's place of importance on Effram. Also, should the invaders reach their valley, someone in command would be needed to rally a fighting force of resistance, and Vankorge held a position of authority among the other breeds of dragon in Effram as well.

"There's Higtrap." Bixby pointed to a city on the horizon. Totobee-Rodolow veered to the left, with the others following.

Patches of land big enough for five dragons to land were scarce. The surrounding area contained scattered woodlands with clusters of houses in between. Some crop fields could have been used, but Bixby knew Cantor would never order them to land where they would destroy a farmer's hard-earned harvest.

They finally set down on a small village green in a community pressed up against Higtrap's high wall.

Cantor slid off first, as soon as he landed. Bixby held Jesha in her arms as she dismounted Totobee-Rodolow.

Lupatzey and Ethelmin chattered with excitement, remarking on the weather, the scenery, the buildings, the people, and anything else that crossed their minds. Rollygon acted more dignified, but Bixby knew that he teemed with wonder and curiosity within. His aura gave him away. It was clear these three mor dragons had never been off of Effram.

As the atmosphere of the quiet village shifted, Bixby dug in her hamper with one hand. Jesha encumbered her search, but the cat did not want to be let down. Finally finding the crown she sought, Bixby settled it on her head and put the directional diadem it replaced in the bag.

People streamed from every street to circle the town square

and stare at their visitors. Under the curious eyes of the villagers, Lupatzey and Ethelmin ceased their string of disjointed remarks. At the back of the crowd, a disturbance churned, demanding to be let through.

The commotion erupted at the front of the circle in the form of the mayor and two township officers. With her ability to discern personality and auras increased by the crown, Bixby recognized their characters immediately. One nervously fought down his fears. The two others controlled blatant curiosity. The shortest man, also the biggest around and dressed in a suit designating wealth and prestige, took three steps forward.

He stood still for a second, glanced over his shoulder, frowned, and made a hurrumphish sound in his throat. A man Bixby had overlooked wiggled around one of the officers, came to stand at the mayor's side, and announced, "Ormando Gefffs, High Mayor of Logtrap."

He bowed and moved one precise step back. Bixby shook her head at the ceremony, but from her experience growing up in all sorts of cultures, she knew some protocol just couldn't be explained.

Mayor Gefffs took off his hat and bowed. He bent at the waist as far as his round middle would let him, his long black tresses falling forward in two sheets beside his head. The mayor straightened. Shaking his hair back, he replaced his hat, and strode across the well-groomed plot of grass to stand before Cantor. He removed his hat once more, gave a smaller, tight bow, and offered his right hand to shake.

Cantor hadn't had the upbringing Bixby had enjoyed. Three years ago, when they first met, she'd hidden her scorn toward his court manners, or lack thereof. She smiled to herself. No one could call Cantor D'Ahma a country rube now. Her mother would probably still like to take him in hand, but she was very picky.

His bow matched the mayor's precisely, establishing through rules of etiquette that the two men were on equal terms. Cantor had to bend to shake the much shorter man's hand, yet he did it with grace, not wounding the mayor's fragile ego.

Watching their auras, Bixby surmised that Cantor was slightly irritated by this delay. The mayor was nervous, perhaps worried should he do something that would not sit well with the authorities within the city. Bixby reached for Cantor's thoughts and found him considering ways to turn this meeting to their advantage.

"We welcome you to Logtrap." The mayor indicated the villagers surrounding them. The people nodded, but their faces reflected awe and wariness rather than welcome. Here and there, an adventurous soul looked eager and curious.

Jesha's growl rumbled low in her throat.

Whispering in her ear, Bixby sought to soothe the cat. "You don't like these people? Let's wait and see what they do." She stroked Jesha's fur.

"My name is Cantor D'Ahma. My traveling companions and I are to meet Chomountain and his companion within the city of Higtrap."

"Chomountain?" Mayor Gefffs' face purpled. "The missing right hand of Primen? Surely you jest."

"Chomountain has emerged from a long sabbatical." Cantor's calm, authoritative tone impressed Bixby. She hoped the mayor and these villagers were equally impressed. "He again moves among the realms to do Primen's will and bless the people."

313

"He's not been here." The mayor still held his hat in one hand. He moved as if to return it to his head and then didn't. He looked around at the citizens of his township and gathered in a great breath. With that breath, his aura firmed and darkened. The mayor was not pleased. He flicked a glance at the two officers.

One came forward to stand at the mayor's side but a half step back. The other disappeared into the crowd.

Bixby would have followed him with her mind, but she had on the wrong crown. He slipped away, and she couldn't latch on to him.

Oh well, she had enough to keep track of here. The three inexperienced dragons fidgeted, their nerves getting the better of them. A quiet yet deep rage boiled within Totobee-Rodolow.

The mayor lifted his chin. "Chomountain has not been here."

"We are to meet him in Higtrap, not here." Cantor's voice and face showed little interest in the mayor's ill humor.

"If Chomountain had been in Higtrap, Logtrap would have been aware. We are not so disregarded by those within as to be totally forgotten when significant events occur."

"I have no doubt of the regard given to you by the rulers of Higtrap. However, Chomountain might not have made his presence known."

Bixby mentally clapped for her friend. Oh, he did sound like a diplomat fully trained at court.

The mayor grumbled. "Now you slight the intelligence of my neighbors. They possess the acumen to recognize the right hand of Primen."

The presence of someone who had just joined the watching

villagers sent a shiver of recognition down Bixby's spine. She glanced over the crowd, trying to locate him. When she did, a small gasp caught in her throat.

"Cantor, a councilman from the guild is here."

He didn't acknowledge her, but she knew Cantor had heard. His aura shifted to a higher level of alertness.

"It's the councilman I gave the message to, the one who was supposed to alert the others that the guild building was about to explode. I thought he'd been killed in the blast."

Bixby sent a message to the five dragons. *"Be ready to leave. One of our enemies is here."* She impressed his image on them all so they would recognize him and be able to follow his movements should the situation get out of hand.

When she turned her attention back to Cantor, he was bowing, shaking hands, and obviously about to lead her and their companions away.

The crowd parted, and they walked one by one out of the town square and down a village street lined with small shops. The doors of these establishments closed just before they came to them. Shades were lowered, curtains drawn, and "Open" signs moved out of the windows.

Bixby put Jesha down. The cat tripped back to her dragon and leapt up onto his shoulders. Bixby skimmed ahead to walk beside Cantor.

"Feeling welcome?" Humor laced his tone.

"Not particularly."

"Tell me what you discerned of their auras."

"For the most part, the villagers were interested in an out-of-the-ordinary occurrence." Bixby did another sweep of the street. In the square, there had been a crowd. Now there were but a few citizens, and those ducked out of their way. She picked up a common thread. A warning had been issued to stay away from the dragons and their company.

"And?" Cantor prodded.

"The villagers at the green were reluctant to participate in anything that would disturb the calm of their lives. A half dozen yearned to go with us, thinking an adventure would be better than their dull existence."

Cantor nodded. "Typical reaction."

"The people we see now are constricted by a mandate spread by word of mouth."

Cantor gave her a swift glance.

"They are to avoid contact with us."

He pursed his lips. "And the mayor's aura?"

"He's finding his persona of influential citizen hard to maintain. He gained his office by fraud. Now, he wishes he'd never succumbed to the temptation. Being mayor brings responsibilities he had not foreseen, and the Higtrap politicians demand a lot in return for their support."

"Do you know where that officer went?"

"I just caught a glimpse of their thoughts, but I know the officer who stayed joyfully accepted his role. He didn't envy the other man's mission to inform the city guard of our arrival. In his mind, the least amount of communication with them, the better."

As they moved farther from Logtrap and closer to Higtrap's gate, they joined a thicker procession of people. Some carried wares to sell. Others had enough to warrant a donkey and cart. All seemed to be in a rush.

Bixby glanced over her shoulder and shivered.

Cantor darted a look at her face. "The councilman?"

"He has someone following us, but I haven't been able to pick out which man it is."

"Look for a woman."

Bixby grinned up at Cantor. It was a good suggestion. Her skirts billowed out as she turned around. With light steps, she approached Totobee-Rodolow. "May I ride?"

"Of course, darling. Having you perched on my neck is like wearing another jewel."

Bixby skimmed up the dragon's scales and took a seat on her head between gem-encrusted horns. Wrapping her knee around one to anchor her, she leaned back against the other.

Totobee-Rodolow laughed. "Sidesaddle?"

"I can watch before and behind us. I'm looking for a spy from the guild."

"I thought you might be. That unpleasant man who almost got you killed was at the village. I wonder what brings him to Derson."

"Could he be trying to capture Dukmee and Cho?"

"Really, child, must you forget your protocol? Chomountain is to be given his full title, and whenever he's mentioned with others, his name should go first."

"I know that, Totobee-Rodolow, but you haven't met him. He doesn't stand on ceremony. He's easier to approach than my own father."

Totobee-Rodolow clicked her tongue and gave a disapproving shake of her head. "Have you spotted the spy?"

"I see several people with dark auras."

"And?"

"I think the auras reflect sadness and loneliness, not evil intent. There are a lot more somber shades than I'm used to

317

seeing. It was like this on Effram, in the market before we found you." Bixby didn't like the atmosphere around them. "Let me examine this more closely."

Totobee-Rodolow remained silent while Bixby chose targets and delved into their thoughts. Bixby sat straight, methodically choosing those whose physical appearance suggested prosperity. She reviewed several, but had to stop. The readings were repetitive and depressing. Moving on to those who wore patched clothing, she found the same sort of thinking. Their similar attitudes puzzled her, and the fact that so many dissatisfied people walked the busy wall road worried her.

She slumped against the convenient horn. "Their sadness is linked to lack of hope. Each one has specific problems, and their troubles are varied. The one thing they have in common is that they each look at their trials and can see no change in their futures. And so they despair."

"We're coming to the gate. How do you wish to present yourself to the guards? Do you want to get down and walk? Or would you rather ride in grandeur and impress them with your social standing?"

"Walk, but first I must change my outfit."

"Of course." Totobee-Rodolow leaned forward so her chin was inches away from Cantor's ear. "The women in your party wish to freshen up. I see bath houses beside the main road. Shall we make a slight detour in order to present ourselves as emissaries of import, rather than dusty ragamuffins?"

She didn't wait for his answer, but broke away from Cantor and led the female dragons away. Bixby heard Cantor's exasperated objection. "When is anyone going to take heed of the time? Am I the only one worried about being late to the battle?"

39

OH NO, NOT AGAIN!

The guards at the gate looked askance at the five dragons but did not prevent them from entering the city.
The friends searching for Chomountain and Dukmee had put
together a plan to attract attention.

Bixby, dressed opulently in shimmering fabrics with glittering accessories and a spectacular crown, rode atop Totobee-
Rodolow's back. Totobee-Rodolow gleamed with iridescent
colors and a rainbow of jewels scattered across her neck and
tail. Jesha, her neck encircled with a shiny gold collar, sat in
Bixby's lap. The other dragons looked drab in comparison, but
that was how they intended to portray themselves.

Cantor acted as spokesman, introducing Bixby as the
Princess Bixby D'Mazeline. The rest of the party were her ser-
vants, including him. Cantor did not mention Chomountain.
After showing papers with the royal seal of Richra prominently

displayed, Cantor was allowed to lead the small procession through the gate.

Once inside, they went straight to the most fashionable inn and took rooms for a week. Bixby felt Cantor shudder as he made the arrangements. He feared they would not be prepared to deflect the Lymen invasion. Her efforts to ease his anxiety had failed, perhaps because she too was growing increasingly apprehensive over the delays.

Sitting by a large window overlooking the street, she and Totobee-Rodolow watched the mass of people passing by. She determined to remain focused on finding Chomountain and Dukmee. That was the most useful thing she could do to help Cantor.

They had calculated that their splashy entrance into Higtrap would draw attention. Rumors would fly. News would spread. Chomountain and Dukmee would hear of their arrival, and the two friends would find the five dragons and two humans.

Cantor approached their seats, though he didn't sit down since his role of servant forbade such familiarity. "Are you ready for the next phase of our deception?"

Bixby carefully controlled her expression. She must look the aristocrat listening to her man of business, and not the friendly girl paying attention to her friend.

She glanced at Totobee-Rodolow, who gave a slight nod.

Lifting her nose in the air, Bixby responded with quiet hauteur. "Yes, we are ready."

The roll of laughter from Cantor's mind jerked her head around. She stared at his placid expression but saw the amusement in his eyes.

"Stop it. You'll make me giggle and ruin my performance."

"I'm sending Rollygon with you. Or would you rather have one of the girls?"

"I'm fine with Rollygon. We meet back here at four?"

"Yes. Send a message if you're tracing down a lead."

Bixby fought the smile that wanted to pop out on her lips. She just wasn't a somber, arrogant person. Being arrogant was hard work.

She nodded regally, and Cantor left the room. Rollygon soon joined them, and the three went out the front door of the inn, intent on causing a stir and giving any messengers a chance to deliver a note without being detected.

In the courtyard at the side of the inn, Totobee-Rodolow paused. "Up on my back, darling. You must look like a princess."

"I want to walk. I can look like a princess while I examine the goods in the market."

"You don't mingle with the riffraff."

"What riffraff? These are well-to-do citizens."

"Beneath your notice, dear Bixby. On my back."

Bixby heaved a sigh and mounted. "How's anyone going to slip me a note way up here?"

"If they are good at their job, they'll manage."

Rollygon took up his position in front of Totobee-Rodolow. Glancing over his shoulder, he winked at the princess.

Totobee-Rodolow poked him. "None of that. You are too in awe of Her Highness to be so cheeky."

As planned, they slowly moved through the streets to the most prestigious market. Once there, Bixby overruled Totobee-Rodolow and got down to shop. She inspected the most expensive clothing and jewelry and made several purchases, endearing herself to the shop owners. By the time they had made a leisurely pass through the booths and indoor stores, no one doubted her legitimacy as a princess.

Rollygon acted as bodyguard. He stepped closer to her as she exited a storefront. "The councilman you pointed out to us was here."

She moved on without comment. The fact that Rollygon had voiced this news without moving his lips almost undid her pretense. She choked on a laugh and quickly raised her handkerchief to cover her grin.

As she paused before a table of embroidered linen, he spoke again. "He pointed you out to three men. Now he is leaving. No. He's moved away, but watches from the next café. The one across the lane and down three shops."

Out of the corner of her eye, she watched her dragon bodyguard. He spoke loud enough for just her and maybe Totobee-Rodolow to hear. But his mouth never even twitched. Amazing. She wondered if she could develop that talent.

This time it was she who Totobee-Rodolow poked. "Pay attention," she hissed. "These men are out to do you bodily harm."

The pointy claw in her side and the tone of Totobee-Rodolow's voice brought her up short. Yes, of course, this was serious. Pretending to be a princess — well, she really was a princess, so it wasn't exactly pretending — had muzzied her brain. Those men wouldn't be pretending to hurt her.

She stepped into the shop close by and took off her crown. Totobee-Rodolow was beside her.

With her hamper in her hand, she explained, "I'm going to wear the circlet that helps me delve into a person's thoughts. Also, my aura enhancer, and perhaps my awareness crown."

The shopkeeper came to offer assistance. "May I show you something in particular, Your Highness?"

Aha! So their ploy had worked. Everyone in Higtrap must be aware of who she was, and probably half of them knew where she was at this very moment. It wouldn't be easy to harm her or snatch her under so many interested eyes.

She communicated that theory to her dragon friend and had it shot down.

"Darling, they need only say that they are emissaries of your father, sent to return you to his palace."

"How about a portal? There must be one around. We can pop through a portal, then come back through it when they've given up on us."

"Excuse me, Your Highness. I carry the most exquisite perfumes, colognes, toilet waters, natural scents, and fragrant wax. What is your pleasure today?"

Bixby tightened her brows, glancing at the man at her elbow. "What?" She looked around. "Oh, this is a perfume shop."

The shopkeeper took a long breath. "Yes, Your Highness. What may I bring to your attention?"

"The strongest scent you have, in the biggest bottle. Make that a very fragile bottle."

The man frowned but went off to do her bidding.

Rollygon poked his head through the open door. "There are more of them now. Two stationed at each way out of this section of the market. You might be able to go out a back door."

"I'll look." Totobee-Rodolow brushed past the returning shopkeeper.

Offering a large green bottle, he said, "Essence of Lalemdice. A fine bath oil with a strong aroma of the lalemdice flower.

Only a small amount in a large bathing basin will provide a long-lasting subtle fragrance throughout the day or night." He uncorked the bottle and waved it below Bixby's nose to allow her a whiff of the oil.

Bixby cringed. "Oh my, that is strong."

"But only a drop ..." The man touched his thumb to the cork, passed his thumb over the fingertips of the same hand, then lifted his fingers to inches away from Bixby's nose.

She didn't bother to breathe in the whiff he offered. "That's fine. I'll take it."

Totobee-Rodolow came back, squeezing past the shopkeeper who was again going the opposite direction.

"It won't do, dear. There are a number of most disagreeable thugs in the alley."

Bixby pulled out her hamper again. "I have a portal locator in here."

Just as the shopkeeper returned with her purchase, Bixby shoved the fourth crown on top of the smaller three. Her scan of the surroundings revealed the man's veiled impatience. His effort to control his dislike of royalty practically slapped her in the face. Startled by the intensity, she offered him a charming smile, hoping to soften his bitterness. His fiery aura dimmed not one bit.

The shopkeeper intrigued her, but she had other claims on her time. Opening another hamper, she found the traps to pay the man for the bath oil.

Totobee-Rodolow took the paper-wrapped bottle and led them out of the shop. She paused in the lane. The people around them didn't seem to notice the loitering men surrounding the market block.

Rollygon edged closer to Totobee-Rodolow. "What is she doing?"

"She's evaluating the force against us. She'll be able to tell us where the weakest link is in the chain."

"Huh?"

"Which men are the least evil, least motivated, least trained, most likely to be overwhelmed if we fight them. She's also looking for a portal."

"I like the idea of a portal much more than a fight." Rollygon surveyed the narrow street, busy with shoppers and wares spilling out to be displayed in front of the stores. "It'll have to be a portal. I couldn't get enough of a wing spread to fly straight up."

Bixby turned her full attention to them. "There is a portal." She surveyed the stores they had already passed. "It is just beyond those men guarding at the cross lane. We'll have to get past them."

She and Totobee-Rodolow exchanged a glance. They both transferred their gazes to Rollygon.

"Are you ready for this?" asked Bixby.

The mor dragon swallowed hard. "Fighting?"

Totobee-Rodolow gave a soft chuckle and winked at her young friend. "Just pretend, darling, that you are wrestling with your classmates at home." She patted his shoulder and leaned closer. "Only hit harder." She straightened. "You'll be fine."

Bixby cleared her throat and spoke louder than her normal tone. "I'm weary. We will return to the inn now."

She climbed onto Totobee-Rodolow's neck, arranged herself to sit sideways, and took the perfume the dragon handed her. Jesha moved to perch on Totobee-Rodolow's head as Rollygon took his position, looking only slightly nervous.

"We must hurry," Bixby told her two friends. "The portal will remain open for only a few more minutes."

She scrutinized the two men in their way as Totobee-Rodolow wound through the crowd. They were well-trained, delighted with the prestige of their job working for the councilmen, and proud of their fighting skills. Not exactly what she wanted to find. At least she and her friends had the advantage of surprise.

Totobee-Rodolow approached the intersection and maneuvered between the two thugs. Bixby kept an eye on the guard on her side, knowing the two dragons watched the man on the other side.

He moved to interfere with their leaving. A flick of his eyes was all the warning she had before his arm shot out, hand snatching at her skirt hem. She smiled, took aim, and swung the heavy bottle. The fragile glass shattered on the man's head, and Bixby held her breath as oil flowed over his hair, face, and shoulders. Stunned, the guard collapsed in a coughing, choking heap on the stone-covered walkway.

A third man stepped out and grabbed Bixby's leg, his fingers digging in to her calf. Her heart rate spiked; then the guard took a breath and the fumes from the bath oil hit him like a physical blow. He coughed and squeezed his eyes shut against the onslaught of tears. She took advantage of his discomfort, hurling a well-placed kick to send the man reeling.

With a glance over her shoulder, Bixby saw the other men running to converge on her and her friends. The townspeople huddled in the doorways, too timid to step out and help either side and too fascinated to disappear into the shops.

Totobee-Rodolow and Rollygon had sandwiched the second man between their tails. With a united effort, they hurled the guard into the air. His body landed on two men racing to give aid to the already conquered thugs. Tearing her gaze from the chaos behind, Bixby searched the area for the shimmer of the portal. *There.* She jumped from one dragon's back to the other and pointed. "To the portal," she commanded.

Rollygon sprinted the few feet and dove through the opening. Totobee-Rodolow followed with such speed that she slammed into them. They went through the portal in a jumble of tumbling bodies, accompanied by Jesha's ear-numbing screech.

Bixby rolled the farthest and came to a stop when she ran into someone's legs. She checked the polished boots and trim trousers. For some reason, they looked familiar.

Stretching out on her back, her gaze traveled up the lean figure to the face of a man looking down at her. He looked tremendously pleased.

"You came back! Will you marry me this time?"

Groaning, she covered her eyes with an arm. "No. I'm still busy."

40

A TEGAN
ENCOUNTER

Bixby stood and brushed dirt and bits of dried grass off her skirts. Still picking brittle brown blades out of the loose weave of her top, she checked to see if Totobee-Rodolow and Rollygon were all right. They sat next to each other. Rollygon grinned as his eyes roamed the surroundings. Totobee-Rodolow used a pocket mirror to examine her face.

When Bixby looked around for Jesha, she was startled to find the cat had made her comfy spot in Tegan's arms. The bothersome man couldn't be all bad if he'd won Jesha's approval.

Still suspicious, Bixby narrowed her eyes. "What are you doing here?"

Tegan stopped stroking the cat to frown at Bixby. "Why do you always ask me questions?"

"Because I like to know things." She watched him tickle Jesha's nose with a feather he pulled from his pocket. When she responded enthusiastically, he set her down, tied the feather to a string retrieved from another pocket, and tantalized the cat by keeping it just out of her reach.

Bixby tried again. "So what are you doing here?"

Tegan shook his head. "I don't remember."

"Try."

He let the cat capture the feather and swooped her up in his arms again. His expression stilled. To look at him, one would think he pondered great and weighty matters. Finally, he shrugged his well-muscled shoulders. "I think I was waiting for something."

Bixby was pleased to have gotten some kind of definitive answer. "What?"

His face brightened. "You?"

Her momentary hope fizzled. "You couldn't have known I would be coming through the portal. We didn't know we'd have to use it until five minutes ago."

Tegan nodded, not terribly upset that his theory did not pan out. With a final rub behind Jesha's ears, he put the cat on the ground with the feather and string. Jesha sat for a moment in a regal pose, then sprang on the feather. Trailing the string behind, she flounced off with her kill.

Moving in a languid manner, Totobee-Rodolow ambled over to stand beside Bixby. "Darling, please introduce us. I don't believe I've met your handsome young man." She batted her dark, thick, and exquisitely shaped eyelashes. "Although she did describe you."

Starting with an impatient sigh, Bixby made the formal introduction. "Totobee-Rodolow, I would like to acquaint you with someone who tried to kidnap me the last time we met. Tegan —"

She stopped, her cheeks warming. Leaning closer, she whispered, "What is your last name?"

He gazed at her for a moment. "I forgot."

She clicked her tongue and shook her head. "Tegan, this is my friend and occasional constant, Totobee-Rodolow."

Bowing with the grace and finesse of a courtier, Tegan smiled at the elegant dragon. "I'm pleased to meet you."

Rollygon sidled up to stand on the other side of Bixby. Bixby realized he wanted an introduction as well. As soon as Rollygon and Tegan exchanged bows and polite greetings, Rollygon came out with a question he'd obviously been holding back.

"Tegan, can you tell us what plane we're on?"

The tall man looked around. "This isn't Effram."

Startled, Bixby peered at the nearby countryside. Rock formations dotted the arid land. No, this wasn't Effram or her home plane, Richra, or Dairine.

"What do you think, Totobee-Rodolow? Are we still on Derson?"

The whoosh of an opening portal caught their attention.

"Now that's Algore." Tegan nodded toward the hole in the landscape. "Algoreans always build fancy homes. Even their shacks have class."

Rollygon's eyes grew big. "You can see that?"

"See what?" Tegan's head jerked back and forth. "What are you looking at?"

"The portal. You can see the portal." Rollygon joined Tegan in front of the entry to Algore.

Tegan shifted his gaze back. He pointed. "That?"

Totobee-Rodolow allowed a contemplative smile to bloom. "Now that's unexpected."

Tegan frowned at her, and then looked to Bixby. "What's wrong?"

"Nothing, nothing at all. You're a realm walker."

He stared at her, his face reflecting deep concern. Then, for no apparent reason, his features relaxed.

"All right." He nodded a couple of times. "Does that mean I have to do something?"

Bixby shook her head. "Look, we have to get back to Higtrap and meet our friends. It was nice seeing you again."

She started toward the open portal.

Tegan's hand stopped her. "That's not the portal to Higtrap."

"I know. We'll go to Algore, and then find a portal to Derson. We may hop around a bit, but we'll get there eventually."

"But the gateway to Higtrap will open within the hour." He glanced around at the others. "You'll save time and effort."

Bixby tilted her head and squinted at him. "How do you know that?"

He blinked.

Tamping down impatience, she kept a level tone. "Most portals open at random. Not necessarily in the same place. Not at any reliable and set time. How can you know that a portal to Higtrap will open within the hour?"

He gave her his considering look, and then shrugged. "I don't know. I think I've been here awhile."

Totobee-Rodolow had widened one of her hands and placed webbed membranes between her fingers. She used the hand to fan herself. Of course, she had removed her rings and decorated the scales. "It's hot here. Alius is noted for dry heat across most of its breadth and width. I'm sure we're on Alius, and I prefer to go back to Derson promptly. Darling, let's do find some shade and something cool to drink while we wait."

Tegan proved to be quite useful. He had hampers and nice, useful things in them. Two scrawny, leafless trees didn't provide more than skinny shadows. Spreading a tarp over them weighed the trees down so they bent alarmingly. Tegan frowned a bit as he stood back to survey the canopy. Then he shrugged and seemed to accept the sag. He'd created shade.

Bixby watched him as he worked. She monitored every nuance in his fluid aura, combining this fastidious study with knowledgeable reading of his body language and expressions. Admitting to herself she was being more than finicky, she also had to concede that not once did Tegan's demeanor brush against a dark influence.

He bowed to Totobee-Rodolow and swept one hand in front of him to usher her under the trees. "A shady spot awaits your pleasure."

One of his hampers yielded fruity drinks in glasses with ice. He provided Rollygon a dish of ice cream when that dragon expressed a yearning for toffee and fudge syrup wandering through vanilla. Bixby had her own hampers with her favorites stored within, but curiosity nudged her to ask for bubbling lemon water. Without a pause, he produced her request.

Rollygon and Totobee-Rodolow chatted amiably with their host. Bixby listened with half an ear. The area in the shade was too small. Feeling trapped, she stood and walked out to sit on a boulder.

Rollygon followed. "Why don't you want Tegan to go with us?"

Bixby studied the dragon's expression. Earnest and young, Rollygon still saw things in black and white, right or wrong, good or bad. No scale between two extremes tempered his judgment. She'd watched his aura slowly taking on the hues of doubt and second-guessing since they'd left Effram. He really wanted to know why she had formed this opinion.

"We don't know much about him. Obviously, he's encountered those who would make him ineffectual. Has he also been seeded with a desire to do us harm? Will he betray us?" Having been under the influence of someone like Errd Tos, Tegan could be carrying a command deep in his mind. One he knew nothing about.

Looking out across the arid landscape, she suddenly longed for the gardens of her parents' palace. Everything green, tidy, coaxed into the best display of blooms, everything predictable. She shut her eyes. When she opened them again, she gave Rollygon her full attention. "He seems to have a convenient memory."

"Even if he has fallen into the hands of one of our adversaries, he's a realm walker. We can't just abandon him."

"He can take care of himself. We aren't abandoning a child."

"Maybe Dukmee or Chomountain can fix whatever's wrong with him." Rollygon's eyes twinkled. "Maybe Cantor can persuade him to stop asking you to marry him."

"That isn't my main concern." Bixby chafed at the smug look on Rollygon's face. "It's far more important to keep our mission from being jeopardized."

"With all of us watching him, he couldn't get away with much."

Bixby shook her head. She couldn't put into words why she didn't want the big friendly realm walker to join them.

Rollygon shuffled his feet. "I could be his constant. I could watch out for him and see that he doesn't get into trouble."

Interrupted by Tegan emerging from under the tarp, Bixby managed a curt, whispered answer. "No! Go talk to Totobee-Rodolow."

The dragon scurried past Tegan with a nod and an all-out gracious grin. The sight of a dragon smile can be unnerving to the uninitiated. Occasionally, Bixby still felt the shiver of trepidation at the appearance of Bridger's toothy grin. Tegan, however, reacted with a friendly nod of his own, not bothered in the least.

He came to stand beside the boulder where she sat. "Hello, Bixby. Are you busy?"

"N — yes!" She managed a smile for him. "Do you need something?"

He nodded absently and opened his mouth to reply.

Her smile faded. Oh no. Had she given him an opening for another proposal after all? "I — we — need to help you put your things away before we go."

"No need —"

"Yes. You've been a good host, and as thankful guests, we'll help pack before we leave you."

A sad expression took hold even as he nodded. Though he managed a few natural-sounding responses to the two dragons as they all gathered things to be stored in his hampers, his eyes tormented Bixby.

Totobee-Rodolow questioned her with a look. Bixby shrugged, shielding her thoughts from the dragons as she pretended she didn't know what had come over Tegan. Rollygon's gaze shifted from the deflated realm walker to Bixby. She watched his aura darken.

Before she could respond with an apologetic gaze in response, a soft swooshing sound, the gentle disturbance of the air, and a change in the light heralded the opening of a portal. They could see the same market they'd been perusing earlier in the day. Totobee-Rodolow, with Jesha on her head, stepped through. Bixby turned to Tegan. "I'm sure we'll meet again. We've got to get back to our friends."

He nodded. "Be safe."

"Yes. Right. You too."

Bixby took several steps toward the opening and stopped. All the teachings of being kind, nurturing those who are afflicted, and being generous even when the desire not to be was strong welled up and prevented her from taking another step. She turned and pulled in a big breath. "Well, come on. I expect you should come with us. Chomountain will want to meet you."

Joy stamped itself on Tegan's face and put a bounce in his step. With one long stride, he was beside her.

He looked down at her with clear blue eyes. Happy wrinkles accented his delight. Little bird feet spread from the corners out toward his temples. The man was too attractive.

He put a hand on her elbow. "Does this mean —"

"No! It doesn't." She grabbed Rollygon's wrist and marched through the portal without looking back.

41

FINDING THE RIGHT CLUES

Cantor walked through the marketplace, wondering where in all the planes Bixby, Totobee-Rodolow, and Rollygon had disappeared to. Several shopkeepers said they had seen his friends some time before. No one knew when they had left.

He approached yet another shop. This one sold fragrances. He'd never known either of his lady cohorts to buy scent. Bixby smelled like a bouquet of flowers and herbs. Totobee-Rodolow carried an air of a sunny meadow after a rain shower. But he was pretty sure these fragrances came from something other than a bottle. Still, he didn't want to leave a stone unturned. Someone had to know *something*.

At first, the shop appeared to be empty.

Cantor looked around for a bell to ring. "Hello?"

He coughed. The combination of bottled scents dulled his other senses and sent an unpleasant sensation to his stomach.

Bixby and Totobee-Rodolow surely had not set foot in this store. He turned to leave.

"Excuse me, sir. I carry the most exquisite perfumes, colognes, toilet waters, natural scents, and fragrant wax. What is your pleasure today?"

Cantor faced the man coming from a curtained door at the back of the store.

"Perhaps there's a lady in your life? One who deserves a bouquet of exquisite flowers? A bottle of perfume lasts much longer than a posy of flowers."

"I'm looking for a girl and two dragons who came shopping this morning."

"Ahhh … the princess and her servants?"

Cantor ignored the fact that the two dragons were hardly servants. That was their cover, after all. "They were here?"

The shopkeeper pinched his upper lip and peered over the top of his glasses at his visitor. He drew himself up to his full height, significantly shorter than that of his customer. His expression changed to determination as he made some decision. Brushing past Cantor, he went to the front door. With a scowl, he searched the crowd in front of his shop and glanced to both ends of the street.

He came back with the demeanor of a man much disturbed. "Are you with the guild as well?"

Possibly, these words were meant to disconcert him. Cantor chose to keep his face blank, something Bixby had taught him.

The shopkeeper's eyes darted to the front door and the back. He licked his lips and returned his hard gaze to Cantor's face. "Well?"

Bixby and Totobee-Rodolow would not have declared they were realm walkers. Bixby rarely told anyone she was of royal blood. But they had been out to attract attention, hoping that gossip would inform Cho and Dukmee of their presence.

Cantor made his judgment. Yes to revealing her heritage. No to admitting they were realm walkers. "I'm not associated with the Realm Walkers Guild. And neither are my friends."

The man breathed a heavy sigh, then pulled in an equal volume of air. He nodded. "I feared they were. I could have given them aid, but I didn't realize your three friends were on our side. Dressed as they were, how could I know they weren't part and parcel with those lying, stealing, murdering cutthroats that run the guild? Or worse, associates in the king's immoral and malevolent court."

"We are on a mission of great import, but we don't answer to the guild."

"Who to, then?"

Cantor did a quick calculation of the risk in telling this man the truth. Truth always won in the end, so he accepted the hazard. "Chomountain."

The shopkeeper's face scrunched into a grimace of disgust. "So you don't belong behind bars, but in a loony bin." He sighed again. "Well, I'll help you find your friends in spite of that." He held up a finger. "One moment."

The shopkeeper went through the curtain and came back in a few seconds. Cantor started to speak, but stopped at the man's finger indicating he wanted another moment. He checked the street in front of his establishment, then returned to Cantor's side.

"The princess purchased a large, fragile vase of extremely potent bath oil. She was very specific about the fragile vase. I wondered about it at the time. However, my main objective was to get these snooty, upper-crust citizens out of my shop."

"I would think that you deal mostly with wealthy patrons."

"I do. So well-to-do that they can't be bothered to come to the market. At least, not this market. The market on Blail Street caters to them. I deal with their servants."

"My friends?"

"They left the shop, and that's when I suspected my mistake." He glanced nervously to both exits in the room. "They were being followed by thugs I recognized as the king's men. It's as that saying goes — if my enemy is your enemy, we must be on the same side of the fence."

That wasn't exactly as Cantor remembered it, but he didn't correct the man. He wanted the rest of the tale. "They followed my friends. Then what?"

"The thugs jumped them at the narrow intersection." He pointed. "There. The princess smashed the bath oil over one man's head, and the one behind him went reeling, overcome by the odor and a good kick from Her Highness." He grinned with pleasure at the remembrance of the scene. "That's when I realized the princess was not a part of the problem, the high and mighty lording over us as if Primen had given them special privilege."

Cantor nearly bit his tongue in frustration. "Did the king's men capture them? Were my friends taken prisoner?"

The shopkeeper's face took on the wary expression he'd worn earlier. "No. They disappeared. I assumed through a portal. But since you say they are not realm walkers, then that possibility is nonexistent." He pinned Cantor's eye with his own. "Is that not so?"

"I didn't say we weren't realm walkers. I said we are not associated with the guild."

"And the nonsense about Chomountain?"

"Is not nonsense."

The shopkeeper raised a skeptical eyebrow. "Well, I hope you find your friends."

Cantor recognized the dismissal. Obviously, the man couldn't grasp the prospect of Chomountain returning to work among Primen's people. Cantor grinned to himself as he left the shop. A lot of people were due to be surprised.

Out on the street, a new surge of pedestrians shopped with the urgency of a deadline. Soon the sun would set, and the citizens of Higtrap had a curfew.

Cantor weaved through the crowd to the intersection. The four shops on the corners looked normal enough. At this moment, no portal hung in the air. He stepped into the boot-maker's and cast an eye over the shelves of footwear. Two customers had the clerk's attention. Unwilling to ask questions in front of the two ladies, Cantor nipped out the door and across the street. Belnora's Bakery's window showed that business had been good. Crumbs on empty platters gave proof of delicious items having gone to fill someone's belly.

A grumble rose from Cantor's own stomach. He started through the door, only to back up and give a courtesy bow to a woman just leaving. Entering the cool interior of the shop, he saw that he was the only occupant other than the baker.

That man wore white garb covered with flour and a funny hat that reminded Cantor of one his Ahma had made for him. It had been destroyed in the caustic Joden Sea on Effram. His hat had been a combination of scraps of bright cloth, but the baker's was stark white, emphasizing the ruddy, round face of the man who wore it.

"I've got some hard rolls, a few teacakes, two loaves of peppercorn bread, and herbed breadsticks. Seven of those."

Cantor had no wish to hear the man's entire inventory. "Are you Belnora?"

"That I am."

"Did you see a disturbance earlier, outside your door?"

Belnora tucked his chin and frowned. "Who's asking?"

"A friend of the lady."

"You're as big as she was small."

Cantor turned and shut the door, sliding the bolt into its latch and moving the closed sign to the window.

"Here now. I'm not ready to close."

"I'll buy what you've got left."

"Then I won't have no day-old for the poor tomorrow."

"I'll pay for the goods but not take them." His stomach rumbled. "However, I would like one of the herbed breadsticks to eat while we talk."

The baker came around the counter to fetch a basket from one of his shelves. He handed it to Cantor and hustled back to his previous position. His face no longer expressed friendly interest.

Cantor sniffed a breadstick. The long golden roll smelled of sweet herbs and butter. He took a bite before putting the basket on the counter.

"I want to find my friends, the princess and her two dragon companions. I have no desire to cause you trouble. Did you see where they went?"

"It's against the law to use portals."

The baker's announcement made Cantor choke. He coughed, then, slowing the rate of his chewing, he waited until his mouth was empty before he spoke. He'd never heard of a law against realm walking.

"Are you saying my friends went through a portal?"

"I didn't say anything about your friends. And I'm not likely to, even with the door shut. That'll be four traps and eighty-nine pins."

Cantor felt his eyes widen. He surveyed the man's leftover baking. "That's an awful lot for this little bit."

"There's more in the back. You didn't let me finish the list, but you did say you'd buy the lot. Four traps, eighty-nine pins."

Counting out the coins into Belnora's outstretched palm, Cantor felt he'd been bilked. "I suppose in the morning you'll charge the poor as well."

"Of course. But they'll pay the day-old price. You're paying today's value."

The man's self-satisfied smirk riled Cantor's usual calm. "If I weren't on important business, it would do me a great pleasure to deal with you as a realm walker is prone to deal with double-dealers."

"You don't worry me none. You came here by breaking the law. Came through a portal, didn't cha?" Belnora laughed through sneering lips. "You can't trouble me."

With a quickness and dexterity that left the baker with his mouth hanging open, Cantor smacked the underside of the man's hand, sending the coins into the air. He snatched them before they could fall again to Belnora's palm. With a deliberate motion, he plucked the value of one breadstick from the pile and placed it on the counter.

"I paid you as to our agreement." Cantor smiled as he dropped the coins back in his purse and pulled the drawstring. "I then discovered I dealt with an unhonorable man. You will not profit from my purse in this way."

His eyes came back to the baker's face as he tucked his money into his tunic. "I'd not make any effort to raise a fuss. My traveling companions are righteous."

Claiming righteousness tied an ordinary man directly to Primen, and in that association, the man could call upon the power of Primen. It was an old-fashioned term, but still held in awe by some.

The man blustered, but Cantor had had enough of his company. He stepped out into the street half lit by dusk. Some of the pale buildings caught and reflected the burnished copper of the sunset. Few people lingered on the street.

The skin on Cantor's arms raised goose bumps in response to a sudden change in the atmosphere. He squinted as he examined every inch of this street crossing. He spied the ripple, heard the whoosh, and sighed as a portal eased open.

Before Cantor could determine the whereabouts of the other side, Totobee-Rodolow stepped through. Jesha jumped from the dragon's head, and Cantor caught the furry creature as she hit his chest.

Craning his neck, Cantor tried to catch a glimpse of Totobee-Rodolow. "Where's Bixby?"

"She's coming, darling," Totobee-Rodolow answered with a lilt of laughter in her tone. "She's found an old friend."

Just then, Rollygon stumbled through the portal, impelled by Bixby, who entered Derson with a face like a thundercloud. One step behind her was Tegan.

"Oh, good," said Rollygon. "Cantor's here. I can't wait to tell him about Tegan."

"What about Tegan?" asked Cantor in a low growl.

"He's a realm walker."

Cantor's chin snapped up. "He is?"

Totobee-Rodolow laughed. "Quite a surprise, isn't it?"

"Quite," echoed Cantor. "What an extraordinary coincidence."

"I doubt that." Totobee-Rodolow patted Bixby's shoulder, nudging her away from the portal and Tegan. "I don't believe in coincidences." She smiled. "Shall we retire to the hotel? Tomorrow is another day. One bound to be full of journeys, explorations, and surprises."

Bixby had been standing on tiptoes, looking over and around anything in her way. "Where is Bridger?"

"Out looking for you. We split up to find you quickly."

Her expression shifted to one of concern. "Is anything wrong?"

He stared at her. A lot was wrong. Should he remind her they were about to be invaded by aliens who would strip them of their resources? He could recount the tales they read in the Library of Lyme about these plant-covered people ravaging the land, pillaging the towns, and massacring the populace. And that was just the external threat. The infighting and corruption in the ranks of the guild added to the pile of what was wrong.

Swallowing his retort, Cantor sighed. "We spoke to the curator at the museum. Dukmee and Chomountain have come, retrieved the artifact, and gone."

Totobee-Rodolow's face didn't flinch. Her charming expression remained. "Just as I said, journeys, explorations, and surprises."

She took Tegan's arm. "Come with us, dear boy. You're bound to be entertained. Perhaps even enlightened. I, for one, shall enjoy the playing out of this remarkable set of circumstances."

Bixby smiled at Cantor and took his arm. "You know, this spot still smells of bath oil."

His lips twitched. "Indeed, it does."

"We'll find them." The light touch of her hand on his arm felt reassuring. They made a good team.

He nodded. "Or they'll find us."

42

ANOTHER ROOM

Cantor felt Bridger approaching before he saw him. The dragon was happy, bubbling with enthusiasm at joining his sister and Bixby at the inn. From what he could determine with his mind, his group and Bridger would converge upon the modest hostel from opposite directions.

Cantor wanted to know more about Tegan before they reached the others. Silently, he communicated to Bixby. *"How did you learn about Tegan's being a realm walker?"*

"When we jumped through the portal, he was there. It appeared to be an isolated spot on Alius, and he said he'd been there quite a while."

"Last time you ran into him, he just happened to be in the same town. And he tried to kidnap you."

"Right."

"And this time he just happened to be in the middle of nowhere?"

"Right again."

Cantor liked this mysterious man less with each encounter. *"Coincidence?"*

"Totobee-Rodolow says she doesn't believe in coincidence."

"In this case, neither do I. But being in an out-of-the-way location does not make him a realm walker."

Bixby sighed. *"He saw a portal open and recognized the plane."*

"That *is conclusive.*"

They reached the inn just as Bridger came up the street. Jesha jumped from Totobee-Rodolow to her dragon. Bridger rubbed her fur, grinned at his sister, and gave Bixby a hug. Jesha, caught in the hug, protested, squirmed out, and climbed to Bridger's shoulder.

Cantor addressed them all. "We have a private parlor upstairs."

Bixby's face went from serene to delighted. "Chomountain and Dukmee are there!" She skipped ahead, the others following.

Cantor waited for all of them to pass through the door and took up a position behind Tegan. He determined to keep an eye on the man, and he wanted to see the faces of Cho and Dukmee when they first spied Tegan. Perhaps they had a better idea of who he was and what role he played in the scheme of things.

They passed through the lobby and up the stairs without speaking to anyone. As Cantor entered their private parlor, he did a double take. Chomountain had rearranged the space to make the room bigger on the inside than the entire inn on the outside. By the time Cantor remembered to look at Cho and Dukmee, he had missed seeing their reaction to Tegan's presence. He'd have to find a private opportunity to ask them what they knew about the man.

Bixby made the introductions as Cantor took in the furnishings and occupants of the parlor. All five dragons were present. Rollygon stayed at Tegan's side. Lupatzey and Ethelmin sat at a long table where platters and bowls of food offered an abundant meal. Bridger, nostrils flared and eyes bright, edged his way to that end of the room.

Within minutes, those who'd come in with Cantor had settled around the table.

Tegan sat beside Bixby, but she beckoned to Cantor. "Come sit by me. I want to hear what you've been doing all day."

"In a minute, Bix. I need to report to Cho and Dukmee." He closed the door to the hall and leaned against it as he observed his comrades.

Chomountain stood behind Bixby and Totobee-Rodolow to give a blessing in Primen's name. Then he went back to sit with Dukmee in one of the cozy chairs arranged in a half circle around a fireplace. The flickering light from the flames danced on the men's solemn faces.

Cantor joined them by the fireplace. Prior to speaking, he glanced over his shoulder to check on his friends. Along with Tegan, they all concentrated on the wonderful feast set before them. The lighthearted group ate, drank, passed plates and bowls and pitchers, and carried on a merry conversation.

Cantor frowned at their lack of concern for the severity of the situation. Invaders and usurpers, that was who they needed to deal with. And possibly a spy in their camp.

In a low voice, he confided his most pressing concern. "This Tegan has suddenly entered our circle for the second time. Now it appears he is a fellow realm walker, but he has a conveniently faulty memory." He turned to Chomountain, whose eyes were trained on the subject of Cantor's disquiet. "Sir, do you know anything about him?"

Chomountain patted his beard, and then turned to answer Cantor. "I see that his confusion is real. I haven't identified its source. Dukmee, do you have anything to add?"

Dukmee's forehead crinkled as he thought. "His aura shows no dark threads. If they are there, they've been skillfully hidden." He shook his head in disgust. "We don't have time to probe into this." He leaned toward Cantor and spoke barely above a whisper. "We have acquired the second stone and instructions for how to use them. In my studies of the sphere, I've discovered an error in my first calculations."

"Not an error, precisely," Chomountain interrupted. "Your equations were accurate to the information you had at the time. These scholars were obsessed with subterfuge. While implementing the orrery room, they fixated on keeping outsiders out. And while gathering the knowledge at the ruins, they devised ploys and ruses to the same end. And with the Library of Lyme, they were obsessed with puzzles. Obsessed."

Dukmee did not add his thoughts to Cho's assessment of the scholars, but nodded to Cantor. "The Lymen invasion will be sooner than we thought."

A lump of dread tightened Cantor's throat. "How much sooner?"

"Four days from today."

Bixby encouraged Tegan to eat.

He said he didn't recognize any of the foods, but that it

didn't bother him. "I'll taste something, and if I like it, that's what I'll eat."

Bixby gasped and looked over the wide variety of foods. None of it was fancy, but all good, standard dishes that most families served often. It looked and smelled wonderful. "Just one thing? You have to try more than one thing."

"Sometimes I try more than one thing before I really like something. But I don't see the sense in trying everything when I've found something to eat."

Bixby had seen her share of picky eaters among the aristocrats who came to her parents' banquets. She'd always thought it was a rather childish behavior. Tegan was just too big and brawny to act like a three-year-old. "You will eat more than one thing tonight."

"I'll get too full and be sick."

Bixby felt her patience slipping away like a silk shawl over a silk dress. She forced her voice to be calm and patient. "You will eat a little bit of many things, and you shall stop before you get too full."

Tegan frowned at her. "I think maybe I won't marry you."

Rollygon, who sat on the other side of Tegan, let out a hoot. He leaned over the table to peer around the mysterious realm walker to see Bixby. "He's discovered you're bossy. Now you'll have to look elsewhere for a handsome beau."

She refrained from sticking her tongue out at Rollygon. Barely.

The others laughed, and soon they all joined in the effort to coax Tegan to try different foods. As the meal progressed, he relaxed under their banter and eventually tasted almost everything.

Bixby withdrew from the talk without calling attention to

herself. She responded when spoken to, but her mind had left the table, moving instead to the group huddled by the fire.

Her eyes returned to Cantor time and again. The three men discussed something of a very serious nature. One of them had put up a guard so she could not visit their minds or tune her ears to understand their words.

Their grim expressions worried her. Each of their problems was critical. But they had more than a month before the invasion, didn't they? The guild assault was scheduled to happen simultaneously. Not a great deal of time to prepare, but nonetheless, they would work out a plan.

Finally, her friends finished their meal and they all joined the three men around the hearth.

Bixby sat on the arm of Cantor's chair. Totobee-Rodolow and Ethelmin were given the two remaining comfortable seats, while the others arranged themselves on the floor or benches nearby.

Cantor stood and gave Lupatzey his chair. He smiled at Bixby, and she gave him a nod of approval. He stood by the fire, his elbow on the mantel, looking peaceful. However, she knew him well enough to see the small signs of tension. His jaw tight and his eyes half-hooded, his breathing deliberately controlled.

The hearing shield had been dropped but not the one protecting their minds. Frustrated, Bixby swung her neatly shod foot with impatience. It peeked out from the ruffled edge of her wine red petticoat and distracted her for a moment. She was picturing a posy of ribbon flowers embroidered there when Dukmee pulled two squarish stones from his pockets.

"These are the two stones that were catalogued in the globe." Dukmee, in his wizard persona, placed the objects in the air before him. When he pulled his hands away, they remained suspended. He gestured, and the stones turned in the air so that everyone might observe them.

Dukmee pointed to one floating on his right. "You see that there are ridges here, and grooves in the other. They line up perfectly, and the stones can be pressed together. Once together, the globe fits in the top. This is a dimension latch. Chomountain and I have tried it, and it worked."

Totobee-Rodolow leaned back in her seat and placed a bejeweled hand against her neck. She rubbed a finger back and forth across a decorative, raised emblem she'd designed in her skin. "A latch? Darling, a latch secures a door. Where is the door?"

Chomountain smiled. "Here, there, anywhere you have the latch. It's somewhat like a hamper. We can see a hamper, and when we put something inside, it's stored in a different dimension. We can't see the object. The object no longer takes up space where we are. But the object still exists."

Bridger peered closely at the revolving pieces. "So the latch is the opening of a hamper we can't see."

"Almost right." Dukmee allowed the stones to fall into his hands. "This latch is more like a lock to a huge hamper. When the three pieces are fit together, a room appears."

Totobee-Rodolow chuckled. "I do hope it's something more exciting than a parlor."

"It is," said Chomountain. "It is the observation post of the universe. Shall we take a look?"

Bixby's first reaction was to give an enthusiastic yes. But then she remembered their solemn faces, and a part of her did not want to see.

Perhaps some things were too grand for mortals, and those select properties should be reserved for Primen's right hand and wizards as worldly as Dukmee.

43

WITHIN FOREVER

Bixby saw the excitement in Dukmee's eyes as he spoke. "It'll be just like passing through a portal to a different realm, only you won't take a step. Don't be afraid. And for goodness' sake, don't touch anything."

Bixby hopped off the armchair where Lupatzey still sat. She slipped past Bridger to stand next to Cantor. She saw her mistake at once. "Oh, I can't see from here."

Cantor lifted her as if she were a child and deposited her tiny frame on his shoulder. "Better?"

"Yes, thank you."

In the silence of a room where everyone held their breath, the click of the two stones coming together sounded clear. Keenly aware of her comrades, Bixby heard them expel the tension just as she released the air from her lungs.

As one, the stones made a neat cube. Then Cho held them steady while Dukmee rested the globe on top.

A flash of light, so bright it stung her eyes.

"They could have warned us," she mumbled. "They did say they'd done this before. So they must have known." Blinking, her eyes seemed to be adjusting.

With her calves against his chest, she felt Cantor's deep voice rumble as he spoke. "Bixby, are you all right?"

"I can't see anything but colorful blobs, but it's getting better."

"Me too."

She reached up to wipe her hand across her eyes as if that would clear her vision. In her mind, she saw Cantor do the exact same motion at the same time. Beneath her, his shoulder muscles rippled with the movement.

"That was strange," he said.

"What?" she asked, but she knew what he was going to say.

The words came out of their mouths in unison. "Did you just wipe your eyes?"

Bixby giggled. The sensation washing through her cut off the laugh. "I want down."

"But you don't want to jump, because you still don't see very well."

"Exactly."

"I know. I'm thinking your thoughts."

"Couldn't we just be communicating the way we've always done?"

Cantor objected. "This is stronger than that. And you're feeling my feelings, aren't you?"

"Because you're feeling mine. It's confusing, isn't it? I still know which are my thoughts and feelings and which are yours, but I feel like they could blend any minute." She squirmed under the uncomfortable feeling of being too close.

"I'll help you down."

His hands went straight to her waist. He didn't have to feel his way along her side or back to find it. With one smooth movement, he set her down. Again with no hesitation. He knew when her feet were safely on the floor.

Bixby became aware of the others. First she recognized voices and connected them to the still-blurry figures around them.

Bridger crouched next to Totobee-Rodolow. "Are you all right, Tote?"

"I'm fine, darling. I'll be better when I can see clearly."

"There, there. Be patient." Chomountain's raised voice rolled around the room like an echo. "Patience. This only lasts a minute."

"See, Cantor? They knew this was going to happen, and they didn't warn us."

"Pull out your forgiving heart, Bix, and use it. They don't skip things on purpose. They're so brilliant, ordinary thoughts don't cross their minds."

"Humph!"

Cantor chuckled. "You sound just like an old lady. I know! Your nanny! Your nanny used to 'humph' all the time."

"I don't think I like your mind and mine being so closely connected."

"Perhaps it'll last only a minute, like the damaged eyesight. Yours is returning at the same rate as mine."

With a few more blinks, both Cantor and Bixby could see. Bixby heaved a sigh of relief, for Cantor had been right. With the returned vision, the uncanny feeling of housing two personalities vanished.

She looked first to see Cantor's face. He seemed to be back

to normal. His gaze wandered the area around them. Vaguely, in the distance, she could see walls, but they appeared to be a good hike away.

"Observatory of the universe, huh?" Cantor shook his head. "It would seem the universe is a rather empty place."

Bixby agreed. In the immediate vicinity, there were five dragons and five humans, and nothing else. Those who had been sitting on the chairs now sat on the floor.

Rollygon went to the lady dragons and offered a hand to help them stand. When they looked comfortable once again, the young dragon faced Dukmee and Chomountain.

He looked disgruntled. "This isn't exactly what I expected." He paused for a moment to survey the surroundings. "You told Totobee-Rodolow that it would be more interesting than a parlor. This is less."

Totobee-Rodolow laughed, her sophisticated lilting voice ringing through the air.

"Good acoustics," said Lupatzey. "We could sing."

"Perhaps later." Chomountain turned to Dukmee. "The globe, if you please."

The wizard removed the orb from its resting place and placed it in a pocket. He plucked the square from the air and disconnected the stones before storing them away. Then he pulled out the clear ball again.

Dukmee smiled at his small audience. "You know that I see letters, numbers, objects, and pictures in the globe." He held the intriguing orb in the air. "In this place, what was inside comes out."

Dukmee tossed the ball in the air. It sailed up and floated down in a long, narrow arc. The globe stopped about nine feet from the floor and began to revolve, slowly at first, but then picked up speed as it revolved. Bits of colored light such as might break off a rainbow seeped through the covering and were hurled into the room. Sparks added to the sporadic flow of textures thrown out by the spinning orb.

Bixby shook her head, trying to counteract the dizziness produced by the free-flowing kaleidoscope. Failing to regain her equilibrium, she closed her eyes tightly for a couple of seconds, then opened them. The room was full. Animals, trees, birds, waterfalls, insects, birds, buildings flew past them and even through them. Anything that could be thought of escaped the confines of the spinning sphere, gained shape and color and whirled away.

Had they stood there for hours or only a few minutes? The orb hung in midair but no longer spun. Things crammed the space around them and cluttered the area as far as the eye could see.

"What is this?" asked Rollygon.

Bridger beamed. "I think it's all the things in hampers."

"Yes," declared Dukmee. "But it's more. Remember? Observatory of the Universe. Come stand close to the globe."

Five dragons and three humans drew near. Chomountain came last with a contented smile upon his face. "I love this sort of thing."

When they had all gathered in a tight circle, Cho stretched up his hand with one pointed finger. The orb floated down and touched the tip of that finger. The globe shimmered, enlarged, then, with a poof and a couple of pffts, surrounded them. They now stood within the orb, which continued to expand. When it stilled, the inside was cool and smelled like a loaf of bread fresh from the oven.

"Sorry about that," said Cho. "I was hungry." He held a

long loaf of bread. Breaking off pieces, he went among the friends, giving warm, fragrant chunks to everyone. "Here's a big piece for you, Cantor. You didn't eat your supper."

Bixby's head spun. "This is very confusing."

Chomountain placed his large hand on her thin shoulder. "I'm not surprised, my dear. This room is difficult for me to grasp as well. We have stepped out of the confines of time and are now in eternity."

Bixby gasped. "We're dead?"

A chuckle rumbled deep beneath his beard. "No, no. Our stay here will be brief. Dukmee will locate the stream of time in which the Lymen planes come within range of their primitive vessels."

"Then what?" asked Cantor.

"We shall watch what they do and plan a way to disrupt their actions."

Another thing to confuse her. Really, this was more complicated than her apprenticeship to the chemist. She needed more thorough explanations. "But —"

Chomountain held up a finger. "You see, we will be watching what is happening then, but when we leave this room, it won't be then but now. And we'll have a day or so to prepare for then."

Their friends had scattered. Rollygon and Tegan stood next to one wall of the confined area. Bixby could see beyond them to a wooded land. Tegan spoke with gestures as he pointed something out in the trees. Totobee-Rodolow and the other female dragons grouped together at a point where a market appeared to be a few feet away from the outside of the globe. Dukmee seemed to be staring into a darkened sky.

"This place makes me dizzy." Bixby put her hand on Cantor's forearm to feel connected with something steady and sure.

"I think Jesha has the right idea."

The cat sat in the middle of the floor, deeply immersed in the strenuous ritual of the feline bath. She paid no attention whatever to the unusual surroundings or the people she regarded as her own.

Bridger sat beside her. Bixby realized he hadn't chosen a subject to watch for himself, but divided his attention among the visions in front of his friends. Very much like Jesha, he was content to wait until some real action came along.

"If you want to know something," said Chomountain, "look out of our enclosure, and whatever is on your mind will appear before you. Bixby, those chemistry problems would be explained in a way you will understand and be able to remember."

She frowned. "That isn't something I feel the need to pursue. Perhaps I could look at textile art."

Bixby chose a vacant spot, and lovely examples of stitched art appeared before her almost immediately. Her mind wandered, though. She turned from the wall to see where Cho and Cantor had gone. They were with Dukmee. She left the display of fabric and joined them.

Her throat tightened in alarm as she recognized their planeary system with two extra planes sliding toward them. The bigger plane, Lyme Major, would pass between Richra and Derson. Lyme Minor would slip between Derson and Zonvaner. As she watched, tiny ovals shot out from the planes' top surface, all headed for the stacked planes.

She wanted to see them better, and the image immediately

grew larger. This time it showed just the three planes being invaded and the renegade realms approaching.

Cantor pointed to the spectacle before them. "We should stop those vessels before they land."

"How?" asked Bixby. The others turned, just now realizing she had joined them.

Chomountain acknowledged her presence with a nod. "Keep watching, my girl. Perhaps we'll see something to give us an idea."

The image enlarged again as the first pods landed on Derson.

Bixby felt tears threaten as she realized her home plane was safe. "They're not going to Richra."

Dukmee put his hand to his chin and whispered. "Why is that? Why is that?"

The violence that followed was hard to watch. The drawings Cantor had made with the pens they found in the ruins should have prepared her, but she found the Lymen invaders hideous. The large green men hoisted themselves out of the plant-like pods they traveled in, then attached the vessels to their backs. Whether the bulk was lightweight or the Lymen were immensely strong, the ships did not encumber the Lymen one bit.

The invaders stood on two legs with a vine tail they often used as a third arm. Their arms resembled huge leaves, but one edge had teeth, much like a saw, and they ripped through wood and people with ease.

A huge bud sat on their shoulders. Multiple eyes lined what would have been a chin on a human. The skin on the face stretched upward to a huge mouth, which opened wide enough to swallow cats, dogs, and lambs. The creatures ate voraciously, as if they hadn't had food in a long time.

Watching them march across the countryside made Bixby sick to her stomach. The invaders had hampers. They ate quite a bit of what they found in their paths, but much was stuffed into the hampers. They sliced the heads off the animals and stored the rest of their kill.

Men ran up to do battle, but the beasts sliced through them with their arms, jagged blades of destruction. The worst happened in the villages. Lymen slaughtered all adults they encountered. With relish, they scooped up babies and children. Apparently, a young baby eaten whole was a great delicacy.

When a youngster was found, an outburst of fighting among the scavengers settled who would swallow the tender morsel. The victor left his comrades behind, while smacking his lips over the snack.

Bixby wrapped her arms around her middle and turned away. Bridger and Totobee-Rodolow stood behind her. She didn't know when they had taken up that position. Totobee-Rodolow opened her arms, and Bixby walked into them. The comfort of the dragon's embrace only slightly nullified the horror of the Lymen invasion.

Dukmee's voice penetrated Bixby's attempt to blind herself to the fierce assault. "Here comes the second wave. These Lymen are gatherers. The first were hunters."

Bixby turned in Totobee-Rodolow's arms. She could see a portion of the vision through a gap between Cantor and Dukmee.

The second surge came in smaller pods. The warriors were smaller as well. They put their vessels on their backs and crossed the countryside, scraping fields of grain into their hampers.

Bixby remembered a tale in the Book of Primen about locusts devastating the land of peace. Could this record really refer to a Lymen invasion?

Bridger shuffled his feet. "The first wave of invaders and the second did the same thing."

Bixby turned her head to look at the dragon. "How do you mean, Bridge? The first ate meat." She swallowed hard. "The second are eating grain."

"Vegetables and fruit as well," Cantor interjected.

Bixby glanced over to see an invasion force sweeping through an orchard. "They both have hampers. They leave nothing behind."

Bridger pointed to one group and then the other. "They left their plane and came down. I don't think they're capable of rising in those weird little pods. I think their only options are straight forward or down."

Rollygon had joined them with Tegan. "If that were true, they wouldn't be able to get back to Lyme Major and Lyme Minor."

Chomountain nodded. "Logical. We shall watch them traverse the plane. Then we shall see them depart."

The men continued to watch, but Bixby had had enough. She left them and found Totobee-Rodolow, Lupatzey, and Ethelmin following her.

"Why are they watching?" Ethelmin's voice wavered.

Bixby lifted her chin, giving herself a façade of courage she didn't feel. Sometimes when she tried to look brave, the false front propped up her weakening resolve. "They're trying to spot weaknesses so they know how to fight them."

"I only saw one die." Lupatzey, with her pale skin even paler, looked like she would lose her dinner.

"I saw that too," said Ethelmin. "He was killed by another Lymen when the two fought over a child."

Totobee-Rodolow snapped her fingers. "That's enough. We shall do something else while they watch."

"What?" Lupatzey had tears on her face. "I don't want to window shop."

Totobee-Rodolow took the younger dragon's arm and patted it as they walked. "No, darling. Of course not. We shall look for Odem and Ahma."

Bixby flung herself at Totobee-Rodolow and gave her a hearty hug. "Oh, thank you for thinking of that. It's the perfect thing to do."

44

GATHERING TO BE DONE

The invasion riveted Cantor's attention, but he knew when the ladies withdrew and left the viewing of slaughter to the men. He had experience with Bixby in battle and counted her as reliable in the middle of bloody chaos. But as the Lymen slashed through everything in their path, he sympathized with her need to turn away.

Cantor, Dukmee, Rollygon, Tegan, and Chomountain sat in chairs provided from Chomountain's vast hamper that no one could see. Occasionally one or the other of the men would get up and peer more closely at a particular scene being played out. The conversation between them was sparse.

As far as Cantor could tell, Chomountain was the only one among the six males who wasn't being dragged down by despair. In the two hours they had been watching, Cantor had not seen one Lymen killed by someone from their planes. A few invaders had met their end at the hands of other Lymen, usually over spoils from their pillaging.

Tegan crossed his arms over his chest and kept most of his emotion from his face, though muscles in his jaw tightened, and his mouth pressed into one hard line.

Bridger had turned part of himself into a chair and sat with his chin in his hand, his elbow resting on a conveniently padded armrest. "Maybe fire," he said. "Perhaps fire-breathing dragons could hold them back."

Dukmee rubbed the base of his skull, rotated his shoulders, and moved his head from side to side before he spoke. "I wonder how many fire-breathing dragons are available."

Bridger gestured to himself and the other dragons in the room. "You have five here. There should be mor dragons still in service to realm walkers. And on Algore, there's a whole tribe of fire-breathing dragons."

Rollygon shook his head. "The gorus dragons are an unreliable bunch. I hear there are over five hundred of them, but they don't play well with others."

Dukmee clapped a hand on Bridger's shoulder. "They fight well, and that's what we need."

Cantor knew about the dragons from his studies, both with Odem and at the guild. They were reportedly a vile, lazy, selfish bunch. "What will motivate them to come to our aid?"

Chomountain lifted an eyebrow. "I shall be persuasive. Being the right hand of Primen does have advantages."

Cantor heard Bixby cry out, "There they are!" The strength of her joy reached him as well and sent him running to her side.

He looked at the image of Ahma and Odem, Ahma's constant, Tom, in his dog form, and Odem's Nahzy in his donkey form. "They're alive!" He grabbed Bixby by the waist and spun around.

When he set her down, he examined the image more closely. "Where are they?"

Totobee-Rodolow clicked her tongue. "I believe they're in the old mines of Richra."

Bixby gasped. "They are. I recognize that geological formation. It exists only in those caverns. Why are they there?"

Lupatzey pulled a disapproving face. "They don't look healthy."

"And they're dirty," Ethelmin added. "I think they're being held against their wishes."

The vision grew smaller, as if the watchers had stepped away, but now they could see more of the area around Ahma and Odem.

"They aren't alone," Lupatzey said.

Ethelmin blinked her eyes rapidly. "There must be fifty people in that cavern. And look at all those animals. Do you suppose they're all mor dragons?"

"I think they are. Dozens of realm walkers and their constants. And that's just those we can see." Lupatzey tore her gaze away from the scene and looked at her friends. "What's going on?"

Totobee-Rodolow scowled. "Those are almost all seasoned realm walkers. Some might say they are beyond their prime, but the collective wisdom in that stony room is phenomenal."

Ethelmin's voice reflected her disbelief. "Then why don't they escape?"

Chomountain and Dukmee joined them. Dukmee gave Ethelmin a scathing glance. "I was trapped in a walled city, and I'm a pretty clever fellow. Sometimes your talents need the assistance of others."

"There's plenty of others," Ethelmin objected.

"Yes, but the others are just as trapped. Probably their gifts have been harnessed in some way."

Chomountain added his opinion. "And I was trapped in a valley. As you dragons were in the cave. There will be a simple key to unlock whatever holds them. Once they know they are free, it doesn't take but a second to revert. You see, deep in their being, they know they belong to Primen."

The right hand of Primen rubbed his hands together, and his face beamed with enthusiasm. "This is just what we need. Bixby, Totobee-Rodolow, Cantor, Bridger, Rollygon, and Tegan will go to Richra and free these realm walkers. Explain our peril and bring them to the western edge of Derson. Ethelmin and Lupatzey will go with Dukmee and me to Gilead and solicit a list of all active realm walkers. Inactive as well. They might come in handy."

Jesha let out a sharp cry from where she sat, still in the middle of the floor. Cho turned to look at her. "Yes, you're going. With Bridger, naturally."

Cantor felt doubt surfacing to quell any plans. "The guild has their own plans for massacre on that day. I doubt they'll be interested in cooperating with us."

Chomountain tilted his head back and looked down his nose at Cantor. He looked every inch the right hand of Primen, haughty and uncompromising. "I doubt they will choose to countermand a direct order from me."

He paused as if waiting for another objection. With their silence, he went on. "I'll send out messengers to gather the realm walkers."

"What runners would be fast enough and able to leap through portal after portal?" Ethelmin nodded at Lupatzey. "You can't think we'll do it. We're not fast enough or strong enough or smart enough in geography. We'd be lost in an hour."

"Thankfully, I do not require your assistance at this point." He surveyed his audience to be sure everyone listened. "I will send Primen's warriors. A desperate time requires desperate measures. Primen probably has them on standby.

"After our work in Gilead is done, we'll go to Algore to recruit the gorus dragons." Chomountain looked pleased with himself. "Everything is falling into place nicely. We'll just watch the end of this bit of mayhem and then be on our way. Must see the ending, you know. How they get off the plane when their pods only go straight or down. Bound to be something clever at play."

45

FOREVER
YIELDS CLUES

Cantor, Bridger, Dukmee, and Chomountain resumed their seats. When Cantor saw that Rollygon aimed to stick to the mysterious realm walker, he didn't object to Tegan wandering away. The newest member of their team pushed a chair over to an unoccupied side of their enclosure. There he sat with Rollygon right behind him. They watched something other than the invasion.

Cantor knew he should investigate, but he liked having a break from Tegan's company. And at least the man was leaving Bixby alone.

At another segment of the enclosure, Bixby and Totobee-Rodolow studied the area of Richra where Ahma and Odem were held captive. The two other female dragons watched as well but didn't seem as interested in the problem of setting his two mentors free.

Cantor left the battle to join them.

Bixby immediately gave him a welcoming smile. A weak smile due to the circumstances, but nevertheless he felt encouraged in seeing it. Her smile proved they weren't mired in the hopelessness of their cause. Not yet, anyway.

Ethelmin sidled closer at the sight of Cantor bending over Bixby's chair. "How do we know what time it is when we look at something?" She waved at the scene before them. "This could be your Mama and Oder ten years ago or fifty years in the future."

Totobee-Rodolow gave the younger dragon a critical look. "Their names are Ahma and Odem, Ethelmin-Tahbeedow." She lifted a fabricated eyebrow and continued in a syrupy tone with just an edge of pepper. "And had you been listening to Chomountain's explanation, darling, you would have heard him say that we see what we are thinking about. We are not thinking about ten years ago or fifty years in the future. And frankly, young one, I doubt that you are thinking at all."

Cantor heard grinding of teeth as Ethelmin clamped her lips together. He wasn't all that familiar with the hierarchy of mor dragon authority, but he did know that Totobee-Rodolow dwelt at the top of the ladder.

The chastised dragon flounced off. Lupatzey looked as if she might follow, perhaps to offer sympathy, but one glance at Totobee-Rodolow changed her mind. Lupatzey edged forward.

Cantor recognized she was trying to be as unobtrusive as possible and at the same time show how willing she was to pay more attention. He caught her eye and gave her an encouraging smile. Bixby's smile had made him feel better. Perhaps he could do the same for Lupatzey.

Cantor stayed long enough to get a good idea of the layout of the prison. Whoever had overseen its construction had connected unused mines and natural caverns. Guards stood at the entrances to the mountain and at checkpoints underground. Barracks above provided living space for off-duty men. One mess hall served them all. The guards carried prepared food down to the prisoners.

"What's keeping them there?" he wondered aloud. He focused on Totobee-Rodolow. "I have no idea how powerful the other realm walkers are, but both Ahma and Odem should be able to leave without much strain on their skills."

"There must be a ward around them. Or perhaps someone has taken their memories." She looked over her shoulder at Chomountain and Tegan.

Bixby nodded. "And on our first adventure together, Cantor and I rescued young men on Effram. They'd been forced into service to the king."

"Only we got there before they'd been put through the ritual that took away the lessons learned at their parents' knees."

Totobee-Rodolow grinned. "My brother would not thank you for that."

Cantor frowned, but Bixby laughed. Her eyes squinted into half moons as they always did when amusement took over her face. "You're right; Bridger was there. And so was Dukmee. They helped."

Bixby's comment poked him in his antipathy for Bridger as a constant. To tell the truth, he no longer felt strongly about the dragon pushing himself into that position. On occasion, Bridger came in handy. Very handy. On quite a few occasions.

He grunted, not willing to concede. Then Bixby'd quit harassing him, and he actually enjoyed her taunts. He gave her the response she expected. "I remember Bridger in a drugged sleep. That wasn't very helpful."

Bixby scoffed. "Now who has selective memory?"

Cantor watched with them for a while longer, then drifted over to Rollygon and Tegan.

He stood beside the dragon and asked softly, "What are you looking at?"

"This is Tegan's life. He's being very clever about retrieving information about his past."

"And?" Cantor nudged the dragon with his elbow.

"Tegan remembers something, then pushes to what happened just before that. It's amazing. Then he goes to the beginning of that memory and pushes back to what happened just before that."

"What have you learned?"

"He's not a spy." The look Rollygon gave Cantor held a bit of reproach. "He's a victim. And Errd Tos did the mind sweeping. However" — now the dragon looked proudly at Tegan — "it appears our Tegan has a very strong will, and most of their stuff didn't work."

Cantor looked at the view before them. "Those are the same caverns where Ahma and Odem are being held."

"We've already been through his escape. He's going backward now, bit by bit. I assume he wants to remember how he got in there."

"He'll be an asset when we rescue my mentors."

"As will I." Rollygon's chest puffed out. "His memories are in my head as well. And I think he'll take me as a constant. So far, it doesn't look like he's had one."

"Cantor," said Dukmee. "You'll want to see this."

He returned to his chair between Chomountain and Dukmee. Even before he settled, he saw why he'd been called over.

The Lymen still marched across Derson and Zonvaner, but without the speed and with far less pillaging.

"What's happened?"

Chomountain chortled. "I believe it's gravity."

"I don't understand."

Cho pointed to a group of people on one side of a hill. They sorted through an odd assortment of items. Cantor decided it was a rummage sale. The marauders approached from the other side, and the citizens did not know their peril.

Dukmee clasped his hands together and propped his chin on the knuckles. He made no effort to contain his grin. "Watch what happens when they run."

The enemy crested the rise and swarmed down the slope. The startled people stood frozen for a moment, then ran helter-skelter. Earlier, no one had been able to outrun the invaders. These villagers sprinted away, taking huge leaps with each stride. The Lymen, bodies bloated with overeating, stumbled in their efforts to catch up.

Dukmee leaned forward. "At first, my thought was that it's as if the Lymen carried a load. But it isn't 'as if,' they do! They've gorged themselves every step of the way."

Cantor shook his head. The sight of the once fleet-footed Lymen barely keeping on their feet relieved some of the tension in his neck and shoulders. The sight was humorous, but also it showed the enemy had weaknesses. They'd discovered one.

Gluttony! A weakness. But could they use this against them? Only after three-quarters of the plane had been looted. Three-quarters of a populace was too big a sacrifice.

He continued to analyze the scene. "But our people are fast. Look at that woman carrying a child. She just jumped over a fence."

"Gravity," said Cho with a smirk on his face.

Cantor turned to Dukmee.

Dukmee closed his eyes. When he opened them, the scene of the invasion had gone. Cantor saw in its place a depiction of the planes. He drew in a sharp breath of air. Not a depiction, but the actual planes.

Lyme Major and Lyme Minor glided into the spaces between three planes. Ample room between the planes allowed them to move without impediment.

Dukmee pointed to Lyme Major making its way between Richra and Derson. "The gravity from Lyme Major is offsetting our gravity. This counterforce lifts our people. It's as if everything weighed less. I'll bet without it, the invaders would be too heavy to move at all. Though they've eaten their way through their advantage and then some."

Bridger rubbed his hands together. "So our people are more agile, while the gluttons get their just desserts by being weighed down by their gluttony."

Dukmee glanced over at Cho. The right hand of Primen had relaxed, leaning back in his chair, eyes closed and a smile on his lips.

Dukmee raised his eyebrows. He turned back to Cantor and Bridger. "I believe this will also answer our question of how they get back to their planes with pods that go only straight or down."

The planes followed their paths in an accelerated pace. As the invaders' home planes moved toward the end of the interpass, the view changed to a close-up prospect of the raiders. The Lymen took their pods off their backs, unfolded them, and climbed in. As Lyme Major cleared the last land of Derson, the invaders lifted off. The gravity of Lyme Major pulled them higher, and at the same time, the plane itself veered lower, almost clipping the edge of Derson.

With his eyes closed, Cho remarked, "I haven't figured out why it does that. I'll think on it after a sufficient rest. A fishing pole and a sunny bank would sure help me unravel the problem." He opened one eye to peer at Bixby and Cantor. "I'd release the catch, of course. No fish dinners for a while."

46

A RESCUE

The three dragons landed behind a ridge overlooking the entrance of the mine. Night clung to them. The heat of the day still made the damp air heavy. Copious vegetation in the form of winding vines snaked over and around everything in sight, and as the dragons settled among the foliage, the mountainous jungle quieted as if listening. Only the insects continued their monotonous rhythms. Slowly, the beasts of the dark returned to their tasks, having overcome the wariness stirred in them by the intrusion of dragons and men.

Cantor signaled for everyone to stay down, using the pile of rocks and boulders as protection from the sharp eyes of the guards posted around the mine entrance. Chomountain had put him in charge of this rescue. Surprisingly, none of the others objected. Bixby and Totobee-Rodolow were as capable of this command as he was, and Richra was Bixby's home. But she accepted his leadership with no sign of resentment.

Bridger had been shrinking ever since they landed. He was

the only dragon who could enter through the southern tunnels. Inside, tight corridors and tighter turns would trap the two dragons who could not shapeshift into anything but their standard forms.

Jesha sat up with a plaintive yeow when the space between Bridger's ears became too small for her comfort. She hopped off and leapt to Cantor's shoulder.

Using his thoughts to communicate, Cantor instructed his team to spread out, scouting for anyone who posed a threat. He didn't want to risk speaking until they were sure no one lurked among the trees and shrouded boulders.

In fifteen minutes, they gathered again with no reports of danger in the immediate vicinity.

"One by one," Cantor said quietly.

The others nodded and went off in pairs to do their assigned tasks. He and Bridger, accompanied by the cat, went to the nearest entrance to the mine.

Two guards stood at either side of the arched opening. Neither spoke. Bridger and Cantor crept close. Bridger took the closer side while Cantor took the long route to get in position on the other. The dense growth of plants aided their approach. Even within a couple feet of the edge, the verdant green shield hid them. However, certain bushes rustled at the slightest touch.

Cantor had just reached his destination when a soft crackle from Bridger's hiding spot alerted the guards. Both men straightened and turned toward the sound.

Cantor allowed his moan to go from his thoughts to Bridger's. *"Your tail?"*

"Sorry."

Jesha sauntered out of their hiding place, sat down in the open area, and proceeded to clean her paws.

"A cat," said one of the men. He jutted out his bewhiskered chin. "I've never seen a cat around here before."

The other guard, taller by a head than his partner, took a step away from his post. "They used to have cats when the mines were worked. Cats and pigs and geese."

"For food?"

"People don't eat cats."

Jesha paused in her grooming, gave the men a brief glance, then started the meticulous bathing of her chest and stomach.

The taller man moved farther away from the entrance and closer to the cat. His speech reached their ears even though he whispered. "For keeping pests away. Cats for the mice, rats, and insects. Pigs and geese for the snakes."

"Snakes?" The bearded guard remained firmly at his post. But his eyes searched the ground around the perimeter of the area where bushes could hide slithering creatures.

"Yeah. They'd get in the caves and attack the workers."

With a swift look over his shoulder, the man still at his post took three giant steps away from the gaping black hole in the side of the mountain. "Pigs and geese eat snakes?"

"Kill 'em. I don't know if they eat 'em." He crouched down in front of Jesha. "Nice kitty. Do you not have a home? You don't look wild. Where'd you come from?"

Cantor and Bridger slipped out of the bushes, sped across the opening behind the men, and dispatched them with a cloth soaked in Dukmee's sleep potion. They trussed and gagged the two men with lengths of vine and dragged them into the thick undergrowth, out of sight.

At least, Cantor dragged his man. He noticed that Bridger

cradled his captive in his arms and settled him gently on the ground.

When Cantor caught the dragon's eye, he furrowed his brow to reveal his puzzlement.

Bridger shrugged, and a sheepish grin revealed his teeth. "He was really nice to Jesha."

They entered the mine and saw the light a hundred yards away. According to the scouting done in the Observatory of the Universe, the lights were spaced evenly unless they marked a corner or a branching of tunnels. Those places had more than one lantern. Single men guarded strategic points in the many passages.

Cantor and Bridger, with Jesha, skulked through the tunnels from the south entrance. According to their plan, Rollygon and Tegan entered on the west and worked their way toward the middle.

In the camp above ground, Totobee-Rodolow and Bixby would first deepen the sleep of the men in the barracks, then slip over to the canteen and tamper with the foodstuffs. By the time the ladies finished tampering with his pantry, the unaware cook would be adding sleeping powder to almost anything he made.

Cantor and Bridger met Tegan and Rollygon when they reached the last doorway at the same time.

"Any trouble?" Cantor wanted to know.

Tegan glanced at his companion. "Not all the passages were as wide as we thought. The assumption that manmade tunnels were more uniform was erroneous."

"A bust." Rollygon sized Cantor up. "You wouldn't have made it through some of those gaps."

"It wasn't too bad." Tegan shifted his eyes away from

Rollygon and tried to hide a grin. "We only had to make detours twice."

The memory obviously embarrassed Rollygon. Cantor wanted to hear the rest of the story, but they had a mission to accomplish. Before he could urge his team on to the next phase, the dragon redirected the conversation.

"How many did you put down?" asked Rollygon with a grin displaying his pointed teeth.

"Seven." Bridger's smile stretched as wide as his friend's.

"Ha!" Rollygon nodded to Tegan. "I told you we had the better route. We nabbed eleven."

Bridger frowned. "Forty altogether. Eighteen between us. That means the women got twenty-two."

Rollygon's face lost none of his delight. He winked at Bridger. "Yeah, but their targets were asleep."

Cantor rolled his eyes. "Another goofy dragon." He looked at Tegan. "Are you going to take Rollygon as your constant?"

The realm walker gave his comrade a considering look. "I think he's already taken me."

Cantor nodded. "It happened that way for me too."

"Are we going to stand out here and talk?" Bridger gestured toward the barred door. "Or open the door and rescue your Ahma and Odem?"

"Bridger does a good job of picking locks." Cantor saw the surprise wash over his constant's face. "He can shapeshift his claw to match the insides of the lock." He backed out of the way and allowed the dragon to step up to the job.

Bridger made a show of holding out one claw and then another, seemingly contemplating which would be best for the job.

Cantor cleared his throat. Loudly.

Bridger took the hint and pushed one claw into the lock. He frowned.

"Something wrong?" Cantor peered around his shoulder.

Bridger shook his head and pulled the door open. "It isn't locked."

"Pretty cocky of them," said Tegan. "Sounds like what you told me about Chomountain's imprisonment. No locks, just the idea in his head that he was home and had no need to go to any other place."

The room before them was dark and quiet. Quiet except for some heavy breathing, a few snorts, snoring, and an occasional half word spoken out of deep sleep. Cantor took a light from his hamper, and the others did the same. Jesha, whose eyes needed no help from artificial light, pranced in ahead of them.

Cantor rushed in after her. The discipline that had brought him thus far in the guise of a cold leader in charge deserted him. Intense excitement tightly bound his chest. Contained longing threatened to burst its confines. He was going to find Ahma, and with her, Odem.

Rollygon began counting the captives as soon as he came through the door. The others stayed behind. Bridger's part was to keep watch for some stray jailer who might turn up unexpectedly. Tegan would wait for Cantor's signal before waking the prisoners.

Several times, Cantor crouched beside a sleeping figure on the thin pallets laid out on the floor. Each time, he stood again and kept searching. Finally, in the middle of the room, he found her.

Holding out his light, he gazed at her. Her face was thinner, her wrinkles deeper, her gray hair hung loose instead of bound in the careful bun he was used to seeing. He wondered if her eyes would snap with life and some hidden amusement when she opened them. He loved her eyes.

Gently, he touched her shoulder. "Ahma. Ahma, wake up."

She smiled before waking. Her eyelids twitched before she opened them fully.

"Cantor, you've been gone a long time." She started to sit up, and he helped her. "Now don't go thinking you need to coddle me. I'm not that much older than when you left."

She put one cool, thin hand to his face and cupped his chin. "No doubt you've been having those adventures you were always so keen on."

He couldn't help but grin. Any minute, she might begin scolding him and telling him he needed to do this or that, and he yearned for that first tongue-lashing. It would mean she loved him, just as her harsh words had always carried the undertone of affection. He scooped her into his arms.

"Put me down. Put me down, you ruffian. When will you ever learn to curb your enthusiasm? Now run along and bring in the firewood. The box was empty last night. And no one's here to do your work for you."

He almost dropped her in his shock. He eased back and carefully studied her face. "Ahma, there is no firewood box. And there are people all around us. A lot of people. And Odem is here as well."

"Where?"

Cantor hadn't seen the old man since coming in the room, but he'd seen him from the Observatory of the Universe. "Here. Somewhere." He placed her on her feet, careful to be sure she could stand before he let go. "We'll look for him together."

She clicked her tongue against the roof of her mouth. "Such foolishness. It's too early in the morning for nonsense."

"Ahma, look. Look around us."

The old woman peered into the darkness. "The floor needs sweeping. Wherever did all those bundles come from? Too big for the broom. Get the shovel, Cantor. You've tracked in enough mud to build a dam."

She leaned against him. "My bones are old." She moaned. "I think perhaps a few bits and pieces of me besides my bones are aging as well. No problem. Cantor will return from his adventuring and help me set things to right."

"I'm here, Ahma."

He put an arm around her shoulder, and she had to crane her neck to look up to his face.

She patted his arm. "Not my Cantor. You're too big. I understand why you'd want to be Cantor. My pride and joy. Primen blessed me the day he had that babe delivered to my door."

Tegan stood behind him. "We need to wake them and get them out of here. Their minds will clear once out of this dungeon."

"Yours didn't." Cantor remembered Rollygon's account of Tegan's internment in this very same prison.

Tegan looked around and shuddered. "I was a special case. I was subjected to more of their foul devices because I'm stubborn." He nodded toward the door. "Rollygon and Bridger have gone to wake the mor dragons." He paused, looking first at Ahma and then at Cantor. "She'll be all right."

Tegan turned and reached for the closest sleeper. "Wake up, dear fellow. We're going for a walk."

47

OH MY, OH MY, OH MY!

A beautiful day for flying. The cool air against Bixby's cheeks refreshed like a dash through a woodland waterfall. And the early morning sun bounced off Totobee-Rodolow's scales, picking out the gems and making them sparkle.

Bixby gasped as she looked over Totobee-Rodolow's shoulder and spotted the camps below. "And this is only half of our forces?"

"No, darling, this is all. They gathered them all here to train them and give them their orders."

In the two days since they'd begun this epic venture, the camps had been set up. The different warriors were separated into groups. Bixby easily identified the gorus area. The uncouth dragons needed no tents, but their grounds had been torn up by their activities.

"What did the gorus do to ravage the land so quickly?"

Totobee-Rodolow shuddered at the sight of the dragons below. "What they are doing this very minute, being rough and rowdy. They constantly compete in races and wrestling and anything else to work off energy. It is said that each day a gorus awakens with enough energy for three days. They either have to expend that energy or stay awake for three days. If they stay awake, at the end of the three days they go berserk from lack of sleep."

As far away as possible from the gorus, someone had set up a camp of elegant tents in neat rows.

"The Realm Walkers Guild councilmen," said Totobee-Rodolow before Bixby could ask.

"What are they doing here?"

"Looking for an excuse to do evil, I imagine, darling. Why else would they bother themselves to leave the comfort of their mansions?"

"They don't look like they've left much comfort behind."

Other groups of less lavish tents scattered over the vast tundra at the western edge of Derson. People milled around. Some pointed up at the swarm of mor dragons and their riders. The sight had caused a stir. People jumped and waved, shouting greetings.

Makeshift corrals penned riding animals. Dogs, cats, and chickens ran free. Although there were few permanent buildings, the area looked as congested as a fair-sized town.

Bixby screwed up her face and, at the same time, tried to keep the whine out of her voice. "Where are we going to land?"

It was a legitimate question. She looked over her shoulder at those behind her. Sixty-two rescued realm walkers on sixty-two mor dragons flew behind her. To either side, Cantor, Tegan, and their two constants added to the number.

They'd gotten the prisoners above ground, fed them a banquet from the hampers they'd brought with them, given them strong-brewed coffee with plenty of sugar and cream, then set up showers for their use and provided fresh clothing. By then, the dawn brightened the air.

All those associated with the prison guard still slept soundly, each of them trussed and gagged. Just before Cantor signaled for everyone to mount up and follow him through a huge portal provided by Chomountain, Bixby and Tegan had gone around leaving knives within sight but difficult to reach. When they awoke, the wardens and jailors would have to tackle the uncomfortable business of getting free.

"There's a meadow beyond that river." Totobee-Rodolow shifted and flew toward the area she spotted.

Bixby slipped off Totobee-Rodolow's back. Activity bustled in the field that had been empty moments before. The realm walkers, after the ride on their constants, shook off the last of their captivity.

Bixby started toward the camps, eager to find her friends. The evidence of their success in their separate missions flourished among the scattered tents.

After entering the confusion, the first person she saw was Dukmee. He took her hand. "We have work to do."

He pulled her toward a tent that she hadn't seen as they came over the swaying grasses. "What kind of work?"

"Healing."

Inside, the tent reminded Bixby of her first look at Dukmee's Three Herb Healing Shop in Gristermeyer. Jars, wooden boxes, and bags sat on every shelf space available. Bunches of herbs in various stages of dryness hung from ropes crisscrossing the ceiling. A work bench held a magnifying glass, an eyedropper, tweezers, mortar and pestle, plus numerous beakers, flasks, and funnels.

Dukmee began loading a hamper with potions he'd already mixed. "The lot you brought in will need strengthening for their bodies and clarity for their minds."

A loud eruption silenced him for a moment. He listened, and when no further commotion ensued, he continued the packing. He loaded a second hamper as well as the first. "The gorus dragons are continually getting into malicious mischief. I've got a compound here that will tame them. But I'm debating whether we want them slightly subdued and cooperative or unstoppable and uncontrollable."

"I vote for slightly subdued up until the Lymen come, then unstoppable."

"Timing. That means precise timing, and I have no experience with their breed or the potion."

"Ask Chomountain."

"I did." He stopped what he was doing and gazed into her eyes. "He said we'd been given what we needed."

"So that means we have the means —"

"And somehow we have the know-how."

Bixby scowled, trying to puzzle it out. "I don't feel like I do. He probably meant just you. I've got you to help me."

Dukmee handed her one of the hampers. "We'll be going to the lot you brought in first. They'll get warm, nourishing food and comfortable beds to get some rest. We'll souse them with herbs to clear their blood and some roots that will restore nutrients to their bodies. They spent too long without sunlight, and we'll counteract the effects of that as well."

Because Bixby was gifted, over the years she'd been sent to numerous mentors. She never stayed with one for more than a couple of months. She learned rapidly and began to ask questions that the scholars found impossible to answer. She exhausted their store of knowledge, and then she exhausted them. But Bixby had been with Dukmee for more than two years.

Now, with a startling realization, she knew why. Dukmee had as many interests as she did. He bounced between different areas of expertise like a handful of beans dropped on wooden steps.

Why did she not get bored? Why didn't he send her away? Because they both did a fast-track cycle in a myriad of disciplines. She broke into a smile.

"What are you grinning about?"

"I'm not bored."

He grimaced, shook his head at her, and headed for the door. "Come on, then. We should be able to stay two steps ahead of your boredom."

They toured through the camp of rescued realm walkers and mor dragons. The ride on their dragons had cleared the cobwebs from the realm walkers' minds. Soon after they landed, they'd begun taking care of each other, which meant the visits from Bixby and Dukmee didn't take long.

Bixby scurried forward when she finally spotted Cantor's Ahma. "Hello." She made a slight curtsey. "We met earlier."

Ahma looked at her without recognition.

"I'm a friend of Cantor's."

That brightened the old woman's face. She reached out to take Bixby's hand and held it securely in her own two. Bixby would've had to tug to get it loose. Her lips twitched into a nervous smile. Perhaps greeting Ahma without Cantor by her side had been a bad idea.

Ahma chirped an inquiry. "Cantor's friend?"

Bixby nodded yes, pasted on a bright smile, and gave her hand a tug. Ahma held tight. Bixby didn't like the gleam in her eye. Hadn't Cantor said something about his Ahma being a bit confused? But the freed realm walkers had all been like that, and they were all better. She hoped Ahma was better too.

The old lady cocked one eyebrow. "Cantor is a dear boy."

"Yes, I know that."

Tug. Tightened grip.

"Are you *that* kind of friend?" Ahma tilted her head, a gesture Bixby had seen Cantor do a hundred times.

Bixby shifted on her feet. She didn't like having her hand in a vise, a gnarly, bony vise. "What is a *that* kind of friend?"

"You know, my dear. He's handsome and kind and would take care of his family."

The light dawned. "Oh, *that* kind of friend. No, we aren't *that*. We're friends, just friends. There's none of *that*."

Ahma dropped Bixby's hand. "That's too bad. Do you have any cranetame in that hamper of yours?"

"Yes, ma'am." She put the hamper on the table to look for the herb. Her wild hair hung down as she leaned forward, covering her face as she pawed through the black opening. She reached in and pulled out a delicate shawl. "Cantor sort of picked this out for you when we were at the market in Gilead."

"What do you mean sort of?"

"He saw it and liked it and said you would like it and put it back."

"So you bought it."

Bixby nodded. "So I bought it."

"For me?"

She almost stated "for you" and stopped herself. A nod would do.

"You're a dear child. But too young and frail for a realm walker's wife."

Bixby's calm smashed against the old lady's condescending tone. "I don't want to be a realm walker's wife. I'm a realm walker in my own right. No one has asked me to be a wife." She nudged aside the memory of Tegan's many proposals. "And it's not a job I'll be applying for any time soon."

"Wife?" Ahma looked truly startled with her eyebrows arched way up on her forehead. "I said life, dear. Life. Not *wife.*"

"Oh. I guess I didn't hear correctly."

Bixby knew she had heard Ahma correctly. What game was Cantor's old mentor playing? She pulled out a packet of cranetame herb and handed it to Ahma with what she hoped was an unagitated smile. "Is there anything else I can do for you?"

"No, dear. Run along."

Bixby strode away, completely unsatisfied with their visit. She didn't know what she had expected, but this wasn't it. Cantor should have provided a common ground between them, a starting point for friendship. One thing Bixby knew for sure—Ahma had no desire to be a friend.

She left the realm walker camp. Some of the constants had remained with their partners, and some had congregated by the river. Finding Totobee-Rodolow and Bridger shouldn't be difficult. They hoped to find old friends and gather news as they mingled with the other mor dragons. They were also imparting information about the threat of the Lymen, the plan for defense, and the status of the Realm Walkers Guild.

She found them easily enough. They were in a deep conversation with Odem and two other mor dragons. She laughed when she saw Jesha on her favorite place between Bridger's ears.

"Hello." She held out her hand to the old man. "I'm Bixby D'Mazeline."

He warmly shook her hand. "Princess Bixby. Cantor told me about you. He was concerned for Ahma at the time. He reassured me that you and Dukmee could cure any side effects we might suffer from our imprisonment."

"Dukmee is a healer. I'm his apprentice."

"Modest as well as beautiful. Now that *is* a good combination."

He let go of her hand but put his arm across her shoulders and turned her toward the four dragons. "This is Tom, Ahma's constant. And Nahzy is mine."

Bixby did her bobbing curtsey. "I'm pleased to meet you."

They acknowledged the greeting as two who were familiar with the ways of court. Bixby preferred to keep her royalty concealed for just this very reason. It would take days for them to start treating her as just another comrade.

Days.

That would be after the Lymen attack.

She hoped they all lived to become well-known friends.

48

LINE OF DEFENSE

They'd used the V of force before. Cantor told himself it would work here in this larger, more sophisticated version. It had to.

The defenders formed two lines, one along the edge of Derson, and the other on Zonvaner. Chomountain centered the one and Dukmee stood at the point of the other. From each leader, a line composed to maximize the strength of their force spread out in both directions along the edges of the two planes. The warriors were arranged in repeated threesomes: realm walker, realm walker's constant, gorus dragon.

Behind this line of defense, a second row offered backup. More gorus populated this line, and there were seasoned soldiers from all three endangered planes. The gorus could be counted on to dispatch any enemy that broke through the frontline. Also, they would jump into any gap should a member of the first string fall. Keeping them back would be more of a problem. The gorus dragons were enthusiastic fighters.

A half mile behind the second line, the councilmen stood with their personal bodyguards, or as Bridger remarked, their personal thugs.

Tension zinged along Cantor's skin. He breathed deeply and whispered a prayer for their success. The words of appeal to Primen veered off to concentrate on the protection of his most cherished. Ahma and Odem must withstand the onslaught. He'd just found them. Bridger must be kept from some foolhardy move. Bixby ... Bixby was actually the first one to come to mind, and he'd shoved her down on his prayer list. Behind every petition for grace and mercy, her name floated as a distraction. She impaired his communion with Primen, his effort to center himself and prepare for battle. He would prefer to be by her side in this fight. Clearly her effect on him was a good reason to not be too close.

Bixby was on one side of Dukmee and Cantor on the other. Cantor felt Bixby knocking up against his thoughts.

"You're supposed to be concentrating. What do you want?"

"Don't be a grouch. I want you to tell me this is going to work."

"It worked yesterday when we did the first experiment."

"Actually, it worked the third time we tried."

"It worked the first two times, but had glitches. That's why we practiced — to get the snags out. The third time was perfect."

"But we didn't sustain it for long."

"Bixby, take deep breaths."

"I wore heavier clothing so I'm less likely to catch fire."

"You soaked your clothes in that liquid Dukmee gave us, right?"

"Yes. It smells."

"Then don't take deep breaths." He looked at Bridger and the gorus dragon just beyond him. Bridger had taken an instant dislike to the brute that had been assigned to them. All the gorus dragons were on the rough side — no manners, loud, boasting, and taken to raucous revelry. Chomountain had gone into the gorus camp and calmed them down. Dukmee had threatened to drug them, but Cho didn't like the idea.

Cantor spoke to Bixby, hoping to soothe her pre-fight jitters. *"Is your gorus behaving?"*

"Yes. I think he's in awe of Totobee-Rodolow."

"Ours keeps belching, and that disgusts Bridger."

"Totobee-Rodolow said they do that because they're nervous."

Bumps rose up on Cantor's arms. The air crackled.

"Did you feel that, Cantor?"

"Yes, they're coming. Stand strong, Bixby. We can do this. Primen is on our side. Who could stand against us?"

"No one."

"That's right. Keep that in the back of your mind."

The renegade planes had been hidden by what Dukmee called a space curtain. He said it was a layer of air gathered at the edge of their own planeary system, and beyond that layer, there was no air. Now Cantor saw one dark disk edge through.

From where they stood, they could see only Lyme Major, since that plane passed above them. Chomountain and his crew would be looking at Lyme Minor.

They waited.

From start to finish, the interpass would take five hours. The warriors defending their planes would need to repel the intruders for only two hours. Then the plane would be directly overhead. From what they'd seen in the Observatory of the Universe, the danger of incoming enemy would end.

A current of power washed over Cantor, and he could sense it originated with Dukmee and traveled outward in both directions. As it progressed, he felt the energy increase with every person it encountered. The force gave strength to and multiplied the power drawn from the conduits. The pulse exhilarated Cantor, and it appeared it had the same effect on the members of the line, intensifying their focus.

The first pod appeared in the sky. The green hull burst into the blue as if someone had pushed a small stone through a piece of material. Unlike a pebble, the pod did not damage the fabric of the blue.

"Hold." The command came from Dukmee.

A dozen more pods slipped into their vision.

"Hold. We want them closer."

Fifty more followed in rapid succession. The first pods were close enough to make out details. The only interruption to the smooth green skin of the vessel appeared at the front, where a window of some kind revealed the head of the lone occupant.

"Hold. Hold. Hold." A breathless pause. "Now!"

Cantor felt the flow of energy leave him in a rush. The stream wrapped around the plumes of fire coming from the mor dragons and the gorus. The Force of V united the individual burst of flame into one barrier of fire. The heat and power of the Force of V pulsed outward, and away from the line of defenders. One by one at first, then ten at a time, the pods burst into fiery conflagrations as they hit that wall of flames. The realm walkers defense devoured the invaders' ships, leaving very little to fall from the sky.

"Hold!"

Cantor obeyed, but it took effort to pull himself out of that flow of energy. He noticed Bridger struggled as well, and it was a full minute before all the gorus had quit blowing their flames.

Cantor examined the empty sky. A few of the gorus let out hoots of triumph, but the celebration died out quickly. In only a few minutes, Lyme Major spat out another assault of pods. As long as they didn't land, Derson was safe.

Dukmee took them through the same regimen, waiting for the ships to come close enough for them to damage. The next volley brought an unpleasant surprise. Instead of a straight-forward assault, a shower of spinning disks pummeled the defenders. The disks were burned, but the effort to destroy them before they reached the ground taxed the strength of the defense line. When the onslaught finished, Cantor picked up several spent disks that had made it past the Force of V.

The palm-sized weapons came from a plant. They reminded him of a flattened grass burr. Nasty, sharp points stuck out around the edge. Several of the warriors had been hit. They moved back and the gaps were refilled. A healer would have to remove the embedded disks.

They went through three additional volleys. These rounds included both the pods and the barbed disks. The stamina of those warriors still in the front line faded. At the end of each encounter, Cantor eased out of the force of strength with greater ease. He noticed Bridger had become more proficient as well. But the gorus dragons held on longer. He relayed this information to Dukmee.

"It's to be expected, I suppose," he communicated in return. *"They have held in there, exercising a discipline they do not*

have. *I'm hoping two more assaults will be the limit of our attackers' strength."*

"Not one has landed."

"Not one," Dukmee agreed, but he didn't sound victorious. *"Those nasty barbs slip through. And they hurt, distract the team from holding the V together. It's too soon to assume we have this problem licked."*

The enemy launched the next foray with greater speed.

The defense line put up their firewall with only seconds to spare. Cantor smelled the singed plants as they fell in front of the line. The defenders had hardly withdrawn and taken a couple of restful stretches with deep breaths before the strongest attack yet came hurtling toward them.

The battles took their toll on the warriors. Many in the second line had been pulled to the front. These men had less training in holding on to the V. If released without the warriors withdrawing the force, the line of powerful fire would whip around like a dropped waterhose spraying at full throttle.

Cantor renewed his hold on the stream of energy. He found the force shifting, slipping from his grasp as if he tried to straighten a cooked noodle and hold it in position. A jolt passed up the line, and he knew someone had fallen. Dukmee gave the command to disengage. But before the line could smoothly and safely withdraw, three jolts in rapid succession whipped the reins of control out of their hands. A few held on.

The force writhed in Cantor's grip, no longer limp like a noodle, but strong and agile like a snake. Without seeing with his eyes, he knew the line of force had broken. Loose ends thrashed back on his fellow warriors. Screeches rent the air. His comrade defenders were being attacked by their own weapon.

Dukmee gave an impassioned order to cease.

Cantor and Bridger dropped the line, but their gorus roared and battled on. With the exchange of a look, Cantor and his constant grabbed the dragon's arms and pulled them back. The gorus struggled to be free, to rage on.

The beast thrashed his tail and connected with Cantor's shin. He yelped and pulled back. Bridger stamped his hind foot on the gorus's tail, immobilizing it. They managed to pull the wild gorus away from the flow of energy, but not without damage. Cantor had singed spots in his hair. Bridger had sores on the palms of his hands and a broken claw.

They sank to the ground, only to jump to their feet when they saw a dozen pods set down in the withered grass before them. An explosion nearby sent them through the air in opposite directions. For a moment, Cantor lay stunned. He felt a pull on his sleeve. Bixby knelt beside him, with Totobee-Rodolow beside her.

"Dukmee says to go four on one. The gorus aren't allowed to fight with us."

He nodded and stood on shaky legs. "Where's Dukmee?"

"He passed out right after he gave the order."

Cantor took a deep breath. That meant he was in charge. He searched the area for his constant. "Bridge?"

The dragon stood from where he'd landed in tall bushes. "I'm with you."

They approached the closest invader. He snarled and whipped his tail toward them. They jumped back, remembering how they'd seen those tails used to swipe opponents' feet out from under them.

United, they gathered a small, mishapened Force of V. Bridger and Totobee-Rodolow shot out a stream of fire. Cantor and Bixby harnessed it, and they quickly overcame the green monster before them.

The next green foe fell as easily, but while they downed one, three others closed a circle around them.

"Take that!" Bridger's outburst alerted Cantor to their predicament. Bridger had swung his tail at one invader, successfully batting him high into tree limbs. But the impact on the beast's blade-like arm had sliced through the dragon's scales.

Cantor launched himself at a second foe intent on killing the weakened member of their team. With his sword drawn, Cantor lopped off one of the beast's arms, twirled in front of him, and with a downward slash, took the other. He turned just in time to see Bixby and Totobee-Rodolow push the next invader toward his sharp sword. The creature raised his arms to attack and Cantor used the exposed torso as a target. The third green beast charged Totobee-Rodolow. Bixby straddled her dragon's tail and was lifted to a height where she could swing downward and remove its head perched on a thin neck.

They looked around. No more invaders lurked in their area.

Cantor cleaned his sword and put it away. "We must see to Bridger's wounds. I'll leave you to help with the wounded, and I'll check the line for trouble."

He started along the ridge, but turned back to quickly cross the trampled ground to snatch Bixby from her perch on Totobee-Rodolow's tail. He held her tight against his chest. With his face buried in her tangle of hair, he breathed deeply. Then set her down again. And left.

"Well!" said Bixby.

"Well, indeed," said her constant.

All along the edge of Derson, other foursomes eradicated

the last invaders. Sentries watched for stray Lymen, but none were spotted.

Cantor worked down the line in the direction that would take him to Odem and Ahma. He wanted to skip some of the wounded in his anxiety to check on his mentors, but he forced himself to tend those before him. Everyone who was able worked to ease the pain of the suffering.

Some had diverse injuries caused by the barbed disks. Cantor had been given a supply of medication. He dispensed pain potions that helped the patients while they waited for other healing measures. Many had been burned by the rope-like force. Most of these wounds were deep and long, but cauterized at the same moment they were inflicted. One realm walker had been lashed across his wrist and had his hand cut off. Again the fire sealed the stub. A dragon had lost a wing, but that would grow back.

The casualties were high among the gorus. They seemed to have been targeted by the untamed force when the realm walkers lost control. These fierce dragons made poor patients, and needed a soothing tonic to lull them to sleep. Cantor shared his supplies, giving a hamper to two young mor dragons with instructions to run along the line in both directions and distribute the medicine to those able to work with the wounded.

Duskflies had come out of the bushes by the time Cantor got to the last group of wounded. He hadn't seen Ahma and Odem. Frustrated, he started back. He could travel quickly now that he didn't stop for every wounded warrior. He wanted to get back to Bixby. Hopefully, she wouldn't be too busy to eat with him. He'd make sure she stopped long enough to rest.

He felt Bridger's approach.

"You're well enough to fly?"

"Yes, and you're needed at the main camp."

"Why?"

"They're gathering those who are mobile, and Ahma and Odem are among those who walked in. Ahma wants to see you."

Cantor ran to the stretch of hillside where Bridger planned to land. As soon as he settled on his dragon's back, he began to ask questions.

"Have we heard from the contingent defending Zonvaner? How severely is Dukmee wounded? Are we running low on supplies? Has a division moved out to cover the departing side of the planes? Has anyone estimated the time when we'll see the last of this hovering plane?"

"Not hovering." Bridger answered the last question. "The renegade plane is moving along nicely."

"What about the rest of my questions?"

"Hmmm? Oh, sorry. I wasn't listening. Wondering when we would have our next meal and what we would have. I'm hoping for noodles and creamy garlic sauce."

Suddenly weary, Cantor leaned forward and rested on Bridger's neck. "Perhaps we'll get a few hours of respite before Cho shows up to direct the next part of our routing of the Lymen."

49

CASTING
ROCKS

Bixby walked with Cantor to where she'd last seen Ahma and Odem. She wanted to ask about the hug he'd given her but when she reached for him with her talents, she ran up against walls and hedges and barriers to keep her at a distance. He'd raised them against her in particular. She could tell they were personal, not general. Because of that, she wanted to corner him and make him talk.

They carried hot meals, enough to share with Cantor's mentors. The idea of having dinner with Ahma, since she had been so strange the first time they met, gave Bixby a dread in her middle. Bridger and Totobee-Rotolow came along. That would make the conversation easier.

As soon as they found Cantor's mentors, Bixby busied herself with serving the thick hot soup, bread, and fruit. Ahma took Cantor to a corner and had a whispered conversation as they ate. Bixby tried to batten down her resentment.

Whispering was rude. Just ask her mother. If the old lady wanted to have secrets, why didn't she just communicate with Cantor through their minds?

The annoyance was shoveled to the side by a powerful feeling of anticipation. Just before she heard Cho's voice, Bixby turned her eyes to the sky.

"To me, Cantor. To me, Bixby. Bridger, Totobee-Rodolow, to me."

In the air above them, Chomountain rode on a magnificent dragon no one had seen before. Dukmee, looking a little wane, sat behind him.

Without hesitation, Bixby and Cantor mounted their dragons and flew to join them.

"Where are we going, sir?" asked Bixby.

"To give our enemies an appropriate send off. We have one more project which must be accomplished before Lyme Major and Lyme Minor are out of sight."

He turned to Cantor. "I hear you have an astonishing aim."

Cantor nodded. "I do, sir."

"Good. We're going to knock those planes out of their orbits. If we put a wicked spin on them, they'll disintegrate."

The right hand of Primen clutched his pointed hat as the wind threatened to whip it away. "We'll go by portal. Much faster that way, and we can have a little nap while we wait for the Lymens to catch up."

They flew through one of the biggest portals Bixby had ever seen. She looked over Totobee-Rodolow's side at the unfamiliar terrain.

"This isn't Derson. Are we on Zonvaner?"

"Yes, darling. And as soon as we finish this little errand with Chomountain, I know of a lovely spa where we can go soak and do the saunas and perhaps have a refreshing body wrap. They might even be able to do something with your hair."

Bixby patted the fringe of hair sticking out from under her helmet hat. She scowled. "What's wrong with my hair?"

Totobee-Rodolow didn't answer.

"Cantor once said he liked it. He said he could find me in a crowd because it shines like a beacon."

"What about Tegan, dear?" Totobee-Rodolow had begun circling in a descent before landing. "Does the dear boy offer you compliments in between proposals?"

"Tegan hasn't proposed in a couple of days. I think seeing his history at the Observatory of the Universe took away his need to have a constant in his life."

"A constant?"

"Not a mor dragon-type constant but someone reliable, always there, an anchor, a place to call home, a helpmate."

"You're not a poet, darling, but I get the point. And I think you're right. Everyone needs a constant."

Chomountain and Dukmee landed. Totobee-Rodolow aimed at a spot beside them.

Bixby chose to think her question. She wouldn't have to shout against the wind and the loud noise dragon wings made at landing. *Do you know Cho's dragon? He's not a mor dragon, is he?*

"No, not a mor dragon. He is a stunning male though, isn't he? Just look at those muscles between his wings. And his color, the white opalescence with an undertone of cerulean blue."

"So you don't know who he is."

"I didn't say that. And it is not polite, darling, to rush someone who is admiring a work of art. His name is X'Onaire. He's a mountain dragon from Cintain."

"A monk?"

"Most definitely, a monk."

Their conversation ceased as Bridger landed with Cantor. It was time to receive their instructions. Chomountain gestured for them to circle around him.

"We are going to damage the planes just before they leave our atmosphere. Our hope is to set them spinning. There are no life forms on Lyme Major or Lyme Minor other than the carnivorous plants."

He must have seen the objection rising to Bixby's lips because he cast a stare her way with steely eyes and one crooked eyebrow. She swallowed her question.

Cho looked straight at her but addressed them all. "I know this from Primen. It is not I but he who has ordered the planes completely destroyed. We are to have nothing to do with them and must not take anything from them to hold as ours."

Bridger gulped. Bixby heard it from the other side of their tight circle. She felt the same tension. Bridger didn't get Cho's stern eye, so he blurted out his question.

"We aren't going to go to those planes, are we? I mean actually walk on their soil?"

"No, no, no. Because of the effects of gravity we witnessed in the Observatory of the Universe." He paused. "There really should be a shorter way of saying that." Again he paused, considering, gave himself a shake, and continued, "As I was saying, the gravitational pull will help us launch explosive rocks at the planes. If we time the bombs correctly and hit the target, the explosions will damage the symmetry of the plane and set it to flip-flop. As it goes beyond the curtain, it will enter space that has no air to resist the turning. The flip-flopping will accelerate. The plane will disintegrate."

He rubbed his hands together vigorously. "Quite simple, don't you see? The simple plans are often the most worthy."

Chomountain looked around the circle, meeting the eyes of each of the participants. Bixby watched as everyone else returned his nod.

Bixby screwed up her face. She wasn't going to nod just to be nodding. Objections and questions hovered on her lips. She wasn't at all sure about this thing they were going to do. Nodding was out of the question.

Chomountain's kind, wise, approving, generous gaze fell on her. He nodded.

If she recognized him as authority and trusted him, then demanding a full explanation only complicated matters. When there was more time, when everyone was not stretched to their limits, and if she still had questions then, he would answer. She remembered she was a minion and she was glad to let him be the boss.

Bixby nodded in return.

When he finished the round of eye contact, he looked over Bixby's shoulder and smiled. "A tree and shade. Dukmee shall take a nap while I show you how to rig the rocks to explode."

Cantor took Dukmee's arm and assisted him to a comfortable spot.

When he returned to the group, he found Cho assigning the first chore, gathering rocks about the size of Cantor's head — his was the largest aside from the dragons. Bixby struggled to lift the cumbersome stones, but she persevered, reluctant to shirk when she knew the others were as tired as she. X'Onaire turned out to be a willing worker. He might look like a fancy painting, but his friendliness and humility brought him acceptance from the group.

When they'd piled up enough rocks to satisfy Cho-mountain, he gave them each a bowl.

"The ingredients in the bowl need to be worked together," he said. "Your fingers are the best instruments to use. Rub the powders together until they combine to make a uniform color. As you knead the materials, they will become warm and then moist. Eventually, the mix becomes a clay."

Bixby sat with the others on the grassy hill, using her crisscrossed legs to hold the bowl steady as she worked at the mixture with both hands. The warm sun felt pleasant, as did the slight breeze. Exhaustion from their morning battle drew her to the edge of sleep. She closed her eyes for a moment and popped them open again. In the dark of her mind lurked the images of burned and maimed comrades. Her mind pulled up words from the Book of Primen to keep the horrors from hounding her.

She ended up singing in her head the Hands Benediction she had once sung with Cantor in the Sanctuary in Gilead. Remembering his strong voice and the promises of Primen soothed her spirit.

The others must have been as weary, for no one talked.

The texture between her fingers changed as she continued to massage the lump of ingredients. The color changed from blue to green, and she busied her mind by imagining what the shade might look like on a pair of gloves.

Chomountain arrived with a bowl of warm water and towels for them to use, and then he passed out a meal. He'd stuffed small loaves of bread with warm meat and crisp vegetables. The drink he produced must have contained a restorative herb. Bixby felt more refreshed by the simple repast than mere food and drink would have provided.

"On to our next project." Chomountain directed them to a crude wooden table, where their bowls and the rocks now waited.

Cho supplied Bixby with a crate to boost her up to a level at which she could toil with the others. They all stood around the work bench and smeared the clay around the rocks, filling cracks and gouges with the explosive.

"This is strange." Bixby gestured with her mud-covered hand to the table and the field around them.

Chomountain paused and gave her his attention. "How is that?"

"We're working here in beautiful surroundings, with songs from the birds and fresh scents of warm grass and flowers." She shuddered. "This morning we were linked together by a powerful force, and we destroyed all that came to harm us." She picked up another rock and smoothed clay over its surface. "And here we labor in comfortable serenity, at ease with one another, and not fretting. But we are quietly creating a weapon that will destroy two planes."

Chomountain's face became still, his eyes squinted in thought, his mouth slightly pursed. He took a deep breath of air and let it out. "You are unsettled by calm and chaos being shoulder to shoulder, so to speak."

"Yes, I think that's it."

"The intensity of feelings is necessary for us to fully respond to life. But that intensity would burn us to cinders if we did not spend most of our time in a softer, more nurturing emotion."

"Isn't that state almost no emotion?"

"No," said Totobee-Rodolow. "We were made to feel. There's rest in contentment, and contentment rests on soft cushions of love, respectability, and generosity."

Cho placed the last clay-covered rock on the table. "We're done here. Three-fifths of the rocks need to be taken to the eastern edge of Derson to be used against Lyme Major."

Chomountain assigned Bixby, Totobee-Rodolow, and X'Onaire to the task of gathering the rocks, storing them in a hamper, and carrying them through a portal to Derson. He pulled Cantor and Bridger aside for a serious conversation.

Bixby wanted to eavesdrop, but Dukmee had been put in charge of her and gave her no time. Chomountain's prescription of rest and the refreshing meal had strengthened him considerably. He hurried Totobee-Rodolow, X'Onaire, and Bixby ahead of him through the portal to Derson. He helped unload the rocks to make a stockpile for Cantor's use.

"Isn't anyone else going to help throw these things?" Bixby objected. "How is he going to be able to throw them so far?"

"When the planes are close, the pull of gravity will do most of the work. Cantor's aim is what is most important."

"Are you going to be here, or are you going back to Zonvaner?"

"I'm going back to this morning's battleground. Chomountain has charged me with keeping an eye on the Realm Walkers Guild councilmen."

Bixby gasped. She covered her mouth. "I forgot."

Dukmee leaned over and kissed her cheek. "Take care of things here."

He walked away and through a portal before she recovered from his unusual action. Her hand now touched the warm spot left by his kiss.

Totobee-Rodolow had come up beside her.

"He kissed me, Totobee-Rodolow."

"I saw, darling. Take your hand away."

She turned to look at her constant and let her hand drift down to her side.

Totobee-Rodolow seriously examined Bixby's face. "Well, darling, there's no bruise. I think you shall live."

Bixby's eyes widened, then she burst into laughter. "If I survived what we did this morning, I'm sure I'll survive a kiss."

They settled down to wait for Chomountain, Cantor, and Bridger. Lyme Minor, being smaller, would pass more quickly over Zonvaner, which was smaller than Derson. The rigors of the day settled on them, and they dozed as they waited.

Bixby sat up abruptly when she heard Cantor holler. He ran through an open portal, scooped her up off the ground, and whirled around. Her feet flung out and her skirts billowed as he laughed. She joined his laughter. It was impossible not to. Before he put her down, he kissed both of her cheeks and the top of her head.

Bridger loped through the portal, with Chomountain making a more sober entrance behind him.

The dragon rushed to Bixby and his sister. "You should have seen him. He didn't miss once, not once."

Bridger pantomimed throwing something, waited a moment, then spread his arms wide, making an explosion noise with his mouth. "We were too far away to see the rocks hit the ground, but it was easy enough to see the flashes of light. And before Cantor was finished with that plane, the rim closest to us had tilted down. Chomountain says once it passes through the curtain, it'll spin. I'd like to see that."

Cantor strode over to Totobee-Rodolow and offered her a hand as she stood.

She patted his cheek. "I'm proud of you, dear boy." She looked over her shoulder at the dark mass in the sky. "And you've come in time to do the same rocky thing to Lyme Major."

Cantor grinned. "Yes, ma'am."

Chomountain greeted Bixby, Totobee-Rodolow, and X'Onaire. He clapped a hand on Cantor's shoulder. "It'll be a couple of hours before the plane is in position. You need to relax that arm." He held up a finger and patted the sides of his beautiful robes. He pulled out a jar. "Have Bixby rub this into your shoulder. The oil will keep your muscles from getting stiff while you rest. And you'll smell nice. Always good to know you're putting off a nice clean, fresh scent."

Chomountain opened the bottle, put it under his nose, and took a huge sniff. He coughed and sputtered, his eyes watered, and he tried to recap the bottle but missed the opening each time he directed the stopper at the top.

Cantor took jar and top from his hands. Without smelling it, he secured the lid.

Through wheezes, Cho told him, "It'll help — just don't push it up your nose."

Totobee-Rodolow put a pointy claw gently against Bixby's back and gave an infinitesimal push. "Go."

Bixby twisted her neck to look at her constant. "He — "

"I know, darling." Her husky voice was just above a whisper. "He kissed you. As before, there are no bruises. So go on now, use your healing hands to keep him from pain."

Cantor had taken his shirt off and sat on a large boulder. He handed her the jar as she came up to him. Without a word, he put his large hands around her waist and lifted her onto the smooth surface of the rock.

"The right shoulder?" she asked.

He nodded and tilted his head down and away from that

side. She poured oil in her hand, put the bottle down, and began to smooth the healing herb over his neck and shoulder.

Once she touched him and began to work the oil along the muscles, she lost her shyness. While she worked, he described the rock throwing and had her laughing at the description of Bridger's enthusiastic cheering.

Later in the day, she watched as Bridger handed him the weapons, and Chomountain gave enthusiastic instructions on where to throw them. Lyme Major had passed over them, slid downward as it skimmed past the edge of Derson, and hung close.

At that point, Bixby thought they could have built a long bridge to cross over. That moment passed quickly, and the explosions urged the renegade plane away. She found herself cheering along with Bridger, Cho, and X'Onaire. After a bit, even sophisticated Totobee-Rodolow added her "Bravo!" to the shouting. Bridger held a rock in each hand, ready to pass them to Cantor. "You've only got two blasters left."

"Hold off while I think." Chomountain stood between Cantor and Bridger, his hand on his beard as he thought.

"Can you throw two at once, young man?"

Cantor only contemplated the distance for a second. "No sir, not with any accuracy."

"All right, then. Here is the alternative. You and your constant will toss the last rocks simultaneously. Bridger, you're to release your control over the throw. Cantor, you are to be as one with Bridger. The two of you will forge a bond much like the V of Force, but Cantor will determine the trajectories of the missiles. He will control your muscles as well as his own."

The right hand of Primen didn't wait for them to agree. He stepped back and nudged Bridger to a position beside Cantor.

A look of doubt crossed Cantor's face, but the fleeting emotion disappeared as a grin took control.

Bixby clutched Totobee-Rodolow's hand. "Look at them. They're beaming at each other like mindless clowns."

Totobee-Rodolow squeezed her hand. "I think my brother has finally convinced his constant they work well together."

Chomountain pointed out the location at which he wanted the explosives to land. The constant pair took up their stances.

Bixby held her breath. "Oh, what are they waiting for?"

Totobee-Rodolow answered with a gentle squeeze and a hissing, "Shh!"

The two pulled back in unison. Aimed. And threw.

"Duck!" yelled Chomountain.

Bixby didn't have the presence of mind she needed. She stood watching as the others fell facedown and covered their heads. From behind, someone tackled her frozen form and pushed her down, covering her body with his own.

The blast reverberated through the air, and it seemed the plane trembled beneath her. Rock and dirt debris showered around them. When all was still, the weight of her rescuer shifted and rolled to the side. She found herself smiling at Dukmee.

They stood. Even as they checked with one another to make sure there were no injuries, Bixby and the others laughed and congratulated themselves. In the distance, half of the renegade realm had entered the curtain. But the plane was tilting. For a moment, it stood straight up and down within the curtain. Then the top edge moved down and the plane was completely upside down and still turning. Bridger gave a final flip in the air and a cheer. The dreaded encounter with two renegade realms had passed. Together they had risen to the need and met the challenge.

Bixby breathed in the evening air, just a trace of smell from the explosive clay clung to the breeze. Tomorrow that would be gone. Maybe tomorrow they'd enter into that comfortable zone between exhilaration and panic. After the last few weeks, she, for one, was ready.

50

ALWAYS A FLY

"I have disturbing news." Dukmee's words forced themselves into the calm.

Every eye turned to him.

"There was an explosion in the tent cluster housing the councilmen."

"Of course," muttered Chomountain, shaking his head. "Leave them alone for an hour, and they begin destroying each other."

"A dozen survived."

Bixby gasped. "That means fifty-four perished."

"More than that, I'm afraid." Dukmee clasped his hands together in front of him at waist level. "Those near the tents were also killed or injured."

Cantor's solemn face told his concern. "We'll return and aid the healers. I wonder if our three loyal members are among the dozen who survived."

"There's more." Dukmee shrugged as if to get rid of the

stigma clinging to his news. "Not all of the pods that carried the last invaders were destroyed."

Chomountain let out a groan. "They must be demolished. The order came from Primen."

"They've disappeared."

"Of course," Chomountain said again. "Everything seems to be all right, and then you discover a fly in the ointment."

Bridger leaned forward. "The pods are flies in the ointment?"

"No, the people who absconded with the pods are the flies."

The dragon bobbed his head knowingly. "The councilmen are flies."

Chomountain gave a snort. "An apt description."

Bixby felt despair rise up and take her by the throat. For a moment, she'd allowed herself to believe that only good would come of this tremendous struggle.

Totobee-Rodolow must have felt the direction of her thoughts. Her mor dragon friend rubbed a soothing hand across her back. "Fear not. Primen is with us. Do not lose hope, for we are alive and can serve Him."

Chomountain added his voice. "Primen is ready to guide us into the next adventure."

Cantor crooked a smile in her direction. "As Ahma says, 'Life marches on ...'"

Bixby knew the rest of the saying. "Should we not put on our shoes and go with it?"